Choosing Us

TARA CONRAD

HIS ONE HER ONLY PUBLISHING

Published by: His One, Her Only Publishing

Cover Art by: Boundless Book Covers

Formatting by: Mr. George Conrad III

Contents

SHATTERED DREAMS

FRACTURED LIVES

MENDED HEARTS

Shattered Dreams

To those who've ever felt broken, this story is for you. For the moments you thought you couldn't go on, for the strength you didn't realize you had, and for the hope that love can mend even the most shattered hearts. Never stop fighting for your dreams.

Svetlana

It doesn't matter that I've been here for three years. I still feel small and inconsequential each time I stand in front of the Moscow State University campus's main building. The rich history and legendary stories surrounding the Soviet-era architecture are not lost on me. I still have to pinch myself to make sure I'm not dreaming. That I'm actually here, in Moscow, walking around on my own.

Well, almost on my own. The only way I was able to convince Papa to allow me to live on campus was if Pyotr, one of his guards, came with me. It shouldn't have surprised me. Pyotr has been my personal detail since I was a young girl. The last thing I wanted was for him to have to follow me to university. I was worried I'd stick out and be ostracized, but I should've known better. Pyotr is well practiced at when to be by my side and when to be discreet.

Papa had assumed I'd stay close to home and attend St. Petersburg University. He should've known I wouldn't do things the way he anticipated. But, after the shock wore off, Papa was elated knowing I took his advice and was pursuing a business degree.

For the past few years, Papa's been grooming me to step into a leadership role at Jelena's Hope after college graduation. It's a dream I thought I shared, but after completing two years in the business program, I waivered in my resolve. Without consulting Papa, I changed my major at the start of this year—something I'm still not sure how to explain to my parents. Which is one of the topics that keep me coming to room 207 each week. When I arrive, I find the door open, a sign that Masha's not with another client.

"Good afternoon, Lana," Masha says when I enter her office.

"Hello again." I close the door, hang my backpack on the coat rack, and sit on her leather couch. Sure, it's a bit cliché, but it's worn in and super comfortable. Given the topics of conversation, I'll take any comfort I can get while I'm here.

"How's your week been so far?"

"It's going well." I can't hide my smile when I think about the recent events that have made each day better than the one before.

"You seem more upbeat than usual."

"A few weeks ago, I bumped into someone I know from back home."

"Would you care to elaborate on that?"

"Not yet." I'm already at odds with Czarenah, my mentor in the BDSM lifestyle. Even though Masha isn't usually judgmental, I'm not prepared to discuss Slava with anyone else yet.

"I'm here if and when you're ready." She pulls out her notebook and pen. "Shall we pick up where we left off last time?"

"I guess so." Until now, we've only covered the easy parts of my past —the happier memories. Last week, we ran out of time right before the awful day when everything changed. This is a big part of why I'm here, so I take a deep breath, forcing myself to return to the past. "It was the day before New Year's Eve. I was ten years old and still believed in Ded Moroz. I was so excited I couldn't contain my energy running round and round Papa's office." I smile and shake my head. "I was probably driving him crazy."

"Papa, may I mail Ded Moroz another letter?" I tug on his arm.

"Did you not already send him three letters?"

"I did. But—" I hold up an envelope that's addressed and decorated. "—I forgot something."

Papa smiles as he stands and walks out from behind his big desk.

Although I'm interrupting his work, again, he never raises his voice or gets angry with me.

"Come moya babochka." Papa leads me out of his office. I take two steps to keep up with each of his. "Where is your sister?"

"She's in the library." Jelena's five years older than me, and she's super smart. She wants to be a doctor, just like Mama. When we're on break from school, instead of playing and having fun, she spends all her time in our library reading. Mama says I should be more like Jelena, but who wants to read books when they can play and enjoy the school holidays.

"Jelena," Papa says as he steps into the room. "Would you mind taking your sister to the post?"

"Of course not," Jelena says as she sets her book on the table. She and Papa exchange smiles as she walks toward us. "Another letter to Ded Moroz?"

"Yes. And it is her last letter. Is it not, Svetlana?"

"Yes, Papa."

"Thank you, malen'kiy tsvetok." Papa kisses Jelena on the head and goes back to his office.

"Come on, let's start bundling up."

Outside our window, snow's falling, and I'm certain it's freezing. But none of that matters. The only thing I care about is getting my most important request to Ded Moroz.

I would've been perfectly happy to throw on my coat and leave. Anything to mail my letter out as fast as possible. But Jelena is much too responsible for that and won't leave the house until we've put on our snow boots, hats, scarves, mittens, and heavy coats. It takes forever for us to get our winter gear on. But finally, we're properly dressed and on our way.

"What have you asked for this time?"

"A puppy."

"You know Papa won't let you have a puppy."

"That's why I'm not asking Papa. I'm asking Ded Moroz." I say as I skip down the sidewalk.

Jelena laughs softly. "Hopefully, that works."

"It will. I know it will. Papa can't say no to Ded Moroz."

"We got to the post office just as Radomir, the post worker, was

closing up," I recall. "I knocked on the glass door with my mittened hand and held up the envelope."

With a smile on his face, Radomir walks towards us and unlocks the door. "What a pleasant surprise this is. What can I do for you today, Svetlana?"

"You must have visited the post office frequently if the employee knew your name?" Masha asks.

"Everyone in our community knew us because of Papa. But that holiday, I did spend a lot of time at the post."

"I have an important letter to mail."

"Well, then, you best come in, and I'll get it posted for you right away."

"Are you coming?" I ask Jelena.

She looks up from her phone. "I'll wait out here. You go ahead."

I shrug and follow Radomir inside.

"Do you have another letter for Ded Moroz?" he asks.

"Yep. I forgot to ask him for a puppy."

"I see," he says as he puts the stamps on my envelope and holds it up for my approval before placing it in the mail bin. "I hope you get your wish."

"I'm sure I will."

Radomir walks me to the door. "Spokoynoy nochi."

"You, too." I smile as I walk back outside and look for Jelena.

She's not out front on the sidewalk where I left her. I look around, trying to find her. Listening closely, I hear voices around the side of the building. I don't want to be seen, so I walk as carefully as possible in that direction and take a quick look around the corner. Jelena is with Gavriil, and he's kissing her. Yuck.

I've snuck peeks at my older sister's diary and know she has a crush on Gavriil. Papa has forbidden her to see him because Gavriil is the son of Rudolf Sergin, another Pakhan in the Bratva. Someone Papa does not do business with. Gavriil shouldn't even be in our community. It could cause a lot of problems.

I'm trying to stay hidden, but my nose gets that tingly feeling, the kind that happens right before I sneeze. I do my best to hold it in, but it's no use. I sneeze loudly and give myself away. Jelena and Gavriil both startle.

"Svetlana." Jelena hurries over to me, grabbing me by the arms.

"Don't tell on me, please. I'll talk to Papa about getting you a puppy," she begs, trying to bribe me.

I look over her shoulder at the brown-haired boy who's leaning against the building. Gavriil stares back. His eyes are dark and frightening. I don't like him at all, but I'd never tattle on my sister. She's my best friend, and friends don't tell each other's secrets. "I won't say anything. I promise."

"Thank you." She grabs my hand, and we start for home.

As we walk away, I glance back and see Gavriil talking on the phone. Something about the way he's watching us doesn't feel right. Papa says I should always listen to that little voice inside.

"If we don't hurry, Papa's going to come looking for us." Jelena tugs on my arm, trying to get me to move faster, but I resist. I want to stay outside, not hurry home and be stuck indoors.

"I should have listened to her," I say. "We didn't even have a chance to argue about it because everything happened so fast. A van came out of nowhere and screeched to a stop in front of us." I close my eyes, and the memories play like a movie. "The back doors flew open, and two masked men jumped out."

One of the men grabs Jelena. He's wearing a mask, but his long, greasy hair pokes out of the sides. "Svetlana, run," she yells.

"Let her go," I scream, trying to go to her, but the other man grabs me. I nearly gag at the smell of vodka on his breath.

"Leave her," the greasy-haired guy says.

Vodka breath pushes me to the ground, but I jump up, knowing I have to save my sister.

"Lana, run. Go get Papa." Jelena's fighting as hard as she can. Kicking and punching. Anything to avoid being pulled into the van.

I don't want to leave my sister, but she's right. These guys are too big for me to fight. I'm too far from home and won't get to Papa fast enough. I look around, hoping there's someone who'll help us. In the next block up, there's a group of people getting out of a car. I'm sure they'll help me. I run as fast as I can.

"Help," I call, but when they see what's going on, they turn away and hurry into their house, closing the door. "No." I try to scream, but nothing

comes out. I'm left standing helpless on the sidewalk with tears pouring down my face.

Even though it's been ten years, the visceral memories of that day are so powerful I catch myself holding my breath from the intensity of my emotions. "I don't know how or why, but I could hear Papa's voice in my head reminding me to pay attention and memorize every detail. So, that's what I did. I memorized as many details as I could and then ran home." I wipe the tears that are sliding down my cheeks. "To this day, I still can't stand the smell of vodka."

"Papa. Papa," I call through my tears as I burst in the front door.

"What is it?" he asks as he rushes from his office.

"It's Jelena. Men took her."

Papa gets down to my level. "What do you mean?"

"We were coming home. There was a van. Men jumped out," I choke on a sob. "They took Jelena."

Papa stands up and turns to Misha, "Gather a team, now."

"Yes, sir."

I was so focused on telling Papa what happened that I didn't hear Mama come in, but now she's standing beside me crying. "Oh God, Maxim," she whispers.

"Moya vozlyublenny," Papa says and puts his arms around Mama. "I will find our daughter and bring her home." Then, he turns to me. "Svetlana, go to my office. I will be right there."

While I wait, I take off my coat and boots. I repeat the details in my head the entire time so I don't forget them. It doesn't take long for Papa, followed by Misha and a few other guards, to come into the office. Papa sits in his big chair and motions for me to go to him.

"I need you to be a brave girl right now and tell me everything you remember."

"Jelena and I were walking home. She wanted me to hurry, but I was giving her a hard time. I wanted to stay outside." My tears fall faster. "I should've listened to her."

"It's okay, moya babochka," Papa reassures me. "What happened next?"

As hard as it is, I tell Papa how the men jumped out and dragged her

away. That there were people. I called out to them, but they hurried into their house. "Why wouldn't they help us?"

"How many men were there?" Misha asks.

"I saw three. Two men grabbed us, and another man was driving. He had a hat on, but I couldn't see what it said."

"Do you remember anything else about them?"

"The man who grabbed Jelena had greasy black hair. The other man, the one who grabbed me, smelled yucky, like vodka."

"Could you see their faces?"

"They had black masks on. The kind that all the boys wear when we're playing in the snow," I say.

"Did they have any scars or tattoos?" Papa asks.

"The man who grabbed me had tattoos on his hand." I think hard, trying to remember exactly what they looked like. "There was an ugly pig with horns. Next to it were some dots. And there were three crosses."

"You're doing great, Lana," Misha praises me. "Just a few more questions, ok? I nod. "What did the van look like?"

"It was white, and it was old and rusty. When the back doors opened, they creaked really loud. And there were no windows."

"Do you remember the license plate?"

I close my eyes again, trying to picture the van. "I don't think there was one."

"That should be enough for us to start looking," Misha says. "Do you need anything else from us, boss?"

"No. I'll be over as soon as I'm done here." Misha and the men begin to file out of the room.

Guilt gnaws at me, knowing I haven't said everything. I don't want to break my promise to Jelena, but I have to tell Papa. "Wait," I call. Everyone stops and looks at me. "There's one more thing. Gavrill was at the post."

"Gavriil? What was he doing there?"

"He and Jelena were talking." Fresh tears trickle down my cheeks, knowing I betrayed my sister by telling her secret. I curl into him, needing the safety of Papa's hug.

"Find the boy," Papa barks out the order.

"I'm on it." Then, they disappear from the room.

"I shouldn't have left her, Papa."

He holds me away from him so I can see his face. "You did the right thing, moya babochka." He kisses my forehead and then stands. "Go to your Mama. I will find your sister and bring her home. Do not worry."

"Even though I was young and didn't understand the extent of the evil at play, something inside me knew I'd never see my sister again."

"That must have been very scary. Especially for such a little girl."

"It was the most terrifying day of my life."

"Given the traumatic events of the day. How did you remember so many details? Most adults wouldn't have had the composure to manage that."

"You have to understand how we were raised. Our lives were never what anyone would consider *normal*. Danger's inherent in Papa's line of work. From a young age, the need to be aware and pay attention to details was drilled into our heads."

"It seems your parents' efforts were successful."

"I guess." I shrug.

"You guess?"

"I mean, yes, I remembered a lot of details. But there's always been one thing I could never understand."

"What is that?"

"They had us both, but they let me go. Why?" My body begins trembling. "Why didn't they take me, too?"

"Many people have similar feelings after experiencing a traumatic event. It's called survivor's guilt."

"I need to stop."

"Okay. Close your eyes and take some deep breaths." I try to relax and focus on my breathing. "Svetlana, you have the power over your memories and emotions. It's okay to put those into a safe place until our next session."

After a few more breaths, I open my eyes. "I'm okay now." I get up and grab my backpack.

"If you need anything, I don't care what time it is, call or text me."

"I will."

As I leave the office, I push the horrific memories as deep as they'll go, trading them for the anticipation of what's to come tonight.

Maxim (Ten Years Ago)

"Papa, Papa." The desperate plea in Svetlana's cry has me running from my office with Misha right on my heels.

"What is it?" My heart pounds as though it already knows what my daughter is about to say.

"It's Jelena. Men took her." Those words are something no parent is ever prepared to hear. I stoop down in front of Svetlana. "What do you mean?"

"We were coming home. There was a van. Men jumped out." She is crying and out of breath. "They took Jelena."

I stand and turn to Misha, "Gather a team, now."

"Yes, sir." Misha wastes no time. He is already on his phone giving orders to my men.

Irina has just made her way down the steps and is now standing next to our daughter. Tears are pouring down her face. "Oh God, Maxim." Her voice is barely audible.

Rage and fear are boiling inside me, but I cannot let my wife or daughter see my barely controlled emotions. "Moya vozlyublenny." I wrap my arms around my wife's trembling body. "I will find our daughter and bring her home." I turn to Svetlana. "Go to my office. I will be right there." Before I do anything else, I must comfort my wife.

"Oh, Maxim," Irina cries. "You have to find her."

"I will not rest until I do." I hold her to me, not only comforting her but also using her physical closeness to ground my rapidly fraying emotions. "I will not allow harm to come to Jelena. You must trust me."

She nods and then pulls away. "You shouldn't be wasting time on me. Go and find our daughter."

I hurry back to my office, knowing every second we are not out searching for Jelena is a second wasted.

My daughter has impressed me with the amount of information she was able to retain. She's shown courage well beyond her years. If not for the details she gave us, we would not know where to start. I dismiss Misha and the rest of my men so they can get ready to go.

Once we are alone, Svetlana lays her head on my shoulder, and her little body trembles in my arms. "I shouldn't have left her, Papa."

I pick up her tiny frame and hold her so I can see her face. "You did the right thing, *moya babochka*." I kiss her forehead and set her on her feet. "Go to your Mama. I will find your sister and bring her home. Do not worry." I watch as she runs up the steps and disappears down the hallway before I hurry in the other direction to get to work.

With each step, I allow the burning rage to become my driving force. When I get to my command room, I find only Misha waiting for me.

"Where is everyone?"

"Timur and Igor are already out looking for Gavriil, and I have two other teams deployed to search Sergin's warehouses."

The world I live and work in is dangerous. That is a fact I have never ignored. However, in my world, there have always been rules. One of which is that women and children are off-limits. Rudolf Sergin does not seem to abide by such rules. He has blindsided me and stolen something very precious to me.

"Fuck," I yell and swipe my arm across the table, sending everything

flying. I grab the edge of the round black table in the center of the room and drop my head. I have never been in a situation like this. For the first time in my life, I am terrified.

"Boss." Misha places his hand on my shoulder. "We *will* find her."

I lift my head and meet his stare. "I do not care how many people die. We will find my daughter," I growl. I check my weapon, ensuring it is fully loaded, and slide it back into the waistband of my pants. With barely controlled rage, I press my finger against the sensor, unlocking the weapons room. I grab a second semi-automatic gun and holster, securing it in place.

"What are you doing?"

"What does it look like?" I do not stop loading up with as much ammunition as I can carry.

"You aren't coming out. Not like this."

"The fuck I am not. Jelena is my daughter. I am not sitting home when she is out there somewhere."

"Boss, I don't think—"

"Move the hell out of my way, or I will not be responsible for what happens next."

Misha must sense the seriousness of my words because he steps out of my way. "The Escalade is out front. I'll drive."

I am getting into the passenger seat when movement catches my eye. Svetlana is standing on the porch. "Go back in the house," I bark out the order, but she does not move. I do not like my little girl seeing me for what I truly am—a killer. Slamming my door closed, I turn to Misha. "Go."

I watch her in the mirror as we drive away. My heart shatters as she wraps her arms around her little body and drops to her knees. I force myself to look away, knowing Irina is there to take care of her while I am gone to bring Jelena home.

Svetlana

Pyotr is waiting in his usual spot, a wooden bench against a wall overlooking the opulent rotunda. Bright sunlight shines through the opaque skylights surrounding a stained-glass star, representing the old Soviet Union. I don't know how the echoing of footsteps and voices doesn't drive him crazy. I watch him for several minutes, impressed by his constant state of awareness. It's only because of his presence that I can relax, knowing he's in control. Even though I fought Papa when he insisted my childhood guard accompany me to university, I can't lie. I'm glad he's here.

Pyotr gets up when he sees me coming. "All done?"

"I am."

"Do you have plans for tonight?" The expression on his face implores me to say no, that I'm staying in. But he knows me better than that.

"Actually, I do." I grin.

"I don't like that look."

"Slava is in town. He'll be picking me up at seven."

"Is he taking you to Ecstasy?"

"He is." And I can't wait. We're going to be doing a scene together.

Shortly after I turned eighteen, I approached my parents with questions about the BDSM lifestyle. My parents have been in a Dominant/submissive relationship for many years. Mama modeled the grace and selflessness of a submissive, while Papa was an example of stern yet loving leadership. They never hid their involvement in the lifestyle from me, but like any other couple, they didn't share what went on behind closed doors.

Most of my friends would never have approached their parents with such a question. So many families in my country are still very patriarchal and don't allow such openness. But my parents are different. They are open and willing to answer any questions I have.

It didn't surprise them that I would be interested in the lifestyle. Although Mama joked that she never thought I would be curious about submission. She assumed that with my more *assertive* tendencies, being a dominant might be more appealing to me. For a brief moment, I considered it. Except the idea of being responsible for another person didn't interest me. Mama gave me an e-reader loaded with several quality books about the lifestyle and asked me to read them before we took any further steps.

When I showed continued interest, Mama brought me to Noire, the dungeon she and Papa go to. She introduced me to Czarenah, another experienced submissive who would become my mentor. Where my parents and I have an open relationship, discussing specifics about their sex life or mine is not a topic either of us is comfortable with. I've enjoyed learning from Czarenah and consider her almost like a second mother. Currently, we have a difference of opinions, though.

Shortly after I moved to Moscow, I started the search for a BDSM dungeon. It didn't take long to find Ecstasy. I've been going there a few times a month for the past three years. There have been several occasions that I agreed to scene with a Dominant, but mostly, I'm just here to watch. That's what I was doing last weekend when a man sat in the chair next to me.

"Excuse me, are you Svetlana Solonik?"

The use of my full name startled me. But when I turned my head, I saw a familiar face. "Slava?"

"I thought that was you." He smiles.

"What are you doing here?"

"I'm in town on business. I read about this place while I was online looking for a club in the area. I thought I'd stop in."

Slava's a Dominant I recognize from Noire. We seemed to hit it off and spent the evening talking. The club was closing for the night, but we weren't ready to say goodbye. So, we found a local bar and had a few drinks. Before parting ways, we exchanged numbers. There was a text waiting for me the following day. Slava wanted to know if I'd like to do a scene with him next weekend. Of course, I said yes.

I dated a lot in high school, but once I started mentoring, I stopped pursuing men who weren't in the lifestyle. During my training, I was able to play with a few of the Dominants at Noire, who helped train new submissives. Several Dominants had expressed an interest in me outside of our training scene. At the time, Czarenah didn't feel I was ready for anything outside of that strictly controlled environment.

In my opinion, everything's different now. I've grown and gained more experience. After I hung up with Slava, I couldn't wait to call Czarenah and share my excitement with her. But, instead of being happy, she was the ultimate buzzkill. She expressed her strong disapproval of me even playing with Slava. Czarenah felt our age difference and my lack of experience are potential red flags. Both were things I disagreed strongly with. Slava is a respected and experienced Dominant. Which, to me, makes him the perfect candidate.

"I assume he's picking you up again?" Pyotr asks as we walk back to my dorm building.

"He is."

"I'll follow you in our car."

"You can stay home, you know. I'm safe with Slava."

"And have your father murder me when he finds out? Not a chance."

I laugh as I put the key into the lock of my dorm room door. "He wouldn't have to find out."

"Not going to happen, little butterfly." His mouth cracks in a rare smile. "I'll stay out of your way, but I will be there."

"You should get yourself a submissive while we're there. It might do you some good." I hurry into my room and close the door before he has a chance to respond.

I'm still in the shower, rinsing my hair when my cell rings. I'm expecting a call from Slava, so I reach out and swipe to connect the call and put it on speaker.

"Hello?"

"Hi," Czarenah says. "Do you have a few minutes to talk?"

"Can you hang on one second?"

"Sure."

I regret not checking the screen before I answered. The last thing I want right now is another argument about not seeing Slava. I hurry and throw a towel around me.

"Sorry about that. I was finishing washing my hair."

"Are you going out tonight?"

"Yes." I may as well get this out of the way since I'm sure this is why she's calling. "Slava will be here in an hour."

"Is there any way I can talk some sense into you?"

"What's that supposed to mean?"

"Slava was at the dungeon earlier this week. He and I had the opportunity to discuss you."

"Okay." I start combing my hair out, partially ignoring her.

"I already told Slava my feelings, and now I'm going to tell you. I don't think it's the right time for you to move forward with him."

"I disagree with you."

"Tell me why you disagree?"

"I don't mean any disrespect. You've taught me well, but I've spent enough time being a student. I'm ready to find an interested Dominant and begin vetting."

"May I explain my point of view?"

"I guess." I'm glad we're on the telephone so she can't see me roll my eyes. I'm certain Czarenah's going to tell me I'm too young. Too inexperienced. But how can one gain experience if they don't get the chance to try?

"This is the first time you're living on your own."

"It's been three years."

"Yes, but you've also just started trauma therapy. You've worked at Jelena's Hope. You understand that as you begin to work through what you've experienced, you'll likely experience many strong emotions. Ones that may cloud your vision. I've known Slava for a long time, and although he's a trustworthy Dominant—"

"Shouldn't that make this a good move?" I interrupt.

"In ordinary circumstances, yes. But what you are going through is far from ordinary. I don't want to see you make decisions that may be clouded by feelings and emotions. It could end badly for both you and Slava. I'm begging you to give yourself some more time."

Czarenah's come to mean a lot to me both as a mentor and a friend. I've always welcomed her advice. Which makes what I'm about to do that much harder. "I can't thank you enough for everything you've taught me. You've made sure I'm prepared for this next part of my journey as a submissive," I say and clear my throat, hoping to hold back the tears that threaten to fall. "But if you're not going to support me with this, I think it's best to part ways."

"Svetlana, please. Don't shut me out."

"I have to go. Slava will be here shortly, and I don't want to keep him waiting."

"Is there anything I can say to get you to wait?"

"You've been very good to me, and I hate that things are ending this way. But I refuse to walk away from Slava without exploring what's between us."

"I see. I'll be here if you need anything."

"Goodbye, Czarenah." I disconnect the call.

Czarenah's made her case, and we're no longer on the same page. I know she thinks I'm being stubborn and reckless. She'll probably run right to Papa, but I don't care. I'm no longer a child. I'm an adult who's fully capable of making her own decisions. She and I have come to an impasse, and it's time for us to go our separate ways.

How long does she expect me to watch from the sidelines before I take the next logical step—beginning to vet a Dominant. And why not Slava? We didn't seek one another out. It happened by chance. I like to think fate had a part in bringing us together. He's well-known and respected in the community. To me, it only makes sense that if we're interested in playing or having a dynamic, we should be able to do so without interference.

Maxim (Ten Years Ago)

From the moment Jelena was taken, we have been one step behind—a position I do not like to be in. If not for Svetlana's ability to retain so many vital details—No. I cannot think about the disadvantages we would face. Knowing Gavriil and his father are involved is a crucial piece of the puzzle. Unfortunately, Rudolf Sergin has left nothing to chance. Within minutes after Svetlana mentioned Gavriil's name, my men were out looking for him. Being the son of a mob boss, he was able to disappear quickly. But no one can hide forever.

It took several hours, but Timur and Igor found the boy and brought him to one of my facilities. I intend to extract my daughter's whereabouts from him. Timur pulls into the gravel parking lot outside the building. I do not wait for the vehicle to come to a complete stop before throwing the door open. I storm into the room where they're holding Gavriil.

"Where is she, you son of a bitch?"

"Wouldn't you like to know," he laughs. "That bitch is one hot piece of ass."

My fist connects with his face. Blood splatters from his now broken nose.

"I am going to ask you one more time. Where is my daughter?"

Gavriil spits on my shoe, infuriating me. "You are a dead man." I pull the gun from my waistband, click off the safety, and aim at his head.

Timur hurries to my side. "Boss, if you kill him now, we'll never get the information we need." He keeps his voice low. What he says may be true, but I remain poised to kill. "Maxim, you're not thinking clearly. Take a step back, and let us handle this."

My body shakes with uncontrolled rage. Killing is part of my life. It is something I have done many times. If it is the choice between them or me, I will pull the trigger without hesitation. But I have never felt bloodthirsty. I have never been blinded by such hate that I long to pull the trigger—until now. I want the satisfaction of watching the life drain from this piece of shit in front of me. However, Timur is correct. Gavriil is the only link we have to Jelena's whereabouts. If I kill him, the trail will go cold. That is a chance I cannot take.

With a click, I put the safety back on and lower my weapon. "Do whatever you need to get him to talk." I give the order and then summon every ounce of self-control I possess to leave the room. I do not stop until I am in my makeshift office, where I call my wife.

"Did you find her?" she asks as soon as the line connects.

"Not yet. We are questioning Gavriil."

"Max, I'm so scared."

"I know, *vozlyublenny*." I am equally as scared, but I do my best to keep my voice calm and even. "Jelena will be back in our arms very soon. I need you to have faith." Faith enough for the two of us.

Sitting here alone, not knowing what is happening in the other room, is killing me. Several times, I have gone to the door with the intent to rejoin the questioning. But Timur was right. I am too close to this situation and will only hamper their efforts. I hire only the best men, a fact which I must trust.

It feels as though an eternity has passed before Misha walks into the office. "Where is she?" I ask, jumping to my feet.

"His father taught him well. He wasn't prepared to give up any information easily," Timur responds as he pulls his bloody T-shirt off and tosses it into the garbage before going into the closet to grab a clean shirt. "Once we employed some non-traditional methods, he broke quickly. The kid gave us two names—Valery and Boris. Says they're *brodyaga* in his father's organization."

"Where are they?"

"They landed in Serbia about two hours ago. Igor made a few calls and got footage from the security system at the Belgrade airport. We were able to confirm Jelena was with them." I grab my phone to call Irina. "I've already contacted Obrad Radovanović. He has boots on the ground tracking them."

I tap the green call button, and the line connects.

"Did you—"

"Have my bags packed. I am going to get our daughter."

Six hours later, the wheels of my jet touchdown on a private airstrip. Radovanović is waiting for us on the tarmac.

"It's good to see you, Solonik. Although, I wish it were under better circumstances."

"As do I."

We waste no time walking to waiting vehicles. While we walk, Radovanović fills me in on the progress his foot soldiers have made. "We tracked the men and your daughter to a holding facility. I was with my team when they arrived, but we were too late. They were already gone."

"*Chert voz'mi.*" We have been doing everything right, yet they continue to slip out of our grasp.

"They're traveling amidst a known trafficking ring," he explains as we get into the back of his black Mercedes S Class. Misha rides in the front with the driver. "That is both a good and bad thing."

"How much do you know about the group?" Misha asks.

"We know the operation and have been on their trail for years. Each time we find a warehouse, we close it down. But they are very organized and have underground networks of their own."

Misha's cell rings. "It's Timur." While Misha is on the phone, Radovanović shares more information about this trafficking ring.

"Where are we?" I interrupt him when the car stops in front of a tall wrought iron gate.

"This is my home."

"What are we doing here? I need to be out searching for my daughter."

"Our combined forces will continue searching. But you are exhausted. You need a few hours of sleep and a good meal."

"Like hell I do," I argue. There is no way I can rest while my daughter is out there, alone.

"Maxim, you cannot go after these men when you are distracted by physical exhaustion." He gets out of the car and waits for me to follow. "You must trust in our men."

"Jelena is my daughter. I need to be out there," I yell and step closer to Radovanović, preparing to challenge him.

"You will be out there as soon as you can think straight." He remains calm despite my anger. "I have known you for many years, Solonik. I can tell when you're off your game. If you go out there like this, you'll get yourself or someone else killed."

I do not want to admit his observation is correct. I am so tired I cannot form a clear thought. I am reacting instead of responding, something I always warn my men against. That is when mistakes are made. "Fine. An hour. Then I join the search." I concede.

We spend the next three weeks chasing in Serbia, chasing Jelena and her captures around the country. Each time we believe we are closing in on them, they outsmart us and get away.

Tonight's intel is solid. Jelena was seen at this location, which turns out to be no more than a flophouse, this morning. Hopes are high that tonight, the tables are about to turn in our favor. I am ready to have my daughter safely back in my arms.

I know we are too late as soon as we breach the entrance and are not met with resistance.

"Boss. Up here," Misha calls from a room on the second floor.

I hurry up the steps, hoping my assessment is wrong and that he has Jelena. But that hope is gone when I find Misha holding the pink sweater Jelena was wearing the day she was taken. He hands me the now dirty sweater that is still warm from being worn. "Fuck," I roar.

"What's wrong?" Timur rushes into the room with Radovanović on his heels.

I hold the sweater close to me. "She was just here. We are too late again."

We go back downstairs and meet up with Radovanović's men, who are returning inside. "We found an underground tunnel in the shed. I sent a group down to track them." He looks to his boss. "These tunnel systems are intricate. They could be anywhere."

Tonight was supposed to be the night. Jelena should be with me on my jet, flying home. Instead, the trail has gone cold, and I am returning home empty-handed. As much as I do not want to leave Serbia, I am confident they are no longer here. We are back to square one, relying on technology to locate them. This part of the work can be done from my home.

I hold onto Jelena's sweater. It is a reminder of how close we got. It is a hope that she is still alive and a prayer that next time, we will find her.

Svetlana

Ecstasy is packed. The energy from the people in attendance is electric.

"Are we going to do a public scene tonight?"

"No."

"Why not?"

"It is our first scene together," he explains. "I want us to have privacy to take things at a slower pace rather than being concerned with putting a show for the onlookers." I'm disappointed, but I'm afraid he'll back out of the scene if I argue. "I've reserved a room if you're ready."

Slava takes my hand and guides me up the stairs to the club's second floor, where the private rooms are located. Although I've played with a few Dominants at this club, this time feels very different. I went into those scenes knowing it was a one-and-done deal. Tonight, all options are on the table. The door closes behind us, blocking out the thumping bass from the music in the main room. Now it's just Slava and me.

"Sit down. We need to go over the rules first."

My heels click on the polished concrete floor as I make my way to the leather sofa. Slava follows, sitting next to me. I've never been in any of the private rooms Ecstasy offers. I take a minute to admire the room's ultra-modern design with minimalist furniture and clean lines. Three walls are covered in creamy white textured wallpaper, while the wall behind the black metal bed is painted a deep purple. Against the wall across from the bed are glass shelves. Various paddles, crops, floggers, canes, and whips are laid out neatly on the shelves. The ceiling boasts several skylights that, during the day, would allow for natural light. Tonight, the recessed lights are dimmed, adding to the dark and dangerous feel of the room.

"Do you have any experience with impact play?"

"Yes. While I was mentoring under Czarenah, I expressed a desire to experiment with it. She oversaw several interactions with a Dominant who introduced me to each implement."

"What were your conclusions?"

"It was a few strikes with each, but I enjoyed it very much."

"Good." He smiles. "Let's discuss limits."

"I don't have any," I answer quickly.

Slava snickers. "*Moya nevinnyy malysh*, I can assure you that you do have limits."

"I guess I haven't encountered them yet." I shrug.

"I will tell you my limits. I feel comfortable using a flogger, crop, or paddle. Whips and canes are off the table."

"Why?"

"You don't have a good gauge on where your limits lie."

He nods. "How do you feel about bondage?"

"I've never experienced it."

"This will be a good first, then. Do you have anything you'd like to request?"

"Yes. I want to be blindfolded and gagged."

He studies me for a moment. "Why?"

"I want to experience everything."

"I'm not comfortable with that tonight."

"Why not?" I want this. I need this.

"I get a great deal of pleasure giving a willing submissive pain. However, your inexperience and this being the first time we're playing together is not the time for experimenting with such extremes. I've seen it too many times. An eager sub who doesn't know their limits or who wishes to impress their Dominant agrees to more than they're going to be able to handle. Oftentimes, they don't safeword for fear of disappointing the Dominant or ending a scene." He pauses.

"I've also witnessed the aftermath of physical and emotional injuries. I've witnessed both Dominants and submissives leave the lifestyle because of the damage done. I don't want that for you. After this scene, I want you begging for me."

"You have years of experience. Doesn't that make me safe with you?"

"Ah, *moya nevinnyy malysh*. I will do everything in my power to keep you safe, but I'm only human. I can't foresee everything and refuse to leave your safety to chance. Do you agree to my limits?"

"Yes, Sir."

Slava sets safewords, and once he's sure we're on the same page, he gives his command. "Strip and kneel."

I bring my hand to the zipper on the front of my dress. His eyes follow as I drag the zipper down slowly, allowing the fabric to slip from my arms, landing on the floor by my feet. The corner of his mouth lifts in a smile as he takes in my naked body. I lower myself to kneel before him. Slava stands and steps closer to me.

"You like to be the one calling the shots, and you challenge anyone who tries to strip that control from you." He gently strokes my hair. "Tonight, I'm going to show you just how good giving up that control can be."

I have to force myself not to move. Slava's assessment of me is spot on. But I plan to show him I can submit to his demands yet remain in complete control. He unbuttons his dark blue dress shirt and disappears from my sight line.

I can hear his footsteps and other sounds behind me. I'm certain he's gathering items for our scene. Given his questions, I'm assuming we're doing something with impact, but he's not laid out the exact details. My mind races, trying to come up with possible scene ideas.

"Stand and come to me," he orders.

I rise from the floor, mindful of being graceful, and walk over to where Slava stands next to the bed. That's when I get my first glimpse of him, and what I imagined is nothing compared to what I see. His upper body has well-defined muscles that lead to a lean chest and abs. I follow the trail of dark hair that dips below the waistband of his jeans. My tongue runs across my lower lip, seeing the outline of his erection.

"Put your arms out in front of you." Slava reaches around me to the bed. "This is bondage tape. If, for any reason, you are uncomfortable and need to stop the scene, I can have it off in seconds."

"Yes, Sir."

He wraps the thin plastic-like material around my wrists. It's not sticky, and it adheres only to itself.

"Are you ready to give control over to me?"

I drop my gaze, unable to answer him.

"Look at me." Slowly, I bring my head back up. "When I ask a question, I expect an answer. Are you ready to give control over to me?"

"No, Sir."

"No?" He raises an eyebrow. "Are you certain you want to proceed with this scene?"

"Yes, Sir."

"Bend over the bed and put your arms above your head." Slava nudges my legs apart and lands his first strike. He continues spanking me with his open hand. "Your skin is the most beautiful shade of pink. Now that you're sufficiently warmed up, let's try something more impactful."

There's a swoosh and then a stinging sensation across my upper thighs.

"How does that feel?"

"It stings. I like it."

He continues alternating between my thighs and my ass. Just as the sting begins to morph into numbness, he stops.

Slava's hand cups my pussy. "Are you wet for me, *moya nevinnyy malysh?*"

I nod, and he removes his touch.

"Are you wet for me?" he asks again.

"Yes, Sir. I am."

He drags two fingers through my folds before plunging them inside my center. I'm so turned on by the spanking that I moan from the small amount of contact. He continues dragging them in and out until I'm a panting mess. Then, they disappear. I groan from the loss of contact.

The next strike is an unexpected thuddy sensation. Slava alternates sides as he increases the intensity.

"You need to relax," he instructs.

"I can't," I argue.

Strike.

"You can."

Strike.

"No." I grit my teeth, trying to hold on to the last shreds of my control.

"Why not?" I gasp at the intensity of the next strike.

"Because I don't want to."

Strike.

"I don't believe that," Slava challenges me. "I think there's more to it."

"I can't give up control."

"Why not, Svetlana?"

"I'm afraid."

The paddle connects with my flesh hard and fast.

"I'll keep you safe. You don't have to be afraid."

"It's too much."

"What's your color?"

"Green."

"Give in to me."

"I don't know how." Almost without my consent, my body begins to relax into each strike, embracing the pain.

"That's it." His voice sounds far away. Although I hear the noise of the paddle connecting with my body, I no longer feel the pain. "Let go, *moya nevinnyy malysh.*"

Everything has faded away, and I'm weightless. The constant thoughts in my head are silent. There's no pain or fear. I want to stay here forever.

"Svetlana. It's time to wake up now."

I blink a few times, trying to get my body to comply. Finally, my eyes open, and Slava's face comes into focus. I'm captivated by the deep blue in his eyes.

"Welcome back."

"What happened?"

"You finally allowed yourself to give in and allow me to have control." He smiles. "And you experienced subspace."

Tears begin falling. "I don't know why I'm crying."

"It's the extremes of the emotions you've just experienced." He reaches out and pulls me close to him. "Stay the night with me. Allow me to care for you."

I agree to return to his hotel, where he spends the night and the entirety of the following day, tending to my every need. He's tender and kind, ensuring I'm not only physically but emotionally cared for.

It's so difficult to walk out of his room knowing he wants me to stay with him again. Unfortunately, I have a presentation for school I need to finish working on.

Svetlana

"How was your weekend?" Masha asks as I take my usual seat in her office.

"It was good." I keep my voice calm and don't go into detail. I'm not ready to dissect what may be developing between Slava and myself.

"Where would you like to start today?"

"I guess we should pick up where I left off."

"As long as you're comfortable with that."

I wouldn't say I'm comfortable, but it seems to be what makes the most sense. I take a deep breath and adjust my position on the couch as my thoughts transport me back in time.

"Over the next few weeks, our lives became even more unrecognizable. Papa hired triple the number of guards for our property. The little time he was home, he spent in his office with the door closed. Most of the time, he was out with his men searching for Jelena.

Mama was home but very much gone at the same time. I could hear her crying when I walked by her bedroom door. I tried to open it several times but couldn't find the courage to do so. How was I supposed to look her in the eyes, knowing I stood by and watched while those men took Jelena away?"

"Hey, kiddo," Dimitri says, sitting beside me on the stairs.

"Dimitri's my cousin," I explain. "He was staying with us for a few weeks before he had to return to Ukraine to serve his conscription."

"I see," she says and jots some notes down.

"Hi," I mumble.

"What are you doing?"

"Sitting."

"I see that." He elbows me jokingly. "Why are you sitting on the steps?" I shrug. "I can see something's wrong." I continue counting the marble tiles on the foyer floor while I debate telling him what's bothering me. "Your secret's safe with me."

"I was in the kitchen with Olga when Misha and the other guards brought Gavrill back here." I was in the kitchen helping Olga get dinner ready. We were peeling potatoes when the SUV stopped, and I froze with the potato peeler in my hand. I couldn't take my eyes off the scene outside the window. "When Olga saw what I was watching, she shooed me from the kitchen. Told me I was slowing her down too much."

"I see."

"Gavriil was handcuffed and beat up." I look at Dimitri. "Papa's going to kill him, isn't he?"

"Of course not." Dimitri's voice rises an octave, giving away his lie.

Masha holds her hand up, stopping me. "Was this the first time you witnessed something like this?"

"My papa having someone brought to our property?"

"Yes."

"It was. Papa never hid what he did from us, but he also didn't allow business to be conducted in our presence. I wasn't meant to see it this time either, but no one knew I was in the kitchen."

"That's a lot of violence for a young girl. How did it make you feel?"

I don't answer for several minutes. I never stopped to think about how seeing that made me feel. "Regardless of what Papa's job is, I always knew he was a good man. He would never set out to hurt innocent people. Gavriil wasn't innocent, and Papa was only doing what was necessary."

"You've explained your knowledge of your Papa's business," Masha says in her usual calm manner. "But you didn't say how it made you feel."

"I don't really know." I shrug. "I've always been immensely proud of Papa. He could do no wrong in my eyes. And Gavriil. Just saying his name brings back my all-consuming hatred for him."

"I'm not a baby, Dimitri. Gavriil was involved with Jelena's kidnapping, and now Papa's going to kill him."

Dimitri sighs. "We shouldn't be talking about this."

"Why not?"

"You're a girl. You're not involved in Maxim's business."

All the emotions I've been trying to avoid boil over, and I shoot up. "I'm not involved?" I yell. "I was with Jelena when they grabbed her. It was me who ran and left her to be taken. But you think I'm not involved?"

Dimitri takes my hand. "I'm sorry. Those weren't the right words. I just meant that your papa doesn't want you affected by the things he has to do."

"Well, it's too late. I'm already affected."

"Those were some pretty big feelings for a little girl."

"I really believed my parents blamed me for Jelena's disappearance, and that's why they were avoiding me."

"You were very close to your parents. Those feelings of alienation must have been difficult."

"I was close to them. Then, almost overnight, they weren't there anymore." I wipe a tear from my cheek and take a second to compose myself. "The new year came and signaled a great deal of change for me. I wasn't a foolish child making wishes to a fairy tale character. I did a lot of growing up and realized such things didn't exist. What did exist were the nightmares I had about my sister being snatched from my side."

I look up at Masha, who's no longer writing. Instead, she's watching me intently while I tell my story. "A piece of my childhood was stolen when Jelena was taken. My childhood, the time of viewing the world through naïve eyes, was over. I started seeing the world as it truly is— cruel and unforgiving. I realized I could never return to the person I was before that day."

Papa got in late last night. Something I wished for because today's my eleventh birthday. Mama and Papa always make a big deal out of our birthdays. We get a special breakfast and a big party. I wasn't expecting a party this year. I don't need a party. I'll be happy to get to spend the day with my parents. I race downstairs to the dining room for my special birthday breakfast with my parents. But when I get inside, I find the room empty.

"I'm sure they'll be here," Olga says as she sets my plate of Syrniki with cheese and honey on top in front of me.

I give her a polite smile, but I know they're not coming.

"I don't like remembering that birthday because of how lonely it was. I hadn't seen Mama. I assumed she was in her bedroom. And although Papa was home, he spent the day in his office with the doors closed. Every time I went by and asked the guard if I could go in, he told me Papa was busy and couldn't see me."

"This seems to evoke more emotion than witnessing the violence."

"I never thought about it that way, but I guess you're right."

"There's nothing wrong with that." Masha tries to reassure me. "It's just an observation."

I nod and continue. "When it was time for dinner, I assumed I'd be eating alone. So, I was surprised when I walked into the dining room and saw Dimitri and Pyotr sitting at the table."

"There's our birthday girl." Dimitri gives me a big smile.

I sit across from the men who do their best to carry on a conversation with me. But neither of them is used to spending time with a girl, so we don't talk about more than the weather and how good Olga's cooking is. All through dinner, my eyes are drawn to the doorway, hoping to see Mama and Papa, but they never come.

After the meal, Olga emerges from the kitchen carrying a pink frosted cake with eleven candles.

"Don't light those yet," Dimitri says and makes a quick exit from the room. He returns a short time later with Mama and Papa, who apologize for running late.

Although everyone has smiles on their faces, I see beneath the masks to the pain they try to hide. After singing Pust' begut neuklyuzhe, I blow out my candles. Dimitri cuts the cake while Olga passes out the plates.

"Classes resume tomorrow," Papa says as we eat.

"Yes, they do." I'm looking forward to finally being able to leave the house.

"Pyotr will be accompanying you."

I drop my fork. "I don't want a guard at school."

"I did not ask if you wanted one," Papa says sternly. "You will have one."

"Fine."

"I must return to work." Papa stands. "S dnem rozhdeniya, moya babochka."

Mama walks out right after Papa, leaving me with Dimitri and Pyotr once again.

"Thank you for trying, Dimitri." I manage a small smile.

"They're doing the best they can right now."

"I know."

"That day marked twenty-one days that my sister was missing. I remember thinking Mama and Papa looked and sounded like the parents I knew, but that's where the comparison ended. No one was the same." I swipe at the stray tear that escapes and look at Masha. "I was scared and sad. I felt invisible."

Maxim (Ten Years Ago)

The door to my office flies open, banging against the wall. "What the hell is wrong with you?"

"Did you forget what today is?"

"What are you talking about?" I'm annoyed by my nephew's unwelcome intrusion.

"It's Svetlana's birthday. The kids spent the entire day alone. Pyotr and I just had dinner with her, but what she needs is her parents."

How could I forget my daughter's birthday? "I will get Irina. We will be right there."

"I'll walk with you."

"I do not need a babysitter." Yet, Dimitri follows me anyway.

"Uncle Max, this has to stop. Your men are more than capable of carrying out this search on their own. You're neglecting—"

"Enough." I slice my hand through the air, stopping my nephew in his tracks. "I will not have you telling me how I should or should not conduct the search for my daughter. Do you hear me? Jelena is my daughter." I start walking away but stop and turn around quickly. "When you have walked in my shoes, you may tell me how to do my job. Until that time, keep your comments to yourself."

I take the steps two at a time, needing to put some distance between

Dimitri and myself. When I get to our bedroom, I find Irina in the same position she has been in for weeks. She is lying on the bed with her back toward the door.

"Irina, I need you to get up." I grab her robe that is draped over the back of the armchair. "It is Svetlana's birthday."

"I can't go."

I sit next to my wife and stroke her forehead. "*Moya vozlyublenny,* we have both forgotten about Svetlana's special day. She is waiting to have cake with us."

Slowly, Irina pushes to a sitting position. Her complexion is pale from lying in this dark room for weeks. I offer my hand to help her stand and am alarmed when I notice the nightdress hanging off her shoulders from the weight she has lost. Now is not the time to bring that up. Instead, I help her into her robe and then take her hand as we go to the dining room.

We are gathered around the table to celebrate my Svetlana's eleventh birthday. It should be a day to celebrate the life of our special little girl. Looking around the table, I see it is not a celebration. My wife sits beside me, but her mind and heart are absent. Rather than Svetlana laughing with her sister, Dimitri and Pyotr are talking with Svetlana, trying to make this as normal as possible. And there is an empty chair where my Jelena should be sitting.

I attempt to interject myself into the conversation. "Classes resume tomorrow," I say.

"Yes, they do."

"Pyotr will be accompanying you."

She drops her fork. It clangs off her dish. "I don't want a guard at school."

"I did not ask if you wanted one. You will have one."

"Fine."

I believed my family was safe in our community. My girls were allowed to grow up and live normal lives. In a matter of minutes, that all changed. We can never go back to the way things were before.

There are new rules for my daughters. They will no longer be allowed off my property without a guard by their side. Jelena is my compliant, good-natured daughter. I know when I find her and bring her home, she will accept my directive with no argument. Svetlana, on the other hand, never misses the opportunity to challenge me. I knew she would fight me on this.

"I must return to work. *S dnem rozhdeniya, moya babochka.*" This is Svetlana's special day. I do not want to spoil it by arguing over insignificant details. Obviously, she is better off without me here right now.

Svetlana

I'm thankful that today's session is over. Recalling the memories from that day was harder than I thought it would be. I really want to go back to my dorm and be alone, but I know my dorm mate, Mei, will be there. I spot Pyotr on his usual bench. When he sees me, he hurries over.

"Is everything okay?"

"That was a tough session. I need some time alone. Can I hang out in your room?" I won't be truly alone, but Pyotr's okay with silence.

"That's fine with me, but I should warn you, Slava's waiting for you outside."

"Did he say what he wants?"

"No."

I take a deep breath and walk outside. Slava's leaning against the building, his arms crossed over his chest. A small group of girls has gathered around him.

"Hi," I say, touching his arm and glaring at the now-silent girls. "Sorry, I'm late."

"Excuse me, please, ladies." Slava places his hand on my lower back and leads me away. "Don't tell me you're jealous?"

"Maybe." I shrug.

"There's no need. I came here for you, not them." His words tamper down the jealousy I'm feeling.

"I'm surprised to see you here. I thought you'd be back in St. Petersburg."

"I'm leaving tonight. I wanted to see you before I left. Can we talk?"

I'm exhausted physically and emotionally, but I can't say no to this man. "Sure. Is everything okay?"

"It is." He leads me to a concrete bench that's under a tree. "I enjoyed our time together this past weekend."

"Why does this sound like goodbye?"

"It isn't a goodbye." He lifts my chin, forcing me to look at him. "I'd like to see more of you."

"You would?" After I say the words, I realize how ridiculous I sound.

"I would," he chuckles. "If you're open to it, I'd like to discuss a contract."

"Um, sure."

"Are you okay, Lana? You don't seem like yourself."

"I had a long day. I'm just a bit tired."

"I'll email you a contract, but I want you to take your time to look it over. Get some rest before you make any decisions."

"I can do that."

"I do hope you say yes, though." He cups my cheek in his hand, and I hope he's going to kiss me. Instead, he says. "I have to go. I'll speak to you later in the week."

I watch as he walks away. Pyotr appears at my side just as Slava gets into his car. "Is everything okay?"

"Yeah, it is." He looks in Slava's direction and then back at me. He's opening his mouth to speak, but I cut him off. "Please, don't. I need one person in my corner."

"I'm always in your corner, little butterfly." Pyotr holds his hand out. "Come on, let's get back to the dorm for your alone time."

Pyotr keeps the lights off. "Go lay down and rest. I'll be here if you need me."

"Thanks." My head barely hits the pillow on his bed before I fall asleep and am thrust right back into my past.

"Are you excited to return to school today?" Pyotr asks.

"Yes." What was supposed to be a fun school holiday turned into a nightmare. Papa said I did everything, and I know he's been working non-stop to bring her home, but it hurts that both he and Mama are avoiding me. I'm sure they blame me for what happened.

I'm looking forward to returning to school where I know I'll have my friends. However, I'm not happy about having to bring a guard to school.

"I know you don't want me to go with you. I'll do my best to give you space."

"Thank you." Pyotr opens the front door for what I think is our walk to school.

"The car's warmed up already," he says proudly.

"The car?"

"Until your sister is found safe and the responsible people have been apprehended, your father is requiring me to drive you to and from school.

"Seriously?"

"I'm afraid so." Pyotr shrugs.

I want to scream and tell Pyotr there's no way I'm driving to school. I'm walking with my friends like Jelena and I used to do. But I know it won't do any good. Pyotr isn't in charge. He's not the one who made this stupid decision. He's always nice to me, so I don't want to give him a hard time. Instead, I get into the car and buckle my safety belt for the short ride to Krestovsky Preparatory Academy.

We drive past my friends, who are smiling and laughing as they walk together. I sink down in my seat, hoping they don't see me being driven to school. A few minutes later, Pyotr turns into the school parking lot. I climb out of my father's gigantic vehicle, thankful we got there before my friends.

When we get inside the school's door, we're met by the director. "Welcome back, Svetlana," Director Valkov greets me. "And you must be the security Mr. Solonik advised us would be accompanying Svetlana?"

"Yes," Pyotr says, standing to his full height and crossing his arms over his chest.

Director Valkov lowers his voice as a group of students walk by. "I understand Mr. Solonik's reasoning, but I'm concerned your presence will upset the other children in Svetlana's classroom. I've set up a chair for you at the end of the hall."

"I will remain outside Svetlana's classroom door."

My eyes dart back and forth between the men. Pyotr's at least a foot taller than Director Valkov. And where the director is round and unfit, Pyotr has lots of muscle—Papa ensures all his guards exercise regularly.

"You must understand, I am tasked with ensuring the safety and security of all my students, not just Svet—."

"I have only one concern, Svetlana's safety. I will be outside her classroom. Unless you need Mr. Solonik to stop by?" Pyotr steps forward.

The hall fills with students who all avert their stares as they walk past the scene unfurling between the two men. I'm so embarrassed I want to crawl into a corner and hide.

"That won't be necessary," Director Valkov puts his hands up in surrender.

"Now, if there's nothing else, we will be on our way. I believe class is starting shortly."

"Yes, it is." He looks at me. "I hope you have a good first day back."

"Thank you," I say quietly.

Pyotr and I walk down the hall until we come to room number five.

"I'll be out here if you need anything." He offers me a kind smile.

"Okay." I take a deep breath and peek through the window of the door. My classmates chat amongst themselves while Ms. Orlova writes on the blackboard, preparing for the day's lesson. When I step into the classroom, everyone goes silent. Ms. Orlova gives me a tight smile but says nothing as I walk past her to the closet, where I hand my coat. All eyes follow me as I make my way to the table I share with my best friend, Sofya.

"How was your break?" I ask as I sit.

"It was fine."

"Do you want to work on our dance during free time?" Sofya and I have studied ballet at the same dance academy since we were three years old. This summer, we're finally old enough to audition for the summer intensive program for pointe students. We've been working very hard on our audition routine.

"I don't think so." She looks across the aisle to where Lavra, another classmate, sits before looking back at me. "Over the holiday recess, my parents enrolled me in a different dance school. Lavra and I are going to be working on our choreography together."

I glance at Lavra, who's whispering something to Nadia, her table-mate. Then, they both look at me and laugh.

"Oh." My fragile heart shatters.

Sofya and I have been best friends for as long as I can remember. Why is Sofya doing this? I'm just about to ask her when Ms. Orlova calls the class to order. I thought coming back to school would be a welcome respite from the loneliness I've felt at home. Instead, I find I'm just as alienated here. Rather than focusing on the morning's lessons, my mind wanders.

Jelena, I need you to be okay. I need you to come home.

I don't realize how much time has passed until the lunch bell rings, startling me. I slide my book into the drawer under the table and file out of the room with my classmates.

I need to talk to Sofya, but she's too far ahead of me in the food line to get her attention. As soon as I'm through, I hurry to the table where she's sitting. "Why did you change ballet schools?"

Lavra whispers something to Sofya, and she doesn't answer me.

"Can I sit here?"

"I'm not allowed to be friends with you anymore. I'm sorry," Sofya says quietly.

"You're not allowed to be friends with me anymore?" I don't understand what's going on.

"None of us want you here," Lavra interrupts. "There's a table over there." She points to a small table in the corner.

I wait, hoping Sofya says something, anything to make this better. But she doesn't. She just ignores me.

I drop my head and walk to the empty table in the corner of the cafeteria. After I sit, I look around the room at everyone else. They're all laughing and talking. I'm the only one alone. As hard as I try, I can't stop tears from escaping. I wipe my face quickly, not wanting the girls to see me cry. They don't need any more ammunition than they already have to hurt me.

Movement catches my eye. It's Pyotr, and he's hurrying in my direction. It's only seconds before he's at the table, pulling out the chair next to me. "What's wrong?"

"Nothing."

"I may not know a lot about children, but I do know they don't cry when there's nothing wrong."

"Everything's different." I swallow over the growing lump in my throat. "My parents don't speak to me anymore. I thought I'd at least have my friends at school, but they're gone now, too."

"It's your first day back. I'm sure everyone's just getting back into the routine of things."

"Sofya," I say, looking in her direction. "Was my best friend. Now, she won't speak to me, and neither will anyone else. Everyone hates me."

"That's not true."

"But it is." I swipe at the fresh wave of tears spilling down my cheeks. "I want to go home."

"Please don't cry," Pyotr says nervously as he searches the room. His gaze stops at the table where Sofya, Lavra, and several other girls point in our direction and laugh.

He wastes no time pulling out his cell phone and typing something. A few minutes later, his phone buzzes. After he reads whatever's on the screen, he turns to me. "Come on." He takes my hand.

"Where are we going?"

"Home."

Pyotr is summoned to Papa's office seconds after we walk into the house. Dimitri's already in there. The door is cracked open, so I sit against the wall with my knees pulled up to my chest, listening while they talk. I know I shouldn't be here, but I want to hear what's going on. I need to know what's going to happen next.

"I do not understand why you brought her home early," Papa says.

"I couldn't make her stay when it was clear she was being made fun of."

"And you gave him permission to bring her home?"

"I did," Dimitri answers confidently. "She's been through too much the past few weeks. There's no reason for her to endure any more cruelty."

"Svetlana knows to ignore such childish behavior. She is a young girl who needs to be in school."

"Maybe you can hire a tutor? At least until things calm down," Dimitri suggests.

Papa's heavy footsteps come closer, and I scramble to get up quickly and disappear.

"I know you are there, Svetlana." Papa's voice stops me in my tracks. "Come back here."

"Yes, sir."

"In." He points, and I step into his office.

"Pyotr and Dimitri." Papa glares at the men. "Feel you will be better served by continuing your studies at home. So, until a qualified tutor is hired, Dimitri will be overseeing your lessons."

"Thank you, Papa." I reach to hug him, and his cell rings.

He looks at the screen. "Go on, now. I must take this call."

Pyotr follows me to the door. "Everything will be okay, little butterfly."

I startle awake and sit straight up. I'm momentarily disoriented and rub my eyes. Slowly, the room comes into focus.

"You okay, little butterfly?" Pyotr asks from his seat across the room.

What he said earlier is true. No matter what's happened, he's always been in my corner, looking out for me.

Svetlana

When I woke up Monday, I had an email waiting for me.

Svetlana,
I enjoyed our time together this weekend and am looking forward to spending much more time together in the near future. I've written a contract that will serve our unique needs as a couple. Take your time reviewing everything. Don't hesitate to call or text me if you have any questions or changes you'd like to make. I'm really looking forward to embarking on this new adventure with you.
~Slava

I've read the contract several times and am pretty confident in my understanding. I don't broadcast being in the BDSM lifestyle because so many still find it a taboo subject. But this is one time that I wish I had let more people get close to me. I could really use someone to talk to about whatever is developing between Slava and me.

"Whatcha looking at?" Mei asks, and I quickly switch tabs.

"Just doing some last-minute research for an assignment."

"Are you still up to going out for dinner tonight?"

"Of course."

"No dates with that sexy guy?"

"What guy?"

"The guy who picked you up last weekend." She smirks. "You've been holding out on me."

"I really haven't. There's nothing—"

"You didn't come back to the dorm. There's much more than nothing," she says, interrupting me. "If I don't leave now, I'll be late for class. I expect to hear every detail tonight." Mei flits out the door before I can argue any further.

I pull the contract back up after Mei leaves. Slava texted me Monday to ensure I got his email, but I haven't heard from him since. He wanted to give me enough space to consider the contract without feeling any pressure from him.

Overall, I'm okay with everything he's proposed in the contract. Except for one thing—I'm not prepared to surrender all my time to a Dominant. Since I don't have class for another hour and I have some time alone, I send him a text.

Me: I'm done reading the contract.

Slava: Tell me your thoughts.

Me: I don't want to commit to anything during the week.

Slava: Can you explain why not?

Me: There are only a few weeks left in the school term. Final exams are coming up. I want to keep this to only a weekend arrangement.

Slava: I appreciate your honesty. I'd prefer more, but if weekends are all you'll commit to, I'm willing to accept that—for now.

Me: I also don't want to agree to anything that extends past the end of my school term.

Slava: I can agree to a short-term contract on one condition.

Me: What is that?

Slava: That you agree to revisit this conversation after school is out for the summer.

Me: Okay. Thank you for understanding.

Slava: That's what this stage is for.

Slava: Now that we're both on the same page. I'd like you to spend the weekend at the hotel with me.

Me: I think that can be arranged.

Slava: I'll text you when I'm in Moscow.

"I still wish you would've been the one to tell me about this weekend," Pyotr complains in the elevator on the way up to Slava's room. "I don't like getting a call from Slava and not knowing what the hell he's talking about."

"It honestly slipped my mind." I've been so busy this week that I didn't have a second to stop and think about the logistics of the weekend. Thankfully, Slava thought ahead and arranged for Pyotr to stay in the room next to ours.

After a long walk down the hall, we stop in front of room 4031. I raise my hand, but the door opens before I get the chance to knock. "You must have ESP or something," I laugh nervously.

"Nothing that fancy. Just a call from security letting me know you arrived on my floor." Slava glances over my shoulder. "Pyotr, good to see you again."

"Likewise," Pyotr answers stiffly.

"Come in." Slava grabs two keycards from the table inside the foyer of his suite. "For your room and mine."

Pyotr takes the offered cards. "Svetlana will keep her phone on at all times. If I text, she has ten minutes to respond, or I will be in."

"That's a bit much, don't you think?"

After spending the night with Slava last weekend, Pyotr has been very overprotective. I don't know what's going on with him, but I don't like it. "I'm a grown woman. I don't need to check in with you."

"That's your choice." He shrugs. "If you don't, I'll be in to check on you myself. And something tells me you don't want that to happen."

"I will ensure Lana's phone is on, and she responds to any messages you send."

My gaze snaps from Pyotr to Slava. "Are you kidding?" I snap.

"You may not have signed the contract yet, but you should watch your tone, *Moya nevinnyy malysh.*"

"I'm sorry."

"Go have a seat. I want to speak to Pyotr privately." Slava waits for me to follow his orders before he turns back to Pyotr. The men step just outside the door, and I'm unable to hear what they're saying. Several minutes later, Slava closes the door and joins me at the table. "Let's get this contract signed, shall we?"

"I like that idea."

"Please check it over one last time to ensure everything is as we discussed."

I skim the pages of the contract, not at all concerned about the accuracy. "It looks good. Do you have a pen?" We take turns signing both copies.

"I'm glad that's out of the way. Now, strip. There'll be no need for your clothes this weekend."

After seeing Slava's reaction when I undressed at the club, I wanted to try to elicit the same response a second time. Grabbing the hem of my shirt, I pull it over my head, exposing my breasts to him.

"I don't like knowing you're wearing nothing under your clothes when you're with other men." He crosses his arms across his chest.

I smile as I shimmy my leggings down and step out of them. "It's all with you in mind, Sir."

"Is it now?" The corner of his mouth turns up. "Get on all fours on the bed."

I climb onto the bed and look over my shoulder. He takes his time unbuttoning his white dress shirt. The outline of his erection is clear. It's empowering knowing I excite him. I grow wet with need as I watch him take off his shirt. Once again, he leaves his pants on, and I feel a tinge of disappointment.

"What's wrong?"

"Nothing."

His hand connects with my ass, and I let out a squeal. "That was the wrong answer. Let's try that again. "What's wrong?"

"I was hoping we were going to have sex tonight."

"Is that so?" His hand makes contact with my body again.

"Yes, Sir."

"And what makes you think we won't?"

"You're wearing your pants like last time."

He leans over my back. His erection presses against me. "*Moya nevinnyy malysh,* we're only just getting started."

His strikes come fast and hard. Each time his hand connects with my body, the repetitive thoughts that plague me on a daily basis begin to quiet until there's nothing left but silence. As my breathing slows, my body relaxes. The warmth of Slava's body near mine returns as his fingers slide inside my wet center.

"Does this feel good?" I nod. His fingers still, and I groan in frustration. "Let's try that again. Does this feel good?"

"Yes, Sir. Very good." He starts moving, and my body climbs to the edge of an orgasm. Just as I'm about to fall over the precipice, they're gone. I drop my head in frustration.

"Get on your back." In this position, I'm able to watch as Slava reaches into a black leather bag pulling out several bundles of red rope. "Curious?"

"Very."

"This is going to be a challenging position. I'll be checking in periodically to make sure you're okay. You are to use your safewords if you feel even the smallest thing wrong. Do you understand?"

"Yes, I do." The reason for his safety reminder becomes apparent immediately. Slava lifts my right leg, binding it to my outstretched right arm. I'm just about to ask where he's going to anchor the rope when he reaches behind the grey headboard attached to the wall, and I hear a click.

"I take it you are not aware this hotel caters to a certain crowd?" he asks as he ties the rope to the hidden anchor. "The rooms are all equipped with discreet features." He moves to my other side and secures my arm and leg in the same fashion. "Last thing." Slava holds up silver nipple clamps connected by a chain. "Have you ever tried these?"

"No."

"I'm looking forward to this even more." His dark eyes sparkle with delight as he places one of the clips over my erect nipple. He slides the ring down, making it tight. Slava makes quick work securing the second clamp and then gives a gentle tug. "Perfect."

Lust swirls in his gaze as he stands back and takes in my body, which is on full display. "Does everything feel okay?"

Slava was right. This is a challenging position. One I don't know that I'd be able to hold had it not been for years of ballet lessons that ensured my flexibility. The clamps make my nipples ache, but instead of being unpleasant, it's fueling my desire. "Yes, everything is good."

Seeming satisfied with my answer, Slava steps out of view. Lady Gaga's "I Like it Rough" begins to play a second before the lights dim. When he comes back into view, he unbuckles his belt and lowers his pants and boxers. My eyes stay glued on him as he fists his erection, pumping his hand up and down his hard length.

"Do you like watching?" The tone of his voice is low.

I'm unable to form words, so I nod.

"Tsk tsk." He shakes his head. "That won't do at all."

"Yes. I like watching."

"That's better," he says, positioning himself between my legs on the bed. "I will not be gentle." The words have barely left his mouth when he rams himself inside me. He sucks in a quick breath. "Fuck, Lana. All week I've been imagining this." He pulls out and enters me again fast and hard. There's no more conversation as he keeps up his punishing rhythm. It doesn't take long before I feel an explosion of sensation, and I cry as waves of pleasure crash over me. My body convulses from the intensity of my release.

"You look so sexy when you come. I want you to do it again."

He keeps one hand firmly on my bound leg, steadying himself as he drives into me. The other hand goes to work expertly, inching my body closer to another climax. His cock grows harder inside me, and I know he's close. "You're going to come with me. Ready?"

Slava's muscles tense and release as his body begins to pulse inside me. He grabs the chain and pulls the clamps off. The sudden rush of sensation causes an explosion of pleasure. I moan loudly as I drown in a sea of blissful sensations.

"Fuck, Svetlana. That was incredible." He drops his head as he catches his breath and withdraws from my body. A trail of liquid drips from me. His eyes narrow as he runs his fingers through our combined arousal, circling the tight ring of muscle. "Has anyone ever taken you here?"

"No, Sir."

"Before this weekend is over, I will have you there, too. I plan to own every part of your body."

Svetlana

The rest of the weekend is spent with me naked and
bound in any number of positions. Pyotr keeps his promise and checks
on me several times. Slava makes sure I'm able to text him right back.
Pyotr knows I'm into BDSM, but the last thing I want is him coming in
here and seeing it.

It's early Sunday morning. The sun is peeking up from the horizon
when my phone vibrates. Slava is still asleep, his arms wrapped around
my body. I move carefully, hoping not to wake him, and grab my phone.

Pyotr: What time are we leaving today?

Me: I don't know. Slava's still asleep.

"Is that your guard already?" Slava asks.

"I'm sorry. I didn't mean to wake you." I lay back down and turn to
face him. Slava's thirty-five, nearly fifteen years older than me. But lying
here with his dark hair messy from sleep, he looks young and carefree.
"He wants to know what time we're leaving."

"We're not even out of bed yet."

Me: Later this afternoon. I'll get back to you as soon as I have a definite time.

"It'll be a long week until I see you again." Slava positions me so I'm straddling him." I plan to get my fill of you before we go. I want you up here." He pulls me toward his face.

In a moment of hesitancy, I resist. His mouth was on me more times than I can count this weekend, but I've never sat on a man's face.

"What is it?" he asks.

"I'm not sure. I've never."

"I won't force you, but I'd very much like it if you did."

I bite my lip, still uncertain. My decision is made when I look down and see the hunger in his eyes. I position myself so my pussy is in line with his mouth. He explores me with his mouth licking and sucking as he goes. Everything he's done until this point was incredible, but it doesn't compare to this right now. I'm already panting with need when he starts to fuck me with his tongue. Oh my God, the feeling is so intense in this position.

"Slava. I can't. I—" My body tenses up as pleasure radiates from my core and spreads through my body in a kaleidoscope of sensations. Every nerve ending in my body feels alive as wave after wave of ecstasy courses through me, and wetness gushes from my body. His tongue doesn't stop until the last contractions of my orgasm subside. My body is limp as he lifts me and lays me down beside him.

Slava props himself on his elbow. His face glistens with my arousal. "That's the perfect way to start a day." He tucks a strand of hair behind my ear. "I'm hopeful I'll have you in my bed every morning after your term ends."

"I need to get through these next few weeks before I can even think about break."

After breakfast and a quick shower, I again find myself at the mercy of Slava's endless desire. I'm currently bound in a spread-eagle fashion while he alternates exposing me to gentle and painful sensations.

I squeal when he drags an ice cube down my belly. My back arches as Slava uses his crop on my hardened nipples. He hasn't gone anywhere near my wet center, and I'm already close to climaxing. He reaches for something that's out of my sight. I hear a vibrator a second before feeling it on my clit. That small amount of contact is all it takes for me to orgasm again. My body has barely come down from the high when something cold presses against my other opening.

Slava's been preparing me for this moment with his fingers and various toys.

"You need to relax, *moya nevinnyy malysh*."

I take a deep breath and do my best to relax the muscles. Gently, he slides the toy in and out until I feel it pass the initial tight ring of muscles. I tense at the sensation that borders on pain. This is the biggest butt plug he's used so far. Sensing my tension, he switches the vibrator back on, massaging my clitoris while gently rocking the toy back and forth until it's fully inside. I'm startled when the toy begins to vibrate. There are so many sensations happening at once. It's almost too much.

"Yellow."

Immediately, he turns the vibrators off. "Talk to me."

"There's so much happening at once," I say between breaths. "It's too much."

"Do you want me to stop?"

"No."

"Take a few deep breaths."

I close my eyes and concentrate on recentering myself. "I'm better. We can keep going."

Slava unties my arms and pushes the vibrator into my hand. "You're in charge of that now." He grins.

Pressing the button, the bullet springs back to life, and I begin pleasuring myself. My eyes close as I get lost in the arousal that's quickly building. Without warning, a dildo is slid inside. "Oh my God," I whisper. I'm stretched to a point where there's almost pain, but then he turns the dildo on, and the pain morphs into pleasure. My mind goes blank as I'm overcome with a torrent of sensation. I writhe beneath him as I ride waves of pleasure. When my orgasm finally stops, Slava makes quick work of untying my legs and removing the toys.

"Get on your hands and knees."

With shaky limbs, I comply with his demand and turn over. He positions himself behind me. I watch over my shoulder as he squirts some lube and penetrates me with his finger. Then, I feel his cock against me. I drop my head as he pushes against my entrance and breeches the muscles.

"I'll go slow," he says. "I don't want to hurt you."

I nod, and this time, he doesn't press for a verbal answer.

He pushes in a little further, and I gasp. Slava's hand comes around my body right to my clit. He plays with the oversensitive area, distracting me with pleasure as he fully sheathes himself inside me. "You're so tight." His voice is strained, and his body trembles. But then his self-control snaps. "Fuck, Lana. I can't be gentle." He grabs my hips as he pistons in and out. "I'm not going to last much longer."

His finger finds my clit once again, and he works me into a panting mess. I come calling his name. He follows me over the edge. Our bodies pulse in shared pleasure. My body collapses underneath him. Slava pulls out and gets off the bed. I roll over and watch the flex of his muscles as he walks into the bathroom. He comes back a few seconds later with a warm washcloth. Gently, he wipes me off before climbing into bed and pulling me close to him. I fall asleep listening to his whispers of how much he's enjoyed every second of his weekend with me.

"*Moya nevinnyy malysh.* It's time to wake up." He rubs my shoulder, and I slowly open my eyes. "I want to take a shower before we leave."

Slava sits up, throws his legs over the bed, and stands before turning around and offering me his hand. I follow him into the bathroom, admiring the flexing of his muscles as he walks in front of me. He adjusts the water and pulls me close to him under the hot stream. I know it's getting late, and he needs to leave, but the erection pressing against my belly gives away his need.

Lowering to my knees, I glance up at Slava as I open my mouth and take in his long, hard length. His dark eyes stay locked with mine as he allows me to set the pace. I've spent the weekend learning how he likes to be pleasured and use every lesson I've learned. I swirl my tongue around the head of his cock before dragging it through his slit, tasting his pre-cum. His hand tangles in my hair as I slowly and gently drag my teeth along his hard length.

As if he can't take it anymore, his hand flies out to brace himself against the tiled wall. With my hair wrapped around his other hand, he takes over. Slava isn't gentle as he fucks my mouth. Tears cascade down my face from the force of his cock hitting the back of my throat. His legs begin to tremble, and he comes inside my mouth. My eyes lock with his as ribbons of cum shoot down my throat, and I do my best to swallow everything he has to give. I feel powerful watching him come undone.

After he catches his breath, he helps me to my feet and then leans over to kiss me. It's the first time his lips have touched mine. Somehow, it feels more intimate than anything we've done so far. "You're making it very hard for me to leave you." He watches me, seeming to gauge my response.

"Then, I've done my job well."

The sun is beginning to set as we leave the hotel. Pyotr follows a short distance behind. Slava walks me to our car and cages me in his arms. "I'll talk to you later in the week."

"Have a safe trip home."

Slava's lips meet mine for a gentle kiss before he turns and walks away. I watch until he drives away. As soon as he's gone, I get into the car and wait for Pyotr to join me.

"I thought you were only in a contractual relationship with Slava," he says as he gets into the driver's seat.

"That's all it is."

Pyotr chuckles. "Someone better tell him that because that guy has it bad for you."

The drive back to campus is quiet. Pyotr's observation caught me off guard, and I'm lost in my thoughts. Slava can't fall for me. Pyotr must be mistaken. All that's between us is a Dom/sub relationship. We have great chemistry in bed, but it's just sex. There are no feelings or emotions involved. He knows I can't commit to anything beyond the next few weeks.

Svetlana

I SLEPT THROUGH MY ALARM THIS MORNING. IT'S A GOOD thing Pyotr was there and woke me up, or I probably would've slept straight through classes today. I'm going to have to start working out more to keep up with Slava's stamina because I'm wiped after this weekend's sexathon. Finally, my last class is over. I don't know how I made it through the day. I'm supposed to have an appointment with Masha, but I don't feel up to it today.

I have to walk past her office to get to Pyotr, who's sitting in his usual spot. It must be my lucky day because her door is still closed. Picking up my pace, I walk past her office with the intention of getting to Pyotr and getting out of here.

I'm almost in the clear when the door opens, and Masha steps out. "I apologize for running late. There was an emergency I had to attend to."

"It's not a problem."

"Come on in."

I look between her door and my guard at the end of the hall. "I need to give my bag to Pyotr first."

"You always bring your bag with you. Is everything ok?" I don't know the correct answer, so I say nothing. "Svetlana." Misha touches my arm. "Coming to therapy is voluntary. If you don't want to have a session today, that's your choice."

"I was going to skip." I don't have any fight in me, so I give up and walk into her office. "I don't have a good reason other than I'm extra tired today."

"I remember my university days. The last few weeks of the term are always stressful." She smiles kindly.

"There's just a lot going on right now." I flop onto her couch.

"I get the feeling this is about more than just school."

I drop my head back and groan. "I thought I knew what I wanted, but now I'm not so sure."

"We can talk whatever this is through if you'd like."

"Papa and Mama don't know that I changed my major yet."

"I thought you were going to tell him over the holiday break?"

"So did I. But it was the anniversary of my sister's abduction, and everyone's emotions were running high. I didn't want to make things worse."

"That's understandable." She taps her pencil against her chin. "Something tells me that isn't the only thing bothering you."

"Did anyone ever tell you that you're very perceptive?" I chuckle.

"That's what they pay me the big bucks for." Masha smiles.

"I guess now's as good of a time as any to tell you. I applied to New York University in the United States and was accepted."

"Congratulations. That sounds exciting."

"I've wanted this for so long. It's a chance to be on my own in a place where no one knows my family or me. Do you know what I mean?"

"I do." She jots something down in her notebook before looking back up at me. "What has you second-guessing your decision?"

"Remember I told you I bumped into someone I knew back home?"

"Yes."

"He comes to Moscow every week for business. We've been spending time together while he's here." I pull my feet under my legs. "It was just supposed to be something fun to do on the weekend. And it has been. What I didn't count on was falling for him."

"And now you're questioning your decision to go to the United States for school."

"Exactly. What should I do?"

Masha laughs. "You know better than that. This isn't about what *I* think you should do. I'm here to help you sort through your thoughts and feelings and to help you look at things from every angle. But in the end, this is your life, and only you're in charge of what decision you eventually come to."

"I wish that were true."

"One of the most important parts of taking charge of your life is communication. You need to voice your plans and your concerns with the people that'll be affected."

"Dimitri used to tell me the same thing, but it's the part I've always struggled with."

I don't know what Papa was thinking, assigning Dimitri to oversee my education. It turns out he makes a good teacher, with the exception of all his supposed-to-be funny computer jokes. He's actually pretty smart and makes my lessons interesting. As a bonus class, he's been teaching me some basic computer hacking skills—something I swore I wouldn't tell Papa about.

Unfortunately, Dimitri's leaving tomorrow. He's going back to Ukraine, where he lives with his mom. He wants to spend the last few weeks with her before he has to serve his conscription.

"I wish I could go with you."

Dimitri chuckles. "You realize I live in a village that could probably fit inside your house, right?"

"At least no one would know I was a coward that ran when—"

"Woah," he interrupts. "You are not a coward. I don't want to hear you speak that way, ever. Do you understand?"

I look down and make no move to answer. Dimitri puts his finger under my chin, lifting my face to look at him. "First, you're a young girl. There was no way you could've fought two grown men. Instead, you did something just as important. You paid attention and gave us details we'd never have been able to get. If not for you, your father wouldn't have had any leads. We wouldn't have known where to start looking."

"Little good it did. Jelena's still missing, and it's my fault."

"Lana, what happened was not your responsibility."

"Then why do my parents hate me?"

"They don't hate you." He closes the textbook we were working in and shifts to look at me. *"I know things have been different around here. Your papa is doing everything he can to find Jelena. You have to try to understand how difficult this is for him. Every day that goes by makes him feel even more helpless. He's channeling all his fear and anger into his search. He barely stops to eat or sleep. And your mama is struggling with grief in her own way. They're doing their best to get through this nightmare one minute at a time. But they don't hate you. You'll see, as soon as your papa finds Jelena, everything will return to normal."*

"I don't think that's true. They're always going to blame me, hate me for what happened."

"Have you considered talking to them?"

"How? Mama doesn't leave her bedroom, and Papa's always working. I used to be able to go into his office to see him, but not anymore. No one will let me in. I know he's looking for Jelena, and that's important. I don't want to take him away from that, but—I don't know." My voice trails off.

"Your parents haven't stopped loving you. I know this is all really hard, but you need to tell them how you're feeling."

"I didn't take Dimitri's advice."

"I'm sensing a pattern.

"Communication was never my strong suit." I shrug. "Dimitri left a few weeks later. He was the only person spending any real time with me, so that was a tough goodbye. What was even worse was the next tutor Papa hired." I let out a small laugh.

In Dimitri's place is this bowtie-wearing guy, Sergei, who calls himself a teacher. Listening to him teach is as dull as watching American football.

I immediately decide I don't like him and make it my mission to give him a hard time—something that's not difficult to do. So far, I've tested this theory with pen clicking, doodling instead of taking notes, playing the different ringtones at the highest volume, and slipping my preferred reading behind my assigned reading. What really aggravates Sergei the most is cracking my chewing gum.

He's so predictable it's not even a challenge. I misbehave, he lectures me on expected behavior. I roll my eyes, and he answers with a ridiculous, frustrated grunt and a threat to tell Papa. I ignore him and continue whatever I was doing in the first place. We play this game of cat and mouse until three o'clock when I'm released from the torture called education.

Today, Sergei is lecturing on Russian history. I stifle a yawn, wishing Dimitri were still here. He made even the most dreadful subjects feel less like splitting frog hair three ways and more like something I actually wanted to listen to.

"Svetlana, you must pay attention," Sergei reprimands for the millionth time.

"I'm listening."

"What did I just say?"

I scan the textbook in front of me, trying to come up with an answer.

"I haven't been on that page for the past fifteen minutes." He sighs loudly. "Your grades are beginning to suffer because of your childish behavior. I'm left with no other choice than to report your deficient progress to Mr. Solonik."

"Whatever." I shrug.

Sergei darts to Papa's office every day after school to give his daily report on my negative behavior. I don't know why he thinks I'll suddenly start caring about it now. I stopped caring about everything and everyone.

"Can you tell me more about why you stopped caring?"

"At that point, I was convinced my parents had all but forgotten about me. I guess I figured if I didn't care, didn't let anyone close to me, that I'd be protecting myself from getting hurt again." I shrug.

"How did that work for you?"

"Before *that* day, my life was perfect. At least, that's what I thought. I had a lot of friends to play with and my sister to talk to. I went to my ballet lessons, which I loved. And I had my parents. I was close to both of them, but especially my papa." Tears prick the back of my eyes. "In an instant, everything changed. My life was unrecognizable. I no longer had friends, ballet, or my parents. That's when I decided to put up walls. I could smile and pretend, but I refused to let anyone get close to me."

"Unfortunately, your family's reaction to a significant trauma is not uncommon. Everyone processes these events in their own way. Oftentimes, without outside support, people tend to struggle in the aftermath."

"Svetlana." Masha waves her hand, getting my attention.

"I'm sorry. Can you repeat what you said?"

"You've done a great job today, but clearly, you're exhausted. Why don't we end it here for today?" Masha closes her notebook and rounds her desk.

"I think that's a good idea." I stifle a yawn.

"I'd like you to do something for me this week."

"Okay," I say hesitantly. Masha's never given me homework.

"I want you to tell your ten-year-old self that none of this was her fault. You've carried so much guilt over your sister's abduction. It's time to let that go. Whether you write a letter or look in a mirror and say it, I'd like you to tell her she's not to blame for anything that happened. Can you do that?"

"I'll try."

It's raining as we walk back to my dorm. Both Pyotr and I are soaked by the time we make it to the building. When I get to my room, I change into dry clothes and prepare to do my homework. As hard as I try, I can't focus. All I can hear is Masha telling me I need to stop blaming myself for Jelena's kidnapping.

The problem is, I don't think I can do that. All these years later, I still replay that day in my head over and over again, trying to figure out what I could've done differently so that my sister would still be here today.

Maxim (Ten years ago)

"I feel Svetlana would be better served enrolled in a more traditional school setting," Sergei drones on.

Every day after Svetlana's lessons conclude, it is the same story. Sergei stands in my office, wasting my time. Precious minutes better spent searching for Jelena, with his constant complaints about my daughter's inattention and negative behaviors.

"Perhaps you do not know how to properly engage a student." I raise an eyebrow.

"I assure you I'm a skilled educator. The problem is Svetlana. Your daughter is—"

I jump from my chair, nearly knocking it over. My sudden movement draws the attention of my guards. "Be very careful with your next words, Mr. Barkov."

He stands in an apparent challenge. "When I was offered this position, I was led to believe your daughter was an advanced student with pristine manners. It has been my experience that she's nothing more than a spoiled brat."

I grab the man by his collar. "What did you say?"

"Your daughter is a sp—"

I cock my fist back, but Pyotr and Timur jump in, saving this pathetic excuse of a man from the recourse he has earned.

"Get this *mudak* out of my house. If I ever see his face again—"

"I've got it, boss." Timur grabs the man by his arm. "Let's go."

"Svetlana would never act that way. He clearly has no idea how to engage and teach a student." I pace back and forth in front of the floor-to-ceiling window that overlooks my property. Behind me, Pyotr clears his throat, and I spin around. "Is there something you want to add?"

"May I speak openly without fear of retaliation?"

Although I have reached the end of my patience today, I nod, giving my trusted guard permission to speak.

"Since Jelena's kidnapping, life has changed drastically for everyone. You've been searching twenty-four hours a day, which has made you unavailable to your family. Mrs. Solonik is held up in her room, losing herself deeper and deeper into depression." He takes a step closer, a brazen move, given my current temperament. "I have no children, so I can't say I would handle things differently. Svetlana is only a little girl. One who was at her sister's side when she was abducted. Arguably, she's endured the most trauma."

"If she needs something, she'll come to one of us. Svetlana knows we are here for her."

"Does she?"

Pyotr's veiled accusations are irritating me. "Of course," I snap.

"I may be overstepping, but I'm asking you to think about it for a minute. Mrs. Solonik used to spend a great deal of time with the girls. Right now, she's struggling to get through each day. Lana used to be free to come and go in your office, but now your door is always closed. I've been out there when the guards turn her away. The look on her face breaks my heart." He pauses, closing his eyes for a moment.

"Then there was school. It may have only been one day, but I saw what she went through. Rather than finding support from her friends, she was ridiculed. Svetlana's scared and sad. Worst of all, she's alone. Her behavior with Sergei is a desperate attempt to get attention from her parents."

Pyotr eyes me cautiously as I sink into the armchair by my desk. I lean forward, holding my head in my hands. His words are heavy and difficult to hear. My nerves have been on a hairpin trigger. Jelena has been gone for eight and a half weeks. With each day that passes, I know my chances of finding my daughter unharmed dwindle.

I have failed to see that my family is falling apart right before my eyes. The Dominant/submissive dynamic Irina and I share came to a sudden stop the moment we learned of Jelena's disappearance. I neglected to care for my submissive, my wife. I am certain the very foundation of our relationship is on unsure footing.

And my dear Svetlana. The day Jelena was taken, I was in awe of her composure as she relayed those critical details to us. All I saw was her bravery. I have not stopped long enough to consider that she is living through this in the same way as her mama and me. As Pyotr pointed out, she is possibly more affected because she watched her sister be dragged away.

"My God, what have I done? Where do I start? How do I fix this mess?"

"Svetlana's in her room. Go talk to her," Pyotr says quietly. "We'll continue working here. If we get any important information, I'll make sure it gets to you immediately."

"I will have my cell on me at all times." I walk to the door and stop to look back. "Thank you." Pyotr nods.

"Svetlana." I knock. "May I come in?"

Her door flies open. "Did you find her?"

"No, I have not."

"Oh." She drops her head and climbs onto her bed, sitting with her legs crossed.

I sit next to her. "Sergei paid me a visit earlier."

"I figured." She shrugs.

"Is there anything you would like to say about your behavior?"

"Not really." She picks up a book that's on her bedside table.

She knows this kind of flippant attitude is unacceptable. I try to remain patient. "Svetlana, we need to talk." I soften my voice. "About Jelena."

Her head shoots up. "What about Jelena?"

I take the book from her hands and set it aside. "Finding your sister and bringing her home has been my top priority—"

"Did Gavriil tell you where she is yet?" My face must give away my shock at hearing her question because she continues, "I know your men brought him here."

My body tenses. "Who told you that?"

My girls know I am in the Bratva and that my job is dangerous. It is something I have never hidden from them. However, they are children, and I work hard to ensure their lives are not affected by what I do. Whichever one of my guards told her about this is a dead man.

"No one. I was in the kitchen with Olga a few weeks ago when Misha and a few of the other guards pulled up. They dragged Gavriil from the backseat. I don't know what happened after that because Olga made me leave."

I must remember to thank Olga. After Misha and the other men finished questioning Gavriil, I had him brought to a holding cell near the guards' housing on my property. Ordinarily, we would have disposed of him right away, but we hoped that, with continued pressure, Gavriil would give us more information. I did not realize Olga had Lana in the kitchen. Gavriil was not in good shape when I left him. Seeing that could only have added more trauma to what she was already dealing with. I cannot imagine the trauma Svetlana has been living with after seeing him.

"Why did you not say anything before now?"

"I've tried to come to your office to see you, but you're always too busy and can't see me."

"I am never too busy to see you. The guards will be informed that you are not to be turned away." She nods. "And I am sorry you had to see that."

"It didn't bother me. Did he tell you who took Jelena and where she is?"

"That is not for you to worry about."

"Why not?" She sits taller, signaling she's ready to dig her heels in and fight.

"Because you are a little girl who should not be involved in my business."

"I'm not a little girl. I'm eleven years old, and I was the one holding Jelena's hand when they took her. I think I've earned the right to ask for some answers."

I study her, considering what she's said. What I see, or rather what I do not, surprises me. There is no trace of the carefree child who was writing letters to Ded Moroz. Whether I like it or not, she has lost the innocence of childhood. And she is right. She deserves answers. "Yes, he gave us some names."

"But you haven't found them yet?"

"No. I have not."

"Did you kill Gavriil?"

I do not want to, but I must answer her honestly. After we arrived home from Serbia, I paid him a final visit. It was clear we had gotten all the information from him. His life was worthless to me, and I took it. I fear she will never look at me the same way once she knows I am a killer. "Yes. I did."

"Are you going to kill me too?"

"Why would you say something like that?"

"Gavriil was responsible for setting up Jelena's kidnapping. He told you the information you needed, and then you killed him." She stands and faces me. "Jelena wanted me to hurry, and I gave her a hard time. When the men were dragging her away, I didn't fight hard enough, and then I ran away. I gave you the information you needed to find Gavriil. So, however, you wish to punish me. If you want to kill me—"

"Stop," I say, raising my voice. Then, I take her hand in mine. "What would make you think I could ever kill you?"

"After I told you everything I remembered, you sent me away. Since then, I'm not allowed to come into your office to see you. If I was stronger or hadn't run away, Jelena would still be here."

"You did exactly what you were supposed to do. If you had not run, they might have taken you too."

"I didn't tell you that the man who smelled like vodka grabbed me."

My heart skips a beat. "What do you mean?"

"He grabbed me. He was going to take me too, but the man holding Jelena told him to let me go and that they didn't want me." A tear slips from her pretty blue eyes. "Why did they want to take Jelena?"

"That is not something for you to worry about."

"Papa." She puts her hands on her hips. "I need to know, please."

I hate that Svetlana has been exposed to evil at such a tender age. I cannot lie or pretend it does not exist. "Gavriil's father, Rudolf, deals in humans. He steals and sells them for large sums of money. He used Gavriil to win Jelena's affection. Then, he waited for the perfect opportunity to get back at me."

"What did he get back at you for?"

"About a year ago, I found out about a shipment of humans coming through St. Petersburg. Rudolf thought I would look the other way, but I did not. I alerted my contact in the *politsiya*. Several of his top men went to prison for a very long time."

She nods, and a small smile appears on her face. "I knew you're one of the good guys. But, Papa, I still don't understand why they didn't take me too."

"I do not have that answer. But I am grateful. My heart would not be able to handle it if you were both taken."

"So, you don't hate me?"

"I could never hate you, *moya babochka*. I am sorry your mama and I have been blinded by our suffering. We failed to see how much you are hurting, too." I open my arms, and she falls into my embrace. Everything my child has been holding in rushes to the surface, and the floodgates open. Sobs wrack her little body. My heart breaks with the realization of just how badly Svetlana's been hurting. Because of my negligence, she has been hurting alone. "Let it all out, *moya babochka*. I am here. You are not alone anymore." When the intensity of her grief subsides, I hold her back so I can see her face. "Things will be different from now on."

That is a promise I refuse to break. I must get my house in order.

Maxim (Ten years ago)

THE SEARCH FOR JELENA CONTINUES. DESPITE HAVING resources and connections around the world, we have not found her yet. I have never felt more helpless. That is why I threw myself into micromanaging every step of this search. Instead, I should have been relying on the men I not only employ but trust to continue working while I tended to my wife and daughter's needs. After holding Svetlana as she cried in my arms the other night, I knew I had failed my family and must do everything in my power to make things right.

I promised Svetlana things would change and have been doing my best to make that happen. Unfortunately, Irina is not in the same place as me, but I coerced her out of the bedroom for several meals. Although she was there physically, she merely picked at her food and did not engage in conversation.

Just a few months ago, my wife was full of life. Since Jelena's abduction, Irina has retreated inside herself. She has chosen to shut out the world. I cannot criticize her because I also did not handle this trial in a healthy manner. But Irina is strong. She is a fighter. She has just lost her way. Today, however, my wife will become reacquainted with her inner strength.

Despite the fact that it is mid-afternoon, our bedroom is drenched in darkness. Irina is lying on her side, facing away from me. With sure steps, I walk to the windows and pull open the heavy drapes, allowing the bright sunshine to fill the room.

"It is time to get up." I allow time for Irina to respond, but she does not. "You have been in here long enough. I need you to get up."

"Go away." She closes her eyes in an attempt to shut me out.

Before this, Irina would never have shown such disrespect. My actions, as of late, have not earned her respect, so I cannot be angry. Instead, I sit next to her on the bed. "I know how much you are hurting because I am, too. But we cannot continue like this. We must do better for each other and for our girls."

"I can't, Maxim." Her voice cracks.

"You can."

"Please. Just leave me be."

I stand but not to leave. "*Moya vozlyublenny*," I say with authority, getting her attention. "You will get up now."

"Yes, *Gospodin*." Her voice is no more than a whisper. Slowly, she pushes to a sitting position and then to her feet. Her head lowered in respect.

I cup her cheek in my palm. "It is time for you to rejoin those who are living. Go and shower. We will be having dinner with Svetlana tonight."

She opens her mouth to argue, but I put my finger to her lips, silencing her. "I was blinded by my own fear and sorrow. I allowed not only our marriage but also our dynamic to suffer. For that, I am sorry." My finger traces the silver chain that threads through a diamond infinity symbol. "I ask that you allow me to retake my place as your Dominant."

"I would never deny you that place in my life." Tears fill her gray eyes. "I'm sorry I haven't been stronger. That I—"

"Shh." I pull her to me. "There is nothing to apologize for. We are both going to do better starting now."

Over the next few weeks, we begin to resemble a family again. Svetlana is excelling with her new female tutor. She has also returned to her ballet lessons, this time without an argument about being escorted by Pyotr. Irina has returned to her medical practice with a part-time schedule. And I am still working hard to find Jelena.

This evening, we are enjoying a quiet dinner together. "Irina, I need you to pack me a bag after dinner."

"Where are you going, Papa?"

Between the team I left with Radovanović in Serbia and the men here, we have been using every resource at our disposal to track down Valery and Boris. It has been trying on all of us.

After the pair departed from Serbia, they seemed to vanish without a trace. But finally, last week, we got a break. There was a hit on facial recognition from a bus station in Madrid. The two have altered their appearances and are traveling under new identities. The more concerning development is that Jelena was not seen with them.

I immediately called Nicholai Federov, a Russian transplant and colleague, to ask for his aid. It did not take more than an hour before he returned my call with information that the men had been successfully apprehended. After losing a few body parts, they told Federov Jelena was sold into a well-known trafficking ring in Patras, Greece.

I wanted to fly right out, but calmer heads prevailed, reminding me that my movements are most certainly being tracked. The last thing I want to do is jeopardize any element of surprise we have. The stakes are higher than ever. We must get there before Jelena's moved, again. So, after a tense conversation with Federov, I agreed to wait until a plan was implemented.

As of two days ago, my team was working remotely with a smaller organized crime affiliate in Patras. The group was more than happy with our offer of key information in exchange for their help locating Jelena. Our new colleagues have been trying to bust this ring for several years. The information we traded gave them the leg up they had been waiting for.

We have learned that this trafficking ring is known for buying people and using them for prostitution. I cannot think about what that means for Jelena. The only thing I am able to focus on is getting her back. And I intend to be there when we do.

I will fly to Madrid in the morning and meet up with Federov. To anyone watching, it will appear that I believe Jelena is still in Spain. From there, Federov arranged a private flight to take me to Greece unnoticed. We could blow the entire plan with one wrong move on our part. Waiting this out is one of the hardest things I have done.

"I am going to Greece."

"Have you found her?" Irina asks.

"We are very close. I am confident this nightmare will be over within a few days."

"When do you leave?"

"First thing in the morning."

Maxim (Ten years ago)

Irina is asleep beside me. From spending several weeks primarily in bed, she still tires easily. But I have laid awake for hours. My mind is racing, imagining every scenario we may encounter in Greece. The sun is beginning to rise when my cell vibrates on the bedside table, startling me.

Pyotr: They're on the move.

Me: I am on my way down.

I intended to be with my men and rescue her myself, but receiving this text means they've located Jelena. They were instructed that if the opportunity presented itself, they should not hesitate. The important part is that Jelena is rescued as quickly as possible. Knowing this was a possibility, I ensured each man was equipped with body cams. If I am not there, I want to be sure I can look into the eyes of the scum who stole my daughter before their time on this earth comes to an end.

I slide out of bed, careful to not wake Irina. After getting dressed, I hurry down to the command center. I want to see my daughter as soon as possible. The hall outside the room is teeming with activity. When the men see me coming, they move out of the way, allowing me clear passage into the room. Misha, Timur, and Pyotr are gathered around the monitors.

"What's going on?" The images are grainy and too dark. "Where are they?"

"Morocco," Misha answers without taking his eyes from the screen.

His answer confuses me. "Why are they not in Greece?" I ask as I take a seat beside him.

"Early yesterday, we received intel that an auction site was located in Patras. Somehow, the group kept it running right under our noses." I watch him, waiting for more information. He takes a deep breath before answering, "As soon as Federov found out, he sent a team in, but the traffickers had already moved. They left behind two lowlifes who were more than eager to talk." He pinches the bridge of his nose. "Several weeks ago, Jelena was in the auction and was sold to a Moroccan named Farouk El Alami."

While Misha talks, my eyes are now glued to the screen. The men are getting into place outside a large mansion. "Are you sure the information was correct?" I need him to say there was a mistake.

"Yes, sir. There's no doubt."

Our conversation is interrupted by the sounds of gunshots and explosions. I watch in silent horror, waiting anxiously for the first glimpse of my daughter in the protective custody of my men. The wait feels like an eternity. My heart hammers in my chest, threatening to burst through my ribcage.

Without warning, the cameras go black.

"What the hell is going on?" I slam my fists on the table. "Get the cameras back online."

Pyotr and Misha's phones simultaneously buzz with incoming messages. "I'm trying, boss," Misha says as he types furiously. No image appears.

"Maxim," Pyotr says, putting his hand on my shoulder. "Our men turned their body cams off."

"Why?" Misha checks his phone and exchanges a worried look with Pyotr. "Somebody better say something. Where is Jelena? I want to see my daughter."

"They found Jelena's body," Pyotr says quietly.

"Give me the damn phone." I spring to my feet, and the chair scrapes loudly against the floor. "I demand to know why the fuck they would say something like that. They cannot make a correct identification. I should have hired a more qualified team. They will regret—"

"There's no mistake, boss."

As if a switch flips, my body transitions into work mode, and I question Misha like I would for any job. "When?"

"A few hours at the most."

"How?"

"Max," Misha says quietly. "You don't want to go there."

"Jelena is my daughter." My fist goes to my chest. "I want to know how the bastard killed her."

Killed her.

She is dead.

My daughter is dead.

My heart sinks into the pit of my stomach, and I struggle to comprehend the reality of the situation. I double over, gasping for my next breath.

Pyotr takes my arm. "Sit down, boss."

My world has been thrown off its axis. My precious daughter has been taken from me in the cruelest and most senseless way imaginable. A wave of guilt and anger washes over me. "Get out of my way," I roar, pushing him aside and hurrying out of the room. I stand in the middle of the hall as the crushing weight of sorrow threatens to consume me. I want to scream, to lash out at the world. Anything to bring my Jelena back. I'm lost in a haze of pain and confusion, unable to think or feel anything aside from an all-consuming sorrow.

I hear a man's voice, but I cannot make out what he is saying. My eyes attempt to blink open, but it takes several minutes for the room to come into focus and for me to recognize where I am—my office. I have no memory of how I got here.

"Boss." Misha's voice cuts through the thick haze.

"What?"

"Irina's asking to see you."

The pain in my heart is unbearable, like a sharp knife twisting inside me. I need to find some way to dull it. I snatch the bottle of vodka from the desk, my lips already anticipating the numbing effect of the alcohol.

"You've had enough." Misha rips the bottle from my hand.

"I am not a fucking child." My words slur together as I swipe at the bottle he holds just out of my reach. "Give it back."

"It's time to sober up." He pushes a plate of food closer to me. "You're going to eat, and then you need a shower. Irina and Svetlana are going to need you."

"I may be drunk." I poke my finger at my chest. "But I am still the one in charge here."

"Then sober up and fucking act like it." Misha's words are harsh.

A fresh wave of pain crashes over me, overwhelming and suffocating. I wish it would drag me under and end this unbearable agony. I whisper the words, barely able to accept they're real. "It was not a nightmare. She is really gone?"

"I wish it wasn't real." Misha's voice cracks. "Jelena's really gone."

I am Maxim Solonik, a *Pakhan.* I do not succumb to weakness or emotion.

Even as I tell myself that, tears spill from my eyes. "How do I tell my wife I did not arrive in time? That our beautiful daughter is dead."

I do not know if I am strong enough to do this.

Svetlana

❧

THIS WEEK I HAVE THE DORM ROOM TO MYSELF SINCE MEI IS away on a university-sponsored trip with the education department. I'm thankful my roommate is easy to get along with and understanding about my guard living in the room next door. Still, I'm also relieved she's away.

Usually, I'd cut classes and, with Pyotr's help, disappear for the week. He's always a knowing accomplice to my avoidance behaviors. However, this year, I'm not able to escape. There's a mandatory three-day conference on campus—something I'm not looking forward to. The only silver lining is all my other classes have been canceled.

I hate this week. I hate the painful memories that always come up.

Ten years.

This week marks ten very long years since the day I learned my sister had become my guardian angel.

Pyotr and I are in the library playing chess. There's constant activity in the hall outside the room.

"What's going on?"

"Nothing."

"That's not true. I know Papa didn't leave today. Do you know why?"

"Please don't give me a hard time. Just take your turn."

"Whatever." I roll my eyes. My hand is on the rook when Mama's blood-curdling wail fills every corner of the room. I jump up and rush to the door, but Pyotr's faster. He grabs me around my waist.

"You need to stay here."

"What's going on? Mama. Papa," I scream.

Pyotr's grip tightens. "Lana, please. Calm down."

Despite my best efforts to break free, I'm no match for his size or strength. My kicks and punches have no effect. He easily keeps his hold on me.

Misha appears in the doorway. "The boss said to let her go to him."

Pyotr lets go of me, and I take off down the hall to Papa's office. My feet skid to a stop when I see Papa on the floor, his arms around Mama, who's sobbing uncontrollably.

"No," I whisper.

"Moya babochka," Papa looks up at me with red-rimmed eyes.

"Please, Papa." I take a step back. If he doesn't say it, then it can't be true. "Don't say it."

"I am sorry, Lana. I did not get there in time. I am so sorry."

My Papa is crying. "Stop." I cover my ears, shaking my head.

"Come here." Papa holds out his free hand. "Lana, please."

"No," I scream and bolt from the office toward the front door.

Barefoot and without a second thought, I throw it open and charge down the steps.

"Lana, come back," Pyotr yells from behind me.

My breaths come out in ragged gasps as my legs carry me further and further away. My lungs burn from the exertion, but the physical pain is nothing compared to the emotional turmoil. I can't stop running because that means facing the reality of what had just happened. And I'm not ready for that yet.

As I make my way into the wooded area behind our property, memories flood my mind. Happier times of running and playing here with Jelena. I spot our tree house in the distance and make a beeline for it. Climbing up the rickety ladder, I scurry across the floor, not caring if I get slivers from the old wood. Huddled in the corner, I pull my legs up to my chest and let the tears fall.

A few minutes later, Pyotr's head pokes from the entrance in the floor. "May I come in?"

I don't answer him. With a slight groan, he enters the small space and sits beside me as he tries to catch his breath.

"Jelena's dead, isn't she?"

"Yes."

"Who killed her?"

"A man named Farouk El Alami." Pyotr doesn't give me a hard time answering my questions.

"Is he dead?"

"Yes."

I look up at Pyotr. "Did Papa make sure he suffered before he died?"

"He did, yes."

"Good. I don't feel bad knowing Papa made sure that man was hurt before he had him killed. Does that make me a terrible person?"

"I don't think it does."

The cold coming through the open windows of the treehouse made me shiver uncontrollably. Pyotr takes off his heavy sweatshirt and passes it to me. I pull it over my head, thankful it's big enough to cover my legs, too. We sit in silence as snow begins to fall outside. Pyotr doesn't push me to talk, which I appreciate. Instead, we sit there, lost in our own thoughts.

I can't escape the memory of Jelena's hand. How it felt as it slipped from mine. I clutch Pyotr's sweatshirt tighter as my body begins to shake harder. "I held onto her as tight as I could. I tried not to let go, but they were so much stronger than me," I mutter between sobs. "I'm a coward." The tears fall harder. I can't control my body as I begin to retch violently. It's painful, but I can't stop it. "I want my sister back," I cry, hoping for some kind of relief. "Please, Pyotr. Please bring her back."

"I'm so sorry, Lana," he says softly. "I wish I could bring her back, but I can't." I throw myself at him, desperate to feel safe. He wraps his strong arms around me, and I bury my face into his shoulder. "I've got you. You can let it all out."

Crying. Screaming. Punching. My body rapid fires through emotions far greater than I know how to handle. Through it all, Pyotr never lets go. I cry until I'm exhausted and numb.

"It's okay to close your eyes." Pyotr strokes my forehead just like Mama does when I'm sick. "I'll keep you safe, little butterfly."

Pyotr holds me close, protecting me from the world outside. His words fill me with a sense of peace, and I know I'm safe in his arms. It's with that thought I allow myself to drift off into sleep.

When I wake, I'm in my bed. Papa's sitting in a chair next to me. He's wearing the same clothes as yesterday, and his usually perfectly groomed black hair is poking out in all directions. His eyes are still red and swollen from crying. But now there are dark circles under them. He must have sat awake all night watching over me.

"Papa," I whisper, and a fresh wave of tears spills from my eyes.

"Moya babochka." He opens his arms to me, and I crawl onto his lap. "I am so sorry I did not bring your sister back as I promised."

"It's not your fault, Papa."

"I failed—everyone." His voice trails off.

A tear rolls down his cheek, and I wipe it away with my finger. I've never seen Papa cry, and I don't like it. I wrap my arms around his neck. "Please don't cry, Papa. We're going to be okay."

We have to—for Jelena.

I don't realize I'm screaming until my door flies open, and Pyotr's rushing into my room with his weapon drawn. "What's wrong?" he asks, panicked.

"It hurts. It hurts so badly."

He kicks the door closed and locks it before sitting beside me on the bed.

"Come here." He holds his arms out to me. And just like he did when I was a little girl, he holds me in his protective embrace as I cry for my sister. "Let it all out. I'll keep you safe, little butterfly."

Svetlana

"THANK YOU FOR SEEING ME." AFTER I COMPOSED MYSELF from my earlier breakdown, I called Masha. Fortunately, she was able to squeeze me in as an emergency this evening.

"I'm glad you reached out." Her smile is warm. "Is it okay if Pyotr leaves?"

"No." I tighten my grip on his hand. "I want him to stay."

Pyotr has been by my side for ten years. Yes, he's paid by Papa to guard me. But he's become much more than just a guard. He's my rock and one of my best friends. The older brother I've always longed for.

"If his presence helps, he can stay." Instead of sitting behind her desk, she sits in one of the chairs by the couch. "Are you comfortable telling me what happened earlier today?"

"I remember sitting on my bed. I don't know if I fell asleep or just started remembering. But suddenly, I was eleven years old again, and it was the day I found out Jelena died." I tell her about that day and how I reacted to it today. "The few weeks following were even worse. It was like I was trapped in a nightmare, and no matter how hard I tried, I couldn't wake up. Her funeral was the hardest day of my life." I squeeze Pyotr's hand tighter. "She looked so peaceful. Like she was only sleeping. I kept watching her, hoping to see her move. Expecting that she'd sit up at any second and tell us she was fine and that there was some mistake. But that didn't happen. She didn't wake up."

For three long days, Jelena's body lays in repose. That's what Mama calls it. During this time, a steady stream of friends, family, and Papa's business associates comes to pay their final respects. The room is filled with the fragrant scent of flowers.

On the final day, Jelena's body is moved to the church for the funeral service. As the mourners enter, they file past her casket, placing flowers and kissing her forehead in a final farewell. Then, they light a candle and take their seats. The sound of people crying echoes in the big room.

Papa leads up to the front row. He sits between Mama and me, his face etched with sadness.

"Why do we have to sit up here?" I whisper to Pyotr, who's sitting beside me.

"It's the rules of a funeral."

"I don't like it." I grab his hand.

"I know, little butterfly."

The funeral service is steeped in tradition, with the priest leading us through ancient rituals and prayers. Papa argued fiercely with him about adding a more modern custom, allowing people to speak. The priest wasn't happy, but Papa won the argument.

Several people, including Jelena's teacher, have stepped forward to share their memories of my sister. Their stories all highlight Jelena's kindness, humor, and loyalty to her friends.

Right now, Innessa, Jelena's best friend, is taking her spot behind the microphone.

"I've known Jelena for almost as long as I can remember. We met on our first day of kindergarten when I was still adjusting to my new foster family. I was so scared and felt like an outsider. Jelena saw me hiding in the corner and walked right over to introduce herself. When I didn't get up, she sat next to me and started talking. Pretty soon, I was laughing and feeling at ease. Jelena was always the brave one, and she never judged me for being a foster kid. In fact, she brought me home after school one day and asked her parents to adopt me." Papa chuckles softly beside me. "I was fortunate enough to be adopted by my foster family when I was ten years old. Jelena was there with me on that special day. She's been by my side for

every major moment in my life." Innessa's voice trembles with emotion as she speaks. "Jelena is, was, my best friend. She means everything to me." She breaks down crying, and her Mama rushes over to comfort her and leads her back to their seats.

"Every now and then, I'd see Innessa somewhere. She never failed to tell me a new special memory she had of my sister."

"Knowing a loved one has not been forgotten is comforting."

"After Innessa sat down, I got up. It wasn't planned. It just happened."

"Jelena was the best sister I could've ever asked for. I have so many memories of us playing together. One of our favorite places was the tree house Papa built for us. Even though she was older than me, she always played my make-believe games and made me feel special. Jelena was also incredibly smart, and I wanted to be just like her when I grew up. I hate saying was because that means something is over. It feels like I'm admitting she's gone, and I don't want her to be gone. It's not fair that she was taken from us. I want Jelena to still be here. I don't want to do life without my sister, but I know I don't have a choice." I swipe at a tear that escapes. "It's hard to walk by your empty bedroom every day and know that you're not there. Jelena, if you can hear me, I promise to always try my best to be good and remember everything you've taught me."

I walk over to her casket, tears streaming down my face, and speak softly. Not into the microphone, but directly to my sister. "Yelena, I miss you so much. I love you, and I always will. Ya obeshchayu, ty nikogda ne budesh' zabyt"

The priest steps back up to the microphone to finish the service. He says some prayers and sprinkles some dirt and holy oil onto Jelena. The burial shroud is pulled up, covering her, and the priest reads one final scripture, Psalm 118. "Blagodarite Gospoda za to, chto On blag. Yego lyubov' dlitsya vechno."

"That was the last day I ever stepped foot in a church."

"Why do you think that is?"

"Jelena was only fifteen. She didn't do anything wrong. She was beaten and raped before some sick bastard killed her. But then, I'm supposed to believe what that priest was saying, that I should give thanks to God and that he loves us?" I shake my head. "How does that even make any sense? What kind of God lets such awful things happen? I still don't understand it, and I refuse to accept it."

"Those are fair questions. One's you're not alone in asking."

"Do you have the answers?"

"I'd be a very rich person if I did, but sadly, I don't."

After the funeral service is over, we walk behind the coffin to the grave-yard. Behind us, everyone is laying Juniper branches on the road.

"Why are they doing that, Mama?"

"It's to confuse the evil spirits," she whispers.

Once we're in the cemetery, everyone gathers around where she'll be buried. I hold Mama's hand and watch Jelena's coffin being lowered into the deep hole. I can't see clearly through all my tears. When the casket is in place, everyone takes turns dropping coins and a small handful of dirt onto the casket.

"Why are they throwing money and dirt on her?" I ask Papa.

"Russians are too superstitious. But if it helps them feel better, then so be it." I decide to be like Papa and not believe in such silly things.

"That must have all been very confusing to a little girl," Masha says.

"Yes and No. It was the first funeral I'd ever attended, so I didn't know the order of events or why certain things were done. Mama, Papa, and Pyotr answered all my questions."

"I'm glad you have so many people looking out for you."

"Me too." I squeeze Pyotr's hand. "I'm a very lucky girl."

When we get back to the dorm, I decide to call my parents.

"Svetlana, I'm so glad to hear your voice," Mama answers the phone. "I'm surprised to hear from you this week, though."

"I wasn't able to leave school this time."

"Is that my little girl?" Papa calls.

"It is. I just put you on speaker, honey."

"Hi, Papa."

"How are you holding up, *moya babochka?*"

"It's been tough."

"Say the word, and I'll have the jet readied. We can be there in a few hours."

"No, I'm good. Pyotr's here. He'll make sure I'm okay."

"I was looking through our family photo albums earlier," Papa says. "I found a picture from your first day of school."

In an instant, I'm transported back in time to that day.

I finally get to go to school just like Jelena. I've been up for a long time when Mama finally comes into my room. "Svetlana, time to get up and get ready for school."

"Yes, ma'am." I hop out of bed.

"Someone's chipper today." Mama smiles.

"I'm going to school today. Just like Jelena," I squeal.

"Yes, you are. Olga's getting breakfast on the table. Run along so it doesn't get cold."

"Okay." I skip past her, and she giggles.

Jelena's already at the table waiting for me. "Good morning, Lana bug."

"Good morning." I sit next to her. "What's for breakfast?"

"It's a surprise." She grins.

I pick up my cup of hot tea and take a sip. It's nice and sweet. Olga must've put an extra lump of sugar in it this morning. The kitchen door swings open, and Olga walks out carrying two plates. She sets them down in front of us.

"Syrniki?"

"Of course." She kisses me on the head. "The first day of school is a very special occasion."

I dig into my favorite breakfast of all time. I love it so much I don't even talk during the meal.

After breakfast, Jelena and I brush our teeth in our shared bathrooms and then go to our rooms to get dressed. Mama has my new school uniform, a dark grey pinafore, and a white shirt, ironed and laid out on my bed. Next to it are white knee socks, and on the floor are my new shiny black shoes. I've been begging Mama to wear them since we bought them, but she said I had to wait for today.

I'm twirling in front of the mirror when Jelena comes into my room.

"What do you think?"

"You look like a proper schoolgirl."

One day, when I'm older, like Jelena, I'll get to wear a dark grey skirt with a button-down shirt. For now, I'm happy with the uniform I do get to wear.

"Come sit down so I can fix your hair." While Jelena braids my hair, I ask her a million questions about what school will be like.

"You'll have the same teacher I did, Ms. Zima. She's the sweetest, and you'll love her," Jelena says as she finishes one of my braids. "You'll have to find your table—"

I spin around, making Jelena drop my hair. "How will I know which table I'm supposed to sit at?"

"That's what I'm trying to tell you, silly." She turns me back around so she can rebraid that side.

"Oops."

"Ms. Zima will have name cards taped to each table so you know where to sit."

"Look at you two," Mama says as she comes into my room. "Where did my babies go?"

"I'm not a baby."

"No, you certainly are not." Mama stands next to Jelena, and I can see their reflections in my mirror. "You've done a beautiful job braiding your sister's hair."

"Thank you, Mama." Jelena beams.

"I have a present for you both." Mama hands us each a box. "Go ahead and open them."

Jelena opens her present neatly, but I pull the lid off my box, toss it onto the floor, and find the prettiest white bows I've ever seen. I remember Jelena telling me that every year, on the very first day of school, all the girls wear the biggest white bows they can find.

"Can you put them in?" I hold the bows out to Jelena as I jump up and down.

"May I put them in for her, Mama?"

"You may."

Jelena stands behind me and carefully clips in my bows. Then, she puts hers on.

"I think we're going to have the prettiest bows out of everyone."

"Lana bug, you can't say things like that," Jelena corrects me. "All the girls will have equally as pretty bows. You don't want to hurt anyone's feelings."

"Oh." I drop my head. "I'm sorry."

"It's okay."

"We need to hurry. Papa is waiting downstairs to take your pictures."

"Pictures," I say and clap my hands. "I love pictures." I take off to find Papa.

"Moya babochka," Papa says and holds out his arms to me. When I get to him, he lifts me and spins me in the air. "My baby girl is going to school. What will I do all day without you?" He kisses my cheek and sets me on my feet.

"Do you need me to stay home to help you?"

Papa laughs loudly. "No. You must go to school. But I will be here when you get home. You can tell me all about your day."

"Okay."

"And look at you, malen'kiy tsvetok'." Papa kisses Jelena's cheeks. "You look far too grown up. Maybe I should lock you in your room before the boys start calling after you."

"Oh, Papa, don't be silly."

"Can we take pictures now, Papa?" I tug on his arm.

"Outside you go," Papa says, and I grab Jelena's hand, dragging her with me.

Papa takes tons of pictures. Some of each of us alone and lots of us together. "I think I got enough." He smiles.

"Are you sure? Maybe you should take a few more."

"We have plenty of pictures. If you two don't leave now, you'll be late."

Jelena and I take turns giving Papa a hug. He wishes us luck on our first day.

"Here are your flowers, girls." Mama walks over with two big bouquets of the yummiest-smelling flowers in her arms.

"What are these for?"

"They're a gift for our teachers," Jelena says. "Everyone brings a gift for the new school year."

Mama and Papa walk us to the gates, where we quickly say goodbye to Misha and Igor, who tell us they'll watch for us when we're walking home.

"Be sure to hold your sister's hand," Mama calls as we walk away.

"I will," I yell over my shoulder.

And then we're off. We meet up with a group of girls and boys down the sidewalk a bit.

"Are you excited to start school?" Innessa asks. She's Jelena's bestest friend in the world.

"I am. Do you like my bows?"

"They're the prettiest ones I've ever seen."

"See, I told you—"

"Svetlana," Jelena says sharply. "Remember what I told you."

"Jelena says I shouldn't say stuff like that, so I don't hurt anyone's feelings."

"She's right." Innessa leans close and whispers, "So, we'll keep it our secret."

When we get to the school door, my feet stop moving.

"What's wrong?" Jelena asks.

"I'm scared. I don't think I want to go to school anymore."

Jelena makes herself smaller so I don't have to look up at her. "Being nervous is okay, but you must try it once. If it's horribly awful, I'll talk to Papa and tell him you don't ever want to come back."

"Promise?"

"Pinky promise." She holds her finger out, and I wrap mine around hers. "Come on. I'll walk you to your classroom."

"I was so scared, but Jelena walked me to my classroom and helped me find my table."

"I did not know about her promise to you," Papa says and chuckles.

"She was always looking out for me."

"From the day we brought you home from the hospital, Jelena adored you," Mama says. "She was like a little mama helping me care for you."

Talking about her, especially on the anniversary of her death, rips open old wounds. The pain is as sharp as it was the day she left us. Tears spill down my face. "I have to go. Pyotr just texted that our food arrived." I make up an excuse to hang up. "I'll talk to you soon."

"We love you very much."

"I love you both, too."

I miss my big sister. Time has not made the loss any easier to bear. I sit in the quiet darkness of my dorm room and cry. Each year, I remind myself of the promise I made to her at her funeral. "*Ya obeshchayu, ty nikogda ne budesh' zabyt.* I promise you'll never be forgotten."

Svetlana

AFTER JELENA'S PASSING, I WAS PLAGUED WITH NIGHTMARES. In my dreams, she would slowly drift away from me until I couldn't recognize her face or voice. These night terrors began to seep into my waking hours. The thought of forgetting my sister terrified me.

My sister has been gone for a month. Thirty days. But it feels like an eternity. I can't imagine missing her this much for the rest of my life. Papa allowed me to take a few weeks off of school, but my tutor returned to restart my lessons last week. I guess it's a good thing. At least for a few hours, I have something to distract me from how much I miss my sister.

After my tutor leaves, Pyotr and I often go for a walk. I talk a lot about Jelena while we're out. Mama and Papa said we could talk about her whenever I wanted. But I try not to mention her because it makes them sad. Pyotr doesn't get sad, so it feels safe to talk to him. Pyotr says it'll get a little bit easier with each day that passes. I'm not sure I believe him because it hasn't gotten any better.

The other day, we took a walk to the treehouse. Pyotr said there was something he wanted to show me. When I climbed up, there was a wrapped present waiting. I tore off the paper and found a white stuffed bear. In his hands is a picture of Jelena and me.

"Squeeze his paw," Pyotr instructs.

"Hey, Lana Bug." Jelena's voice plays.

"I know how worried you've been about forgetting what Jelena sounded like. Now, anytime you want to hear her, you can."

I try my hardest not to cry, but I can't help it. "Thank you, Pyotr." I throw my arms around his neck. "This is the most special present in the whole world."

I reach over to my desk to grab the bear. Whenever I get lonely, I press his hand and hear the eternally young voice of my sister calling me Lana Bug. Holding the bear close to me, I drift back in time once again.

I don't wait for my tutor to leave before I sprint from the room and crash into something big.

"Hey, little butterfly. You're in quite a hurry."

"Sorry."

"It's okay. You didn't get hurt, did you?"

"Nope."

"Is today the big day?"

"It sure is."

"Good luck."

"Thank you." I hurry down the hall, not wanting to waste another second.

When I get to my room, I reach under my mattress and pull out my black notebook.

At the funeral, I promised Jelena I'd make sure she was never forgotten. When I made the promise, I wasn't sure what I could do to keep it. Luckily, Pyotr's pretty smart and gave me some ideas. I'd do anything to bring her back, but I can't do that. So, the next best thing is that her death might be able to help other people. I have an idea I'm hoping Papa will like.

Before I go to talk to him, I have to get changed. Papa needs to take me seriously, and he won't do that in jeans and a T-shirt. I look through my closet, but I don't have anything to wear to a business meeting.

I creep down the hall to the door of Jelena's bedroom. No one's been in here since she was taken. Slowly, I turn the handle and push the door open. It looks just like Jelena left it. Her bed is made, and all her pillows are fluffy. Her favorite stuffed animal, a brown and white stuffed horse named Sasha, is nestled in the center. She named it after Papa's American business associate Alexander, whom she had a huge crush on. On the table next to her bed is the book she was reading, War and Peace. It's a super big book that's required for school. I pick it up and take it with me. If Jelena was reading it, I want to read it, too.

Jelena's desk is in front of a big window overlooking the back of our property. Unlike mine, hers is neat and organized. Her math text is open, and a pencil rests in the center. Next to it is her notebook with math problems written on the page. It looks like she was in the middle of a homework assignment. It didn't matter that we were on school break. Jelena always asked for extra credit work. I don't want any more homework, but I decide I'll tidy up my desk, so it looks like hers.

The reason I came in here is to go through her closet. Jelena has clothes that are more grown-up than mine. Setting the book down, I go into her closet and search for the outfit I want—a navy blue skirt and matching jacket. Jelena wore it to volunteer at Mama's office several times. After looking through a bunch of outfits, I finally find the one I want.

My white school uniform shirt works perfectly, and even though I need to use a belt for the skirt and I have to roll up the blazer sleeves a little to make it fit, I think it works well. I pull my hair back and put it in a bun to look older. Then, after putting my black school shoes on, I grab my notebook and go downstairs to Papa's office, where I find Misha outside the doors.

"Is Papa busy?"

"He's on a phone call. Is there something I can help you with?" he asks.

"No. I need to talk to Papa about it."

"Misha, I—" Papa says, opening the door startling me. "Moya babochka, you look like you are ready to go to work."

"I am." I nod. "Do you have some time to talk?"

"For you, any time." Papa smiles and steps aside, allowing me to enter. "Please excuse me, Misha. I have an important meeting with Ms. Solonik. Can you make sure we're not interrupted?"

"Sure thing, boss."

Papa sits in his big, comfy chair with his hands folded. "What can I help you with today?"

I open my notebook and clear my throat. "I made a promise to Jelena that I wouldn't let her be forgotten."

"That will not happen."

"I know we won't forget her, but other people might. They'll forget how good she was." I pull my feet under my legs. "I don't want that to happen."

"I see. What do you have in mind?"

"I don't know for sure." I bite my lip while I look at the notes I made. "I know Jelena wasn't the only person who's ever been trafficked and that it happens to lots of people." I look at Papa. "Pyotr said many of the people that are taken don't have anyone who loves them or looks for them."

"That is very true."

"There has to be something we can do to help."

"You are a remarkable young lady. Do you know that moya babochka?" I shrug, not thinking I'm anything other than normal. "I have been thinking precisely the same thing."

"You have?" I ask, surprised.

"Yes. I've been busy getting some colleagues together to form a network to go after people like Rudolf Sergin and Farouk El Alami. I want to make sure no one else ever has to lose a loved one."

"I like that very much. But what about helping the people that were stolen? I want to help them."

"How so?" Papa tilts his head.

"When I was talking to Pyotr, he told me your men found other people, even kids, who'd been taken from their families."

"Yes. That is true."

"And that when they're rescued, they are usually sick or hurt." Papa nods. "Who helps them?"

"I would like to get your mama. She should be here for this conversation, don't you think?"

"Yes." I smile.

Papa texts Mama, and a few minutes later, she joins us in the office. Papa catches her up on what we've talked about so far.

"I'm on board. How can I help?" Mama asks.

"Well, you're a doctor. You can help fix whatever's hurt, right?"

"I can fix a lot, yes. But often, there are things in the mind that have been hurt. I can't fix those."

"Who can?"

"Doctors called psychiatrists and therapists."

"Can we get some of them, Papa?"

He grabs a pen and starts writing notes of his own. "Yes, I will look into hiring some mental health professionals."

"And some more doctors. I'm only one person," Mama adds. "And where are we going to do all this?"

"We are going to need a building," Papa says. "And a name."

"Yelena Nadezhda," I say.

"Jelena's Hope," Mama whispers. "I love it."

"It is perfect," Papa says. Svetlana, you have done something truly remarkable here. It is not often that adults even consider helping trafficking victims. You have created something special that will provide care and support for so many people. It shows what a tender and caring young lady you are. I am incredibly proud of you."

"As am I."

It's been a year since Jelena passed away, and today is a big day. There are so many people here to support us. It feels like the whole community is cheering us on. It's a little scary to be the center of attention.

"I wish Jelena was here."

"She is here, little butterfly," Pyotr says. "She's always watching over you."

Papa, Mama, and I are all here to cut the ribbon and officially open Yelena Nadezhda, Jelena's Hope. A special treatment center where recovered trafficking victims can come to heal. A place that will bring hope back into their lives.

My bear holds a photo, a moment frozen in time of Jelena and me. It's one of the last pictures Papa took of us over the holiday the year she was taken.

"I miss you so much," I whisper, feeling the weight of Jelena's absence in my heart. "When I first brought the idea of Jelena's Hope to

Mama and Papa, I had no idea what I was really asking for. I didn't know how many families like ours were suffering or how many people were living in captivity. We've helped so many and won't stop until everyone is safe and free."

The world is darker without Jelena's bright light, but Papa is right. Jelena will never be forgotten. Her legacy lives on in each one of us.

Svetlana

AFTER YESTERDAY, THE LAST THING I WANTED TO DO WAS get up bright and early to go to the symposium for a session on balancing big tech versus society. I sat in the very last row so that I could get out as soon as the presentation concluded. The last thing I wanted to do was get stuck talking to anyone.

I've spent the rest of the afternoon studying for finals next week. Part of me can't wait for this term to be over. The other part is wishing it could last forever. I'm not ready to answer the questions I know are heading my way. A loud argument outside of my room interrupts my quiet study time.

"Maybe I didn't make myself clear the first time," Pyotr yells. "I will not let you in. She doesn't want to be bothered."

"I don't remember asking for permission," Slava answers equally loudly.

"This is the last time I'm going to tell you before my fist meets your face. You need to leave."

I jump from my bed and hurry to the door before there's a physical altercation. "What's going on?"

"I'm trying to tell your *boyfriend* that you don't want to be bothered."

"Svetlana, please tell your *bodyguard* to stand down?"

The men are nearly chest to chest. "It's okay." I try to slide in between them. "He can come in."

"If you need me, just call." Pyotr glares at Slava before stepping back.

"Thank you." I smile and watch him disappear inside his room.

"He lives in the dorm with you?"

"Not *with* me. He has his own room." Slava's presence inside my room makes it feel smaller than it already is. "What are you doing here?"

"I've been calling and texting all night. I got worried when you didn't answer, so I flew up to check on you."

"You didn't have to do that." Slava joins me, sitting on the bed.

"Yesterday marked the anniversary of your sister's passing. I figured this week is going to be difficult for you," he says while extending his arms. I seek refuge in his embrace, curling up against his chest. "As your Dominant, it's my responsibility to care for you, especially during difficult times."

"I miss her so much," I admit.

"I know," he replies, tracing calming circles on my back. "You don't have to carry this burden alone. Let me help ease your pain."

I allow myself to be vulnerable and release my emotions. Tears stream down my face.

Slava doesn't loosen his hold on me until I stop crying.

"Thank you," I say quietly.

"There's no need to thank me."

"Well, I'm thanking you anyway."

Slava looks around my tiny dorm room. "I don't suppose you have anything to eat in here."

"I have a few granola bars, but that's it. We're not allowed to cook in our rooms." Not that there's space for anything other than our beds and desks.

"I'd like to take you out for dinner."

"You want to take me out?"

"Why do you seem so surprised?"

"I thought we were just, you know, a contract thing."

"Svetlana," He runs his knuckles down my cheek. "I like you a lot. I'd like to have more than just a *contract thing* with you."

"Slava, you know I can't commit to anything right now."

"I know. And I'll continue to respect your boundaries. But I will also keep telling you and showing you so you have no doubt about my feelings." My stomach grumbles loudly, giving away the fact that I haven't eaten anything since this morning. "Come on, let's go."

"I can't go out like this." I motion to the sweatpants and T-shirt I'm wearing.

"You look fine."

"I wore these to bed last night."

"You win." He laughs.

While I get changed, I text Pyotr.

Me: Slava and I are going to go out and grab a bite to eat.

Pyotr: When are you leaving?

Me: I'm getting changed now. Give me five minutes.

Pyotr: Okay. I'll be out front.

Slava gives me the choice of where to eat, so I bring him to Semplice Trattoria, a small restaurant within walking distance of campus. It's mid-week, so the restaurant is empty, and we're able to get a quiet booth in the back corner.

"Finals are next week?" he asks.

"They are."

"Are you prepared?"

"I'm getting there. Between the symposium this week and everything else going on. I'm a little behind, but I'll be okay."

"I don't envy you. I'm glad my college days are way behind me."

Slava is unlike any of the men I've met in Moscow. He's much older and settled in his career. I have no doubt that if I declined my acceptance at NYU to accept his offer of a relationship, I'd be cared for and loved. I'd simply slide into his life and join him on the path he's already on. But where does that leave me, and what I want from life? If I take his offer of something more, will I end up regretting not pursuing the goals I have for my future?"

"Svetlana," Slava says, waving his hand in front of my face to get my attention.

"Can you repeat what you said?"

"I was pointing out that you haven't touched your pizza." He reaches across the table and takes my hand in his. "Would you feel better if we have this wrapped and go back to your dorm?"

"It's past visiting hours now. Maybe we can go back to your hotel?"

"We don't have to. I don't want you to feel pressured."

"I really don't want to be alone tonight."

After we get our pizza wrapped, we walk back to campus. While I pack an overnight bag, Slava gets his car.

"Are you sure about this?" Pyotr asks from my doorway.

"What do you mean?"

"You usually don't do anything this week. Are you sure you're up for this?"

I put my toothbrush in the bag and zip it closed. "Why do you seem so against me being with Slava?"

"There's a huge age difference between the two of you. I want to make sure you're not being taken advantage of."

"Really? I can't believe you would say something like that."

"I'm just looking out for your best interest."

"I don't have to answer to you about who I spent my time with," I snap. "I'm not a child anymore. I don't need you monitoring my every step."

Pyotr holds his hands up in front of him. "I'm not trying to start a fight. I'm just—"

"I can assure you I'm not being taken advantage of." I lock the door, and we walk to the stairwell. "It doesn't really matter, though. After next week, I won't be seeing him again."

Svetlana

SLAVA'S SUITE HAS A HUGE SOAKING TUB THAT WE'RE TAKING advantage of. My head is laid back while I enjoy the foot massage he's giving me. I swear his fingers are magic.

"I must confess. There's another reason I flew up early. I've been waiting for the right time to tell you, but I don't think there is a right time.

"What is it?" I lift my head.

"My business in Moscow has concluded early."

"Okay?" From the tone of his voice, I can tell that isn't everything.

"My investment firm is opening a new location in Tokyo," he explains. "My partner and I take turns flying out to our new site locations. It was supposed to be his turn, but he's having a family emergency and can't go."

"What does all that mean?"

"I'm going to have to fly out."

"When?"

"My flight leaves tomorrow evening. I won't be here for our last weekend together." The past two months have flown by. We were supposed to have one more weekend together, but this news changes everything. "I can't lie. I'm disappointed that we have to end our dynamic sooner than we planned."

"I am, too." I change positions, getting on my knees and straddling his lap. "So, I guess we better make the most of tonight."

"What do you have in mind?" He grabs my ass, pulling me closer to him. His erection rubs against my pussy.

"Anything you want, Sir."

Somehow, he manages to stand us both up. I wrap my legs around him as he carries me toward the closed bathroom door. He reaches to open it, but his wet hand slides off the handle.

"Fuck it," he says, backing me up against the door. His lips crash against mine.

Slava wastes no time sliding his cock inside me. He grips my legs tightly. I'm sure there will be bruises there tomorrow. His movements are desperate—primal. It's as if he's trying to ensure I'm ruined for any other man. He comes with a deep growl, and I follow him. My inner walls squeeze his cock. He drops his forehead against mine while we catch our breath.

"That was just the appetizer," he says as he withdraws his still erect cock. "To the bed, now." He follows me. "Bend over and spread your legs."

He takes me from behind with just as much desperation as before. His hand reaches around my waist, and his fingers go to work on my clit as he works me to another orgasm. I cry out in pleasure. He pulls out and drags his finger through the wetness, spreading it to my other entrance.

The head of his cock presses against the tight muscles. I take a deep breath and relax, allowing him to enter without resistance.

"Good girl," he praises me. "You feel so fucking amazing."

I can't speak. The feel of him there is still overwhelming and takes all my concentration.

Slava grabs my hips as he begins moving. My hand slides between my legs as I pleasure myself.

"That's right, *moya nevinnyy malysh*. Make yourself come for me."

Each thrust of Slava's cock stokes the spark burning inside. As the flame grows, tension builds, and my breathing becomes erratic. A burst of white-hot sensation consumes every part of me, and everything around me fades away as shocks of pleasure pulse through my body. Slava thrusts one more time and then explodes inside me. The two of us are lost in the whirlwind of our shared orgasm.

After we've come down from our high, Slava gets in bed and pulls me against him. "I'm going to miss you, Svetlana."

My eyes close before I'm able to respond.

The bright sunlight shining through the half-open curtains wakes me. I grab my cell from the table beside the bed to check the time.

"Shit. Slava, wake up." I shake his shoulder.

"What's wrong?"

"I forgot to set my alarm. It's after nine. I'm late."

"Are you sure you have to go?" He pulls me to him, and the hair on his chest grazes my nipples. "I can come up with better ways for you to spend your time," he says between kisses.

"Yes." I kiss him. "I have to go."

"Fine." He groans but releases his hold on me. "Let's get you to school."

I shoot Pyotr a quick text.

Me: We overslept. Why didn't you call?

I get dressed while I wait for his reply.

Pyotr: You're a grown woman who doesn't need me monitoring your every step, remember?

I can't believe he's using my own words against me. I roll my eyes in frustration.

Me: I'll be ready to go in a minute.

Pyotr: I'll call for the car.

While I'm putting my hair into a messy bun, Slava's behind me getting dressed. I shift my position so I can watch the show.

"What time is your flight?"

"Six."

"Will you let me know when you've landed? I'd like to know you got there safely."

"Certainly." His lips meet mine. "I'm going to miss you."

"Me too." It's much harder to leave than I thought. But if I don't go, I'll fail the term, which can't happen. I will already have some explaining to do as to why I'm late. "I really have to go, though."

Slava walks me to the door. "I'll speak with you soon, Svetlana."

Pyotr's waiting in the hall. When he sees me, he grabs my bag and walks toward the elevator. I take a final look over my shoulder at Slava, who's standing in the doorway watching me walk away. There's something about the forlorn look on his face. It's almost enough to make me forget school and run to him. I stop walking for a brief second and look between the two men.

"You're going to be late. Are you coming?" Pyotr asks, breaking the spell.

"Yeah. I'm right behind you."

The mood in the car is tense.

"I'm sorry." I shift in my seat. "I was rude to you and shouldn't have been."

"And I'm sorry for overstepping."

My relationship with Pyotr is complex at times. He's my bodyguard, yes. But at the same time, he's so much more. We've been together for ten years. He's watched me grow up and held my hand through so many dark days. The bond we've formed is strong. It's because of that connection the lines sometimes get blurred.

"You didn't overstep. You were looking out for me. Just because I disagree with your thoughts doesn't give me the right to lash out at you."

"I forgive you, little butterfly." Hearing my nickname gives me the confidence that everything is okay.

Pyotr drops me off outside the conference hall while he parks the car. I sneak into the already-in-progress lecture and am thankful my professor doesn't seem to notice my late entrance. I do my best to take notes and pay attention, but my mind keeps drifting back to Slava. To the look in his eyes as I was walking away.

Me: Thank you for last night. It meant a lot to me that you came.

Slava: I'd do anything for you.

My professor chooses right then to look back at me. When he sees the phone in my hand, he gives me a disapproving shake of his head. I mouth *I'm sorry* and slide my phone back into my pocket.

Svetlana

I'VE SURVIVED FINALS AND AM PACKING THE LAST OF MY things to go home.

"I can't believe we've just finished our third year," Mei says.

"I know. It's crazy, isn't it."

"When does your train leave?"

I check the clock on my phone. "In an hour."

"You should be on your way to the station. You don't want to miss your train."

"And if I do?"

"It's not too late to come home with me."

Yet again, I managed to get myself into quite a predicament. I made some major changes and didn't tell my parents about any of them. I don't know why I thought keeping them in that dark was a good idea. It didn't cross my mind at the time that, eventually, they would find out. Now, I not only have to tell them what I did, but I also have to explain why I've kept it from them. Neither of which I've quite figured out just yet.

Which is why I opted for the train. Papa wanted to send his jet to fly us home, but I was desperate for any extra time to formulate a plan. I wish Jelena were here. This is the part she always helped me with. She was an expert at talking to Papa and Mama and smoothing things over for me. No matter how many years pass, I'll never get used to living without her.

Pyotr pops his head around the door we have propped open. "Little butterfly, we need to leave now, or we'll miss our train."

Mei giggles at his childhood nickname for me.

"I'll call you when I get settled at home." I turn to Mei and give her a big squeeze. I have to fight the tears that prick my eyes. Even she doesn't know about NYU.

"Everything will be okay," she reassures me.

"I hope so." I grab my bag and head for the door. "Have a safe flight home. I'll talk to you soon."

Pyotr parks in the long-term garage, and we rush through the station to get to the correct terminal. We arrive with only minutes to spare. We're barely in our seats when the train begins to pull away.

"I'm going to take a nap. I'm pretty tired."

"Not a problem. I'll be awake."

I pop my headphones in and close my eyes, pretending to chase sleep. I didn't lie. I was out very late last night with some friends, and I'm exhausted today, but I don't have time to sleep. There are a little under four hours before I have to face my parents.

Every scenario I can imagine goes through my mind, and none of them end well. Pyotr knows I changed my major, which, in the whole scheme of things, is the lesser of the two issues I'm struggling with. What he doesn't know about is my application and acceptance to NYU. I knew Papa was going to explode, possibly literally, and I didn't want Pyotr getting in trouble. I figured if I didn't tell him, he could claim plausible deniability and hopefully escape my father's wrath. The problem with my theory is other than Masha, I've had no one to talk to about this. No one to help me come up with a solid plan.

"Are you awake?" Pyotr shakes my shoulder gently. "We're home."

I take out my headphones and pull up the shade on my window. "Already?"

"Time flies when you're snoring."

"Haha. You're so funny." I elbow him. "I can't snore if I'm not asleep."

"I'm pretty sure you were snoring. Everyone on the train was staring."

"You're lucky I like you. Otherwise, I'd have to tell Papa to fire you," I joke.

"You'd be lost without me, butterfly."

Pyotr's one of the better guards my father employs. And he's right. I wouldn't know what to do without him. I came close to not having him and almost got stuck with Viktor instead.

After Dimitri's conscription, he returned to work for Papa. When he arrived at our house, he brought Viktor. They were friends in Ukraine and served their military time together. Papa took an immediate liking to Viktor and had him shadow Pyotr, whose main job was guarding me. I didn't do much other than go to ballet lessons on Saturday. Pyotr was a highly trained guard who would've been a better asset back on his regular duty. Papa felt Viktor would be an appropriate choice for my security detail.

At the time, I was thrilled. Thirteen-year-old Lana was totally boy-crazy and only saw blond hair, blue eyes, and a gorgeous face. The fact that he was twenty years older than me and wouldn't see me as more than a child never crossed my mind. Which turned out to be a good thing. Even if I was closer to his age, I don't think I could've managed to stay in the same room with him for more than five minutes without a fight. Viktor was the most overprotective guard I'd ever met. Papa got tired of our constant bickering and decided to reassign Viktor to the United States to work with Alexander. Which meant Pyotr stayed with me.

We exit the train and wait for our bags before going outside to find the driver we're expecting. Pyotr and I are shocked to see Papa, Mama, and Misha waiting for us.

"There she is," Mama exclaims as she rushes over to me. "I've missed you so much." She squeezes me in a tight hug.

"I missed you too, Mama."

Papa takes his turn, hugging me. "You guys didn't have to meet us here."

"We couldn't wait another minute to see you." He kisses both cheeks and whispers, "It appears we have much to discuss."

I try to keep a neutral look on my face. There's no way he knows anything, right?

"Let's go to the car." Mama links her arm with mine. "I'm sure you're exhausted and eager to get home."

This is one scenario I didn't plan for.

Svetlana

Misha slows the car to a stop in front of our house. Papa gets out first and goes straight into the house. I take it as a good sign that maybe there's something important waiting for him. Misha walks in with Mama while Pyotr and I grab our bags.

"Is something going on?" Pyotr asks.

"Dunno." I feign ignorance and walk into the house.

I reach the bottom of the staircase before Papa's booming voice halts me in my tracks. "Just a minute, Svetlana." I don't turn around. "Pyotr, please take her bag. Irina and I would like to speak to our daughter in the office."

"I'd really like to freshen up after traveling first."

"It was not a request."

Pyotr takes my bag and gives me a questioning look.

"Thanks," I say and offer him a small smile before turning and walking in the direction of the office.

"Go right in. I will be there in a moment."

"Yes, sir," I mumble as I walk past him.

Mama is already seated in one of the antique armchairs across from Papa's desk. I take my seat next to her just as Papa steps into the room. I grew up playing in here and have never been afraid of my father. But right now, as he takes his place behind his oversized desk, I can't help the feeling of intimidation I'm experiencing.

"Now that we are alone." He leans forward, resting his elbows on the desk. "Perhaps you can start by explaining why you changed your course of study without telling us."

"Well," I say and fidget in my seat. "I decided to take my future career in a different direction."

"I was under the belief that you were studying business to help run Jelena's Hope." Papa keeps his voice steady and even.

"I was. Except I decided a degree in business isn't where my heart is."

"So, you transferred to the law department?" Papa asks.

"Yes. Wait. How did you know?"

"The department chair and I are colleagues. He called to congratulate me on your win in the criminal court competition contest as well as your outstanding academic success."

"Right."

"That's a lovely plan, Svetlana," Mama says, putting her hand on my arm. "Why didn't you tell us?"

"Because I didn't think you'd approve of me changing my major or the *other* part of my plan," I say quickly.

"What's the *other* part of your plan?" Mama asks.

My parents are both staring at me. I may as well be in an interrogation room with a spotlight shining on me. There's no turning back now, so I blurt it out. "I want to continue my education in New York City."

"No," Papa states firmly.

"You can't just say no. That's not fair."

"I can and did."

"Can you talk some sense into him, Mama?"

"Svetlana, you know—"

"Please, Irina. I would like to hear your thoughts on this."

After a moment of contemplation, Mama responds, "Your Papa and I were quite shocked when the department chair phoned to congratulate him on your academic success," she says, glancing briefly at Papa. "We are incredibly proud of you, of course. We wish you had told us yourself rather than us finding out secondhand. And now you're saying you're interested in attending school in the United States. It's a lot to process all at once."

"I'm not just interested. I've already been accepted. I *am* going to study there," I say firmly, bracing myself for Papa's reaction.

Papa's expression remains unreadable for a moment before he finally asks, "You did what?"

I sit up straighter, determined to stand my ground. "I applied to New York University and was accepted for the Fall term. I will be going to the United States to study."

There's a long silence as Papa processes my words. I can feel the tension in the room building, like the calm before a storm.

"Svetlana, you should go to your room so your Papa and I can talk," Mama says quietly, her eyes flickering between Papa and me.

"Gladly," I say, pushing my chair back and standing up. As I walk towards the door, I can feel Papa's eyes burning into my back. I pause for a moment and turn around. "I know you don't approve, Papa, but this is something I have to do," I say firmly and walk out of the room.

Outside, I lean against the wall and listen intently to the muffled voices coming from the office.

"You do realize how thick those doors are, right?" Misha asks.

"Shh." I strain to hear what they're saying, but it's too quiet. After a few minutes of unsuccessful eavesdropping, I give up and head back to my room, my mind already racing with plans for the future.

As I comb through my damp hair, there's a soft knock on my bedroom door.

"Who is it?" I call out.

"It's me," Mama replies. "May I come in?"

"Sure." Mama enters the room, closing the door quietly behind her. "Let me guess, you're here to scold me for arguing with Papa earlier."

She takes the comb from my hand and sits beside me on the bed. I turn towards her, allowing her to comb through my long hair. "Do you remember when I used to braid your hair at night? I miss those moments," she says wistfully. "It feels like you've grown up overnight."

"I'm still the same person, Mama."

"In some ways, yes. But you've also become so much more than the little girl who used to run barefoot through the backyard with pigtails bouncing."

I face Mama, meeting her gaze. "Have you come to tell me Papa said no to New York?"

"He hasn't made a decision yet, but that's not what I came to discuss with you."

"Okay. What is it then?"

"We saw Slava at the dungeon a few weeks ago. He mentioned that you've been spending time together in Moscow."

"Yes, we have. Is Papa upset about that, too?"

"He wasn't pleased, but Slava explained it was temporary. That's probably why he's still alive," Mama chuckles softly. "But your father and I wish you had told us about it first."

"I understand."

"I'm curious. How does Slava fit into your plans of going to the United States?"

"I don't think he does."

"Have you discussed this with him?"

"No."

"Svetlana."

"Before you say anything, please listen to what I have to say." Mama nods. "A few months ago, Slava showed up at Ecstasy. It was purely coincidental. Seeing someone familiar was comforting, and we talked all night. We spent some more time together at the club and a few weeks later decided to discuss a contract," I explain. "He's been coming to Moscow pretty much every weekend. We kinda had a dynamic going."

"Lana, there is no *kinda* in this lifestyle."

"We had a contract, but it really wasn't anything serious."

"Is that what Slava believes too?"

"I don't know." I look down and play with a loose string on my blanket. "It doesn't matter now. It's over."

"I fear you see this differently than Slava."

"What did he say?"

"It was more what he didn't say."

"What do you mean?"

"I urge you to speak with Slava. It's something for him to tell you, not me. You must be completely honest with him."

My phone buzzes with a text alert. I glance at the screen.

Slava: Have you arrived home yet?

Instead of answering, I set it face down on the bed.

Mama stands up and plants a kiss on top of my head. "The longer you wait, the more difficult it will be."

After Mama leaves, I sink back onto my pillows. I'm unsure how to have this conversation with him.

Me: I did. I meant to text but got sidetracked.

Slava: I'd like to speak to you. Can I call?

I'm not in the mood for any more *important* conversations tonight.

Me: Things are pretty tense here right now. Can we talk tomorrow?

Slava: Sure. Sleep well, *moya nevinnyy malysh.*

I drop the phone on the bed beside me and close my eyes, wishing I had someone to talk this through with. At this moment, I feel very lost and alone.

Maxim

"Irina, *vozlyublenny*, would you please pack me a bag?"

"Yes, *Gospodin*," she answers. "May I ask where you're going?"

"I am taking a trip to New York City."

A few days ago, my strong-willed daughter approached me with this seemingly crazy notion of moving to New York City. To study law, of all things. The irony of her decision is not lost on me.

At first, I was inclined to forbid her from going, but that only strengthened her resolve. I am puzzled as to why she cannot be satisfied with staying on the same continent as me. Svetlana has never been to the United States, let alone New York City, and cannot possibly comprehend the workings of a city like that. The potential danger she might be putting herself in is worrisome. How can I ensure her safety if she is halfway across the globe?

My mind inevitably drifts back to the terror-filled day ten years ago when Jelena was abducted only a few blocks from my home. It serves as a reminder that danger lurks all around. I cannot keep Svetlana locked up in her room in the name of keeping her safe. Despite my concerns, I must permit her to live her life to the fullest, even if it means allowing her to study in the United States.

After careful consideration, I arrived at an idea - Alexander Montgomery.

"You're really going to let her go?" Irina asks, surprised.

"I am."

My wife quietly continues packing clothes without arguing. "Irina." I stop her, place my hands on her shoulders, and make her look at me. "You must trust me."

"You can't guarantee her safety," she replies, her voice trembling.

"Safety is never a guarantee. You are right. But I will do everything in my power to ensure no harm comes to her."

"I trust you, *Gospodin*," she says, but her struggle is evident in her eyes.

Our daughter's abduction ten years ago changed us both. Irina quit her job as a pediatrician and fell into a deep depression while I threw myself into work. Our Dom/sub dynamic was nonexistent, and our marriage nearly fell apart. We neglected Svetlana, who had witnessed her sister's kidnapping. It took a conversation with Svetlana for me to realize the extent of her grief and the need for change.

We have done a great deal of healing. But even now, I struggle with my overprotective nature. I would prefer to keep Svetlana locked in the house where I can control every variable. But Svetlana is a tenacious young woman who challenges me constantly. I will never tell her, but my daughter keeps me in check. I can't stifle her dreams, even if it means letting her go to New York City.

It has been almost a decade since the night I walked into Alexander's office only to find a young, inexperienced, and broken young man sitting behind a desk. His business was failing, and he was ready to throw in the towel and call it quits. I offered him an opportunity to join forces with me in my fight against human trafficking. I do not know if he was brave or just desperate, but he agreed.

. . .

Me: I just landed at JFK. Do you have time to meet with me today?

Alex: I'll clear my schedule. Where do you want to meet?

Me: Fire and Ice. I can be there in an hour.

Alex: See you then.

Over the years, we have worked closely, and he has taken on more responsibilities in my business. I have had the privilege of watching Alexander heal and grow in confidence. He has more than proven himself to be a trustworthy man. And, for the most part, gets along well with Svetlana. A necessary skill to possess for what I am about to ask.

Alex

Maxim's text requesting I meet him at Fire and Ice has disrupted my plans for the afternoon.

"Can you clear my schedule this afternoon?" I ask my office assistant Paul.

"Sure, Mr. Montgomery."

"Thanks."

"Is everything okay?"

"I hope so." I have a secure line in my home office. That's the usual method of communication for something important. The fact that Maxim's flown in from Russia without warning has me concerned. "Hey, Brand." I pop my head into his office. "I'm going to be heading out in a few. Paul's rescheduling this afternoon's meetings." Over the past few years, Brandon has become not only my best friend but also an irreplaceable part of my company.

"What's going on?"

"Maxim just texted. He's in the city and asked me to meet with him."

"I didn't know he was in town."

"Me either. I'll be at Fire and Ice if you need me."

"Let me know how it goes."

Viktor pulls up in front of the club, and as I step out of the car, I spot Timur leaning against the building. He appears to be engrossed in his phone, trying to blend in with the crowd. However, I know better than to think he's just another New Yorker buried in their device. His eyes are constantly scanning the area for any threats of danger.

"Nice to see you, Alex."

"You too."

"The boss is inside."

"Has he been waiting long?"

Timur checks the time on his phone. "Only about fifteen minutes."

"Viktor's parking the car. He'll be here in a few minutes."

Since the club is closed, it's easy to spot Max sitting in the café. He stands when he sees me.

"Thank you for meeting with me on such short notice."

"It's not a problem." I take my seat. "Is everything okay?"

A server arrives with our meals.

"I took the liberty of ordering for us." Once the server leaves, Max reveals the reason for his impromptu visit. "Svetlana has been accepted at New York University."

"Congratulations."

"I wish I could share in your excitement." Maxim's lack of enthusiasm doesn't surprise me. I've known Svetlana since she was a girl. She's always been an intelligent and independent young woman. Which is part of the problem. Svetlana has a mind that is very much her own. She never backs down from an opportunity to challenge her father. Max will never admit that she gets her strong-willed nature from him. Even though he's struggling with her choice, he adores her, and I'm sure he's proud of her achievements. "It has been a lot to process."

"That's understandable. But I'm sure she'll do great there."

"Yes. I have no doubt."

Max eats in silence for a few minutes. I know he didn't fly all the way to New York to tell me Lana would be attending college here. He doesn't seem in a hurry to tell me what is going on, though. I've known Max for long enough to realize I need to be patient, but curiosity is about to get the better of me.

"As you know, Svetlana is in the lifestyle."

"Yes," I answer hesitantly, unsure where he's going with this.

"She is a submissive without a Dominant."

"Maxim, I'm not interested in having a—"

"I am only asking if you will be her protector. And her friend," he says. "I'm planning to send Pyotr with her, but I need to know she will have someone familiar with the city and the people at Fire and Ice."

I don't know what I expected Max to say, but it wasn't this. "What would agreeing to this entail?"

"I trust you to oversee any Dominants who express interest in approaching Svetlana. As someone familiar with both the individuals here and Svetlana herself, I am confident that you will prioritize her safety and well-being in this matter."

"She would wear my collar of protection?"

"If you agree, yes."

I run my hand through my hair. A collar of protection is much different than a permanent collar, but I'll still be responsible for another person. This is not a simple yes or no question. "Can I take some time to think about it?"

"Of course. If you did not ask for time, I would be worried."

"When is she planning to arrive?"

"We have not discussed that yet. Alexander, I understand the gravity of what I am asking."

"I know you do. I'll have an answer for you tomorrow."

We spend the remainder of our meal discussing business. One of the most recent events is that Irina left her position in the pediatric office where she's worked for years. She's not the medical director for Jelena's Hope.

"Leaving her private practice must have been difficult for her."

"It was. As much as she loved working with the children, her heart is at Jelena's Hope. She was exhausting herself going back and forth."

"She's a hard worker. This will ease things up for her." I take a drink of water. "How long are you in town for?"

"Only a few days."

"I'll have my housekeeper get a guest room ready."

"Timur reserved a suite at the Ritz-Carlton."

"There's no need for that. You're always welcome at my home."

"I do not want to be an imposition."

"I have plenty of room, and Timur can stay downstairs with Viktor."

"Thank you, Alexander. I appreciate your hospitality."

Brandon

Once again, I find myself working late in the office, but I don't mind. There are still moments when I wonder how fortunate I was to land a job like this. Memories of my first encounter with Maxim Solonik and Alex come to mind.

By the time I get to Fire and Ice, the lobby is empty except for Star and two large men who appear to be guarding the main doors of the club.

"Good evening, Star. What's with the security?" I motion with my chin.

"We have a guest tonight."

"Must be someone important."

"Maxim Solonik. He's been here a few times."

"I've heard his name mentioned in passing." This is the first time I'm here the same night as this mysterious Russian.

"He has a great reputation at his dungeon in Russia. Maxim is also a whip master," Star says, getting my attention. "He's teaching a special class."

"Sounds like I came on the right night.

"He also brought a young man with him—Alexander. He lives in the city but has been struggling after the death of his mother. Maxim seems to

have taken him under his wing. Maybe you can introduce yourself?" she asks, uncertain.

"I'll be sure to find him."

"Excellent. So, are you here to play or just a voyeur tonight?"

"Just here for dinner and show." We share a laugh.

"In that case, enjoy your evening." She nods at the guards, who step out of my way so I can enter the club.

Working in Brooklyn and having to drive across town to get here takes forever. So, by the time I step into the main room, tonight's action is already underway. My first stop is the café. I'm starving. Lucky for me, it seems most everyone is gathered around the stages tonight, so I get a table right away. While I eat, I watch the scenes.

Vivian, one of the club's regular Domme's, is doing a teacher/student scene with her sub, Haven. It seems the student hasn't been achieving her full potential in class and has landed in detention. The teacher is educating her with a violet wand. Given the pleasure-filled moans coming from the stage, it's clear the ladies are both having a good time.

Stage two's scene is just getting started. Master Emiliano is prepping his slave, Avalon, for her punishment. The two had been in a Dom/sub dynamic for several years but recently have transitioned into a Master/slave dynamic. Although Avalon was the driving force to take their relationship to the next level, she's struggled to get used to her new role. Emiliano is patient, but only so much can be tolerated—even in a learning situation. There are rules and boundaries in place for a reason. Their dynamic will fail if Emiliano doesn't follow through with the punishments spelled out in their contract.

On stage three, I spot Maxim Solonik. He's taking some practice swings with his whip, no doubt warming up his arm. I'm glad I haven't missed his class.

As I finish my meal, I attentively listen to the experienced Dominant as he discusses the different grips and stances a person can take while using a whip. Then, he demonstrates using the various instruments.

"He's very impressive," I say quietly as I take the last empty seat by the stage.

"Maxim has a lot of experience."

"You know him?"

"I do." The guy sticks his hand out. "Alex Montgomery."

"Brandon Carpenter. Nice to meet you."

I return my attention to the stage. The whip is my impact implement of choice. I've taken several classes and have become comfortable using it. My goal is to become as skilled as the man on the stage. It's clear he has a wealth of knowledge that he's eager to share with anyone willing to learn.

"That concludes my demonstration." He pauses while his audience applauds. "Would anyone be interested in doing some one-on-one work?"

My hand shoots up. There's no way I'll pass up an opportunity like this. It appears I'm the only one who's volunteered and am invited onto the stage. After a quick introduction, Maxim has me choose the whip I'm most comfortable with.

"I am interested in why you chose this particular tool."

"The stock whip is the one I learned first. I'm comfortable with the level of control I have when using it. And—" I hesitate. "I get a certain amount of satisfaction watching a restrained submissive squirm when she hears the crack. They're often unsure of how much it'll bite and are surprised when the sting isn't as big as the sound."

"That is a good assessment. I would like to see your technique."

He steps a safe distance away. I'm confident in my movements and precision with the stock whip. With every swing, I skillfully adjust the intensity of impact and strike my intended target with accuracy. "Very good," Maxim says. "I would like to see you wield a bullwhip."

"I've never used one."

"There's a first time for everything. Would you like to learn?" Maxim asks me.

I'm at a crossroads, faced with a choice I knew would come at some point. Do I continue to avoid it out of fear, or do I take the leap and reclaim this part of me? "Yes, I'd love to."

Maxim brings two chairs from the audience to the stage and suggests we sit down and go over the basics of the bullwhip. He starts by explaining the history of its design and then demonstrates the best ways to execute a strike. After finishing, he hands me the whip and says, "Let's see what you can do."

Nervously, I take a few swings, but Maxim interrupts, "Wait. Try holding it like this." He adjusts my grip on the handle, explaining that it will give me better control and produce a louder crack.

Following his advice, I'm able to precisely hit my target and create a louder sound each time. I continue to practice until my arm tires, and my accuracy begins to falter. "I think I need to stop for a while. My arm is done."

"That was a good call. Many Dominants are so focused on their submissive that they fail to see the signs their body gives to end a scene."

I look out into the club and realize it's empty. The only people left are Star and Montgomery, who are sitting in the chairs watching. "I'm sorry, Star. Time seems to have gotten away from us."

"Not at all. Alex and I were enjoying chatting."

"You are always most hospitable, Mistress," Maxim says with a smile.

Not wanting to keep Star any longer, we quickly clean up the stage. I hate that it's gotten late and the instruction has ended. There's so much more I can learn from Maxim.

"Would you care to grab a bite to eat?" I ask as we exit the stage.

"Thank you for the invitation, but I am no longer a young man. I am going to head back to my hotel and get some much-needed sleep. Alexander, maybe you would like to join Brandon in my place?"

"Do you mind?" he asks.

"Not at all." I turn to Maxim. "Thank you again."

"It was my pleasure."

We wait with Star while she locks up.

"May I offer you a ride home?" Max asks Star.

"That would be lovely."

Alex and I see them off and then head out for something to eat and a few drinks. We sit in the quiet back corner of a little bar situated in a fancy upper-West side neighborhood. Although I don't live here, this is my bar of choice when I want to escape the constant noise and craziness of Manhattan.

"How do you know Maxim?"

"He's a business associate." Alex takes a swig of his beer.

This strait-laced guy and the Russian are business associates. Something doesn't add up. "What do you do?"

"I own a marketing firm—Montgomery Advertising." He quickly changes the subject. "Have you always lived in the city?"

"I was born and raised in Brooklyn," I respond to Alex's question. He watches me closely, waiting for me to elaborate. My story's not all that interesting, but here goes. "I have a sister, Quinn, who's eighteen years older than me. Needless to say, I was a bit of a surprise for my parents, who thought their days of raising children were over. Instead, they found themselves parents of a newborn. Quinn had already moved out of the house by the time I was born. She and I aren't very close." I stop and take a drink. "My parents were wonderful people and hard workers. Two years ago, Mom had a major heart attack and passed away. Dad never recovered from the loss and died six months later."

"I'm sorry to hear that. That must've been rough."

"I guess that's one of the worst parts of having older parents. Having to say goodbye too soon." I shrug.

"Does your sister still live in the city?"

"No. Her husband is career military. Currently, he's stationed in Germany, so they and their three kids are there. We talk every now and then, but that's about it."

"So, you're pretty much on your own here."

"I am."

"What do you do for work?" he asks.

"I graduated high school and slipped right into the role of caregiver for my parents. The city's a pretty expensive place to live, so I'm currently working a few odd jobs."

Alex leans forward, resting his elbows on the table. "What would you think about making a career switch?"

"Considering I don't have an actual career, I'm open to hearing the details."

"Come work for me at my firm."

"I don't know anything about marketing."

"I can teach you what you need to know."

"You don't even know me. Why would you offer me a job?" Either this guy's drunk, or he's just plain crazy.

"I have a feeling about you."

I raise my eyebrow and consider that my second thought must be right—he's crazy.

"It wasn't long ago someone took a chance on me. If that hadn't happened, I would've been forced to close up shop and move back to Seattle." He sits back. "So, what do you say? Will you come work for Montgomery Advertising?"

"What the hell, sure."

Brandon

My cell rings as I walk into my house.

"He wants me to agree to be a protector Dom for his daughter, Svetlana," Alex says.

"Hello to you, too."

"Hi."

"A protector Dom. Wow. That's a big ask."

"It is. But she'll be busy at school most of the time."

"You're actually considering this?"

"I am."

"You're crazier than I thought."

"That just might be true," he laughs.

"Are you going into the office tomorrow?"

"No. Max is staying at my place."

"Okay. I'll catch up with you on Monday then."

Nothing Maxim Solonik does is anything less than over the top. Even though I should be used to his way of doing things, I can't help but be shocked.

First thing Monday morning, I find myself in a dress shirt and tie as I walk into Montgomery's office to report for my first day of work.

I step off the elevator and into Montgomery Advertising. A younger guy sits behind the desk. He's currently on a call, so I stand off to the side and wait.

The office takes up the entire floor. Down the right side of the space are doors that I'm assuming lead to private offices. The center is open with lots of natural light from the building's windows. Desks are arranged in groups of four. Several people sit at their computers, appearing to be hard at work. I gotta say, I'm impressed with the place.

"Brandon?" the guy asks when he hangs up.

"Yes."

"Sorry for keeping you waiting. I'm Paul. It's nice to meet you." He extends his hand. "Mr. Montgomery is expecting you. His office is the last door on the right."

"Thanks."

"Thank you," I reply, aware of the curious stares from employees as I walk past them. Despite feeling out of my depth, I resist the urge to turn back and go home.

"Good morning," Alex greets me as he opens his office door.

"Morning," I reply.

"Please come in," he says, gesturing me inside.

To my surprise, Maxim is sitting on a black leather sofa. He stands up to greet me. "It's good to see you again, Brandon."

"Likewise," I reply and take a seat in a sleek leather chair. Alex sits down at his desk and gets straight to the point.

Montgomery didn't specify the position when he asked me to work for him. I came in anticipating discussing something entry-level where I'd be filing, photocopying, and making coffee, but that's not what is being described.

"I'd like to offer you the position of Chief Marketing Officer," he says.

"Wait a minute," I interrupt. "I think you misunderstood what I told you last night. I don't have a college degree or any experience in marketing."

"I didn't misunderstand." Alex leans back in his chair.

"I guess it's me that doesn't understand."

"Alexander does a great deal of work for me." Maxim joins the conversation. "Due to the sensitive nature of my accounts, my business *cannot be handled by just anyone. As Alexander already knows, I have high requirements for an employee."*

"Neither of you knows me. Why would you offer me a job like this?"

"We don't know you personally. You are correct. But my sources have informed me that you fit the description. "

His sources? Who is this guy? "I get the feeling there's more to this job offer than meets the eye."

Maxim tells me about his daughter, Jelena. Then, he provides a detailed explanation of his business operations. As it turns out, Maxim's a powerful player in the Russian Bratva. He leverages Montgomery's company to distribute sensitive information to a network of individuals working together to combat the global issue of human trafficking.

"Why me?"

"I got a feeling about you, and I've learned to trust my gut on these things," Alex says matter-of-factly. "If you need some time to think about it—"

"I'm in." Rarely do I go with my gut reaction. I'm more of a think things through until I have a contingency plan for my contingency plans. For some reason, this is different. There's a voice urging me to say yes. That this is something I need to be involved in.

"You did not ask about salary," Maxim adds. Rising from his seat, he grabs a pen from the desk and writes something on a piece of paper before sliding it over to me. I'm shocked when I pick it up. Confident that he put too many zeros on the number, I go to open my mouth, but Max stops me.

"There is no amount of money too great in this fight."

Alex and Maxim spend the next few hours explaining how the network operates and outlining my role within it.

"We'll be working closely together, and in six months, you'll be a marketing expert," Alex says.

"I'll take your word on that."

"Come on, I'll show you to your new office." Which is just a few doors down from his.

The nameplate on the door reads 'Brandon Carpenter.' The office is almost as large as Montgomery's, with a stunning city view. A large modern desk with an ergonomic chair sits in front of the windows. The wall to the right of the desk is lined with bookshelves.

"Through this door is our shared conference room, and that door"—He points to a second door— "leads to your private bathroom."

"Right." My head is spinning.

"I know how overwhelming this all is. I felt the same way when all this was getting off the ground."

"Overwhelming is putting it mildly."

"Max has a big personality. He can be a lot," Montgomery chuckles. "But he's a really good guy who's doing some very important work."

"I guess I'm still trying to figure out why me." I lean against the desk.

"When he first approached me, I had the same questions. I've since learned that fate has a way of bringing the right individuals together at the right moment," he responds before walking back to the door. "There's a paper on your desk with the company login information and a website. Order whatever you want to furnish your office. After you're settled here, head up to Human Resources. They're on the next floor up. They have all your onboarding paperwork. You're free to go when you're done there."

"Thank you. I really appreciate this opportunity."

"You're welcome." Alex raps his knuckles on the door frame. "I'll see you tomorrow."

I sit behind my desk and attempt to let the reality of all this set in. If you had told me when I walked into Fire and Ice on Friday that I would be offered a new job, and not just any job, one that could change my entire life, I would've said you were crazy. But here I am.

As I leave my office, I feel a newfound sense of purpose. I've been given the opportunity to work on a project that's bigger than me. Fate put us together, and I get the feeling she isn't done with me yet.

Alex

TIMUR MAY BE OLDER THAN VIKTOR AND ME, BUT THAT didn't stop him from kicking our asses in my private gym. I'll never question Maxim's choice of guards again. On the way to my room for a shower, I pass my office, where I hear Max on the phone. Judging by the tone of his voice, I'd hate to be whoever's on the receiving end. Max was planning to stay in town for a few days, but he received an urgent call late last night that has him rushing to prepare his jet for an immediate return home.

While I shower, I contemplate Max's request to take Svetlana on as a protected submissive, a decision that kept me up all night. My first instinct was to say no. The idea of being responsible for someone else's well-being is daunting. However, Max has been a steadfast friend and mentor to me. The night Maxim walked into my tiny office changed my career. I was days away from going bankrupt and having to return to Seattle as a failure. I owe the success of my company to him.

As if that wasn't enough, eight years ago, Max found me at my lowest. It was the first anniversary of my mom's passing, and I was a drunken mess. Maxim understood such profound grief and didn't judge my poor coping mechanism. Instead, he sat with me all night while I sobered up. Then, he brought me to Fire and Ice and re-introduced me to the lifestyle I'd turned my back on.

Although I've remained a member and visit the club a few times a month, it's usually to observe. I've done a few non-sexual scenes, but that's as far as it's ever gone. Having a permanent submissive is a big commitment. Too often, feelings get in the way, and when that happens, it leaves open the possibility of getting hurt. That's not an avenue I'm interested in pursuing.

So, why am I still considering it? It's not because I'm interested in Lana, even though I get the feeling Max wouldn't be opposed to that. I know he'd never hold it against me if I declined his request. But there's something else, something bigger than gratitude toward him, that's urging me to say yes.

Svetlana will have two more years of school left when she transfers to NYU. Then, I'm assuming, she'll return to Russia. So, this isn't long-term. But am I able to make a commitment to being a protector Dominant? By the time I finish dressing, I'm confident with my answer.

When I emerge from my room, I find my office door open. The three men are in my kitchen, discussing something in hushed tones.

"Alexander," Max says when he sees me. "Thank you for letting me use your office."

"I hope everything's okay."

"There are some developments at the center that need my personal attention."

I lean against the counter opposite the island where Maxim sits with a cup of coffee. "Do you have a few minutes to talk before you leave?"

"We're going to get the bags in the car. Let us know when you're ready to go," Viktor says as he and Timur leave the room.

"I've given your request a great deal of thought. If Svetlana is agreeable, I will be her protective Dominant."

"Thank you, Alexander. This eases my mind a great deal." Max's body visibly relaxes. "I will speak with my daughter when I arrive back home."

Svetlana

"SVETLANA," PAPA SAYS WHEN I COME UP FOR AIR.

"I didn't know you were home." I push myself onto the side of the pool.

"I got in a short time ago." He passes me a towel. "I would like to speak with you."

"About?"

"Dry yourself and get dressed. We will talk in my office."

"Okay. I'll be there in a few minutes."

I guess I'm done swimming laps today. Papa said he was going to New York for business, but I'm hopeful at least part of the trip was to consider my request to study there.

After I've dried and dressed, I pad barefoot through the house and find Timur outside the office.

"The boss is waiting for you." Timur opens the door for me.

"Thanks, T." I smile nervously and walk into Papa's office.

"Take a seat, *moya babochka*."

I sit, tucking one leg under me. My fingers trace the ornate carvings on the antique chair. "Did you have a good trip?"

"I could have used more time with Alexander, but there was some business I had to return to deal with."

"What's going on?"

Since the day I asked Papa about Gavriil's involvement in Jelena's abduction, he's allowed me to know bits and pieces about his business. Of course, I wanted to learn more. Over the years, I've pushed, hoping to take on a more significant role. That's part of the reason I chose to study business. I thought if I did that, Papa would finally give in and allow me to be a part of his organization. But he refuses. He's adamant that women do not hold positions in the Bratva. I'm all for breaking stereotypes, but Papa is not.

"Nikolai Federov's men busted a trafficking ring and apprehended someone we have been after for a long time."

"He couldn't handle it on his own?"

"Federov knew I would want to deal with this personally."

"It was someone involved with Jelena's kidnapping, wasn't it?" Even though she's been gone for a decade, Papa has not given up on tracking down every last person involved.

"Yes. She was the one person who has evaded us all these years."

"She? It was a woman?" That news rattles me. How could another woman participate in an act so disgusting?

"This is not what I brought you in here to discuss." Ugh. Papa's a master at shutting down and changing the subject. "I have made a decision on you going to New York?"

"I already told you. I'm going whether you ag—"

"Svetlana." Papa holds his hand up, silencing me. "I went to make arrangements with Alexander for your arrival."

"You did?"

"You may go on certain conditions."

Here we go. "What are they?"

"You will stay with Alexander until the dorms open at the end of August, and Pyotr will accompany you. I'll make arrangements for him to live on campus."

"I don't want a guard with me."

"We are not having this argument, Svetlana."

"Papa, I need the opportunity to live on my own. I'm asking you to trust me."

"My dear daughter." Papa softens his voice. "It is not you that I distrust. It is others that seek to do harm that I do not trust."

"I know all too well the evil that exists in the world. It was me that was with Jelena when she was taken. I watched her be dragged away." I swallow the knot that's forming in my throat. "When I open my eyes each morning, I renew my vow to live despite whatever danger may be around the corner. If I didn't, fear would rule my life, and evil would win. I can't let that happen."

I'm just about to give up hope when Papa speaks. "There is not a day that goes by that I do not thank God you were spared. I know how close I came to losing both of my girls that day. And yes, at times, it has made me a little overprotective."

"A little?"

"Well, maybe a little more than a little bit." Papa smiles. "But you have made an excellent point. I am willing to offer a compromise."

This is progress. "What are you proposing?"

"For my sake, Pyotr will accompany you at all times, but he does not have to live in your dorm."

"No. Going to New York is meant to be a fresh start. I can't do that with security following me around."

"I am willing to have him out of sight. As long as he's there."

"Totally out of sight?"

"Totally out of sight."

A smile spreads across my face. "It's a deal."

"On to the next point. Alexander."

Papa informs me that Alex has agreed to be my protector Dominant. I feel a tinge of embarrassment, knowing that he went behind my back to arrange it. Rather than resist, I decide to accept his offer. It's my part of the compromise for Papa not forcing Pyotr to live in the dorm with me. I'll deal with Alex once I get there.

"Thank you for doing that, Papa. I appreciate you looking out for me," I say, grateful for his concern. "When can I leave? I'd really like to explore the city before school starts."

"Alexander is willing to accommodate your schedule."

I pull out my phone and open the calendar app. I want to pack and leave tomorrow, but I suspect Papa will have something to say about that. "How about the first week of July?"

"That works well. I will inform Alexander of your plans."

"This means a lot to me. Thank you, Papa."

Brandon

"I can't believe you agreed to this. You're crazy."

Alex shrugs. "Possibly. But if I was in his shoes, which I never will be, I'd hope someone would do the same thing for me."

Alex has known Svetlana since she was a young girl. I've never met her, but he's told me countless stories about what a handful she is. You'd think she would've outgrown it, but it doesn't seem like she has. She sounds like a spoiled little rich girl to me. There's no way I would've agreed to babysit her.

"When is she coming?"

"She'll be here the first week of July."

"So, these are your last few weeks of being single." I chuckle.

Alex rolls his eyes. "Lana and I aren't a couple. I'm just going to be looking out for her."

"We'll see about that."

"I'm sure you have work or something to do. " I don't want to keep you," Alex says, heading to my office door. "I have an errand to run."

"Are you going anywhere fun?"

"The jeweler to pick up her collar."

"You're going to collar her?" I'm beginning to think he's completely lost his mind.

"A protective collar, yes. If I'm doing this, I'm doing it right."

I've been too busy ribbing Alex to notice the tension in his body. He's taking this very seriously, and it's already weighing heavily on him. I close my laptop. "Actually, I don't have anything pressing to do. How about I go with you?"

"Thanks. I'd appreciate the company."

He's quiet as we ride down the elevator and exit the building. Once we're outside, he lets out a big sigh.

"You good?"

"I don't know. This is a big commitment. I don't want to do anything to screw it up. If something happens to her on my watch."

"You aren't going to let anything happen to her."

"I'll do my best, but I'm only one person."

"I've got your back."

"Really?"

"Of course."

"Thanks." He slaps my shoulder.

Rather than take the subway, Alex and I walk the ten blocks to the small jewelry shop.

We aren't all the way into the store when a curvy brunette spots Alex and bats her fake eyelashes at him. "Mr. Montgomery. It's so nice to see you again."

"Harvey called to let me know my order came in." Alex ignores the woman.

"Yes, it did. I'll go get it." She turns and sways her hips as she walks into the backroom.

"Someone's happy to see you," I whisper.

"She's married."

"That doesn't seem to matter to her."

"I know."

"Here it is," she says as she approaches us.

Alex takes the offered velvet box and lifts the lid. "What do you think?" Inside the box is a delicate chain. A silver charm with a garnet dangles from it. A lowercase p and the initials A.M. are engraved on it. "I wanted it to be something she can wear to school without attracting unwanted attention," he explains.

"Because a garnet is discreet?"

"It's her birthstone."

"That makes more sense."

"Do you like it?"

"I'm flattered, but I don't think it's my color," I grin, and Alex rolls his eyes.

"Do you think she'll like it?"

"Yes. I think Lana will love it."

Whether or not Lana likes this collar is of little interest to me. I'm more concerned about whether Alex has gotten himself in over his head. He hasn't had a submissive since I've known him. Not only hasn't had one but also hasn't been the least bit interested in finding one. Now, this. I'll give him that it's for protection, but women get attached easily. Svetlana will want more from him, and knowing Alex, he'll cave and try to give it to her. This can only end one way—disaster.

Svetlana

Delaying my departure until July turned out to be a wise choice as it allowed me to get everything ready without rushing to leave for New York City. Over the past few weeks, I've purchased most of the things I need for my dorm. For convenience's sake, I'm having them shipped directly there.

Now that the move is approaching, my excitement has turned to nerves. I enjoyed living in Moscow, but it wasn't a true test of my independence. Moving to New York City is both exciting and terrifying.

I am also faced with the dilemma of Slava, an issue I've yet to tackle. We've had some contact since our contract expired. He's still in Japan and has asked me several times to fly out and visit him. Slava has mentioned he'd like to discuss another contract. Although I enjoyed my time with him, accepting his offer would mean giving up everything I've worked so hard for. That's not something I'm willing to do. I have to figure out something, though. He doesn't know I'm leaving in two days, and I'm unsure how to tell him.

"Svetlana," Mama says, popping her head into my bedroom. "Are you ready to go?"

"I just have to grab my shoes."

Any decisions about Slava are going to have to wait. Today, Mama and I are doing some last-minute shopping for new clothes and shoes. Although I was content with waiting until I got to the city, Mama insisted on the one-on-one time, which I don't want to miss. Once I leave, it'll be a while until I see her. She can't just up and leave Jelena's Hope without having enough staffing to care for the people we have there. I can't think about stuff like that, or I may lose my nerve.

Even though I know Pyotr and Misha hate shopping, they've been extra patient today and even pretended to enjoy themselves. I'm sure Pyotr hopes this means I won't drag him shopping when we get to New York. I don't want to burst his bubble yet. He'll find out soon enough that I plan on taking full advantage of shopping in a new place.

Our last stop is for a late lunch at a lovely little café. The guys grab a table in the corner, giving Mama and me privacy.

"I can't believe you're leaving in two days. The month seemed to go by so quickly."

"Neither can I. But I'm really excited to go."

Mama watches me intently. "You don't look like someone who's excited."

Before I can respond, the server appears with our food. I wait until she's gone before I speak. "New York University is a highly regarded institution. This is the opportunity of a lifetime, and I know how lucky I am. But at the same time, I'm leaving my family and everything I know behind."

"Did you have these doubts when you applied to the school?"

"No. I suppose I didn't think it through very well."

"Or is it perhaps that your circumstances have changed since then?"

"What do you mean?"

"Does Slava have anything to do with your current reluctance to go?

"Our contract ended, and then he left for Japan."

"But you keep in touch."

"We do."

"What does he think about you leaving?"

I knew this was going to come up. I promised Mama when I came home from Moscow that I'd have this conversation with Slava, but I never did. "He doesn't know."

"Svetlana." Mama's voice is stern. "I thought we discussed this."

"We did. But since our dynamic is over, I didn't see the need to tell him."

"It may be over on paper, but you know as well as I do that there are still unresolved feelings between you. You owe it to Slava to be completely transparent. Honestly is one of the keys to how this lifestyle works."

"I wasn't dishonest with him."

"Withholding information is dishonesty," Mama says sharply. "I know you say you want to be a submissive, but if you aren't prepared to be honest at all times, then perhaps you should consider if this lifestyle is really where you belong."

I can't believe she'd even suggest that. "Our contract was a short-term arrangement. Nothing serious. There was no need to tell him about New York."

"I disagree. There's more to it than *nothing serious*." I shrug. "I saw the look on his face when he spoke about you. That man is very taken with you. Whether he's said the words or not, he's hoping for something more serious."

"I guess."

"He's a good man."

"I know, and I'd have a solid future with him." I sigh. "The problem is, if I agree to a long-term dynamic with him, I'd be giving up the things I want."

"You wouldn't go to New York to study, but there are schools in Japan. Slava won't hold you back. As your Dominant, he'll want to see you flourish."

I pick at the food on my plate while I think about what she's said. How Slava would react isn't something I've given much consideration to. The only thing I thought about was not going to New York. "I guess not."

"Have you spoken to Czarenah about this?"

"No."

"Why not?"

"We haven't spoken in months. She didn't tell you?"

"No, she didn't." Mama looks surprised.

I add to her disappointment by explaining how I cut Czarenah out of my life because she disagreed with me.

"I'm beginning to think Czarenah may have been right," Mama says.

"And that's why I didn't tell you. I knew you'd take her side."

"It's not about taking sides. We all care about you and don't want to see you get hurt."

"Can we change the subject? I don't want to spend my last few days at home arguing with you."

Mama steers the conversation toward the upcoming developments at Jelena's Hope. The center is expanding by adding elementary school classrooms to accommodate the increasing number of young children needing rehabilitation. The children we recover require a supportive and specialized learning environment. Their unique needs cannot be met in a traditional school setting.

While it's a significant undertaking, my parents are glad to support it. However, it's also a bittersweet moment. More children being recovered means more are being sold into slavery, and their young lives are forever changed. Jelena's Hope having to grow isn't something that excites any of us. We're just grateful that our center can provide the necessary support and care to meet their needs.

Svetlana

Misha pulls up to the tall wrought iron gates that grant entrance to our property. They slowly open, allowing our vehicle to pass through. As we get closer to the front of our house, I notice an unfamiliar car parked in front.

"Are we expecting company?"

"Not that I'm aware of," Mama answers.

It takes the four of us to carry all my packages. I'm going to need another suitcase for all this stuff. We're barely ten steps into the foyer when Timur appears.

"Lana, your father would like to see you. He's in the library."

"I'll get these." Pyotr takes my bags. "Do you want them in your room?"

"Yes, please." I look to Mama. "Are you coming?"

"No. Your papa only asked for you." That wasn't the answer I was hoping for. And why is he in the library? Normally, he uses his office for business. "Do you know what he wants?" I ask Timur as we walk down the hall.

"I'm not at liberty to discuss it."

"Go figure." I blow out a frustrated breath. But as soon as I step into the entrance to the library, all my questions are answered. "Slava, what are you doing here?"

He stands and walks over to greet me with a kiss on my cheek. "I wanted to speak with you. In person."

Papa rises from his chair. "It was good catching up with you, Slava. I will leave you two to talk."

"Thank you, Max."

Papa closes the door behind him, leaving Slava and me alone. After talking with Mama over lunch, I was prepared to text him about my moving to New York. His being here changes that plan.

"Can we talk?" he asks.

"Sure." I sink into one of the plush reading chairs. "You know you could've just texted or video-called me. You didn't have to fly back just to talk."

"This is a conversation we need to have in person."

"That sounds serious."

"I want to discuss our future."

"Our future?" I ask quietly.

"Svetlana, I loved every second of our time together. I think you did as well."

"I did."

"I don't want this to be the end for us. I want you in my life."

"I'm not sure what to say."

"Say you'll come to Japan with me. We'll figure out where we go from there."

"Slava, I—"

"I'll give you a good life. Much like the one you're used to."

"It's more complicated than that."

"I'm in love with you, Svetlana." His words knock the air from my lungs. "I want to spend forever with you."

"You barely know me." I jump from my chair and walk to the windows to put space between us. "You can't mean that."

Slava follows behind me. "I know everything I need." He turns me to face him. "All you have to do is say yes."

"There's something I haven't told you."

"What is it?"

"I've been accepted at New York University. I'm leaving for the United States in two days."

"I see." He drops his arms. "Why haven't you told me this until now?"

"I didn't think there was reason to. Our dynamic was over, and I had no idea how you felt." My heart sinks with the realization that Mama was right. Even if I didn't think it was important, I should've told him about my plans sooner. Because right now, the look of hurt on his face is almost too much to bear.

"Wow," he says and takes a step back. "I'm not sure what to say." He runs his hands through his hair.

"I'm so sorry. How can I make this right?"

"I don't know that you can."

"Our contract was short-term. Just some fun while you were in town." The words spill from my mouth. "I had no idea you had real feelings for me."

"I told you I wanted more than just a contract with you."

My mind drifts back to his last trip to Moscow. Slava's right. He did tell me, but I blew it off. Or maybe I didn't want to believe what he was saying.

"I think it's time for me to go." He turns his back to me and starts walking out of the room. I can't let him leave like this.

"Slava, wait." I grab his arm. "Let me make this right, please."

"There's nothing you can do right now to fix this. I won't hold you back from New York. I wish you would've told me. Would've allowed me the opportunity to adjust my life to fit your plans."

"You would've gone to New York with me?"

"I would've gone anywhere if it meant I could be with you."

"There's still time. Come with me."

"Svetlana." He cups my cheek in his hand. "You need to find your way, and I deserve to be more than an afterthought."

"Can you ever forgive me?" Tears drip down my face.

"Already done." He leans in, his lips meeting mine.

This kiss is unlike any we've shared before. It's full of unspoken promises and bittersweet goodbyes. Then, without saying anything, he turns and walks away.

I feel the loss immediately and realize there's no one to blame but myself. The man who may have been my forever has just walked out of my life.

"Slava is gone already?" Papa asks as he enters the room.

"He told me he's in love with me. But I ruined everything."

Papa opens his arms to me, and just like when I was a small child, I cry in the safety of his arms.

"I am sorry that you are hurting," Papa says when my tears subside. "I hope this situation shows you the importance of honesty and communication in a relationship."

"I have." I wipe my cheeks with the back of my hands. "I tried to make it right. I told him I'd like him to come with me, but he said no."

"Moya babochka, your actions hurt Slava deeply. How could you expect him to forget that and move forward?"

"I don't know."

Czarenah was right. I wasn't ready to enter a contract with a Dominant. I wasn't prepared for the depth of the commitment or the level of transparency necessary to make a Dom/sub relationship work. Unfortunately, Slava paid the price for my mistakes. My hope is one day when this pain has passed, he'll give us a second chance.

Svetlana

THE VIEW OF NEW YORK CITY FROM PAPA'S JET IS breathtaking. Although it's night, you'd never know it. The lights from the city's buildings illuminate the sky. It's so different from anything I've seen in Russia.

"I wish I'd come with you before this. I had no idea it was this amazing."

Papa laughs. "We haven't even landed. How do you know you like it?"

"I just have a feeling." I smile. Although the pain from losing Slava is still raw, I also can't quiet the voice inside telling me this adventure will be my best yet.

The plane's wheels slow to a stop, and I unbuckle my safety belt, anxious to take my first steps in the United States.

"After you, little butterfly." Pyotr motions for me to go before him.

As soon as I exit the plane, I'm hit with hot, humid air. It wasn't what I was expecting, especially given the late hour. "I should've worn shorts," I say to Papa, who's waiting at the bottom of the steps.

"Alexander's apartment has air conditioning."

"It's a good thing."

Pyotr joins us as a shiny red Tesla pulls up beside the plane. Alex and Viktor step out of the sleek sports car.

"Max, it's good to see you," Alex greets us as he shakes Papa's hand. "Did you have a good flight?"

"We did," Papa replies before excusing himself to call Mama.

I look around, unsure of what to do next. "Thanks for letting me stay at your apartment. I hope it's not too much of an imposition."

"It's not a problem. I've got plenty of room," Alex reassures me.

"I offered to stay at a hotel, but Papa refused." I sigh loudly.

"He's just looking out for you. It's your first time in the city, and you're a long way from home."

Papa rejoins us. "That was quick."

"She has a busy morning. I caught her in between appointments," Papa replies.

Viktor interrupts, "We're ready to go, boss."

Papa nods. Alex opens the car door. "Let's get going then."

Alex's apartment is supposedly a half hour from the airport. At least, that's what I was told over an hour ago. I've never seen so many cars fill the streets and these crazy yellow taxis that dart in and out of the traffic recklessly.

"If there's this much traffic in the middle of the night, I can't wait to see it during the day," I say sarcastically.

"Traffic is always a guarantee," Viktor says, glancing back at me in the mirror.

"Great." The backseat is not big enough for Alex, Pyotr, and me, making the ride even worse.

"Patience, *moya babochka*," Papa says from the front seat.

After what feels like an eternity, Viktor turns into an underground parking garage. I'm thankful to get out of the car and stretch my legs.

Alex types some numbers on a pad outside the elevator. "I'll make sure you have all the codes to get in and out."

"Thanks." The elevator doors open. "Are you coming, Papa?"

"You two go on ahead. I'll be along shortly."

It's just Alex and me in the elevator. We both fidget nervously, unsure of what to say.

"Are you hungry?" Alex asks.

"A bit, yes."

"I have some takeout menus. You can look through them and pick something to order."

The elevator dings, and the doors open. Alex motions for me to step out before him.

"Is this your apartment?"

"It is."

Everything in the open floor plan is modern and sleek. And we're so high up. Floor-to-ceiling windows offer views of the water and brightly lit buildings.

"Viktor will be up with your bags in a few minutes. In the meantime, I'll show you to your room." Alex leads me down the hall. As we walk, he points out the various rooms we pass. "This one's yours." He opens the door. "I hope you like it."

"It's perfect," I say as I step inside and look around.

"Shall we go order some food?" He looks as nervous as I feel.

"Do you mind if I take a few minutes to freshen up?"

"Sure. Take your time. I'll be in the kitchen when you're ready."

Alex closes the door, leaving me alone. I walk over to the windows that overlook the city. I'm used to looking out and seeing St. Petersburg, where I grew up. Outside this window are modern skyscrapers and streets full of cars—it's a totally foreign sight. The excitement I felt when I stepped off the plane has already disappeared. In its place is anxiousness at just how much my life is about to change.

The reality of what my life is about to be like hits me. After Papa leaves, I'll know exactly three people here. Pyotr, who'll likely be feeling at least some of the anxiety I am since he's also never been to New York City. Viktor, who I don't really get along with. And Alex, the man who's tasked with being my babysitter. He's not a total stranger. He's been around to some degree throughout my childhood. But I don't actually know anything about him. Maybe Papa was right, and I didn't think this through very well because I'm already homesick.

"May I come in," Pyotr calls. I cross the room and open the door. "I've got your stuff."

"Thank you."

"Where do you want them?"

"The bed is fine."

He sets my bags down and studies me for a moment. "You good?"

"I think so. There's going to be a lot to get used to."

"Give yourself some time, little butterfly. Once you become familiar with the city, you'll be okay."

"I'm sure."

"You coming?"

"I'll be out in a few minutes." After freshening up, I find my way back to the kitchen. "Your apartment is lovely," I compliment Alex as I step into the kitchen.

"Sometimes I wonder if I should find something smaller, but the thought of packing and moving isn't appealing." He smiles. "Have a seat. I have the menus here."

"Where's Papa?"

"He's downstairs with Viktor."

"Downstairs?" I ask as I sit on the stool beside him and look through the menus.

"Viktor has an apartment one floor down. They'll be up shortly."

"Is there anything you'd rather?"

"Nope. It's your choice tonight."

I suspect Papa arranged for me to stay with Alex because he's hoping we connect romantically and end up together. Alex is handsome, and he's a Dominant. Those things are attributes in his favor. But he's Alex. He knew me as a child. Saw me wearing braces. Watched me go on my first date and was there when I came home with a broken heart. He's a nice guy, but I see him as more of an older brother.

"How about this one?"

"What do you like on your pizza?"

"I'm a plain kinda girl." Alex raises his eyebrow. "What?"

"Plain?"

"At least for my pizza," I smirk.

Alex

Svetlana's been here for two weeks. Although she says she's doing okay, I get the sense she's struggling. The only thing she's done since she got here is shop. Lana's had poor Pyotr out almost every day. Whatever Maxim pays him isn't enough to compensate for his being dragged around from store to store. Somehow, Pyotr does it without complaining—much.

I'm sure it's difficult trying to acclimate to an entirely different culture. But despite her retail therapy, Lana's not her bubbly, outspoken self. I've been holding off on collaring her. Trying to wait for the perfect time. But perfect doesn't exist, not even for timing. I'll put my collar around her neck this evening, and then we're going to Fire and Ice. It's time to introduce Svetlana to the BDSM community here in NYC.

Me: I'm getting off early tonight. Be ready by 6 to go out.

Lana: Where are we going?

Me: Fire and Ice. I'm on my way into a meeting. I'll text when I'm on my way home.

I was hoping Brandon could go to the club with us tonight, but he hasn't returned home yet. He's been on a business trip in California for the last two weeks. A big tech company is expanding to New York City, and Montgomery Advertising is handling their marketing campaign.

Brandon was supposed to have been back a few hours ago, but his flight was canceled because of mechanical issues with the plane. Last I spoke to him, he was still in Denver trying to book a new flight home.

I grab my laptop and head into my conference room, where a group of people is beginning to gather. Once everyone's seated, I motion to two of my newest hires, Ben and Michelle, to start the meeting. They're about to give a presentation to a local client and friend, Ian. He owns a chain of fitness centers and is looking for a creative marketing campaign to increase membership.

While Ben and Michelle give their presentation, I find myself distracted. I'm trying to come up with the best way to give Svetlana my collar of protection later. Several days ago, I spoke to Star, hoping to get some guidance. Other than discussing the importance of what I've agreed to, she had nothing to offer regarding how to collar her. Star said it was entirely up to me, and I'd know what to do when the time was right. I'm beginning to doubt her wisdom because I still have no idea what I'm doing.

Applause draws my attention back to the room.

"I'm impressed with what you've come up with," Ian says. "It's almost as though you were in my head."

"We're delighted you like it," Michelle responds with a smile.

"You have some rising stars here, Alex."

"I think you're right."

Ian spends a few minutes sharing his ideas on how to fine-tune the ads before walking out with Michelle and Beb.

Me: I'll be ready to go in about 15 minutes.

Viktor: The car will be out front waiting for you.

I need a few minutes alone to put my thoughts together.

I texted Lana that I was on my way home, but she didn't text back. I've tried calling twice, but I keep getting her voicemail. My mood goes from bad to worse when the elevator doors open, and I'm assaulted with music so loud I'm surprised the windows aren't shaking. I drop my stuff on the table and pull my phone out to shut the music off.

"Who turned my music off?" The last word is cut short when a towel-clad Lana nearly collides with me.

"I did."

Her hand flies up to her chest. "Holy shit, Alex. I didn't hear you come in."

"How could you with the music up so loud." I cross my arms. "I tried texting and calling you."

"You did?" She looks at her phone. "Obviously, I didn't hear that either."

"You have ten minutes to be dressed and in the living room. We need to talk."

I turn to leave before I explode.

"Great. I'm with another bossy man."

"I heard that," I call over my shoulder.

"And?" she yells back.

I freeze midstep. Part of me wants to turn around and put her over my knee for disrespecting me. The other part knows we have no formal agreement. I choose not to engage her any further for fear that I'll choose option one. Instead, I go to my bedroom to get changed.

I'm sitting on the sofa waiting for Lana. She has thirty seconds before she's late, and I cancel tonight. With five seconds to spare, she hurries into the room.

"You're lucky. Your time was almost up."

"Fifteen minutes was barely enough time to blow-dry my hair."

"If you didn't have the music on so loud, you would've known when I was coming home. That won't happen again, will it?"

"No."

"Sit." She lowers herself onto the cushion at the far end of the couch. Here goes nothing. "You are well aware that your father asked me to serve as your protector Dominant."

"About that. I don't think it's necessary, do you?"

This girl isn't for real. "Maxim told me you agreed. Is that not true?"

"Well, I kinda agreed."

I sit back and motion for her to keep talking.

"I didn't want to say yes, but it was one of Papa's stipulations before he agreed to allow me to come to New York. So, I said yes, but figured you and I could work out something else once I was here."

"Absolutely not. I promised your father I would do this. Unlike you, giving my word means something to me." The smile she was wearing disappears. "So, you have a choice to make. Either you will follow through on your word and wear my collar of protection, or we'll call your father and see how he wants to proceed."

"You'd do that?"

"Yes."

"Fine." She crosses her arms. "I guess we'll do this your way."

"Svetlana, I'm not your enemy."

Svetlana

"I'm sick of being told what to do. It makes me feel like a child."

"My role as your protector isn't to boss you around. It's to ensure your safety. You're in an unfamiliar place, and you're going to meet a lot of people you don't know. I can guarantee men at the club will be interested in you."

"You think I can't handle myself?"

"In my opinion, I don't think you're prepared for that."

"I've had a Dominant before." I know I sound like a petulant child, but I can't help it. Alex is driving me crazy already.

"And how did that go?"

"It was really good. Until it wasn't."

"Can I ask what happened?" Alex softens his voice.

"I screwed up." I get choked up thinking about the look on Slava's face before he left. "I kept things from him and ended up hurting him." I'm waiting for the lecture that I'm sure will come, but what Alex does next surprises me.

"I've made some pretty bad decisions in my past, too. Before my mom passed away, I had a submissive. We'd been together for a little over a year. I really cared about her. After my mom died, I spiraled out of control and left her without so much as an explanation." He runs a hand through his hair. "I hurt her badly. It took time for me to see how my actions affected her and to make it right."

"How did you fix it?"

"I didn't say I fixed it. I said I made it right. There's a difference."

"Did you ask her for a second chance?"

"No."

"Why not?"

"Because even though she forgave me, she didn't want me in her life." My heart sinks. "It was hard to accept, but I had no one to blame other than myself."

"Things are different with Slava and me."

"If you keep trying when he already said no, he's only going to see that as disrespect," Alex says softly. "You need to accept that you messed up, and that door's closed."

"If I don't keep trying, he'll think I gave up. That I don't care."

"Knowing when to walk away isn't easy. But if you really care about Slava, you'll respect his wishes."

I don't like what Alex is saying. It's not what I want to hear. "I never meant to hurt him."

"Making mistakes is part of being human. But it's important to learn from your experience and not repeat it."

"I guess."

Alex smiles. "Now, back to the matter at hand. The collar." He grabs a small box from the table. "Are you ready to move forward?"

"Yes. Do I have to call you sir?"

"No. Alex will be fine," he chuckles. "I do have some expectations, though."

"What are they?" I roll my eyes, certain he'll have a long list for me to follow.

"While you're staying here, I'm going to ask that you're respectful. Playing music is fine. Blasting it is not."

"I'm sorry. It won't happen again."

"I forgive you. I also need to know that you'll respect my place as your protector. When we're at the club, you will not approach a Dominant or do anything behind my back."

"What if there's someone I'm interested in? I can't talk to them?"

"Not unless it's cleared through me."

I was right. He's just another person who wants to tell me what I can and can't do. "I can take care of myself."

"I'm sure you can." Alex sighs loudly. "But for now, you don't have to. I'm assuming that responsibility for you. I'm not trying to limit you or hold you back."

"Then, I guess I don't understand."

"My goal is to ensure your safety and, hopefully, your happiness. I want to get to know you as more than Maxim's kid. I want to know who Svetlana is. This way, I'll have an easier time pre-vetting Dominants for you. I want you to enjoy this transitional time."

His explanation sounds reasonable. "Okay. I won't approach any Dominants without your consent."

"I hope you like it." He lifts the collar, which is more like a delicate necklace, from the box. "I wanted it to be something you could wear without attracting unwanted attention. What you choose to tell others is up to you."

I examine the silver chain, the pendant with his initials, and the lowercase *p*. It's something only people in our lifestyle would recognize. It's clear he put a lot of thought into this. That's evidenced by the garnet that dangles under the charm. "It's beautiful." I turn around and hold my hair up so Alex can put the collar on.

"I promise I'll do my best to be understanding and fair. And to keep the lines of communication between us open," Alex says as he does the clasp.

"I promise to do my best to submit to and respect your guidance."

"Are you ready to go to Fire and Ice?"

Svetlana

HOMESICK. THAT'S A WORD I NEVER THOUGHT WOULD COME out of my mouth. But I'm terribly homesick. I've spoken to my parents several times since moving. Papa's main concern is that I'm not going out without Pyotr. He's always focused on my safety first. Mama asks how I'm adjusting and if I've started making friends. She realizes the challenge of living with three men. I've gotten good at giving my parents a polished speech to reassure them I love living in a big modern city. The time difference makes having lengthy conversations tricky. Something I'm not complaining about. If our phone calls went any longer, I'm sure they'd see through my story. Because the reality is, I'm doubting everything.

New York is unlike anything I've ever experienced. I'd read it's called the city that never sleeps, but until I got here, I didn't realize how literal that statement is. It's like there's a power switch that's always turned on.

The first few days, I was mesmerized by the fast pace and the convenience of having anything I could dream of available at all times. Shopping was just as good, if not better than the stories I'd heard. For the first few weeks, I dragged Pyotr out almost every day to add to my wardrobe and buy more things I didn't need for my dorm. But that got old fast.

The constant go, go, go that is Manhattan is exhausting. I find myself longing for the quiet seclusion of our home in St. Petersburg.

I think the worst part of all this is that I'm lonely. The only people I know here are the men I live with. Until school starts in September, meeting people is going to be difficult. Pyotr is just as unfamiliar with the city as I am. The difference is I'm okay with exploring, but Pyotr insists we stay in the small area Alex and Viktor told him is safe. Viktor promised to take Pyotr out and show him more of the city so we could branch out, but that hasn't happened yet. Alex works a lot, so Viktor's always gone. I'm hoping tonight signals a change in all that. Alex is finally taking me to Fire and Ice.

My fingers go to the collar around my neck. I'm still not entirely comfortable with it. I knew Alex had made an agreement with Papa. I didn't anticipate that he would expect me to follow through with it. I mean, why would he want to be tied to a girl he barely knows? Unless he's thinking that I'm going to fall for him. There's no chance of that ever happening. Alexander Montgomery may be handsome, but he is definitely not my type.

Viktor pulls the car up to the curb. "Is there a particular time you want to be picked up?"

"I'm not sure yet. I'll text you later."

"No problem. Have a good evening."

Viktor jumps out and gets my door. "Thanks, Vik."

"Have fun."

"But not too much fun, little butterfly," Pyotr calls from the front seat.

"Aren't you coming?"

"Nope. Viktor's taking me out for the tour he promised."

"I guess I'll see you later." As much as I complain about always having Pyotr with me, I already miss his presence. It feels foreign being without him.

"You ready?" Alex asks.

"I think so." I try to maintain a calm exterior, but inside I'm freaking out. "Do I look okay?"

"I would've preferred you wear something a bit more substantial."

"For real?" It took me forever to pick out an outfit earlier. Finally, I settled on a red bodycon dress with a cutout mid-drift and a pair of black Louboutin heels I bought the other day. It's a sexy choice that I'm sure will draw some attention my way. "Don't women here wear similar clothes?"

"They do."

"Then, what's the problem?"

"I'm going to have my hands full with the men and women who'll be inquiring about you. I won't be able to enjoy my evening." He laughs.

I roll my eyes. "Very funny."

"Come on." He places his hand on my back. "Let's go in."

My first impression is that of confusion. We're standing in a lobby with no indication that this is a club. If not for the discreet sign indicating bracelet colors and meanings, I'd question if we're in the right place.

"Good evening, Alex."

"Good evening, Star. I want to introduce you to Svetlana Solonik."

"It's a pleasure to meet you," the woman says. "I've heard so much about you from your father."

"It's good to meet you as well."

"How are you finding our city so far?"

"I haven't gotten to see much of it yet."

"I've been swamped at work," Alex explains. "I'm afraid I haven't been the best host."

"Shame on you, Alexander," she says, half joking. Alex shrugs. "May I steal your submissive for a few minutes? I promise to return her in one piece."

"Sure. I'll be inside."

Alex pulls open one of the tall wooden doors, and I quickly glance inside to what must be the main room.

"Let me text Owen so he can cover the desk, and then I'll give you the grand tour." She swipes at her phone screen. "He'll be out in a minute. In the meantime, let me explain our color levels."

After I'm given a purple bracelet, the color indicating not to approach me directly, we set off on our tour.

The club's main room is brightly lit and has a modern warehouse vibe. It's very different than Ecstasy and Noire, but I like it. Music plays in the background but is not so loud that you can't hear the person next to you.

Although I don't recognize faces, I see familiarity in the people around me. For the first time since I got here, I feel at home.

"As you can see, we have three stages for members who wish to do public scenes." Two of the stages are set up, but nothing is happening at the current moment. "We have a café if you get hungry while you're here."

"Whatever they're cooking in there smells incredible."

"It's a popular spot for club members." Star leads me to a hall. "These are our private rooms. They're all in use, or I'd give you a tour."

"Are they all the same?"

"The rooms at the end of the hall are our themed rooms." She motions to the doors that are closer. "These are the aftercare rooms. They're done in more muted tones. I'm sure Alex will show them to you when they're not occupied. Do you have any other questions?"

"Not right now."

"Then, I'll return you to your Dominant. He's probably wondering where you are."

"I'm sure Alex wouldn't mind if you kept me all night."

"I doubt that."

"He's not very happy to have me with him."

"What gives you that impression?" she asks with genuine interest.

"I don't know. I just have a feeling."

"Alex is a complicated man. But he's kind and fair. I promise you're in good hands."

"I'll try."

We search the club for Alex and find him in the far corner, speaking with several people. As we approach, all heads turn my way.

"Looks like you're attracting attention already," Star whispers.

"I'm sure Alex is going to love that."

"Give him a chance before you make a judgment."

Although Alex isn't a total stranger, I really don't know him. I knew he was in the lifestyle, but I've never been privy to this part of his life. Because of our age difference, we were never more than acquaintances.

Whenever he was at our house, I was just the kid he had to be nice to because I was the boss's daughter. Being roommates who are in this Dom/sub protective relationship is uncharted territory for both of us.

"Did you enjoy your tour?" Alex asks when Star walks away.

"I did," I answer without looking at him. Instead, I'm checking out the guys Alex has been talking to. One, in particular, is drool-worthy. "Are you going to introduce me to your friends?"

"No."

"Seriously?" I cross my arms. "I can't believe this."

"If you men will excuse us, I need to speak to my submissive private-ly." Alex wastes no time taking my hand and leading me away.

I pull out of his grasp. "You didn't have plans to introduce me to anyone tonight, did you?"

"I'm not discussing this right here. Come with me." He doesn't stop walking until he finds who he's apparently looking for. "May I use your office for a few minutes, Star?"

"Sure." She looks between us. "Is everything okay?"

"No."

"Come with me. I'll unlock it for you."

"Let's go." Alex's tone is icy.

We follow Star down the hall with the private rooms and turn the corner. This is part of the club that wasn't included in my earlier tour. Mistress Star swipes a card, and the lock clicks open. Alex enters her office, but I don't move.

"Are you just going to stand there?"

"Maybe."

"I think inside the office is a more appropriate place to sort out whatever this is," Star suggests. I follow the Domme into her office.

"I cannot believe you behaved that way in front of those men. You do realize they were Dominants?"

"How would I know that? You didn't bother to introduce me."

"There was no reason to."

"Isn't that the point of all this?" I wave my hand around.

"The point is that you need someone to look out for you because clearly, you're too immature to do it for yourself."

"Okay, you two." Star intervenes. "Take a seat, and we'll discuss this calmly." After we sit, Star asks Alex what happened, and then she turns to me for my take. She listens attentively to both our sides. "Svetlana, I'm going to have to agree with Alex on this. That kind of behavior from a submissive is disrespectful."

"How will I meet anyone if *he* refuses to introduce me?"

"When and who I choose to introduce you to is up to me," Alex interrupts.

"I knew this was a mistake. You probably have no intention of letting me meet anyone."

"Svetlana, that'll be enough," Star says sternly. "Remember that you are a submissive."

"Isn't his job to help me meet a Dominant?"

"That's part of his job, yes. But it will not happen on your terms. This is only your first night here. There's no reason to jump into meeting a Dominant."

"But—" Star holds up her hand, silencing me.

"It's more important for you to acclimate to Fire and Ice and meet other submissives. Becoming part of our community is an important step in your journey. You must trust that Alex will introduce you to the Dominants when he feels the time is right."

"And if he never thinks it's the right time?"

"If you keep acting like this, there won't be—" This time, Star interrupts Alex.

"Did you discuss your expectations for this dynamic before you came here?"

"Yes," we both answer.

"Alex, did you explain how you'll handle any introductions to Svetlana."

"I did."

"And did you agree to respect Alex's dominance in this relationship?"

"I did."

"I've worked hard to develop high standards for both the Dominants and submissives who come to my club. Alex is a respected member of this community, and I don't doubt he's acting with your best interest in mind. If I see him, or anyone else, out of line, I don't hesitate to step in. Your dynamic is no different. Do you understand?"

"I do. I'm sorry for being rude." I look to Alex. "This move hasn't been easy for me."

"I know that, and I apologize for being largely unavailable the past few weeks. Work needed to take priority. I wasn't going to tell you yet, but I'll be off all next week. I planned to take you out to show you more of the city."

"Really?"

"Yes, really." He lets out a frustrated breath. "I need you to trust me."

"I understand."

"Are we okay now?" Star asks.

Alex looks at me, and I nod. "We're good," he says.

"You two go on ahead. I have a few things to do in here."

On the way back to the main room, I notice one of the private rooms is no longer in use. "These were all occupied earlier. Star suggested I ask you to show me one when they were free."

"Sure." He swipes his card and opens the door.

It's as if I've stepped into another realm. "It's a dungeon."

"It is." Alex stays in the doorway while I walk around.

"This room is incredible." The faux stone that covers the walls looks and feels authentic. On the ceiling are wooden beams that only add to the dark aesthetics. Electric candles provide dim lighting. This room has everything from a St. Catherine's Wheel to a stockade. Chains hang from the ceiling for bondage and suspension. There's even a throne. "I'd love to play in here."

"Duly noted."

"I take it you don't like torture and pain?"

"It's not my thing."

"You don't know what you're missing out on."

A couple appears in the doorway.

"Hey, Alex," a woman says. "Did we have the wrong time?"

"No." He motions to me. "I was letting Lana take a look around."

"Did you get a new sub?"

"Not exactly. Lana, I'd like to introduce you to Kate and her submissive, Raul."

"It's a pleasure to meet you," I say and keep my gaze down.

"You as well."

"We'll get out of your way. It was nice seeing you." I follow Alex down the hall. "I'm impressed. You can behave."

Over the course of the night, Alex introduced me to several submissives. We exchanged numbers so we could keep in touch. Alex chose not to introduce me to any Dominants. I hoped he'd change his mind, but he didn't. Although the evening got off to a rocky start, it ended on a much better note. It's the early hours of the morning when we exit the club. Viktor and Pyotr are waiting outside next to the car.

"Are you an expert on the city now?" I ask Pyotr.

"I have a much better feel for it. How was your evening?"

"I had a great time."

"I hope she wasn't too much of a handful?" Pyotr asks jokingly.

"She could use to be bent over someone's knee."

"As if."

"Come on, let's get you home."

I'm quiet on the ride back to Alex's apartment. Alex asked me to trust him, but I behaved like an entitled brat instead. I drop my head back onto the seat. Screwing up seems to be my lot in life, and to be honest, I don't know how to change it.

Brandon

"Hey." I pop my head into Alex's office. "How was the rest of your weekend?"

"Less eventful than Friday night." I got back into town about three a.m. on Saturday and called Alex. I'm glad I called because he needed to discuss what happened between him and Lana at the club. "Come on in."

"I only have a few minutes," I say as I close the door.

"I don't know what I'm doing," Alex confesses.

"What do you mean?"

"Lana spent the rest of the weekend in her room. She barely said two words to me." He runs his hands through his hair. "Do you think I was too hard on her?"

"From what you described, no. She overstepped, and you corrected her. It's a necessary part of any Dom/sub dynamic."

"That part was always hard for me. I guess I thought it would be easier not being in an actual relationship. I was wrong."

"She'll eventually meet someone, and your work will be done."

"I don't know anyone who's looking for a sub that's as challenging as Lana's going to be. She's very—" Alex hesitates. "—Spirited."

The alarm on my cell goes off. "Sorry. I have a video conference in five minutes."

"Do you have plans tonight?"

"No. What's up?"

"Why don't you come over. We'll grab some takeout, and you can meet Svetlana."

"Sure. From what it sounds like, this might be a good show. I'll make sure to bring some popcorn."

"You're a regular comedian, Carpenter."

"I called Tony for dinner," Alex says as we take the elevator to the ground floor. "We have to stop by the restaurant on the way home."

Tony's been a regular at Fire and Ice since the club opened over twenty years ago. He's a master with wax and often does scenes with his sub, Leo, showcasing his talent. But his mastery doesn't end there. He also owns what I think is the best restaurant in the city, Italiano Deside-rio. "I'll never say no to his food."

"Me either. I was glad he squeezed in a takeout order on such short notice."

Viktor double parks outside the restaurant while Alex runs in to grab the food.

"What do you think of Svetlana?" I ask Viktor.

Viktor glances at me through the rearview mirror. "Lana might come off as rebellious and indifferent at first, but I suspect it's just her way of guarding herself. Her sister's abduction was traumatizing for her. I suspect she's never fully processed that. It's easy to overlook that aspect of her when you're around her." His observation is intriguing. I've never heard anyone describe her like that before. "She's certainly giving Alex a run for his money," Viktor adds, grinning.

"I've heard."

Alex and Tony walk toward the car, their hands full. Viktor jumps out and grabs the bags from Tony. He gives a small wave and hurries back into his restaurant.

"Tony apologized he couldn't stay and talk," Alex says as he slides into the back seat. "He's got a packed house."

"It looks like he made enough for an army." There are five bags filled to the top with food that smells delicious.

"He went over and above as usual."

As we finish the drive to Montgomery's apartment, Viktor's insights about Svetlana linger in my mind. His depiction casts a fresh perspective on the girl I've only heard about. I find myself intrigued and eager to meet her.

"You ready for this?" Alex asks as we exit the car and grab the bags.

"Of course."

"I don't know what Lana or the apartment will be like when we get up there."

"I'm sure it'll be fine."

It's a short trip to his penthouse apartment. The elevator doors open, and his place is quiet as usual.

"I don't know what's worse. Walking in here with the music blasting or complete silence?" We set the bags on the island in his kitchen. "I'll go find Lana."

While he searches for his houseguest, I get the food out of the bag and grab place settings for us.

He returns a few minutes later. "She'll be out shortly."

We're just sitting down to eat when she enters the room. I look up to find the most beautiful woman walking on planet Earth. I'm immediately drawn to her eyes, which are a striking shade of sapphire. They're unlike anything I've ever seen. Her chestnut brown hair with hints of caramel and honey hangs long down her back. I envision it wrapped around my hand while I'm driving into her.

Alex clears his throat. "Svetlana, this is my good friend, Brandon. Brandon, this is Maxim's daughter, Svetlana."

"It's nice to meet you," she says.

"You as well. I've heard a lot about you."

"You have?" She looks at Alex.

"Brandon's a Dominant at the club."

"Is that how you two know each other?"

"That's how we met. But now we also work together," Alex explains. "Brandon's aware of your father's involvement in my company."

Lana's the picture of submission throughout the rest of dinner. She's polite and only answers when spoken to. There's no sign of the stubborn, outspoken girl I've heard everyone describe her as. I'm starting to think Viktor's assessment of her is more accurate than he realizes.

Svetlana

ALEX: I'VE INVITED A FRIEND FOR DINNER. PLEASE BE ON your best behavior.

Me: I'm not a child.

Delete

Me: Really, Alex? You sound like Papa.

Delete

I go through several more texts that I delete without sending. I want to do the right thing, but I'm not sure what that is.

Me: I've made a mess of things and could really use someone to talk to.

I hit send, and then I wait. It's over an hour when my phone finally rings.

"Hello?"

"I got your text."

"Thank you for calling."

"I'm glad you reached out."

This is harder than I thought it would be. "I screwed up and ruined everything."

"Want to tell me what's going on?" Masha asks.

I take a few minutes to fill her in on my last interaction with Slava as well as everything that's occurred since I got here.

"Do you remember what we talked about before you left? That there'll be setbacks."

"I remember. But this is more than a setback."

"We all make mistakes. The important thing is that we learn from them."

I've only learned that I have a special talent for hurting the people around me. "Masha, I need your help. I embarrassed myself, but I don't care about that. What I care about is that I made Alex look bad. And now I don't know how to face him again."

"You know I'm not a part of that lifestyle. However, it sounds like his reaction was fair."

"I didn't like it, but it was fair."

"Is he still holding it over your head, or has he put it behind him?"

"He didn't say a word about it after we stepped out of Mistress Star's office."

"So, what's your plan for moving forward?"

"I have to respect him and not be so outspoken."

"You're very good at giving the expected answers."

"What do you mean?"

"Svetlana, ever since I met you, you've been the perfect patient. You answer each question with what you *think* is the correct answer. What I'm hoping to hear."

"Isn't that what you want?"

"No."

"I don't understand."

"I want to hear what you really think. What you really feel. I need to know what's underneath the mask. The stuff you don't let others see."

Although that's not the response I was expecting, I recognize this is a pivotal moment. If I don't lay everything out in the open, I may lose this chance and never experience the growth I need to become a proper submissive.

"You're right. I've become quite good at playing the game. But I'm done. I'm so tired and can't do it anymore."

"Is that all?"

"I'm scared." Tears begin to fall. "I'm terrified to give up control."

"That's what I've been waiting for you to admit for so long." She softens her voice.

We discuss how my sister's abduction and the helplessness I felt watching her being taken away. She's right. Even though I went to therapy while I was in Moscow, I never allowed her past my protective exterior—never dealt with the trauma I've carried around my entire life.

"When you meet the right Dominant, your submission will be a true gift. One that you'll freely give."

"I already met him."

"Have you met someone since arriving in the United States?"

"No. It's Slava. He's the one."

"Is he?"

"Yes, I'm certain of it."

"Before you say anything else, I need you to hear me out, okay?"

"Okay."

"Slava swept you off your feet. You were attracted to him both in looks and the knowledge that he's solid and settled. You had fun with him. But the entire time you were together, it was on your terms. Is that an accurate description?"

"I agreed to weekends only and that the contract would end when my school term finished. Was I wrong to have asked for those things?"

"From my understanding, there's no clear right or wrong during negotiations. It's something unique to each couple. Much like any *vanilla* relationship, the important part is that both members feel heard and have come to an agreement."

"We did."

"Yes, you did. But from the outside looking in, it appears you set the boundaries, and Slava did the compromising. He asked one thing of you, to discuss a more committed relationship after school. When the time came, you refused to do that. You went so far as to withhold information from him that directly affected that."

"Yes, but—"

"It doesn't matter what kind of a relationship you're in. Complete honesty is essential. Didn't I stress that when we spoke?"

"You did."

"Why do you think you weren't honest with him?"

"That's a complicated answer."

"I'm okay with complicated," Masha chuckles.

"Slava's everything any submissive would want in a Dominant. Heck, he's everything any woman could ever wish for in a man. And the time we spent together was phenomenal." I smile at the memories. "But every time I thought about being with him long term, I felt like I'd be giving up a part of me that I was unwilling to sacrifice."

"Can you explain that further?"

"Slava's so settled. I assumed he was looking for a submissive who would be willing to slide into his already perfect life. But I wasn't ready to do that. I still had dreams and goals for my future that I thought I'd be giving up if I stayed with him. I didn't tell him because I feared he'd reject me. It was easier for me to reject him and blame it on circumstances."

"That's an excellent observation."

"I was wrong, though. I didn't know that Slava would've changed his life for me. And because I wasn't honest, he was hurt. But I'm going to make it right and get him back."

"Did he offer you that option?"

"Not exactly."

"Not exactly?"

"No, he didn't."

"Svetlana, you need to respect his decision to walk away. When you meet the right Dominant for you, submitting to him won't feel like you're giving up who you are to be in their life. You'll grow as a person and as a couple. Your past, present, *and* future will make sense, and you won't fear losing yourself. Slava's a good man, but he was not the right one for you."

"If I was honest, like everyone told me, things would be so different. I'd still have Slava."

"That's not a guarantee. We can't go back in time and ask for a do-over. What's done is done."

"What do I do now?"

"First, you need to stop hyper-focusing on the past." Sometimes her keen observations scare me. "I've said this before, and I'll say it again, you must start looking at the bigger picture."

By the time we hang up, I feel I have a better handle on myself and what I need to do from now on.

Me: Thank you for letting me know. I'll do my best.

Alex: I appreciate that.

I'm reading a book when there's a knock on my door. "Come in."

"It's just me. I wanted to let you know I'm home and brought dinner."

"Okay. I'll be out in a minute."

"Right." He looks puzzled, but he doesn't say anything else.

After he leaves, I put my book away and give myself a once over in the mirror. I don't know who Alex has brought home, but I want to ensure I'm presentable.

When I get to the kitchen, Alex is sitting at the table with another man who turns when he hears me enter the room. His dark eyes are soft and gentle. I'm momentarily captivated by his intense gaze.

Alex clears his throat, breaking whatever spell I'm under. "Svetlana, this is my good friend, Brandon. Brandon, this is Maxim's daughter, Svetlana."

"It's nice to meet you," I say and sit in my usual chair.

"You as well. I've heard a lot about you."

"You have?" I look at Alex.

"Brandon's a Dominant at the club."

"Is that how you two know each other?"

"That's how we met. But now we also work together," Alex explains. "Brandon's aware of your father's involvement in my company."

While we eat, Brandon and Alex discuss some upcoming projects at work. I eat silently, avoiding any intrusion into their conversation. It isn't until they begin talking about a Fire and Ice event and whether either of them has plans to attend this weekend that I take notice. Apparently, a Dominant named Anthony is doing a sensual wax scene with his submissive, Leopold.

After polishing off the massive portion of chicken parmesan and pasta on my plate, I make a mental note to ask Alex the name of the restaurant. It's the most exquisite Italian food I've ever tasted.

As soon as everyone has finished eating, I rise from my seat. Alex looks at me with uncertainty about my next move.

"May I take your plate, Sir?"

"You may. And you don't need to call me Sir."

"I didn't want to be rude in front of your guest."

"I appreciate that, but Alex is fine no matter who's around."

"Thank you." I turn to Brandon. "May I take your plate?"

"Sure. Thanks." He smiles.

"You can leave that stuff in the sink. We'll take care of it later." Alex says as he and Brandon move to the living room.

I struggle with what I should do. Do I go ahead and wash the dishes or leave them in the sink? I settle with following Alex's instructions and leave everything for later. Then, I walk toward the hall leading to my room.

"You're more than welcome to hang out with us," Alex says, stopping me mid-step.

"I don't want to intrude."

"Don't be silly."

I sit in the extra wide chair across from the couch the guys are on and tuck my feet under my legs.

"Alex tells me you'll be attending NYU in the fall."

"I am."

"What are you studying?"

"Political science."

"Nice. What do you want to do with that degree."

"I hope it will help me get accepted to law school."

"That's terrific. Will you be staying in New York for your graduate degree?"

"That's my plan. If everything works out, I'd like to stay here permanently."

Alex's cell rings. He checks the screen. "If you two will excuse me, I need to take this."

"How are you finding New York so far?" Brandon asks.

"It's an incredible city. Although it can be a bit overwhelming at times."

"That's an understatement."

"Have you lived here for long?" I ask.

"I was born and raised in Brooklyn."

"And you still find it overwhelming?"

"I do. That's why I keep my house in Brooklyn. Sometimes, I need a break from the craziness of Manhattan." The conversation comes to an awkward pause. "Are you coming to the club with Alex this weekend?"

"I don't know. Alex hasn't said anything about it."

"Right. I hope he decides to bring you. The things Anthony does with wax are amazing."

"Sorry about that." Alex comes back into the room. "Looks like I'm going to have to go into work on Monday after all."

"Maxim?" Brandon asks.

This time, it's my phone that rings. "It's Papa."

"Go on and answer it."

"It was nice meeting you, Brandon." I smile.

"You, too."

I leave the guys in the living room to talk to my parents.

Brandon

been able to get her out of my head. During our meal, there was a palpable tension between her and Alex. I know he was worried about how she'd act. She maintained her polite demeanor, but I could sense the fiery nature that people often attribute to her just beneath the surface. I want to see her again and get to know her better, but I'm uncertain how to broach the subject.

"Got a minute?" Alex asks from my doorway.

"Sure."

His movements are stiff as he closes the door and sits across from my desk.

"Is everything okay?" I take my glasses off and set them on the desk.

Alex takes a deep breath. "When are you going to ask about Lana?"

"What?"

He leans forward. "You've asked me about her every day for the past month."

"I have?" Here I thought I was being subtle. I guess not.

"You have. When are you going to take the next step?"

"I have been uncertain about what to say and when to say it." After the rough start she and Alex got off to, he wanted to make sure all that was in her past before he moved forward with pre-vetting Dominants for her. The three of us have spent some time together, and all my interactions with Lana have been positive. She appears to have adjusted and is in a better state than before. Although she still challenges Alex, she does so privately, which is more appropriate. A submissive always has a voice. It seems she needed practice using it effectively. "I would like your permission to pursue Svetlana."

"You have my blessing."

"How do you think she's going to feel about this?"

"I don't guess anything when it comes to Svetlana." He holds his hands up. "The best way to find out is to ask her. Why don't you come over tonight? I can find something to keep myself busy while you two talk."

"Thanks, Montgomery."

"I have some real work to get to now."

After he leaves the office, I lean back in my chair. It's been a long time since I've pursued a submissive, and I've never been interested in someone as complicated as Lana. She's younger than anyone I've considered. Even though she was raised in this lifestyle, she doesn't have a lot of personal experience. And I can't overlook her sometimes unpredictable nature. Then, there are the demons I've yet to face. I'll have to proceed cautiously so that neither of us gets in over our heads.

When the elevator doors open to Alex's apartment, we're hit with the smell of something mouthwatering coming from the kitchen.

"She cooks, too? You've been holding out on me, Montgomery."

"I had no idea, but I guess we're not ordering out," he says as we enter the kitchen, where we find Svetlana at the stove. "What are you making?"

"Beef Stroganoff," she says as she turns around. "Brandon, I didn't know you were coming over tonight."

"I hope you don't mind."

"Not at all. I made more than enough." She looks at Alex. "I hope you don't mind. I invited Viktor and Pyotr for dinner. This is Pyotr's favorite meal."

"Actually, I'm going to need to steal them for a bit. There's something important we have to take care of. Do you mind entertaining Brandon for me? We'll grab leftovers later."

"Umm. Sure, if that's what you want."

"Thanks." Clasping my shoulder, he says quietly, "Good luck." Then, he disappears.

"Is there anything I can help with?"

"Dinner will be ready in a second. I have a bottle of Barolo chilling. Would you mind opening it?"

"Not at all."

I've spent enough time at Montgomery's place to know where everything is. I grab the corkscrew and find the bottle she mentioned. While I pour the wine, Lana makes our plates.

"I hope you like it."

She watches me intently as I take my first bite. "Wow. This is incredible."

"Thank you." She blushes.

"Where did you learn to cook like this?"

"Mama and Olga."

"Is Olga your grandmother?"

"No, Olga is our cook."

"They obviously passed their talent to you."

"I'm afraid it wasn't that simple. Being in the kitchen was of very little interest to me. In my country, women need to be able to cook. So, I was forced to learn."

"If this meal is an indication, I'd say you learned well."

"It took a while. Poor Papa was subjected to some very questionable meals," she giggles. "Fortunately, I've improved since then and have grown to enjoy being in the kitchen."

We eat silently for a few minutes, but it's not awkward. On the contrary, it's comfortable. As if we've done this many times.

"Alex tells me you're getting ready to move out. You must be excited."

"Actually, I'm terrified," she confesses. "I don't know what uni will be like here compared to Moscow. And what if my roommate hates me?"

"I don't have experience with college, so I won't be much help with that. But I don't think there's any way your roommate could hate you."

"You didn't go to college?"

"No. My parents were older when they had me. By the time I graduated from high school, they needed extra help. So, instead of attending college, I got a job and cared for them."

"That's a very selfless thing to do. They must appreciate the sacrifice you made."

"They did. They're both gone now."

"I had no idea. I'm very sorry."

"It was a tough loss, but I'm learning how to live with it."

"I understand loss. Obviously, you know about my sister."

"I do. I can't imagine how difficult that was for you."

"I still have nightmares about it sometimes." She sets her fork down and takes a sip of her wine. "People always say that the pain gets better or goes away, but it doesn't. It's always there. If not at the forefront of my mind, it's just below the surface. Somedays, it feels like it was just yesterday she was taken, and other days, I struggle to remember what she looked like—what her voice sounded like."

"I know what you mean. I don't believe grief goes away. We learn how to live in spite of it."

"That's exactly it. Not many people understand that."

"I think they do. Whether we like it or not, we're going to lose people we love. The problem is that because grief and loss are uncomfortable, people try to sweep it under the rug and pretend it doesn't happen. Then, we're taught to give these pretty answers that supposedly make people feel better."

"You may be right. I know I've tried to do that myself. But pretending it hasn't happened or because it's been so many years, everything is suddenly okay doesn't work."

"You're not the only one who's tried that." Lana gets up to clear our now empty plates. I follow her into the kitchen. "Can I help you with the dishes?"

"There's no need. I can do them."

"I know you can, but I'd like to help."

"If you really want to."

If she only knew what I really wanted to do with her. But I can't jump right to that. I need to keep my body under control and take this one step at a time. I've made mistakes in the past. Skipped necessary steps with a submissive, and the results were disastrous. I don't want to do that with Svetlana.

There's something different about her. About the way I feel when I'm near her.

Svetlana

I'M CAUGHT OFF GUARD WHEN ALEX SAYS HE WON'T BE HERE
for dinner. He tries to be around in the evenings, especially for dinner.
But I know sometimes Papa calls with an emergency that needs to be
addressed immediately. Usually, Pyotr stays with me, though. Knowing
Alex needs both men is concerning. I want to call Papa and find out
what's going on. But Alex asked me to entertain Brandon, and I don't
want to be rude.

While Brandon pours the wine, I prepare myself for an uncomfortable dinner. Every time we hung out, Alex was there too. Brandon seems
like a nice guy, but I really don't know anything about him and have no
idea what to talk about. That situation is quickly resolved when we start
talking about our families. Brandon's experienced a great deal of loss, as
well.

Now, he's helping me do the dishes. It feels oddly familiar. We work
side-by-side as though we've done this routine many times before.

"Would you like to go for a walk?" Brandon asks as I'm putting the
last dish away.

"Sure. But I need to ask Alex first."

"Not a problem."

I take out my phone to send a text.

Me: Brandon asked me to go for a walk. Is that okay with you?

It's a few minutes before the bubbles begin dancing on my screen, indicating Alex is typing.

Alex: Is that something you'd like to do?

Me: Yes.

Alex: It's fine with me. Have fun.

"He said yes."

Brandon's face lights up. "Great. Let's go."

We're quiet on the elevator ride down to the ground floor. When the doors open, Pyotr is waiting at the building's entrance.

"And here I thought I'd get to go out without an escort."

"It's fine. I don't mind," Brandon says and smiles.

"I'm glad *you* don't. Nobody ever asks me if I mind."

"Your safety is important."

"Are you saying you wouldn't keep me safe?"

"No, I'm not saying that. But I appreciate Pyotr coming along. It means I can pay more attention to you without worrying about everything around us."

"Smooth," I say and shake my head.

Pyotr maintains a discreet presence while Brandon and I walk down the sidewalk.

"Have you been to Riverside Park yet?"

"Yes. Alex brought me here when I desperately needed a quiet place amid all the chaos. Now, Pyotr and I come here for our afternoon runs."

"It's one of my favorite parts of the Upper West Side." We stop at a bench overlooking the water. "Care to sit and watch the sunset?"

"I'd love to."

Several other people had the same idea and have gathered at the water's edge. The sun is just beginning to disappear behind the buildings across the river. Hues of orange and purple are painted across the sky. The reflection on the water is breathtaking.

"I'd like to get to know you better," Brandon says, surprising me. "I've already talked to Alex and got his permission."

Now, the odd events of tonight all make sense. There was no emergency. That was Alex's made-up excuse so Brandon and I could spend time alone together.

"That was very unexpected. I'm not sure what to say." My heart is pounding.

"I know you have a lot of big changes coming up. I don't want to stress you out. We can take things as slowly as you need." He pauses. "I'd like the opportunity to get to know you better. If you'd be open to it?"

"And you're sure Alex is okay with this?"

"I'm positive. But if you'd feel better discussing it with him first, that's okay, too."

I don't know what the right answer is. Alex and I didn't discuss how he'd like me to handle this. "I'm not against it, but I'd like to talk to Alex about it before I give you a definite answer."

"I can respect that."

"Thank you." I smile, feeling much more at ease.

Once the sun sets, we slowly walk back to the apartment.

When we arrive, Viktor, Pyotr, and Alex are at the table eating.

"Thank you again for cooking," Alex says when he sees me. "The stroganoff is wonderful. It tastes just like Irina's."

"You're welcome. I love cooking."

"I wish I had known that weeks ago." He laughs.

"Thanks for letting me borrow her, Montgomery."

"Anytime. Within reason."

"I had a great time tonight," Brandon says.

"Me, too."

"Do you need a ride home?" Viktor asks. "I can drive you home."

"Nah, I'll take the subway."

I watch as Brandon walks toward the elevator and steps inside. When he turns back to face me, the smile on his face nearly makes my knees give out. But I force myself to maintain my composure. When I lead with my heart, I tend to get in trouble. This time, I'm determined to think things through before I act on them. Who knows. Maybe it'll lead to a better result. Only time will tell.

Brandon

I GRAB A SEAT IN THE NEAR-EMPTY SUBWAY CAR AND POP MY headphones in so I can try to figure out where things went wrong tonight. I thought Svetlana and I were getting along well. I could've sworn there were the beginnings of a connection. Could I have imagined it? Maybe I misread the cues because when I asked to get to know her better, she froze. I fear Svetlana's complexities exceed what anyone suspects. I don't think I could walk away if I tried, and that worries me. I don't want to repeat the sins of my past.

I was the luckiest guy in the world. It's what I thought every day after Celia Baldwin, the prettiest girl at Fort Hamilton High School, agreed to be my girlfriend. Even though I'd lost my virginity long before I met her, I was honored she chose me to be her first. I might have been a teenager, but I was a kinky bastard who liked to be in control in and out of the bedroom. Lucky for me, Celia was open to experimenting.

After graduation, I got a job as a bartender at a popular bar in Manhattan. That's where I first met Angel. He and I often worked the same shift and would go out after work. One weekend, he invited me to go to Chains. I'd never heard of it, but I assumed it was another NYC nightclub.

I was wrong. Chains was a BDSM club. That night, my eyes were opened to a whole new world that I didn't know existed. It was a world where everything I liked to do was on full display. The air smelled like sex, which was no surprise because that's exactly what was happening in every corner of the seedy club.

Celia and I quickly became regulars. She was agreeable to doing anything and everything I wanted. I loved parading my submissive's flawless body in front of the club attendees. We often fucked while others watched. Knowing men were getting off watching her didn't bother me.

Then, I started getting asked if others could join. Hell yeah. Countless nights I fucked Celia at the same time as another man. Sometimes, I'd invite women to join us. Other nights, I stayed on the sideline and watched others use her. Celia never said no. She got off on it as much as I did.

Celia was not only insatiable, she also loved pain—and I loved giving it to her. But she quickly outgrew the things I felt confident doing to her. Fortunately for us, there were plenty of other Dominants in the club who were more experienced and willing to take a scene to the next level for her.

One night, we went down to the dungeon to do a private scene with Diablo, a club regular, and a master with a bullwhip. Everything was planned beforehand, and I was confident nothing could go wrong. I bound her wrists together while Diablo bound her legs to a spreader bad. We placed her on her hands and knees. It was a challenging position.

I started the scene with a flogger to warm her up while Diablo stimulated her nipples. It didn't take long before her arousal was dripping down her leg. Then we switched places. He took a few practice swings with his whip before turning to Celia. Over and over, his whip landed on her skin. Her moans grew louder. I was so fucking hard and couldn't wait any longer.

Freeing my erection, I ordered her to open her mouth. I wasn't slow or gentle as I thrust into her. Diablo dropped his whip and began to fuck her ass, just like we had planned. I wasn't thinking clearly. I didn't realize he—

My phone vibrates in my hand, pulling my attention out of the past.

Alex: How did everything go tonight?

Me: I don't know.

Alex: What do you mean you don't know?

Me: Didn't she talk to you?

Alex: Viktor and Pyotr are still here, so we haven't had a chance to talk.

Me: I asked her, but she said she'd get back to me.

Alex: That's odd, even for Lana. I'll talk to her and let you know.

Me: Sounds good. I'll see you in the morning.

Svetlana

～

"Let me know when you're done eating. I'll be in my room," I say, leaving the men to finish dinner. I really need to talk to Alex, but not until we're alone. While I wait, I grab the book I'm reading. I want to finish it before the term starts and I have to put all my time and energy into textbooks and school assignments. Unfortunately, I can't seem to focus on the words and make no progress.

"Got a few minutes?"

"Sure. Come in." Alex steps into the room but leaves the door open. I set my book aside. "Did you know what Brandon was going to ask me tonight?"

"I did," he says as he sits in the chair across from my bed.

"And you didn't think to give me a heads up?"

"I thought about it and decided not to."

"Seriously?"

"Yes, seriously." He crosses his arms.

"I would've liked a heads up."

"Think about it. If I told you he wanted to spend more time with you but decided not to ask, you'd be crushed. I didn't want you to get hurt."

I study him for a minute, weighing his words. "I guess you're right."

"Can you say that a little louder?" He grins.

I toss a pillow at him. "No. That was all you're getting." We share a laugh.

"So, what's up with you not answering him?"

"I thought you'd be happy I'm coming to you first."

"I didn't say I wasn't happy."

"And they say women are confusing."

"What's that supposed to mean?" He raises an eyebrow.

"The whole trust you and ask you first bit. I was trying to do the right thing and come to you first. But now you're wondering why I didn't give him an answer."

"Brandon already asked me for permission. I thought you'd get the hint when I left the two of you alone for dinner."

"I might've if your excuse for leaving didn't sound so real." It's not uncommon for Papa to call Alex with an emergency that needs to be handled immediately. Instead of seeing Brandon's intent, I was too busy worrying about what might be happening. "I don't know if now's a good time to do this."

"Why not?" Alex asks, genuinely concerned.

"There's a lot of big changes about to happen. Should I be adding more to the mix?"

"It's completely your decision, but if it makes a difference, I think you'll be able to handle it just fine."

"Why him and not any of the other Dominants at the club?"

"Do you not like him?"

"I mean, he seems very nice, and we have more in common than I'd realized."

"Brandon and I have been friends for years. I can tell you that you'd be completely safe with him."

"I don't question my safety with him."

"Then, what's the hesitation? Is it because he's black?"

"What? No. Brandon's your best friend. You know how badly I screwed things up last time."

"And you're afraid you're going to do it again." I nod. "It seems you have two choices. You can let the fear of making another mistake keep you from trying again, but who knows what you might miss. Or you can take that first terrifying step and see what the possibilities are."

"You really think Brandon and I might be a good match?"

"You can be a pain in the ass sometimes," he chuckles. "But yes, I think you and Brandon would get along quite well."

"Do you have his number?"

"I do."

"Do you think it would be okay if I called him?"

"I'm sure he'd like that."

Alex texts me Brandon's number and then leaves my room. I fall back onto the pillows, picturing the incredibly sexy man I spent the evening with. There's a quiet confidence about Brandon. He's a Dominant, but he's soft-spoken and kind. He too, is settled in his career, but his work is directly involved with Jelena's Hope—it feels familiar.

I've heard from the other submissives that Brandon's a master with his whip. That's something that appeals to me. I've often imagined what it would feel like to be bound and whipped. While training at Noire, I enjoyed playing with a Dominant whose implement of choice was a whip. Even though it was a very short and controlled scene, I loved every second. He had expressed an interest in being more than play partners for a night, but Czarenah didn't feel I was ready for a dynamic yet. I resented her for that judgment call, but looking back, she was right.

Exploring that side of Brandon might be fun. But as excited as I am for the possibilities a dynamic brings, I'm equally as nervous. I have a history of screwing up anything good in my life, of pushing away people who get too close before they can hurt me.

Now, I'm face to face with the opportunity to submit to a man, a Dominant, who is worthy of my submission. But can I do this the right way, or will I screw this up like I do everything else? For both our sakes, I hope I can do this.

My hands shake as I input his number and tap the green call icon. The phone rings several times. Just when I think it's going to voicemail, he picks up.

"Hello?"

"Brandon?"

"Yeah."

"It's Svetlana."

"Hi."

"Alex gave me your number. I hope that was okay."

"Of course. I'm glad you called."

"I had a chance to talk to Alex."

"Okay."

"If you're still open to it, I'd like to get to know you. To see if we might work as a Dom/sub couple."

"I'm glad to hear that."

"I have one request."

"What is it?"

"Can we take things slowly?"

"*Mon petit papillon*, we can do this however you need."

Svetlana is learning what it means to submit, but trust doesn't come easily. Will she give Brandon her heart—or will she run before he can claim it? Continue their story in *Fractured Lives*.

Fractured Lives

Svetlana

"Yes, Papa. Pyotr checked out the dorm. He was happy with the security," I explain for the tenth time. My cell is propped on the small counter so I can keep the call on speaker while I finish putting away the groceries I picked up.

"Does he have a key for your room? In case there is an emergency."

I love Papa with all my heart, but he tends to go overboard. "Yes, he has the key card." I roll my eyes.

"Would you consider him staying in the dorm for one semester? I will make the arrangements."

Putting some distance between myself and everything that comes with being a Solonik is one of the biggest reasons I wanted to come to New York City. I thought going to Moscow would be far enough, but it wasn't. Papa's reputation runs far and wide, especially in Russia. I hoped by coming here, I'd have a fresh start as just Svetlana Solonik. If Pyotr lives in the dorms like he has in the past, it's going to raise red flags with my classmates, and they'll avoid me like they did in Moscow.

"Papa, we talked about this. I don't want Pyotr living in the dorm with me."

"I know, *moya babochka,*" he sighs in defeat. "I had to try."

The door to my dorm opens, startling me. An older man and

197

woman walk in, followed by a petite girl with long blonde curls. "Papa, I have to go. My roommate just arrived." I end the call and, slide my phone into my pocket, and am ready to introduce myself.

"I thought you had a single room." The woman whispers loudly.

"They're first come, first serve. I guess they ran out." The girl turns to me and smiles. "Hi. I'm Natalie."

"I'm Svetlana. It's nice to meet you."

"These are my parents, Charlo—"

"Mr. and Mrs. Clarke," the woman interrupts.

"It's a pleasure to meet you both. Is there anything I can do to help?"

Natalie goes to speak, but Mrs. Clarke steps in front and answers for her daughter. "We've got it just fine on our own."

Sensing the hostility from her mother, I decide it's best to give them some privacy. "Okay. I'll get out of your way."

The dorms at NYU are much different than in Moscow, where Mei and I shared a single space that was both our sleeping and study area. Here, the rooms are set up like small apartments with two private bedrooms that share a kitchen and bathroom.

I go into my room and close the door. Unfortunately, the walls in our rooms are paper-thin, and I can hear everything.

"I'm going to find whoever's in charge here and speak to them. You need a room by yourself."

"I'm fine. I think it'll be fun to have a dormmate."

"Did you hear her accent? She sounds like she's from Russia or some foreign place like that."

What's this woman's problem? My impulsive side wants to text Pyotr and ask him to come over. That would definitely give her something to complain about, but I don't want to ruin any chance of becoming friends with my roommate.

"Charlotte, I think it'll be good for Natalie to share the space." Mr. Clarke makes his opinion known.

Just like she did with her daughter, Mrs. Clarke overrules her husband. "You're far too permissive, Stanley."

"I'll be fine, I promise. If you guys don't get going, you'll miss your flight."

"Are you sure you want to stay?" Their voices grow louder. They must be in the kitchen. "It's not too late to come home. You'll be much closer to Thomas."

"I'm positive."

After what sounds like a tearful goodbye on the mother's part, they finally leave. A few seconds later, there's a soft knock on my door.

"I apologize for my parents' behavior," Natalie says when I open the door. "They aren't thrilled that I'm going to school here. They're even less happy that I have a roommate."

"My parents weren't exactly over the moon with me choosing NYU either. But why wouldn't they want you to have a roommate?"

"They, well, mostly my mother, are afraid I'll be negatively influenced by people who don't live the way we do." She shrugs. "Other than the times they've dropped me off here, they rarely leave the smalltown I live in."

"Parents," I chuckle. "There's nothing to apologize for. Where are you from?"

"Northmeadow. It's a small town in Missouri." I must look as clueless as I feel because I'm not sure where that is in relation to New York. "It's in the Midwestern part of the country," she explains. "Where are you from?"

"St. Petersburg, Russia."

"Wow. What brought you here?"

"I was looking to experience something different."

"New York certainly fits the bill for that."

"It certainly does."

"Would you like to grab a bite to eat?" she asks.

"I'd love to. Do you know any place good?"

"I know a little Russian restaurant a few blocks away."

Svetlana

The restaurant is only three blocks from our dorm. Although the food isn't exactly the Russian fare I'm used to eating, it's not bad, and having food that's somewhat familiar is comforting.

"You said you were from a small town. How small is small?"

"There's less than one thousand people."

"Excuse me?" I nearly choke on my bite of food. "Did you say one thousand?"

"Yep. It's the kind of place where everyone knows everyone."

"I kind of understand that. St. Petersburg has over five million citizens, but our direct community is small."

"It can be suffocating," she says.

We finish our meal and start our walk back to campus just as the sun's beginning to set. As much as I fought Papa to let me be more independent, being out alone is an unfamiliar feeling, and I find myself looking around to find Pyotr. I texted him before I left the dorm, so I know he's following us. But just as Papa promised, Pyotr's staying out of sight.

"Is everything okay?" Natalie asks.

"Yes. Why?"

"You look nervous."

"A little. St. Petersburg may have a lot of people, but it's nothing like this. I guess it's going to take a little getting used to." I don't want to talk much about myself, so I attempt to change the subject. "What brought you here?"

"My brother."

"Does he live here too?"

"I wish. But, no. Michael committed suicide two years ago."

"I'm so sorry."

"Thank you," Natalie says sadly. "His death changed my whole perspective on life."

"Loss has a way of doing that."

"Before he died, my only plan was to marry my boyfriend and become a mother. I still want to do those things," she says quickly. "But I also want to get my degree and have a job."

"What are you studying?"

"Psychology. I plan to become a therapist."

"That's terrific. I'm sure your parents are very proud of you."

"Not exactly."

"Why not?"

"My parents expected me to get married right after high school like they did. They weren't thrilled when I told them I wanted to attend college. Then, I told them I wanted to attend NYU. Mom was completely against it. If it wasn't for my scholarship, I wouldn't be here." Natalie's phone dings. When she checks the screen, a huge grin spreads across her face. "It's my boyfriend, Tommy." She holds it up, and I see a picture of a handsome guy with dirty blonde hair and a mega-watt smile. He's wearing a sports jersey and holding an American football.

"He's gorgeous."

"He is," Natalie says dreamily. "Give me a second." She types a quick text and sends it off.

"How long have you two been dating?"

"Since we were fifteen."

During our meal, Natalie told me a little about Northmeadow, the ultra-conservative small town she grew up in. Now, all this about getting married and popping out babies immediately after secondary education. That's a crazy old-fashioned idea—even for Eastern Europe.

"Wow. That's a long time. Does he go to NYU, too?"

"No. Tommy would never leave Missouri. He got a full-ride football scholarship at Mizzou."

"What's a *Mizzou*?" I struggle with the word.

"It's the nickname for the University of Missouri."

"It must be hard being so far apart."

"It's been challenging, but we're making it work."

It wasn't easy only seeing Slava on weekends, and we weren't even really dating. One of the reasons I didn't sign another contract with him was because of the extreme distance my going to school in the United States would put between us. I give her a lot of credit for being able to handle a long-distance relationship.

"Do you have a boyfriend?" she asks.

"I was seeing someone back in Russia, but we broke up shortly before I came here. It's all good, though. New York is a big city with lots of possibilities."

"I guess," she says.

"What do you like to do on weekends?" I ask as we arrive back at our dorm, hoping to get the scoop on places to hang out.

"Except for a few local restaurants, I don't go off campus."

I stop dead in my tracks. "You mean to tell me you've been in this city for over a year, and you haven't gone to any clubs or bars?"

"Tommy doesn't approve of me going to places like that." She shrugs, and before I can respond, her phone rings again. "It's Tommy. I better take this. Hello?" Natalie answers her phone as she walks into her bedroom, closing the door behind her.

Her boyfriend doesn't *approve* of her going out? Something tells me he's not sitting in his dorm every weekend worrying about her. Why should Natalie have to miss out on everything college life has to offer? The more I dwell on this, the more I decide I don't like this Tommy guy.

Brandon

MUCH TO MAXIM AND PYOTR'S DISMAY, ALEX AND I MOVED Lana into her dorm a few weeks ago. They would've been happy if she had decided to stay with Alex rather than move onto campus. I understand her need for autonomy, especially given her father's high profile.

"You looked stressed," Alex says from my office doorway.

"It's nice to see you, too," I say as he walks in.

"What's going on?"

"Svetlana."

Alex sinks into one of the chairs. "What did she do now?"

"She didn't do anything." I close my laptop and sigh. "I'm nervous about seeing her tonight."

Alex is bringing Svetlana to Fire and Ice. I'm looking forward to it since I haven't seen her in several weeks. We've kept in touch by text and phone and have gotten to know one another better. Svetlana's an intelligent young woman with a mind of her own, which I've found surprisingly attractive. Nothing compares to spending time in person, though. My mind has been wandering all day, which makes working next to impossible.

"That's all?" Alex chuckles.

"She keeps herself pretty closed off. I don't exactly know what she's hoping for between us."

"Svetlana's a difficult one to figure out. Just when you think you understand her, she sheds a layer, and you have to start over again," Alex chuckles but shifts his mood back to seriousness when he notices I'm not laughing with him. "Something tells me that's not what you're worried about."

"I don't want to repeat past mistakes."

"What happened between you and Celia was a long time ago," Alex tries reassuring me.

"The past has a habit of creeping up on us when we least expect it."

"That night was awful. I'm not trying to downplay what happened. But it wasn't your fault. You were young and didn't know anything about the lifestyle."

"That's not an excuse."

"I'm not trying to make excuses. You took the advice of people you were supposed to be able to trust. You were as much a victim as Celia."

"Don't ever say that. Celia was the only victim that night."

"Brand," Alex says, lowering his voice. "You suffered as much as she did."

"I shouldn't have had that drink. If I didn't make that choice, things would be—."

"If I thought for a second that you weren't trustworthy, I wouldn't have agreed to let you pursue Svetlana," Alex interrupts. "How she'll react when you offer her a contract is anyone's guess."

"She's really not like everyone makes her out."

"Lana's a challenge, and she's often unpredictable," Alex says thoughtfully. "But you're right. Underneath her protective exterior is a kind and caring young woman."

"It sounds like your perspective on her has changed."

"Living with her all summer, I've seen a different side of her. There's still plenty of days I'd like to wring her neck, though," Alex chuckles.

While Svetlana was staying with Alex, I was able to spend a good amount of time with her. Alex is right. She does a remarkable job of maintaining a prickly disguise, ensuring most people don't stick around for long. For those that aren't chased away, they earn the opportunity to see the real Svetlana. The one who's fun-loving and flirty but who's also incredibly vulnerable.

"She's complex," I admit.

"And I think you're the right man to help her let her guard down once and for all."

"I don't know about that."

"Enough of the self-deprecating talk." Alex waves me off. "Are you going to propose negotiating a contract tonight?"

"I have a private room reserved," I say, leaning back in my chair.

"That sounds like it could be fun."

"Don't get excited. It's only so we'll have a quiet place to talk." Alex raises his eyebrows, clearly not believing me.

As much as I miss seeing Lana whenever I'm at Alex's, her being busy with the start of a new semester hasn't been entirely negative. We've discussed the lifestyle and what we both want for our future. I know she wants a permanent Dominant, and she knows I'm interested in her as a submissive.

Tonight, I plan to ask my little *papillion* to begin vetting and negotiating a contract.

Brandon

Alex is running late, which means Lana is also running late. I alternate between leaning against the building and pacing back and forth on the sidewalk in front of Fire and Ice, waiting for them to arrive. My nerves are on a hairpin trigger, thinking about the many ways tonight could turn out.

Finally, I see Alex's car coming down the street. Viktor slows to a stop, and I step forward to open the backdoor and help Lana out. Once she's on her feet, I allow my gaze to travel up and down her body. She's wearing tight jeans that accentuate her long, lean legs and a black top that's low cut and held together by several thin straps.

"You look amazing."

"Thank you," she answers.

"Montgomery," I greet my friend as he exits the car. He holds up a finger, and I see he's on his phone.

"He's had that thing glued to him all afternoon," Lana complains.

"It must be important."

"It's Papa. There's information he needs pushed through the network."

"One minute, Max," Alex says, moving the phone away from his ear. "You two go ahead without me. I have to go back to the office."

"Do you need a hand? I can go with you."

"I'd prefer if you stay and keep an eye on Lana."

She crosses her arms. "I don't need a babysitter."

That's when I realize whatever's going on with Max must be important because Alex doesn't engage. Instead, he puts the phone back to his ear and slides into his car.

"Shall we?" I hold the club door open for Lana and follow her inside.

Like most other weekend nights, Fire and Ice is busy. The three stages have scenes in progress, and the private rooms are either in use or reserved. I'm glad I called ahead. "I reserved one of the suites. Are you comfortable with that?"

"Of course." She smiles.

We make our way through the main area where the majority of the action is taking place. The hallway is empty as we walk down to room three. I swipe my member id under the scanner on the door, and the lock clicks open.

Lana steps in and looks around. I reserved a role-play room that's set up like a classroom with a blackboard, a teacher's desk, and several student desks arranged in neat rows. Several of the desks have built-in restraints, and there's a variety of paddles and rulers to discipline any deserving pupils.

Lana leans against one of the desks. "Are you into a teacher/student kink?"

"Not particularly. This room is the most conducive room for talking."

"Talking, right," Lana says, sitting at a desk. "Where should we start, Mr. Carpenter?"

"You can call me Brandon." I grab the chair behind the teacher's desk and drag it around to sit across from Lana. "How's school so far?"

"It's been quite an adjustment. University here is much different than in Russia."

"How so?"

"In Russia, we choose our major, but our classes and schedule are chosen for us. No changes can be made to the schedule. Classes start at eight a.m. every morning and don't end until well into the afternoon."

"That sounds pretty strict."

"It is. But here, I was able to choose my classes and schedule. It's a very different experience, but so far, I like it."

"I'm glad to hear that." My statement is followed by an awkward silence. I'm not sure what to ask or say next. When we're texting or on the phone, we never run out of things to talk about. But sitting here alone together is a different story. I don't know what to say next.

Lana's the first one to break the silence. "What are we doing here?"

"What do you mean?"

"This." She motions around us. "We haven't seen each other in weeks. You went through the trouble of reserving a private room. And you only want to talk."

"Yes." The word comes out sounding just as uncertain as I'm feeling.

"Look, Brandon, I'm really interested in you."

"I'm interested in you, too."

"Why am I getting the feeling there's something you aren't saying?"

"There is."

"Tell me."

None of this is going like I planned. "I'm not ready to discuss a Dom/sub contract. I want to keep seeing you, but I understand if you aren't interested." The words come out fast, and they were not the ones I intended to say. What the hell was that, Brandon? I mentally chastise myself.

"That's all?" Lana gets up and walks around the desk until she's standing before me. "I'm okay with that, for now." She runs her finger down my chest. "So, do we have this room all night?"

"We do."

"How about we put it to good use?"

Even though I know I shouldn't do this, I can't help myself. My hands grip her waist, pulling her onto my lap. "Before we go any further, I need to know this is okay with you. That this is what you want."

"It is."

"What is? I want to know exactly what you want." I allow myself to slip back into the Dominant role I'm most comfortable in.

"I want you to fuck me, Mr. Carpenter."

Those words are exactly what I needed to hear. My lips crash against hers, and she opens, granting my tongue access as I deepen the kiss. She pulls away and slides off my lap. Her hands slide her shirt up and over her head. It lands on the floor. Then she moves to her jeans, unbuttoning them and shimmying them down her legs. She kicks them aside. Lana stands before me in nothing but a black lace bra and a scrap of fabric that covers her pussy.

"How can I please you?" she asks seductively.

"Turn around and bend over the desk," I say in a low, deep voice.

Lana's graceful as she turns her back to me and folds herself over the desk.

I grab the ruler off the teacher's desk and bring it over to show her. "Is it okay to use this on you?"

"I would love that, Mr. Carpenter."

"If it's too much, all you need to do is tell me to stop. Do you understand?"

"Yes, I understand."

Lana's already told me she loves impact play and that she craves pain, so I feel comfortable with the way this is going.

The wooden ruler makes contact with Lana's ass. I know it stings, but she doesn't flinch. I do the same on the other side. Her pale skin turns pink. "How's that?"

"Not hard enough."

My strikes don't have to be hard to make a significant impact. Instead, I hit her five times quickly, all in the same area. A soft mewl escapes her lips.

I pause to pull my shirt over my head and toss it to the teacher's desk. "Your ass is a beautiful shade of red, *mon petit papillon*. How does it feel?"

"It feels good. May I have more?"

"You're a greedy little thing, aren't you?"

"Yes," she says.

Without warning, the ruler makes contact with her skin. "Do you act this way with other professors?"

"No, Mr. Carpenter. Only you," she says in a breathy tone.

"Good. If I'm fucking you, no one else better come near you."

Dropping the ruler, I take her black panties and pull. They tear easily, and I let them fall to the floor. Then, I reach my hand between her legs. "This pussy is all mine."

"Mhm."

"Say it, Svetlana. Tell me it's mine."

"My pussy is yours." I slide my finger inside her. "I'm wet for you."

"You're dripping." I add another finger, pumping them in and out. "Spread your legs."

I open my pants and free my dick. I line it up with her opening and push inside as far as her body can take me. Then, I pull out. Lana whimpers and my hand smacks her ass before I slide back inside.

"Hold onto the desk, and don't let go." Her hands reach over the top of the desk and grasp it tightly. As soon as they do, I pull almost all the way out before I thrust into her hard and fast. With my hands holding onto her hips, I repeat the punishing move over and over.

I know I should slow down and ease up my hold on her. She's going to have bruises from my fingers, but I don't care. I want to mark her—make her mine.

"Come for me, Svetlana," I demand. "Fucking tell me your mine while you come on my cock."

"I'm yours," she yells as her body squeezes mine, sending me into my own orgasm. "Oh my God, you feel so good, Mr. Carpenter."

When I pull out, I watch my cum drip from her pussy. It's an erotic sight that I can't take my eyes off.

"Did I pass your test?" she asks, looking over her shoulder.

"I think I can give you an A for today." I take her by the hand and help her up. "Are you okay? I didn't hurt you, did I?"

"You don't have to worry about hurting me," she says. "Contract or not, I like it rough."

I don't know how or why I was lucky enough to meet this woman. But now that I've had her, I'll be damned if I let anyone or anything take her away.

Svetlana

After straightening myself up in the attached bathroom, I return to the classroom where Brandon's finishing cleaning up.

"It seems we've missed tonight's scenes," he says.

"I guess it's good I didn't come to see them."

"True. It wasn't *them* you came for," Brandon grins.

"Was that a joke?" Brandon's always so serious. I like seeing this side of him, too.

"Alex texted. He's still tied up at the office. If you'd like, I can drive you back to your dorm."

"I'm planning on staying at Alex's tonight. Natalie doesn't know about all this, and I'd like to keep it that way."

Our lives are polar opposites. It's not only our geography but how we were raised. My parents live the BDSM lifestyle and have always been open and willing to talk about anything. Well, almost anything. Stanley and Charlotte Clarke are ultra-religious and conservative. Natalie was raised with such closed-minded views. It's a wonder she's as open as she is. Natalie's sweet and innocent—I adore that about her. But she's also very naïve. I'm afraid if I told her about this part of me, she'd run in the opposite direction and never look back.

"That's fine. I can take you there," Brandon says, taking my hand in his as we walk across the club's main room. "I don't have a fancy driver like your father or Alex."

I stop walking. "I don't care about any of that stuff." Brandon cocks his head. "I know you've been told I'm a spoiled princess, and in some ways, I guess it's true. Papa's job ensured I was raised with advantages not everyone had. But I don't care about money or status. Actually, I think I'd be happier with nothing."

Brandon takes a few steps, closing the distance between us. "I don't give a shit what anyone else thinks. I know what I see when I look at you, *mon petit papillon*, and that's all that matters."

"What's *papillon?*"

"It's French for butterfly. You," Brandon cups my cheek in his hand. "Are a beautiful and mysterious butterfly."

"Why did you call me that?"

"Butterflies symbolize hope, bravery, and transformation. Everything you embody." Goosebumps cover my arms, and I shiver. "Are you okay?"

"I'm good." This is getting too personal, and I try to pull away.

"No, you aren't." His hold on me tightens. "Why did that bother you?"

I want to run, but for some reason, my mouth betrays me and opens, allowing words to spill out. "Papa and Pyotr have called me butterfly since I was a little girl. There's no way you could've known that, yet you called me butterfly, too."

"Then, you know it's true," Brandon says. I lean in to kiss him and am interrupted by my phone rings. "You should answer that."

I nod and take a step back, then reach into my pocket to pull out my phone. "Hello?"

"Hey. I'm sorry I got tied up here," Alex says. "I wanted to check in on you."

"There's nothing to be sorry for. Is everything okay there?"

"Your father had some critical information that needed to get into the right hands. Thankfully, it did."

"I'm glad to hear that."

"Brandon texted to let me know he's driving you home."

"Is it okay if I stay at your apartment tonight?"

"Of course."

"Thanks." I smile.

"I'm wrapping everything up here, so I shouldn't be much longer. I'll see you in a bit."

After I hang up, I join Brandon, who's talking with Star. "Is everything okay?"

"It is." I'm not sure what, if anything, Star knows about Alex and Brandon's involvement in Papa's business, so I don't say anything else.

"I'm going to have you wait with Star while I get the car." Brandon kisses my cheek before turning to walk away.

I watch him until he's out of sight.

Most everyone has cleared out of the club. With the lights low and the music off, it's quiet in here—too quiet. Star's finishing some paperwork, but she keeps stopping and looking at me. I scroll down my social media, trying to appear busy. I hope she thinks I'm too busy to talk, but of course, that doesn't work.

"How was your evening?" Star asks.

"It was nice." I glance up quickly and then go back to scrolling.

"I didn't see you and Brandon for most of the night."

"We were around."

"Mhm." She taps her papers on the table. "By around, I suppose you mean in a private room all night."

"Yes." I put the phone down. "We had some important matters to discuss."

"I know Brandon and am certain of your safety with him. Otherwise, this conversation would be very different. I'd be remiss if I didn't remind you of the need to vet a Dominant before being intimate with them."

"Yes, I'm aware. That would only be if the relationship were of a contractual nature, correct?" My reply comes out snippier than I intended, but at the same time, I get tired of always being treated like a child.

"That's correct."

Brandon: I'm out front in the red Mustang.

"Brandon's here. Have a good night." I quickly head for the door.

"Svetlana," Star calls.

"Yes?" I stop and turn around.

"I'm not the enemy here. If you're open to it, we might even get to be friends."

It isn't what I expected her to say, and I find myself momentarily at a loss for words. I recover slightly and mumble, "Goodnight."

Brandon

"WHAT THE HELL WERE YOU THINKING?" ALEX YELLS, AND I hold the phone away from my ear.

"Hello to you, too." I roll my eyes.

"Whatever. Answer my question."

"Why?"

"Because that's my collar around her neck."

"Collar of protection," I say, irritated. "She's not your submissive."

"Svetlana's my responsibility to protect."

"Weren't you giving me the lecture earlier on how much you trust me?"

"Yes, but that didn't mean you should go and fuck her tonight."

"Wait a damn minute. How do you know what we did or didn't do?"

"After Lana didn't respond to my texts, I called Star. She informed me you and Svetlana were in the private room all night. That can only mean one thing."

"We're both consenting adults."

"Who should be vetting one another, not—"

"There's no contract, so there's no need for vetting."

"Right."

"I'm serious."

"What happened?"

"I told Lana I'm not ready for a contract, and by some stroke of luck, she was okay with it. What happened after that is between Lana and me."

"You're serious? You're not pursuing her as a submissive?" Alex asks, lowering his voice.

"Don't mistake this for being disinterested. I'm still very much pursuing her. We're just not looking at a dynamic right now."

"Oh." There's an awkward pause. "I apologize for jumping to conclusions."

"It's all good. But Montgomery, you're way too uptight. You need to get yourself laid." I laugh.

"Fuck off, Carpenter."

"I'm hanging up now. I need to get back to the club."

"Where the hell are you?"

"I'm walking down west twenty-third."

"Where's Lana?"

"I left her on a street corner," I say sarcastically.

"What the hell?" Alex yells.

"Lana's with Star at the club. I went to get the car."

"You're lucky. Now get off the damn phone and get back to Lana."

I can't contain my laughter, earning me side-eyed looks from people who try to avoid walking by me on the sidewalk.

The garage I use when I'm at the club is only a few blocks away, but I didn't want Lana to have to walk. I get the car and return to the club in less than fifteen minutes. There's no parking, so I put my flashers on and text Lana, letting her know I'm here. She comes out almost immediately.

"Nice ride," she says appreciatively.

"You like Valkyrie?" I run my hand along the dash.

"I did until I knew it was a she." Lana pouts.

"I didn't take you for the jealous type."

"You're running your hands over another woman. What do you expect?"

"Valkyrie is beautiful, but she has nothing on you."

"Smooth," Lana chuckles.

I reach over her and grab the safety belt, clicking it into place. "Being properly restrained is important."

"I'm a huge supporter of restraints." I love that she keeps up the witty banter.

The radio plays in the background while I drive up Riverside Blvd. "Tell me something about you I don't know yet."

Lana responds quickly, "I don't have a driver's license."

"Really?" I don't know why that surprises me. It's fairly normal for people who've grown up in Manhattan to not have a license. Public transportation can take you everywhere you need to go. Anyone who's ever driven downtown will attest to what a nightmare it is. I only got mine to drive my parents back and forth to their many doctor's appointments.

"Since I've always had a guard to bring me wherever I need to go, there's never been a reason for me to have one."

"Do you want to learn to drive?"

"I never really thought about it." She shrugs. "Living in the city, I don't see a reason to have one since I can walk or take the subway anywhere I need to go." Lana shifts in her seat to face me. "Tell me something about you."

"What do you want to know?"

"Do you have any siblings?"

"I have an older sister."

"Are you close?"

"No. By the time I was born, she was grown and out of the house."

"Does your sister live in the city?"

"She's in Germany with her husband. We don't really keep in touch."

"I'd give anything to have my sister back," Lana says pensively. "You should try to talk to yours more."

I glance over at Lana. The faraway look on her face makes me realize how callous my words must've sounded. I know how much Lana misses her sister, and I've taken for granted that I still have mine. "You're right. I should."

I enter the parking garage under Alex's building and pull into the guest parking spot.

"I had a nice time tonight," Lana says.

"Tonight's not over."

"It isn't?" Her face lights up.

"I'll wait with you until Alex gets home."

Svetlana

Brandon and I are enjoying a glass of red wine when Alex strolls into the kitchen.

"Hello, you two," he says as he loosens his tie.

"You look like shit," Brandon says.

I look at Brandon and raise my eyebrow before turning to Alex. "Would you like a glass of wine?"

"That'd be great," Alex says, ignoring Brandon's smart-ass comment.

While I get a glass, the guys talk quietly. "What was going on that had you tied up all night."

"A large shipment was on the move from Cyprus to Venezuela. I needed to push the information through to Max's contacts in South America and wait for their reply."

"Were they successful in intercepting?"

"The raid was wrapping up when I left," Alex says as I hand him the glass. "Tomorrow, we'll start placing the recovered persons in treatment facilities."

Papa works tirelessly, trying to stop human trafficking. One of the biggest hurdles is trafficking is a multi-billion-dollar business. Where there's that kind of money, there's sure to be a fight. Over the years,

Papa's network has grown, expanding all over the globe. Unfortunately, the traffickers have shared the same growth. That doesn't stop Papa and all the others from continuing the fight with the hope that one day, we'll live in a world free from this evil crime.

"Where will they go?" I ask. "Jelena's Hope is almost at capacity."

"There are a few smaller facilities," Alex explains. "We'll do our best to ensure no one is left without the services they need."

I swirl the wine around my glass.

"What are you thinking?" Brandon asks.

"After we found out Jelena had been murdered." The sting of those words is still as piercing as the day it happened. My thoughts come out disjointed. "Sometimes I wonder what I'm doing here. Going to school seems like a waste of time when I could be back home working at the center and making a real difference."

"Just because you aren't there doesn't mean you're not making a difference. You're studying to become a lawyer to help put the criminals involved in trafficking behind bars." Brandon reminds me.

"I guess."

It's not that he's wrong. In my mind, that was my plan from the beginning. Looking back, I can't help but think how naïve I was. Why did I think I could go head-to-head with traffickers in a court of law? First off, how many of them actually get arrested? Out of those, even fewer end up in front of a judge. And if by some chance they do, realistically, what are my chances of winning a trial? They pay their legal counsel a fortune to keep them out of prison. Corruption runs deep in these circles, and I'm no match for them.

"I don't want to hear, *I guess.*" Brandon places his hand over mine. "You've already made a huge difference in so many people's lives through Jelena's Hope. You'll continue to do so through the legal system. Will it be easy? Of course not. But if there's one thing I know about you, it's that you don't back down from a challenge."

"Sometimes it just seems like it's all for nothing. Papa works day and night, yet the trafficking industry hasn't really been affected. Who has he stopped?"

I don't know how Papa gets up every day and looks evil in the face, knowing that no matter how many traffickers he eliminates, there's more waiting in the shadows to step in and pick up where their predecessors left off.

"Svetlana," Alex interrupts my thoughts. "You're right that we'll never eradicate trafficking, but that doesn't mean our efforts are wasted. I'm certain every person who's walked through the doors of Jelena's Hope has a different opinion. None of this is for nothing."

I know Alex and Brandon are right, but that doesn't stop the doubt that creeps in, making me question everything.

Svetlana

"Thank you for tonight," I say as I walk Brandon to Alex's private elevator.

"I'd like to see you again."

"I'd like that, too."

Brandon leans in to kiss me goodnight. His erection presses against my abdomen, and I almost ask him to stay.

"When?" he asks as the elevator doors open.

"Maybe next weekend. I'll let you know if I'm going to be here."

"Can I see you before then?"

"I don't think so." I'm unsure how to navigate these waters. I'm looking for a Dominant, not a boyfriend. I know I told Brandon I'm okay with not pursuing a dynamic right now. I'm hoping I can convince him to not wait too long. "I'll text you during the week."

Brandon steps into the elevator. "Goodnight, Svetlana," he says as the doors close.

After he leaves, I return to the living room and sink onto the dark grey sofa. Alex follows me into the room and sits across from me. "How was your night?" he asks.

"It was nice."

"Nice?" He raises an eyebrow.

"Yes. Nice." I don't know how much Alex knows, and I'm certainly not going to be the one to kiss and tell.

"How were the scenes tonight?"

"Okay."

"I'm sorry I wasn't able to make it. I hope Brandon kept you entertained."

"I haven't seen him in a while, so it was nice to talk and catch up." It's a true statement.

"I see."

"Why the inquisition?" I ask, mildly annoyed.

"Look, I know what happened tonight." Alex leans forward, resting his elbows on his knees. "I need to be sure you know what you're doing."

"You're not my father, Alex."

"I'm well aware of that."

"Then, why are we having this conversation?"

"Because you're both my friends."

"And?"

"I don't want to see anyone get hurt."

"Thanks a lot," I snap and stand from the couch, intending to walk away.

"Lana—" Alex reaches out to grab my arm.

"Don't Lana me," I say as I spin around. "I know what everyone thinks about me. Do you think I don't hear what they say?"

"That's not what I'm doing. I'm trying to look out for you."

"I don't need you prying into my personal business." Alex runs his hand through his hair and lets out a frustrated sigh. This argument is pointless. Instead of continuing down this path, I decide to shift the direction of the conversation, hoping I can convince Alex to give me some information. "How long have you known Brandon?"

Sometimes, when we're together, I see a haunted look come over Brandon's face, but as quickly as it comes, it's gone. I assume whatever it is would explain why he's apprehensive about pursuing a Dom/sub dynamic. He's told me a little about himself, but I sense there's something important he's holding back.

"Nine years or so."

"How long has he been going to Fire and Ice?"

"Why do you ask?"

"When we talked tonight, I was sure he would ask me to start vetting. Instead, he said he wasn't interested in a dynamic, and I'm curious why not."

"What did he tell you?"

"Nothing."

"Then you won't get anything else from me either."

"What happened to wanting to protect me?" I cross my arms.

"That's exactly what I'm doing." Alex takes a step back. "When Brandon's ready, he'll tell you himself."

"So, you admit there's something."

"Goodnight, Svetlana. I'll see you in the morning."

I let out a frustrated groan. These men are infuriating.

Brandon (Two Years Later)

I'M STARTLED AWAKE FROM A NIGHTMARE. SWEAT DRIPS from my forehead, and I'm breathing heavily. Nightmares about that night with Celia have plagued my dreams for the past two years—since I started dating Svetlana.

Getting out of bed, I open the door to my small balcony and step outside. The clear sky allows the full moon to illuminate the night. A warm breeze blows and makes my sweat-drenched skin feel cool. I can't shake the memory of Celia's face when I finally realized what was happening.

Celia's eyes water and mascara drips down her face as I fuck her mouth while Diablo thrusts himself into her ass. The scene is erotic as hell, and I come in her throat. Celia swallows everything I give and then, with long, slow drags of her tongue, licks me clean.

I step away while Diablo continues to thrust into her. I won't leave Celia alone, but I need a drink. Cracking the door open, I spot Angel. "Would you grab me a beer?"

"Sure."

Behind me, Diablo's still balls deep inside Celia. "Do you like being a whore?" he asks.

"I do, Diablo." Celia loves to be shared, especially with Diablo.

He grabs her hips and comes with a roar. He pulls out and smacks her ass before going into the attached bathroom.

"Here you go." Angel looks over my shoulder into the room. "Fuck, Brandon. She's smoking hot. Do you have room for anyone else?"

With my glass in hand, I walk over to Celia. "Are you good with adding one more?"

"Yes, Master," she says and licks her bottom lip.

I motion for him to join us.

Angel walks into the room and straight over to Celia. I chug the rest of my beer, watching Angel whisper to her while he strokes her hair.

Diablo returns from the restroom and gives Angel a nod. "Are you almost ready, Brandon?" he asks.

"I'll be there in a minute." My words come out slurred. That's odd. I've only had one beer.

Angel steps away from Celia and grabs a ball gag from the wall. I try to ask him what he's doing, but when I go to open my mouth, nothing happens. My legs feel weak, and blackness creeps into the edge of my vision until there's nothing but blackness and silence.

A shiver runs through me. It's over, I remind myself. Except when I considered entering a serious dynamic, I became paralyzed. I know I'm not the same person I was back then, but fear is a cage holding me hostage. Its bars are made of my insecurities and doubts.

Shortly after I expressed interest in Svetlana, Alex removed his collar of protection. The plan was we'd vet and enter a dynamic. I've thought about it non-stop since then but haven't brought it up again. Since she's not in a dynamic, other Dominants have approached her asking to enter vetting with her. Hell, I don't blame them. Svetlana's a brilliant young woman who's also stunning. She told me she'd wait, and so far, she's turned them all down. But how much longer will that last? I'm afraid she'll get sick of waiting for me to man up. That Lana will take one of those men up on their offer and leave me in her past.

There's nothing that can be done right now. So, I force myself to take deep breaths to slow my heart rate. Once I'm sure I'm calm, I go back to bed and fall into a now dreamless sleep.

Svetlana

Undergrad school is finally in our rearview mirror. After my parents flew back to Russia, Natalie and I traveled to Northmeadow with her parents, where we've spent the past month. When I say she comes from a narrow-minded small town, I'm not exaggerating. I've never seen anything like it.

Charlotte treats Natalie like she's a child who's incapable of making any decisions on her own. If Natalie tries to assert herself, she's reprimanded and reminded of her *place*. Each time that happens, I look at her father, who sits quietly on the sidelines. Quite frankly, I think he's afraid of his wife.

Then there's her boyfriend, Tommy. They've been dating since Natalie was fourteen. My mind is blown at the thought of being just shy of twenty-two and having only dated one guy. Her parents thing the sun rises and sets around this guy. But I see right through him, and in my opinion, I think he's a total asshole.

He makes her parents look like a dream. As far as he's concerned, Natalie has absolutely no voice. She's supposed to stand by his side, look pretty, keep her mouth shut, and do as she's told. I've tried to express my concerns, but she won't hear it. This is all she knows. To her, it's normal. Which is a sad reality.

Tommy blew a gasket when he found out she was coming to Russia for a few weeks with me. That's when I went behind Natalie's back and stepped in. Tommy was sitting on her parents' front porch while Natalie was helping Charlotte make dinner.

"Do you mind if I sit?" I ask and motion to the empty spot on the porch swing.

"Shouldn't you be in the kitchen with the women making dinner?"

"Charlotte and Natalie have it under control," I say sweetly. "I wanted to talk to you."

"About what?" He doesn't bother looking up from his phone.

"About the trip Natalie's taking to Russia."

His head pops up, and he glares at me. "She's not going to Russia."

"There's where you're wrong. Tomorrow morning, we're flying back to JFK, and from there, we're going to St. Petersburg."

"I already told her she's staying here."

"And I'm telling you that's not happening." I stand up and point my finger in his face. "You may be able to silence Natalie, but you can't silence me."

"Who the fuck do you think you are?" Tommy asks, raising his voice. "Natalie belongs to me, and she'll do as I say."

The front door swings open, and Pyotr steps out. "Is there a problem out here?"

"Not at all." I put my hand on Pyotr's arm. "I was just telling Tommy that Natalie and I are leaving for home tomorrow, and he's not standing in the way of our plans."

Tommy stands and gets in my face. "And I was just telling Svetlana to fuck off."

Pyotr steps forward and nudges me out of the way. "I suggest you change your tone, or I'll change it for you."

"Dinner's—" Natalie steps onto the porch and stops mid-sentence as she looks between the three of us. "What's going on?"

"Tommy was just asking what time our flight leaves tomorrow," I say, not breaking eye contact with him. "He didn't know if we needed a ride to the airport."

"My parents are going to drop us off," she responds, taking Tommy's hand. "Do you want to come for the ride to see me off?"

Tommy pulls his hand from hers. "I have plans," he says and walks into the house.

The smile fades from Natalie's face. "He's worried about me going to Russia," she says nervously.

"I'm sure that's all it is," I lie, afraid if I tell her the truth, she'll back out of the trip.

"Dinner's ready."

"We'll be in in a minute."

I wait for Natalie to go inside and ensure she's out of hearing distance before turning to Pyotr. "Can you believe that guy? What a piece of shit."

"He better watch his step tonight. I've about had enough of him."

"Please don't do anything. We just need to get through tonight and get on the plane tomorrow."

Dinner was tense, but that's not out of the ordinary. It's clear Charlotte is as unhappy with my presence as Tommy is. Thankfully, Tommy went home early last night, and according to Natalie, she hasn't heard from him today. In my opinion, that's for the best. Once we land in Russia, I'm hoping she forgets all about him.

After a nearly thirteen-hour flight, the wheels of Papa's jet finally come to a stop on a private airstrip at the Pulkovo Airport. I see a familiar black Escalade parked a short distance away and know my parents are already here. It feels so good to be home.

"I'm nervous," Natalie says between biting her finger nails.

"What for?"

"All of this." She motions out the window. "Until now, New York City was the furthest I've traveled. I never imagined I'd be in Russia."

I've been trying to get her to come home with me since we first met, but she's always had an excuse why she couldn't. When I was home for the winter break, Papa jumped on our video chat to insist Natalie come stay with us over the summer—to celebrate the end of one journey and the beginning of another. He tends to be pretty insistent, and Natalie was unable to say no. Once we were both back in New York, we worked on getting her a passport so she'd be all ready to travel come summer.

"You're going to love St. Petersburg. Come on." I grab her hand. "I can't wait to see my parents."

Papa's already waiting at the bottom of the steps when the door opens. I hurry down and nearly throw myself at him.

"*Moya babochka*, I have missed you," Papa says while hugging me tight. Unlike many other Eastern European men, he's never been afraid to show emotion or affection.

"I've missed you too."

"Let me look at you." He holds me away from him. "You look well. Happy."

"Thank you. I feel good, too." I look over my shoulder and motion for Natalie to come closer.

"Natalia, it's a pleasure seeing you again," Papa says, surprising her by wrapping her in a hug.

"You as well, Mr. Solonik."

"You must call me Maxim."

"Yes, sir."

The corner of Papa's mouth lifts in a smile. "Come. Let us get you girls home."

While we walk to the car, Pyotr and Misha grab our bags and put them in the back of the SUV.

"Where's Mama?"

"There was an emergency at work."

"Is everything okay?"

"It will be," Papa says as he slides into the front seat.

Once the car is loaded, Misha begins the drive home. It's about an hour before the familiar St. Petersburg sites come into view.

"Svetlana," Natalie says, grabbing my arm. "It's breathtaking."

Tserkov' Spasa na Krovi is lit up, highlighting its iconic onion domes. I didn't realize how much I missed the comforting sights I grew up seeing until they weren't part of the landscape I looked out on every day.

"We'll go see it while we're here. The inside is even more beautiful."

Natalie nods but doesn't look away from the window, watching the beautiful historic architecture that makes up St. Petersburg pass by. As we emerge from the other side of the city, the sights morph into large and equally stunning homes.

Misha slows to a stop at the guard house that sits on the perimeter of our property. The guard on duty gives a slight wave as the tall wrought iron gates open, and Misha drives through.

"Where are we?" Natalie whispers.

"Home."

"You live here?" she asks, eyes wide.

"Yes."

I look at our house and try to see it through Natalie's eyes. A sprawling three-story limestone home sits at the end of a winding drive-way. Mahogany double doors are flanked on each side by two pillars. Pristinely manicured greenery lines the front. I've never taken the time to really look at the place I was raised. It's always been just home to me, but for the first time, I see the opulent beauty and realize how lucky I am.

Misha's just shut the car off when the front door flies open, and Mama rushes out. I jump out of the car quickly and run into her embrace.

"I missed you so much."

"Not as much as I missed you." She kisses me on both cheeks. "I'm sorry I didn't make it to pick you up."

"Is everything okay at work?" I ask, concerned.

"It is now." Mama looks over my shoulder and smiles. "Let me go say hello to my other girl." She pulls Natalie in for a hug.

"Thank you so much for inviting me to your home, Mrs. Solonik."

"Irina, please. And we're so glad you're here. Come on in and get settled."

Natalie follows us into the house and lets out a gasp.

"Is everything okay, Natalia?" Papa asks from behind us.

"Your home. I've never seen anything like it."

The foyer is a grand space. The centerpiece is the sweeping Carrara marble staircase that gleams under the light of the crystal chandelier hanging from the high ceiling. At the top of the steps is a balcony. It's one of my favorite spots in our house. On the walls hang centuries-old artwork my parents have collected. The floor is an intricately crafted mosaic made of precious stones, including Jade, Carnelian, Amethyst, Quartz, and Lapis Lazuli.

"It is older than most anything you will find in America."

"Now I'm embarrassed," Natalie says, turning to me.

"Why?"

"For having you stay at our house when you're used to living here."

"Don't be silly. I love going home with you."

I've stayed at Natalie's parents' home several times over the past few years. Natalie says her house is a farmhouse, even though they don't have a proper farm. Something that's always confused me. They do have a relatively large piece of land where Charlotte spends a great deal of time caring for her flower and vegetable gardens during the summer months. Despite the house being older and slightly run down, it's comfortable.

"Come on, I'll show you to your room." I thread my arm through hers and lead her up the staircase.

Brandon

Lana's picture flashes on my screen as the phone rings. "Hello?" I hear her voice a second before the video connects.

"Hi there," Lana says. "I hope I didn't call at a bad time."

"Not at all. Did you just get in?"

"About an hour ago. Papa insisted we have a bite to eat before going to bed." She smiles.

"How did Natalie do?"

"She seems a bit overwhelmed, but I think she'll be okay. It's good for her to get away and see the world."

Although I've yet to meet Natalie, Lana's told me about her parents and boyfriend. I'm not impressed with anything I hear. For people who claim to love her, they're incredibly controlling.

"What time is it there?" I ask.

"Almost two a.m."

"We should keep this short. You must be exhausted."

"Sleep isn't in my near future. My body's all messed up. It thinks I'm still in New York." Lana bites her lip. "I was hoping you and I could spend some time together."

"I see." Even though she's not here, my dick is hard as I imagine the possibilities. "Do you have anything in mind?"

"I do." The camera shakes, and I momentarily have a view of the floor while she props it on the dresser. I travel quite a bit for work, so we've played long-distance plenty of times, but it never grows old.

"Butterfly" by Crazy Town plays in the background, and Lana steps into view. One by one, she sheds each piece of clothing as her hips move to the beat of the music. While I watch her strip tease, I pull my T-shirt over my head and open my pants, freeing my cock. Her hands go to her breasts, kneading the flesh and playing with her nipples. She slides one hand down her toned abdomen to her neatly pussy.

"Are you wet for me?"

Lana's finger disappears between her legs. She drags it languidly along her slit. "Very."

"I wish I was there to taste you." I pump my hand up and down, imagining it's Lana's lips wrapped around me.

Bringing her finger to her mouth, she teases the tip with her tongue like she does to my cock. I groan, wishing it was my mouth on her. She reaches behind her and holds up the purple vibrator we've used in the past when she's been away.

I go to pull the app up and am distracted when I hear a feminine voice in the background.

"Lana, are you awake?"

"Yes. I'll be there in a minute," she calls.

"Who's that?"

"It's Natalie," Lana answers as she grabs a robe and hides the vibrator under her blanket. "I'll call you back."

The call ends, and I drop my head back and groan. Natalie's timing was horrible, but I'm too far gone to stop now. With my free hand, I find the private folder I have on my phone and pull up the video Lana and I made the last time we were together.

Svetlana's spread out over my dining table with my head buried between her legs. I'm eating her like a starving man while my fingers thrust inside her. She's panting and moaning as I bring her to the edge countless times before I curl my fingers inside her, and she explodes on my tongue.

Before her orgasm is finished, I flip her over and pull her feet to the floor. With her bent over, I thrust inside her and fuck her hard and fast.

My hand moves, matching my pace on the video until I'm spurting waves of hot cum. It takes the edge off, but my hand is no replacement for Svetlana.

Me: Dream of me, *Mon petit papillon.*

Then, I take a cool shower, hoping to calm my body. Being apart gets more difficult every day.

Svetlana

I ADJUST MY ROBE AND RUN MY FINGERS THROUGH MY HAIR before I open the door.

"Did I wake you?" Natalie asks.

"No. I was getting ready to take a bath."

"I'm sorry. I'll go back to—"

"It can wait." I step aside. "Come on in. Is everything okay?"

"I don't know." She lets out a frustrated sigh.

"Want to talk about it?" I sit on the bottom of my bed.

"It's Tommy." Natalie joins me. "We just hung up. He's really upset."

"Why?" I resist the urge to roll my eyes.

"Tommy thought we'd get to spend more time together before he had to go back to school."

"You were home for a month, and he was barely around."

"He's been picking up a lot of hours at the pharmacy. He needs the extra money, and Dad plans on having Tommy take it over one day."

If it were anyone other than Natalie, I'd be furious that she's making up excuses for his behavior. The problem is Natalie believes everything she's saying. She's been sheltered all her life—brainwashed, in my opinion. She's learned to accept that she has no voice in her own life. That this is how a healthy relationship works, but she couldn't be further from the truth. Showing her otherwise is a tricky scenario. If I push too much, I'm afraid I'll alienate her, and that's the last thing I want to do.

It's taken years, but Natalie's beginning to loosen up a little. She's gone shopping with me and now owns some more *normal* clothes like jeans and shorter skirts. I even convinced her to go to dinner and a Broadway show with me.

Natalie did well until we returned to Northmeadow at the beginning of summer break. Her demeanor shifted back to mousey, and she left all her new clothes in New York, choosing only to wear ankle-length skirts and blouses that even my *babushka* wouldn't have worn.

"I think he'll survive."

"He was crying."

"Why?"

"Tommy's going back to school next week. Football practice starts. We won't see each other until Thanksgiving."

"He's not even going to be there, and he's giving you a hard time?"

"You don't have a boyfriend. You wouldn't understand." She flops back on my pillow. "Ouch. There's something." Before I can stop her, she's reaching under my blanket. "What's... Oh my God." She holds the silicone dildo in front of her. I grab it and toss it in my top dresser drawer. "Is that what I think it is?" Natalie's cheeks are flaming red.

"It's a sex toy," I say matter-of-factly.

Natalie jumps off the bed and hurries to the door. "I think I should go back to my room."

"You don't have to go."

"I didn't know you had," she hesitates. "That thing."

"There's nothing to be embarrassed about." I try to explain. "It's perfectly normal to have toys and to use them."

"I'll take your word on that. Thank you for the chat, but I think I should probably try to get some sleep now." She hurries from my room.

"Nat, wait," I say before she gets too far down the hall. She stops and turns around. "There's a whole world out there waiting for you to explore it. Please don't let Tommy hold you back." The words are out of my mouth before I can stop them.

"I'll see you in the morning." Natalie goes into her room, closing the door behind her.

This time, it's me knocking on Natalie's door. "Come in," she calls.

After the way things ended last night, I'm nervous about how things will go today. "Good morning."

"Morning."

"Are you hungry? Breakfast is almost ready."

"I'm starving, actually." Natalie smiles.

"Come on. I'll show you where the kitchen is." We walk down the hallway to a second staircase at the back of the house. "Olga isn't here today, but even when she is, you're more than welcome to go in and grab a snack."

"Who's Olga?"

"She's our chef."

"You have a chef?"

"She not formally trained, but she could outcook any of those people on the American TV cooking shows." I hold the door to the kitchen open. "Here we are."

"Good morning, girls," Mama says as she opens the oven, pulling out a tray.

"Morning," we answer in unison.

"How did you sleep, Natalie?"

"Not the best. You know, the first night in a new place." She shrugs.

"That's understandable." Mama smiles. "I hope you both brought your appetites. I made *Vatrushka* and Lana's favorite, *Syrniki*."

"I'm not sure what either of those are, but they smell heavenly. Is there anything I can do to help?"

"Would you carry that one to the table?" Mama points to a platter filled with preserves, sweet sour cream, and maple syrup.

"Sure."

Natalie takes the filled platter, and I grab the plate of *Syrniki*. We make our way into the dining room. "Morning, Papa."

"Good morning, *moya babochka*." He kisses my cheek. "Good morning, Natalia."

"Good morning, mister, I mean, Maxim."

Mama enters the room with the fresh pastries, and we all get settled at the table. One of the ways Mama honors Papa's place as her Dominant is to make his plate before anyone else is served. Natalie watches curiously, and I wonder what she's thinking.

Once Papa's plate is set before him, I don't waste any time grabbing some of the steaming pancakes. "I've missed these so much," I say as I fill my plate. "Our kitchen's very tiny, and the stove hardly works. We end up using the microwave more than I care to admit."

"Then you will be all the more pleased with the surprise I have for you."

"A surprise?"

"In honor of the next step in your educational journey, I've rented an apartment in Greenwich Village for you and Natalia."

"For real?"

"Do I usually joke?"

"Oh my gosh. I can't believe it." I jump up and wrap my arms around his neck. "This is amazing. Isn't it Nat?"

"You didn't have to include me," she says in disbelief.

"We didn't have to. We wanted to." Mama covers Natalie's hand with hers, giving it a slight squeeze. "You're part of our family now."

"I have already contacted your school and arranged everything with the bursar's office. Your belongings are being moved into your new apartment this week."

"We don't have to live in a tiny dorm anymore," I squeal.

"I don't even know what to say," Natalie adds. "I have no way to repay your kindness."

"Your smile is enough," Papa says.

My parents have visited us in New York on several occasions. Each time, they comment that Natalie always appears nervous. I've told them a little about where she comes from and how she's treated by her parents and boyfriend. It's helped them to better understand why she's so reserved.

"I can't wait to tell my parents."

"You might want to wait on that call. It is the middle of the night for them," Papa chuckles.

"Oh yeah, the time difference. I almost forgot."

While we finish breakfast, Papa shows us pictures of the apartment he has saved on his cell. It has two bedrooms and two and a half bathrooms. It's huge, especially for New York City standards. The recent renovations reflect a sleek and modern style.

Not having to live on campus is something I didn't see coming. I'm surprised and elated that Papa is allowing it. I've put a big focus on personal growth, and I can only hope he sees that I've grown and matured since coming to New York.

Brandon

CELIA'S MUFFLED SCREAMS PIERCE THE DARKNESS, BUT I can't reach her. I struggle to open my eyes. To chase away the suffocating blackness I'm shrouded in. When I finally pry my lids open, everything around me is fuzzy. Celia's cries are louder—closer.

With painstaking slowness, the scene around me comes into focus, and what I see horrifies me. Angel, Diablo, and several other men I don't recognize huddle around Celia. Some are stroking their erect cocks while they watch the others take their turns with their unwilling victim.

What the hell is wrong with me? I try to move, but my limbs feel like lead weights. My efforts to move them are in vain. I open my mouth to yell something, anything to make them stop, but no sound comes out.

"Hey guys," Angel says, pointing at me. "Look who's awake."

"Now he can watch how a real man fucks a woman," Diablo says, laughing.

Time passes in agonizing increments while I'm trapped in a useless body, watching my girlfriend being tortured. I watch as her head drops. Her cries are no more. It's as though she's resigned herself to her fate. I beg my body to cooperate. First, a finger moves, then a toe. Little by little, my body and mind become one again, and I pull myself to an upright position.

"Get the fuck away from her." My voice cracks as I speak. "I said get the fuck away from her."

"What are you planning to do about it?" One of the men says while he thrusts inside Celia.

I sway on my feet and grab the nearest thing to me. Despite my best efforts, I fall to my knees.

"Forget about him," Diablo says. "He won't be interfering any time soon."

Celia turns to look at me. Her beautiful blue eyes are red and swollen from crying, but the fact that she appears miles away scares me. I grab the table and again get to my feet, my legs a little stronger than before. She watches my every move as I reach into my bag and pull out my gun. It's illegal for me to have it in here, but I don't care. I don't leave the house without it. And this is why.

"I'm not going to say it again. Get the fuck away from Celia." I click the safety off. The sound echoes in the small room. The men stop what they're doing and look at one another.

"There's no need for a gun, Brandon," Angel says. "We're just having some fun with her."

"It's not fucking fun when she's not given consent."

"You know what a whore she is. She's loving it." He cackles.

His comment infuriates me. Everything in me itches to pull the trigger. It's only the terrified look on Celia's face that stops me. I don't want to traumatize her any further. "Remove the gag." When no one moves, I yell, "Now."

Angel unbuckles the gag, and it falls to the floor.

"Ask her."

"What are you talking about?"

"Ask her if this is what she wants."

"Come on, Brand. There's no need for this. We'll get our stuff and get out of here." Angel looks at the other men in the room. "Get your things, and let's go." The men, in various stages of undress, replace their clothes.

My hand trembles, but I don't take my finger off the trigger until the last man leaves.

"Brandon," she says my name softly. "I think they hurt the baby." Her head drops as she loses consciousness.

The baby? Reengaging the safety, I rush over to her. "Cece, talk to me," I say as I frantically untie her. "What baby?" Gently, I roll her onto her back. Her bruised body is limp, but it's the blood pooling beneath her that scares me the most. "Fuck." I find my pants and pull out my cell, and dial 911.

"What's your emergency?"

"My girlfriend was assaulted. Raped. She needs your help."

"What's the address?"

I rattle off the address and drop my phone. I find my discarded T-shirt on the floor and carefully pull it over Celia's head. "I'm here, Cece. Everything's going to be okay." I talk to her while I put my pants on. Her eyes don't open. She doesn't stir. "God. Please let her be okay."

It feels like an eternity before the paramedics are pounding on the door. "I'll be right back." I carefully lower her head to the floor to let them in. "She's over here. Hurry, please."

The EMTs crowd around Celia, leaving no room for me. "Is she going to be okay?" No one answers. Their focus is solely on her.

I watch as they load the stretcher into the back of the ambulance. They start to close the doors, and I step forward. "Can I ride with her?"

They look at each other before answering. "I'm sorry. We can only allow family—"

"I'm her fiancé," I interrupt.

"Go ahead," an older male says. "She's going to need a familiar face when she wakes up."

We're halfway to the hospital when her eyes blink open. "Brand?" she asks.

"I'm here, Cece." I jump from my seat, earning a disapproving look from the paramedic who's taking her vitals, and take Celia's hand in mine.

"Where am I?"

"You're in the ambulance on the way to the hospital." Her eyes close once again. I look at the man. "Is she okay?"

"She's lost a lot of blood."

"You can't leave me," I whisper. "Please hang on, Cece."

The doctor forces me to wait outside the treatment room while they work to stabilize Celia and collect a rape kit. I pace back and forth in the hall outside her door, praying she's okay. The door opens, and I spin around, but instead of the doctor, it's a female police officer.

"Are you Ms. Baldwin's fiancé?" she asks.

"I am."

"And your name is?"

"Brandon. Brandon Carpenter." She writes my name in her small notebook.

"I'm Officer Weber. I'd like to ask you a few questions."

"Okay. Whatever you need."

"There's a private waiting room down here." She starts walking, but I don't follow.

"Can't we talk here? I don't want to leave Celia."

"Brandon," she says softly. "This is a sensitive subject that shouldn't be discussed in the hallway. You can come right back to her as soon as we're through." I nod and follow her into the room, where we get settled in the cold and uncomfortable hospital chairs. "Can you tell me what you remember from tonight?"

Tears slip down my face as I recount the details. "We had a written agreement with Diablo about what would and would not happen tonight. Angel was the only thing we didn't discuss beforehand, but I asked Cece, and she said he could join us." Officer Weber writes down everything I'm saying. Then, I explain what I saw when I woke up. "I shouldn't have had the beer." I drop my head into my hands.

"How many drinks did you have?"

"One." I look up. "Only one."

"And you blacked out?"

"Yes."

"Would you consent to a blood test?" she asks.

"Yes. I'll do whatever I need to."

"I suspect your drink may have been drugged." She scribbles something

in her notebook before continuing. "Can you tell me the names of the men you saw assaulting Ms. Baldwin?"

"Angel Vega and Diablo. Shit." I look at Officer Weber. "I don't know what his real name is."

There's no judgment in her tone when she asks, "Was there anyone else?"

"There were three other men, but I don't know who they were. I've never seen them before."

"Do you know where I can find Mr. Vega and Diablo?"

I give the officer Angel's contact information. "I don't know where to find Diablo. We only communicate when we're at Chains."

"Is there anything else you want to add?"

"I didn't mean for this to happen. I love Celia."

Officer Weber offers me a kind smile. "Let's go find the doctor to get your labs done."

I follow her back down the hall to the nurses' station. She talks quietly with the man there.

"Mr. Carpenter," she says, getting my attention. "This is Bill. He's a physician's assistant and will draw your blood."

"Okay."

"Thank you again for your cooperation," Officer Weber says. "I'll be in touch."

After my lab work, I return to Celia's room and find the door cracked open. I walk in and see Celia awake. A nurse is standing by the bed, checking a monitor.

"Brandon," Celia says my name quietly.

"You're awake." I force a smile as I walk over to her.

"If you need anything, just push the red button," the nurse explains, leaving us alone.

Sitting on the edge of her bed, I take her hand in mine. "How are you feeling?" Tears spill over her eyelids. "Don't cry, Cece."

"I'm so sorry, Brand," her voice cracks.

"There's nothing for you to apologize for."

"I was pregnant. I was going to tell you after our scene tonight. But I lost the baby." Celia's body is wracked with sobs. "I'm so sorry."

Pregnant.

A baby.

Our baby.

"Please say something," Celia begs, but no words come. I'm in shock, trying to process what she said. "Are you mad at me?"

"No," I say quickly and take her face in mine. "I could never be mad at you."

"I just found out. I was going to tell you. I promise. I wanted it to be a surprise," she says without taking a breath.

"Shh. It's okay."

"I'm sorry to interrupt," the doctor says as he enters the room. "I was able to reach your parents. They're on their way, but I don't want to wait to take you to the OR."

"The OR?"

The doctor pulls up a chair as he patiently explains everything. "Celia is still bleeding heavily. Part of that is from the trauma of the assault. I also suspect there is remaining tissue in her uterus." Celia clings to my hand. "She and I discussed taking a wait-and-see approach or having the procedure."

"I opted for the surgery," she says quietly.

"Is it dangerous?"

"It's a fairly routine procedure. Like any surgery, there are risks, but they're minimal."

"I'll be okay, Brandon. Will you wait here for my parents?"

"Yes, of course."

"Are you ready?" She nods. "We'll be back in a minute to take you to the OR."

We only have a minute before several nurses enter the room. Everything happens quickly as they transfer Celia to a portable stretcher and push her out of the room.

I stand in the hallway helplessly as I watch them wheel Celia away from me.

Brandon

Work has been nothing short of torturous this morning. My mind focuses more on Svetlana than the accounts in front of me. Which is why I'm shocked when I finish typing this email and find I'm caught up on everything.

Me: Are you busy?

Alex: No, why?

Me: I'll be over in a min. I need to talk to you.

Lana and I have been dating one another, but we've not made any further steps toward a Dominant/submissive dynamic, and I'd like that to change. I'm ready to take the next step and begin vetting each other. I've written up a loose outline for a contract. I'm hoping she and I can discuss it and take the next step toward becoming an official Dom/sub couple.

I grab the manilla folder and cut through the conference room to Alex's office.

While he looks over the document, I sit on his couch, tapping my fingers on my leg. "What do you think?"

"It's a good starting point," he says as he finishes the last page. "It should be fine."

"Good."

"I thought you didn't want another dynamic. What made you change your mind?"

Since we first met, so much has changed in my life and Lana's. She's the first woman I've ever opened up to about what happened that night with Celia. I was certain Lana would be disgusted and walk away, but she didn't. She cried with me for Celia and everything we lost that night. Instead of putting a wedge between us, it brought us closer together.

I still had to face a hurdle but didn't know how.

"I bumped into Celia a few months ago," I confess.

"I thought she left town."

"She did. She and her husband flew in from Texas to visit her parents."

"Her husband?" Alex lifts his eyebrow. "How did that go?"

It's late, and I'm hungry. I don't want to cook, so I walk the few blocks to get a tray of Krispy's pizza. I'm distracted watching a video on my cell while I pull the restaurant's door open.

"Brandon?"

The familiar voice steals the breath from my lungs.

"Celia? What are you doing here?"

"We're visiting my parents." I look behind her and spot a tall man holding a sleeping baby close to his chest. "Brandon, this is my husband, Donovan."

"It's nice to meet you," Donovan says. "I've heard a lot about you."

That can't be good. Part of me wants to turn and run.

"Van, do you mind going back without me. I want to talk to Brandon."

"Sure." He kisses her cheek and walks away.

"I should've asked you first," she says. "Do you mind company?"

"Not at all." My eyes follow her husband as he disappears around the corner. "You have a baby."

"Clover's our youngest. We also have a two-year-old boy, Jax." Pain squeezes my heart like a vice. "I'm sorry. I didn't mean to upset you."

"You haven't." I manage a small smile. "Do you want to walk to the park?"

"Didn't you come here to eat?"

I suddenly have no appetite. "It can wait."

Celia and I walk a few blocks in silence. I haven't seen her in over ten years, but she hasn't changed. She's still petite with long, silky black hair and eyes that are the color of the sky on a cloudless day. So many thoughts go through my mind, but I can't voice any of them.

"How have you been?" she asks when we get to the park entrance.

"I'm well. How about you?"

"I'm doing good."

We continue further to the other side of the park, where there's a lone bench. In front of us, the water from Gravesend Bay laps onto the rocky shore. Off to one side, the Verazzano Bridge lights up the evening sky. When we were teenagers, we spent so much time sitting here. Celia would curl up against my side while we dreamt about our future together. The future we didn't get to have.

"How are your parents?" I ask as we sit.

"Mom's doing well. Dad, not so much." She looks down at her hands folded in her lap. "He was diagnosed with cancer."

"I didn't know that. Is it bad?"

"Yes," she says quietly. "It's pancreatic cancer, but it's metastasized to his bones."

"What can I do?" I ask, instinctively reaching for her hand but pulling away at the last second. I'm no longer a high school kid with no resources. I make more money than I can spend. "I'll have a doctor brought in to consult on—"

"That's very kind." Celia touches my arm. "Donovan already had a colleague review his case. There's nothing that can be done."

"Your husband's a doctor?"

"He's a pediatric neurosurgeon."

"I see."

"That's why we came in. Dad doesn't have much time left."

"I'm so sorry, Cece."

"No one's called me that in a very long time." We sit silently for several seconds before she asks, "Are you married?"

"No," I answer quickly. "I don't think I'm marriage material."

"Why would you say something like that?"

"You, of all people, know the answer to that."

"Brandon, you are not responsible for what happened that night." I get

up and walk a few steps away. Celia follows and moves to stand in front of me. "You were as much a victim as me." I shake my head. She reaches out and touches my face with her hand. "Bran, look at me, please." I shift my gaze down to her. "I don't blame you for anything that happened. You need to stop blaming yourself and move forward."

"How can you say that?"

"Because I know you're a good man. We were both young and stupid—and we paid a steep price for our foolishness."

"I was supposed to protect you."

"And you did."

"After you were hurt doesn't count."

"Of course, it counts. I would've died in that room if it wasn't for you."

"Things would be so different today if I hadn't—"

"Shh." Celia places her delicate finger against my lips. "We're exactly where we're supposed to be right now."

Instinctively, I wrap my arms around her tiny frame and pull her against my chest. She doesn't resist. Instead, she puts her arms around me and rests her head against my body. Lowering my face, I kiss the top of her head. Her hair still smells like strawberries. I close my eyes and allow the happy memories of our past to wash over me, remembering all the other times I held her in this exact spot.

"I've missed the feel of your arms around me," Celia says, her voice catching on a sob.

"Does he treat you well?" I ask, tears trailing down my face.

"He does. Donovan loves me and is a good father to our children."

All these years, I've worried that Celia had to live with the memory of being raped. Of knowing the life she carried inside her died in that room. "Are you happy?"

"I am." She looks up at me. "But a piece of my heart has always been yours. It will always belong to you."

"And mine yours." I hear footsteps and spin around, pulling Celia protectively behind me.

"Sorry, I didn't mean to startle you," Donovan says with his hands up.

"What are you doing here?" Celia asks, stepping out from my protective hold.

"I didn't want you walking back in the dark by yourself. Your mom *said I'd probably find you here." He looks between the two of us. "Is everything okay?"*

"It is." I attempt to reassure him.

"Clover's starting to fuss. She's getting hungry," he explains. "Are you ready to go?"

"Give me one more minute."

"Sure." Donovan walks away, giving us a few more minutes of privacy.

"I'm glad we bumped into each other," Celia says. "Can I give you my number so we can keep in touch?"

"I can't— I don't think that's a good idea, Cece. I can't be in your life and not be with you." I glance over to where Donovan is waiting for his wife. "There's someone I met a while ago. I've been holding back, but I think now's the time to take the next step with her."

"I understand," Celia says, using the backs of her hands to wipe her face. "Whoever the woman is. She's very lucky to have your heart." Then, she stands on her tiptoes and gently kisses my cheek before she turns and goes to her husband.

He says something quietly to her. She nods and threads her fingers with his. They walk away, leaving me standing there, alone.

"I'm glad you saw her," Alex says. "Hopefully, now that she's told you the same things we've been saying for years, you'll listen."

"You're one to talk." Alex has sworn off relationships and love.

"We're not here to talk about me." He holds up the contract. "This is about you and Lana."

"Right," I chuckle. "I'll talk to her when she comes back from visiting her parents."

"That's a great idea."

Lana hasn't brought up the idea of a contract since we met, and for a long time, that was okay with me. I was living in the past and drowning in guilt. There was so much that was wrong about that night at Chains. Things I had no idea about at the time.

It wasn't until I met Alex and started going to Fire and Ice that I learned about the BDSM lifestyle for what it really is. What I experienced there was the complete opposite of everything I saw and did at

Chains. I've always been a Dominant but feared making a lasting commitment.

That chance meeting with Celia was something I desperately needed. She is the only one who was able to grant me true forgiveness. The kind I needed to forgive myself. That night marked a new beginning for me as a Dominant.

Svetlana

Pyotr trails behind Natalie and me as we sightsee in St. Petersburg. Today, we're spending the afternoon at The State Hermitage Museum. It's the second-largest art museum in the world and has over three million pieces in its collection. I haven't been here since I was a schoolgirl, so I'm enjoying it as much as Natalie.

"Your parents are wonderful," she says. "They're still so much in love with each other, and they're so easy to talk to. I wish my parents were more like them."

"I'm fortunate to have been raised with their example." Their relationship is the model for what I hope to have one day.

"I hope one day Tommy looks at me like your father looks at your mother," Natalie says wistfully. "I guess that's something that comes with time."

"Did you ever consider that Tommy might not be the right one?" I ask without taking my eyes off the painting on the wall.

"What do you mean?"

"Maybe you should go on a few dates while you're away at school?"

"That would be cheating." Natalie looks horrified.

"Not if you tell him you're doing it," I explain. "Tommy's the only guy you've ever dated. I know you plan on marrying him, but I think you should get some more experience before you take that step."

"I can't believe you're saying this." She picks up the pace of her walking.

"I didn't mean to upset you," I say as I catch up to her.

"What did you think my reaction would be?"

"I hoped you'd see reason."

"Tommy loves me. We've never dated anyone else, and I'm just fine with keeping it that way."

"You're positive he's not seeing anyone while he's away at school?"

"Of course, he isn't. He'd never cheat on me."

"I'm sorry. I don't want to fight about Tommy or upset you."

"I love him, Lan. And he loves me."

"The only thing that really matters is that you're happy."

"I am." Natalie smiles.

"Then, I'm happy." I link my arm with hers, and we walk to the next exhibit.

I'm far from an expert on relationships. Lord knows I've done my fair share of screwing up in that department. I guess I should be happy she's seeing an example of a healthy relationship. Hopefully, it's something she'll continue to think about and compare it to her relationship with Tommy.

Natalie's enjoying time in the sun by the outdoor pool while I'm in my room. Everyone suspects I've come up to call a guy. And it is, but not the way they all think. In reality, my phone call is to have a long-distance session with my therapist, Grayson.

After a particularly loud and intense fight with Alex, Star pulled me aside for a heart-to-heart talk about my attitude. At first, I was defensive, assuming she was going to tell me why I was wrong and why Alex was right. That was part of the conversation because, like it or not, Alex was right. But instead of lecturing me, she told me a story about a submissive she knew many years ago.

The girl was gorgeous, which attracted the attention of many Dominants. But every dynamic she entered ended in failure. The problem—the girl could never get her attitude under control. She was disrespectful to all of her Dominants, making them look bad in front of the rest of the community. She didn't respond to their correction and was always released. Several experienced Domme's and submissives approached her, trying to mentor her. They wanted to see her succeed, but she wouldn't take advice from anyone. In the end, she walked away from the lifestyle.

Star told me I reminded her so much of that girl. That I have a lot of potential to be a good submissive, but I need to work on myself. She explained that before I could submit to a Dominant in a meaningful way, I needed to be strong and confident in myself.

Her words struck a chord in my heart, and I let my guard down enough to take the constructive advice. She put me in touch with a kink-friendly therapist, something I'd never heard of. I called him the next day and started therapy that week. The twist is I didn't tell Alex or Brandon anything about it. Not because I was ashamed or wanted to hide it, though.

The last time I spoke to Masha, she opened my eyes to the fact that I never truly let my guard down when I saw her. Because of that, I didn't make any real progress toward the goals we set. This time, I promised myself I'd be completely honest with my therapist and, most importantly, myself. My hope was the people around me would eventually see a change. And that's exactly what's happened.

About six months after I started my sessions, Alex removed his collar of protection.

When I get to Alex's house, I'm surprised to find him sitting on his sofa. "What are you doing here?"

"I live here."

"Very funny. You know what I mean."

"I left the office early. I want to do something before we go to the club tonight." He pats the couch. "Come sit down."

"Okay," I say hesitantly as I take a seat.

"We've gotten to know one another quite well. Don't you agree?" Alex asks.

"Yes."

"When you first came, I seriously doubted if we'd make it until you moved into the dorm. When you did, the oddest thing happened."

I wait for him to tell me, but he says nothing. "Well, what happened?"

"I missed having you around." He laughs, and I join him. "You've come a long way from the impulsive and argumentative girl you were."

"Thank you. I think."

Alex takes a deep breath. "It's time to remove your collar."

His words shock me, and my hand instinctively reaches for the chain around my neck. Why?"

"You no longer need it."

When Alex first put his collar around my neck, I thought I'd suffocate under its weight. I hated it and wanted to tear it off, but I knew if I did, Papa would find out, and I'd be on his jet returning to Russia. But now I've grown used to it—like it even. The thought of being without it is scary. "What do you mean? Aren't you supposed to be protecting me? I don't have a Dominant—"

"Svetlana," Alex interrupts me. "You no longer need the collar. That doesn't change the fact that I'll always be your friend and will be the first, well maybe the second in line, to protect you."

I carry Alex's collar with me all the time. It's a physical reminder that I'm never alone.

That night, Alex said he noticed a new sense of maturity and complimented the personal growth I showed both in and out of the club. At that point, I confided in him about going to therapy. The look of pride on his face is something I'll never forget.

"Svetlana," Gray says when the video connects. "How are you?"

"I'm doing well. Thanks for asking."

"Are you enjoying your trip home?"

"I am. I didn't realize how much I missed it here. Being around familiar sights and sounds is really nice."

"Is there anything specific you'd like to address today?" Gray always gives me a choice as to how the session will proceed.

"Brandon asked me again about introducing him to my friends."

"What did you say?"

"I told him I wasn't ready yet."

"Can you help me understand your reasoning?" he asks and jots something down.

"I like to keep my circle small, so I don't feel they need to know that much about me."

"That's fair."

"And part of me is embarrassed."

"Why?" he asks with genuine curiosity.

"I think Brandon thinks I'm some popular girl with tons of friends. I don't know what he'll think if he finds out that, with the exception of Natalie, there's no one else."

"Do you really think he'll care?" I shrug. "From everything you've told me about Brandon, I don't think the quantity of your friends is important."

"Even if he doesn't, Natalie is a whole other kind of issue."

"What does he know about her?" Gray asks.

"We've discussed Natalie. He knows I love her dearly, and she's my closest friend. I've explained that she grew up sheltered. Let me correct that, *very* sheltered." I fill Gray in on my latest visit to Northmeadow and explain exactly how naïve Natalie is. "I know Brandon and I aren't a Dom/sub couple, at least not yet. But I have no explanation for how we met, and I don't want to keep anything else from her. There's enough as it is."

"There's a lot to explore there. Which of those issues do you want to cover first?"

I really don't want to discuss the things I keep from Natalie, so I opt for talking about the pros and cons of a Dom/sub dynamic with Brandon. "He hasn't said anything about it in a long time, but I can feel it coming, and I don't want to be left unprepared if and when that conversation comes up."

"How does that make you feel?"

Whenever I think about submitting to Brandon, it brings up a lot of feelings about Slava and what happened between us. Things I thought I'd resolved within myself. "I just remember feeling so constricted. Like I'd suffocate in the shadow of a Dominant. Does that make sense?"

"It does. Why do you think you feel that way?"

Sometimes, I wish Gray would give me the answers instead of making me try to figure them out. "I don't know."

"I think if you allow yourself to reflect on the situation, you'll find your answer."

"Maybe I'm not made to settle down with just one person?" I shrug.

"What makes you say that?"

"I have to think that if I was supposed to be with one person, I wouldn't have reservations about it. That I'd look forward to submitting to a Dominant rather than fear it."

Gray pauses before speaking. "I hear what you're saying, but I think you're confusing two different things."

"How so?"

"Submitting to a Dominant in this lifestyle and choosing a life mate are not one and the same," he explains. "Signing a contract is not a life sentence, if you will. It doesn't have to signify the end of your freedom but the beginning of the next amazing adventure. You're also only looking at a dynamic from your point of view."

"What do you mean?"

"When Slava wanted to negotiate another contract, instead of talking with him, you imagined what you thought he wanted and how the conversations would go. You didn't allow him to tell you his thoughts."

"I don't want to make those same mistakes with Brandon."

"I know you don't," he says with a smile. "Unfortunately, we're out of time for today. I'd like you to take some time to explore those thoughts this week. Perhaps you'll view this situation and Brandon in a new light."

"I'll do that."

"And Lana."

"Yes?"

"You avoided the whole part about Natalie. We'll talk about that next week."

"I'll hold you to that." We share a laugh.

After we hang up, I take my time changing into my swimsuit. What Gray touched on has me thinking about my feelings for Brandon. I have a great time with him, and our chemistry is off the charts. The sex is some of the best I've had. Gray's right, though. I'm doing exactly what I did with Slava. We haven't had any serious conversations about what a dynamic between us might look like. Yet, I'm assuming what his answers will be. I need to not put the proverbial horse before the cart.

There are also questions I feel I need to ask myself, such as do I want to settle down with one man? Are marriage and children something I see in my future? If and when Brandon and I have those conversations, I want to know what my answers are so neither of us is left with unrealistic expectations.

There's so much going on in my head right now. Fortunately for me, I'll be in Russia for the next few weeks, so I don't have to make any decisions today.

Brandon

I'M LEAVING THE GYM WHEN I GET A TEXT FROM ALEX.

Alex: Max's jet landed a few minutes ago. Pyotr's dropping Natalie off at the dorm before bringing Lana to my house.

Me: Thanks for the update.

Alex: You're welcome to stop over this evening.

Me: I think I'll give her a few days to settle in.

Alex: Whatever you think is best.

And that's the problem. I have no damn clue what's best. I sat down with Star and Owen earlier this week to get their opinions on the contract. Owen pointed out a few details he felt should be added due to Lana's and my past that I overlooked. The most critical part was discussing potential triggers that either of us was aware of. He also suggested I add a spot for Lana to tell me her fantasies because that's a great way to create role-play scenes. I left Fire and Ice confident with the contract.

Lana: Hey. I'm back in town. Care for some company tonight?

Me: Welcome back. I have plans tonight.

Lana: Are those plans going to take *all* night?

Me: Unfortunately, they are.

Lana: Oh.

Me: Maybe we can get together during the week?
Lana: I'll see what my schedule looks like.
Me: Ok. Talk later.

Before Lana and I go any further, we need to talk—with our clothes on. I'm looking for something long-term with Svetlana, hopefully, a relationship that will continue to grow outside of any contractual dynamic we establish. I don't want to get into this tonight when she's just returned from a long plane ride and will undoubtedly be jet-lagged. With so much on the line, I feel it's important we take the time to discuss every aspect of a Dom/sub relationship. I need to know what kind of a submissive she is, and she needs to know that I'm capable of being her Dominant.

I've learned a lot since everything that happened with Celia. I've trained under experienced Dominants and am surrounded by responsible people who practice the BDSM lifestyle. Those who know about my past remind me I'm not the same person I was in my early twenties. Sure, I'm human, and mistakes happen, but I have knowledge now that I did not have back then.

After Celia's rape, Chains was shut down. The two men, who I didn't know then, are each serving a fifteen-year-sentence for rape in the first degree. Angel is serving a twenty-five-year sentence for rape in the first degree and additional charges for drugging me.

Diablo, the mastermind behind their plan, is serving thirty years. He was charged with rape in the first degree, false imprisonment, and a slew of other offenses. The trial for him was brutal, especially for Celia. Sitting in the courtroom, watching her on the stand reliving the most horrifying night of her life, was gut-wrenching.

When Diablo took the stand, he was so sure he'd be off the hook since we'd done other scenes together that he forgot this time we had a written contract. It was the first time Celia was going to be whipped. After searching online for some guidelines, I read that we should have everything in writing, just in case. That way, there'd be no confusion about what is acceptable or not. Included in that was that I was to be present at all times. Celia was not to be gagged or otherwise restricted from using speech, and no one else would be included without Celia and my prior consent. Diablo's signature was on that paper, alongside ours, showing he understood and agreed to the very rules he broke.

It was vindication to see them escorted from the courtroom in handcuffs, knowing they'd each be spending a good number of years in jail. But at the same time, it did little to bring back the life that was taken from us.

After the trial concluded, Celia's parents whisked her from the courtroom. Her attorney approached me before I could catch up to them with a request from Mr. and Mrs. Baldwin to have no further contact with Celia. He informed me she would be relocating to a small town in Texas with a family member. Despite how much their request broke me, I agreed. I didn't want to cause Celia any more pain. That was the last time I saw her until we bumped into one another a few months ago.

Our chance meeting came at the perfect time. Having the opportunity to talk to her gave me the closure I never had. It was the missing piece I needed to feel confident moving ahead with Svetlana.

Svetlana

"Is everything okay?"

"Yes. Why?"

"You're gripping your phone so tight it looks like you're going to break it," Natalie says.

I loosen my hold. "Everything's good."

Pyotr pulls up in front of our new apartment. "The building's beautiful. I can't wait to see the apartment." Natalie smiles and gets out of the car. When I don't follow, she bends over and looks into the car. "Are you coming?"

"Actually, no. I'm staying at my friend's place for a few days."

"Maybe I should stay in the dorm then?"

"Don't be silly. Go ahead and get settled. I'll be back later in the week."

"Are you sure?" she asks uncertainly.

"Positive." I smile, trying to reassure her.

"Okay, I guess."

Pyotr waits until Natalie is inside before pulling away. "I thought you were going to Brandon's?" he asks.

"So did I, but apparently, he has *other* plans tonight," I say through gritted teeth.

"I see." Pyotr's response is clipped.

The rest of the drive is silent as I will myself not to cry.

Me: I hope you don't mind. I'm on my way to your place.

Alex: That's not a problem, but I thought you'd be anxious to see your new apartment.

Me: I was anxious to see Brandon, but he's unavailable tonight. Do you know where he is?

Alex: Nope. It is not my weekend to Brandon-sit

Me: Your comedian skills need work. Don't quit your day job.

Alex: I'll be at the office late. See you later.

Between being one of Manhattan's top marketing firms and all the stuff Papa sends his way, Alex's going to work his way into an early grave.

I pace back and forth in front of the floor-to-ceiling windows overlooking the river while I obsess over Brandon's text. He has plans for tonight—all night. I've gone from hurt to mad to furious. "I'm not sitting here while he does whatever he's doing with another woman tonight." I decide there's no way I'm just going to sit here tonight.

I shower quickly and, with a towel wrapped around me, take my time drying my hair so it hangs long and silky down my back. I apply my makeup, making sure I have smoky eyes and sexy red lipstick. My dorm was too small to bring all my clothes, something I'm thankful for now as I find the dress I'm looking for.

The satin fabric is cool against my skin. The front of the dress has a plunging cowl neck. Halter ties allow for a backless design. The bottom of the dress hits mid-thigh and features a sexy slit that leaves very little to the imagination. Stiletto heels complete my look.

I take the elevator down to Viktor's apartment, where Pytor stays while I'm here. I find him chilling on the couch watching television. "Pyotr, do you mind driving me to Brandon's?"

"I thought he had plans?"

"He does."

"Did you let Alex know?"

"I'll send him a text on the way."

We hit the rush hour traffic from all the commuters making their mass exodus from the city for the weekend, which makes the ride to

Brooklyn take forever. The subway would've been much faster, but Pyotr isn't a huge fan.

Finally, we're in Brandon's neighborhood. "Don't pull in his driveway. I don't want him to know I'm here."

"Are you sure you know what you're doing?"

"I'm positive," I lie. Because, in reality, I don't know if I can handle what I'll find when I walk into his house.

"Did you text Alex?"

Just sent it. I hold up the phone.

Me: I dropped my stuff off at your place. I decided to go out. Don't wait up for me.

"Can you wait out here?"

"I'd rather come in."

"I doubt this will take long."

"If you're not out in fifteen minutes, I'm coming in."

"Deal."

For a brief second, I almost let my nerves get the best of me. I pause and look back to where Pyotr is waiting in the car, but I can't back out. With my key in hand, I pull my shoulders back and unlock the door.

Other than a small light, the downstairs is dark. I hear music coming from upstairs and walk in that direction. Once I'm upstairs, I walk toward Brandon's room, where the music is coming from. His door is closed. My stomach turns as I reach out to turn his doorknob.

"I hope I'm not interrupting your other plans," I say as I open his bedroom door.

Brandon

"Are you still at work?" I answer my ringing phone.

"I just got a text from Pyotr," Alex says.

"Is everything okay?"

"Did something happen between you and Lana?"

"Not that I'm aware of. She called earlier and asked about getting together tonight."

"What did you tell her?"

"I told her I had plans tonight." I pause as the realization hits me. "Lana must've thought I meant with another woman."

"Where are you?"

"I'm at home."

"Why did you tell her you had plans tonight?"

"I knew if she came over tonight, we wouldn't get any talking done. I wanted to wait until we could discuss a contract and vetting."

"She just got back in town after being away for over a month."

"I'm very aware of that."

Pyotr: What the fuck are you up to, Carpenter?

"I have to go." I don't wait for Alex to say goodbye before I hang up.

Me: I think there was a misunderstanding.

Pyotr: Oh?

Me: I told Lana I had plans tonight, but it's not what she thinks.

Pyotr: Keep talking.

Me: I want to take our relationship to the next level and officially become her Dominant, but I didn't want to do it tonight. I wanted to let her get settled in after her trip.

Pyotr: Are you alone?

Me: Of course.

Pyotr: Good, because she's on her way in, and I didn't want to have to kill you.

I'd laugh if I didn't think Pyotr was serious. I'm well aware that if I did something to fuck up and Lana got hurt, my life may very well be on the line.

I hurry out of the bathroom, still wet from my shower, and look out my window. Sure enough, Lana's walking up the steps to my house. I can only imagine what she's expecting to find. I only have seconds to throw a pair of pants on and get out of my room.

She's downstairs, so I move quickly and quietly. Her heels click on the hardwood floors as she walks past the guestroom on her way to my bedroom.

"I hope I'm not interrupting your other plans," she says, and I hear the door hit the wall. "Brandon?"

Quietly, I come up behind her. "Yes?"

She jumps and spins around to face me. "Where is she?"

"Where is who?"

"Your *plans.*" She puts her hands on her hips.

"There's no one here but me."

"Mhm." She lifts an eyebrow.

"Feel free to check." I motion with my hand.

"I think I will." She purposely nudges me with her elbow as she storms by.

While she throws open the doors to the guestrooms, I lean against my doorframe with my arms crossed. I'm enjoying watching her in the sexy little dress she's wearing.

When she gets to the last door, she turns around. "There isn't anyone here."

"I know."

"You said you had plans," she says quietly.

"I wanted you to settle in and get a good night's sleep." I push off the wall. "Because I knew when I saw you the last thing you were going to get to do is rest."

"Why didn't you just say that?" She swallows.

"I didn't choose my words wisely."

"I thought you were spending the night with someone else."

"Why would you ever think that?"

"I've been gone all summer, and I guess I assumed—"

"I love you, Svetlana." I blurt out, cutting her off.

She freezes, her eyes wide. "You love me?"

"Yes." I take a step closer, closing the distance between us. "I love you." My mouth crashes into hers, and I thread my fingers through her hair. "You are mine," I say between breaths. "Do you understand?"

"I do."

"I need to hear you say it."

"I'm yours, Brandon."

Hearing those words sparks something inside me. I lift her, and she wraps her legs around my waist as I carry her back into my bedroom, where I kick the door closed behind us.

Lana unhooks her legs, and I slide her down my body. "Strip for me."

Svetlana

BRANDON MORPHED FROM HIS USUAL SWEET DEMEANOR INTO a jealous alpha male. When I got here, I was furious with him, thinking he was cheating on me. I made a total fool of myself, checking his house like he was hiding another woman. But then something in him changed. A switch flipped, and my misplaced anger transitioned into intense arousal. I've never had a man go crazy possessive over me. I love it.

"Strip for me," Brandon commands.

Slowly, I lower the zipper on the side of my dress. The satin fabric slips off my body as it billows to the floor. I'm left standing completely nude.

Brandon steps toward me, and I instinctively move back until I'm against the bed and fall onto it. He spreads my legs and pushes them apart, stopping to look at me like I'm a feast about to be eaten. Then, his head lowers, and he runs his tongue along my slit. It's a slow and languid movement. "I need more." I squirm, trying to encourage him, but it has the opposite effect.

"Stay still," he says, grabbing my hips. I whimper in protest, and he looks up at me. "Are you going to be obedient?"

"Yes." He raises an eyebrow, and I know what he's silently asking. Although we don't have a contract or any kind of official dynamic,

Brandon's always been a Dominant in the bedroom. "Yes, Sir. I'll stay still."

Then, his head disappears between my thighs again, his tongue skillfully caressing every inch. He dances between passionate caresses and rough intensity, eliciting a symphony of sensations that leave me breathless and yearning for release. With each flick and tease of his tongue, I find myself on the precipice of bliss, panting and whispering fervent pleas for him to grant me the sweet surrender of ecstasy.

"I love hearing you beg," he says.

"Please." My voice is barely above a whisper.

"Please, what?" He looks up with a grin on his face.

"I need—" My eyes close as he spears two fingers inside me. "Yes, that."

"Is this what you want?" I nod, and he stills.

"Yes. And your mouth." Oh God, I need his mouth on me.

"You're a greedy girl, aren't you?"

"I am. I want all of you, please, Brandon."

Without warning, his mouth envelops my sensitive bud. I'm overwhelmed by the intense sensations. His skilled fingers thrust in and out, propelling me toward the precipice of desire. In a swirling whirlwind of ecstasy, I lose myself completely. My body arches as euphoric waves crash over me. Lost in my pleasure, I am oblivious to Brandon removing his clothes until he thrusts inside me.

"Fuck, Svetlana." He holds my hips tight. "I missed you."

"I missed you, too."

"I need you to listen to me. I would never cheat on you. No one could capture my heart and soul the way you have. From the moment our paths crossed, it's been you. It'll always be you. Do you understand?"

"I understand."

He keeps up his punishing rhythm, and my body tenses as another orgasm builds from deep inside.

"Let yourself fall, *papillion*. I'll catch you."

I've never had a man claim me the way Brandon is right now. It's as if he's marking me as his own. I can't hold back any longer. The overwhelming surge of pleasure becomes too much to contain, and an explosive orgasm radiates from the core of my being. As my body convulses around his rigid length, it triggers his release. His eyes squeeze shut, and his head falls backward as he surrenders to the intensity of our connection.

"If getting jealous causes this, maybe I should let it happen more often," I giggle.

His head snaps up, and he pulls out. "I'm not joking, Svetlana."

"Me either." I push up on my elbows. "I like this side of you."

"We need to talk," Brandon says, picking up his T-shirt and passing it to me. "Get dressed." He slides his legs into his jeans while I pull his shirt over my head. "I'll be right back," he says, disappearing from the room.

I sit cross-legged on the bed, waiting for him to return. When he does, he has a manilla folder in his hand. "What's that?"

"This is why I wanted to wait until another day."

"What is it?" I crane my neck, trying to see what's inside, but he holds it just out of sight.

Brandon

This is not how I planned to have this conversation. Hearing Lana mention the possibility of me being with another solidified my decision to do this tonight. I've never experienced such a fierce sense of possession and desire for a woman as I do for Lana. She's mine, and mine alone. Tonight, I intend to deepen that connection between us.

"I'd like to discuss a contract," I say, gauging Lana's reaction.

"You would?" she asks.

"Yes."

"When did you change your mind?"

"I told you this is what I wanted when I met you, but I had a few personal hurdles to overcome before I felt ready to begin negotiating a contract." I sit on the bed beside Lana. "We need to discuss my past. The reason I've been holding off on doing this."

My hands tremble as I tell Lana about Celia. It's uncomfortable recounting this part of my past. But I can't move forward with a Dom/sub relationship without being completely transparent about one of my biggest regrets and most important life lessons. Svetlana listens quietly, her features giving nothing away as to what she might be thinking or feeling as I lay everything at her feet.

"For years, I've replayed that night in my head, wishing I'd done things differently and berating myself for not coming to sooner. There's been times I imagined I'd pulled the trigger." My voice cracks, and I pause to regain control of my emotions. "I bumped into Celia a few months ago. It was the first time we've spoken since then. All these years, I assumed she hated me, but I was wrong. She never blamed me for what happened."

"Why would she?"

"Because I failed her."

"You saved her," Lana says, wiping a stray tear from my cheek. "How is she today?"

"She's happily married and has two children." I smile. "Celia encouraged me to forgive myself and to be happy."

"She's right. There was nothing you could've done differently—"

"Yes, there was. I should've asked more questions and learned more about BDSM before we went to a club and especially before I allowed anyone to play with us. That will never happen again."

"You aren't open to playing with other people?"

"No," I answer without hesitation. "I will not share you with anyone. That's a hard limit for me."

"May I see the contract?" she asks. I pull out her copy and pass it to her, watching her read. "You know how to use a whip?" she asks.

"I do. But if that's not something you're interested in, we can put it on the hard limit list."

"Don't take it out. I'm very interested in it," she says, smiling.

"Do you have any experience being whipped?" I'm curious to learn more about Svetlana as a submissive.

"A little, yes, and I liked it very much."

"I take it you're willing to begin vetting and negotiating a contract?" Lana bites her lip as she looks between the papers and me but says nothing. "Tell me what you're thinking."

She sets the papers on the bed in front of her. "I feel like I'm at a crossroads. This is what I've wanted for so long, and I want to say yes."

"But?"

"I'm scared. I don't want to ruin what we have."

"I'm terrified, too."

Over the past two years, Lana and I have gotten to know each other, and we've had a lot of fun dating, but something's always been missing —being an official Dominant and submissive couple. We have a good sex life full of kink, but that does not encompass the totality of what the BDSM lifestyle offers.

After I started going to Fire and Ice, I had a submissive for a short time. Owen introduced me to Wynter, an experienced submissive. We got along well and, after a period of vetting, signed a contract. My relationship with her allowed me to practice my fledging skills with someone who wouldn't let me go too far. Was it a conventional Dom/sub dynamic? Probably not. But that's the beauty of this lifestyle. It's not a one-size-fits-all kinda thing. Wynter and I designed a dynamic that met our needs and provided her with the safety net I insisted be built in.

We ended the dynamic when Wynter's job offered her a transfer to Finland. It was an opportunity that was too good for her to pass up. She asked me to go with her, but I wasn't willing to walk away from my life here. It wasn't easy to release her, but our dynamic ended on good terms.

Since then, I've played with subs here and there. Everything was extremely short-term—nothing longer than a weekend here and there. I didn't trust my skills or judgment enough for anything more. I'm not that same man, though. I've grown in confidence and have faced the demons in my past.

"I'm a Dominant, Svetlana. I want to be *your* Dominant."

"If I decided to move forward with this." She holds up the contract. "Couples negotiating a contract shouldn't be sexually involved."

"That's true. If we'd just met, I'd insist on it." Lana narrows her eyes. "But we're already together. It doesn't make much sense for us to take a step backward. Unless you want to."

"I wouldn't agree to this if sex was off the table." She gives me a cheeky smile.

"I do think we should put some rules into play, though."

I grab a pen, and we make a list of fair negotiating guidelines, including not using sex as a bargaining chip. We're still talking when Lana yawns. "You must be exhausted."

"I am."

"It's time for bed. We'll pick up where we left off tomorrow." I reach out to pick up her copy of the contract.

"Wait. I want to take a picture to send to Grayson."

I pull my hand back as though the papers are on fire. "Who the hell is Grayson?"

Svetlana

I DON'T REALIZE WHAT I'VE SAID UNTIL AFTER THE WORDS are out. I wasn't purposely keeping Gray a secret. Well, maybe I was. Telling the guy you're dating that you're still going to therapy because you've not come to terms with your sister's abduction, rape, and murder is not the easiest thing to do. I've thought about it but could never find the right words, so I let it go.

"Grayson's my therapist. Star put me in touch with him."

"When?" Brandon asks through gritted teeth.

"I've been seeing him for a little over a year."

"Why are you sending him a copy of the contract?"

"Gray's a kink-friendly therapist." I reach out and take Brandon's hand in mine. "He knows what happened between Slava and me and about you. I want to get his thoughts on the contract."

"Why didn't you tell me? Did you think it would change my feelings toward you?"

"I don't know. I guess I didn't realize." I stumble over my words. "I didn't think we were anything more than—"

"Fuck buddies? Wow." Brandon gets off the bed and walks to the other side of the room. "Now I feel like the fool."

"It's not like that." I get up and go to him. "I've been waiting for the other shoe to drop. For you to get sick of me. Like everyone else does," I say that last part quietly. Then, I walk around to stand in front of him. "I didn't think someone like you could care about someone like me. My negative self-thoughts are one of the things Gray and I have been working on."

"Svetlana, I could never see you as only someone to warm my bed until the next pretty thing comes along. Whether you consent to become my submissive or not, I need you to know that you're worth so much more than that."

Brandon's words burrow their way deep inside my heart, where I'm hoping they take root. "I'm learning."

"And if you let me, I want to be the one here every day to remind you."

"I'd like to negotiate the contract. If you're still okay with that. But I need to go slow."

"We can talk about that tomorrow. Right now." Brandon turns me around to face the bed. "You need to sleep."

I wake before Brandon and carefully slide out of bed to grab my phone. I quietly go downstairs to the kitchen to grab a coffee. After Alex took his collar off, I was certain that Brandon would offer me a contract, but he never did.

My first term at NYU is coming to a close. Natalie's packed and ready to return home for the Christmas holidays. Since we don't celebrate American Christmas, I decided to stay with Alex and see what the holiday is like here.

"Are you sure you don't want to come home with me?" Natalie asks. "I hate the idea of you staying here alone."

"I won't be alone. I'm going to stay at my friend's house."

"The same mysterious friend you visit almost every weekend?" she asks, her voice rising in pitch.

"Yes."

"I'm convinced this friend is a secret boyfriend."

"I can assure you this is not a secret boyfriend," I smile.

Several times, I have considered telling Natalie about Alex and Brandon. Every time I go to open my mouth, I stop myself. Even though we're roommates and have become fast friends, Natalie knows relatively little about my personal life. She was raised to not ask questions about things she isn't directly involved in, and even then, she doesn't pry. In this case, it's worked to my advantage. I keep a lot hidden from most people. Secrets I don't want to talk about. Things Natalie could never understand.

Living in New York has been everything I dreamed it would be. It's my chance to be me, not the daughter of a mob boss. Not the girl whose sister was trafficked and murdered. Not even the girl who's involved in BDSM. Just plain Svetlana Solonik.

Natalie's phone chimes. "It's my ride." She surprises me by throwing her arms around my neck. "I'm going to miss you."

"We'll see each other in a few weeks," I say, squeezing her back. "Have a nice time at home."

"I will." She grabs her rolling suitcase and strolls out the door.

After she leaves, I grab my bag and head outside to find Pyotr, who's just pulling up in the car with Viktor.

Over the years, I convinced myself it was never going to happen. I knew Brandon was holding something about his past back. At one point, I asked Alex, hoping he'd tell me Brandon's secrets, but being a good friend, he did not.

Waiting was a difficult thing for me to do, especially at first. My initial reaction was to do something stupid and force Brandon to tell me. Looking back, I'm so thankful I didn't do that. After I started seeing Grayson, one of the things we worked on was giving others space to tell their story if and when they were ready.

Last night, Brandon opened up to me about Celia and everything that happened that night, including the loss of their unborn child and how that affected him. It was a moment that brought us closer together.

While I sip the hot coffee, I check my texts to see if Gray replied to my text from last night.

Grayson: I got the pictures you sent. Before I comment, I'd like to get your thoughts.

Me: Brandon caught me off guard with the whole idea.

As much as I don't want to, I tell Gray everything that happened last night. It wasn't my finest moment, but I've learned telling him everything is important.

Grayson: Do we need to go over the importance of proper vetting?

Me: No. He and I have already talked about it.

Grayson: I can already hear it. *But...*

Me: You're very perceptive.

Grayson: That's what I'm told. Now spill it.

Me: But this isn't a typical scenario. We've been together for a long time and already know so much about each other.

Grayson: That's true. However, this represents a considerable shift in your relationship—in the dynamics of it. Not taking your time here or skipping this step entirely could cause problems in the future.

Since when is Gray so gloom and doom? I don't see the point in vetting. We've already done that without putting a label on it. And I'm sure there won't be a long and drawn-out negotiation. Sure, we need to discuss limits, but beyond that, I don't see much else.

Me: I'll take that into consideration.

Grayson: Since I'm already on the subject of things you don't want to hear. I'm also going to urge you to take a step back on your physical relationship through this stage.

Me: Probably not

Grayson: Lana...

Me: Gray...

Brandon appears in the doorway wearing only his pajama pants.

"Why didn't you wake me?"

"You never sleep in. I figured you needed the rest."

"Who are you talking to?"

"Grayson."

Brandon doesn't respond. The subject of Grayson will take a bit more hashing out. While I wrap things up with Gray, Brandon grabs a mug and makes himself a coffee.

Me: I have to go.

Grayson: Please think about what I said.

"What's on your agenda today?" I ask as Brandon sits across from me.

"Negotiations," he says with a smile. "If you're okay with that."

After breakfast and a quick shower, we sit across from each other at the dining table. The first part of the contract outlines any medical issues we need to be aware of. Next, we discuss safewords. We've already been using red, green, and yellow, so we decide to keep those. Brandon also suggests adding hand signals if we do a scene where I'm gagged.

"Let's talk about triggers," Brandon says, moving to the next section. "In your previous experiences, has anything come up?"

"Not really."

Brandon leans forward on his elbows. "This section is important. Not that the others aren't. We've both experienced traumas. I want to be sure we don't rush through this and overlook anything."

"I agree. Maybe it's because I haven't had any long-term dynamics, but I haven't run into anything triggering."

"Nothing that happened with Slava that you feel should be addressed in this section?"

I'm sure he's referring to my refusing to talk to Slava after our contract expired like I agreed to. I don't consider that a trigger so much as a mistake I've learned from and hope not to repeat.

"No, I don't think so."

Brandon watches me closely for a few seconds. "I'm okay to move on, but I'd like to revisit this topic before we sign anything."

Brandon

~~

"What about this section?" Svetlana points to the paper. "What we'll call each other."

"I'm partial to *papillion*." I smile. "Is there anything you'd like to call me?"

"I like Master."

"No," I answer quickly. "Anything but that."

"Why?"

"That's what Celia called me. I think we just found my first trigger." I flip back a few pages and make a note of that.

"I'm sorry."

"It's okay. You didn't know. How about we go with Sir?"

"I can agree to that, Sir," Svetlana says, then bites her bottom lip. "What about when other people are around? People who aren't in the lifestyle?"

"I'm fine with you calling me Brandon in those scenarios," I say, turning the page. "Limits. This is another area that we'll start discussing today, but we'll leave it open for anything that comes up."

I've already listed some hard limits, things I already know are also limits for Lana. There will be no illegal activities, sexual or otherwise, no toilet play, infantilism, cutting, catheters, or guns.

"No fire play?" she asks. "Why not?"

"I have no experience with it."

"I've never done it either, but it's something I'd like to try. Can we move it to soft limits pending more education?"

"That's fair." I jot down a note to ask Owen and Star about education on fire play.

"Humiliation is a hard no for me," Lana adds. "One of the Doms I played with in Moscow was really into that. I agreed to it for a scene one night and had to safeword. I can take all sorts of physical pain. Actually, I quite like pain, but not from words. I can't handle that."

"I'll put that on the hard limit list."

We take our time reviewing a list of common and not-so-common things and assigning them to hard, soft, or acceptable limits. There's still a lot more to go through. "Why don't we stop here for today." We don't have to force the conversation into one afternoon. "Are you planning to stay here tonight?"

"I told Natalie I'd be home tonight. Is that okay?"

"It actually works out well. I'm supposed to go to the club with Alex, and I felt bad about leaving you here alone."

"What's going on at the club tonight?"

"There's a roundtable for the Dominants."

"I'm glad you brought up Dominants. I have to call Alex and make arrangements to get my things. I left it all at his house."

"Go call him while I clean this stuff up."

After I gather the papers, I go in search of Pyotr. He has a key to my house and let himself in last night after Lana's search for the invisible woman. I find him downstairs watching television.

The basement level of my home is its own apartment. When my parents were still alive, this is where I lived. It allowed me the freedom to come and go while being right here if my ailing parents needed anything.

I think Pyotr enjoys the downtime he gets when we're here. I don't think he's heard me come in, but he turns my way. "Everything okay?"

"Lana had to make a few phone calls. She's going back to her place this evening."

"I'll be here when she's ready."

"Great. I'll let her know." I turn to go back upstairs.

"Do you have a minute?" Pyotr asks.

"Sure. What's up?"

"You know I've known Lana since she was a little girl."

This sounds like it might get serious, so I sit on the other end of the couch. "Yes."

"I've been by her side when she was at her lowest. The past few years, I've witnessed a lot of personal growth in her," Pyotr says, clearly proud of her. "I know she can be a challenge at times. Lana does her very best to push people away before they have a chance to hurt her."

"It's understandable, given what she's experienced."

Pyotr nods. "She's made some questionable relationship choices in her past. I'm sure she's told you about Slava."

"She has."

"I didn't approve of him."

"Why not?" Lana hasn't told me anything about this. I'm curious to hear Pyotr's thoughts.

"Lana was barely twenty at the time, and Slava was in his mid-thirties. I'm still not sure why Max didn't kill him," Pyotr chuckles. "Ordinarily, I could care less about a person's age, but this situation was different," he explains. "Lana talked a good game, but in reality, she was very impressionable—naïve."

"I thought he treated her well."

"He didn't hurt her, but in my opinion, Slava didn't take the time to get to know her. If he did, he would've seen the little girl inside that was begging for attention. She clung to anything or, in his case, anyone seeking comfort. Those are not the right reasons to be in a relationship." Pyotr is tense as he speaks. Although he's never said anything out loud, I know he cares a great deal about Svetlana. "I don't know much about this BDSM stuff other than the relationships can be complex. Which is all the more reason to not enter one with someone who isn't on a level playing field."

"That's a very good observation."

"Slava did it anyway. Because of that, Lana was hurt. Slava was, too. He isn't my responsibility, and frankly, I was glad he was out of her life."

Listening to Pyotr's observations, I'm beginning to grow nervous. Is he trying to tell me he doesn't approve of my presence in her life? What will I do if that's what he says next? My fears are put to rest with his next statement.

"I'm glad you came along," he says. "You see beneath the mask Svetlana wears."

"Before I met Lana, I'd heard a lot about her from Maxim and Alex. The topic of conversation was always about how difficult she was. One evening, Alex invited me for dinner. I had a few minutes alone with Viktor, so I asked him what his thoughts were," I say. "Viktor told me there was more to her that most people miss. I didn't want that to be me, so instead of going into it with preconceived ideas, I chose to forget everything I was told. I paid attention to the young woman telling me all about living in a new country and her excitement about starting school."

I smile, remembering that night as though it were just yesterday. "Sure, I saw the strong-willed girl she wanted everyone to see. But it was when she didn't think anyone was watching that I saw it. A scared, vulnerable young woman with a soft heart—one that deserved to be treasured."

"I was waiting for you to find her," Pyotr says with an emotion I can only describe as love.

"What do you mean?"

"I don't have a family of my own. Svetlana's the closest thing I'll ever have to one. I've watched men come and go. The one thing they all had in common was none of them ever deserved the love she has to give." He pauses. "You're different, Carpenter. When you look at her, I have no doubt you see what's beneath her protective exterior. You very well might be the right man for her."

"I'm in love with her." Pytor's the only person, other than Lana, who knows the depth of my feelings for her.

Pyotr smiles approvingly, then the smile slips from his face. He puts his finger in my face. "Don't do anything to fuck it up."

"Got it."

"What time will she be ready to leave?" And just like that, the threatening bodyguard disappears, and the mood lightens.

It takes me a minute to get my thoughts together after Pyotr's warning. He's fiercely protective of Lana. At times, I thought that maybe he was interested in her romantically, but that couldn't be further from the truth. All this time, he's been waiting for someone deserving of her to come along. I'm honored he believes that man is me. I'll do everything in my power to live up to his expectations.

After I make arrangements for Lana's ride, I go in search of her. My bedroom door is open, and I hear the shower water running. Lana's curvy silhouette is visible through the steamy glass door. She hasn't heard me come in, and I use that to my advantage, watching her run her hands over her body while I remove my clothes.

I pull open the shower door and Lana shrieks. "You scared me," she says, trying to catch her breath.

"Were you expecting someone else?" I raise an eyebrow.

"You're so funny." She reaches to smack my chest, but I grab her wrist and spin her around.

"Put your hands on the wall and bend over," I instruct, and use my foot to spread her legs. Reaching around her to the shelf, I grab the lube and squirt a generous amount on my fingers, then slowly slide my fingers in, stretching her and readying her for my cock. "Every part of you belongs to me."

"Mhm."

"Tell me." I've never felt the need to hear that a woman is mine as strongly as I do with Lana.

"Every part of me belongs to you," Lana says, looking over her shoulder.

"Are you ready?"

"Yes."

I pull my fingers out and add more lube to my dick before lining it up at her entrance. I push the tip past the tight ring of muscle and pause. As much as I want to plow into her and take her rough against the wall, I don't. All it would do is hurt her and tear her body. I don't want that, so I wait for her body to relax and allow me inside.

Inch by slow inch, I push my way into her. Taking her ass feels different than anything else. It's tight, almost painfully so, but I'm addicted to having her this way. I love walking the fine line between pain and pleasure with her. "Are you ready?"

"Yes," Lana says, her voice low and breathy.

Slowly, I start moving. The sensation of being squeezed by her body is overwhelming, and I struggle to not finish quickly like an inexperienced schoolboy. I have to remain focused so this can last for as long as possible.

Hot water streams over my back as my hand tangles in her long brown hair, wrapping it around my hand. "I'm getting close, *papillion*. I want you there with me."

Lana's hand drops between her legs. "Can you do it harder, Sir?"

Her words cause my fraying self-control to snap. With my free hand, I grab her waist to steady her as I give her exactly what she asked for.

"Yes, just like that," she encourages me.

"Fuck, Lana," I growl. "Come with me, now."

Lana's body squeezes my cock. Every nerve ending in my body is on fire, and I come deep inside her.

"It's too much, Sir. I can't." Lana's legs begin to give out from the force of her orgasm. I wrap my arm around her, holding her up as we ride out the ecstasy of our orgasms together.

The sound of our breathing mixes with the falling water from the shower. Lana inhales sharply as I pull out of her. When I'm sure she can stand, I loosen my hold on her. She turns around to face me. "That was incredible."

"We're made for each other, *papillon*. I want forever with you."

"I'm not—."

I place my finger on her lips, stopping her. I'm aware that I asked for more time when Lana was ready for more. The tables have turned. I'm sure of what I want, but now it's Lana who's asking for more time. "What do I need to do?"

"Just keep being you."

Svetlana

NEGOTIATING A CONTRACT WITH BRANDON WAS SUPPOSED to be easy. It's what I'd been waiting for since we first met. So, why, now that it's happening, am I having second thoughts and dragging my feet? It's been one month, and I'm still unable to sign and make the commitment.

While Brandon finishes his shower, I make breakfast. Whenever I stay at his house, which is more and more often, I cook the meals. It's a simple domestic thing to do that usually brings me great pleasure, but today, it's making my heart pound and hands tremble.

"You look tense," Brandon says, coming up behind me and wrapping his arms around my waist. "Is everything okay?"

"I'm a bit preoccupied thinking about an important paper due this week." I'm not ready to discuss the second thoughts I'm having yet. Mostly because I don't know what they are or why I feel this way. But I do know that I don't want to risk losing him.

"My office is at your disposal if you need the computer," he says as he sits at the table.

"I appreciate that, but everything I need is at my apartment," I say as I plate his French Toast. "I need to go home this afternoon so I can finish it up."

"Oh." The smile fades from his face. "I thought you'd spend the rest of the weekend."

"I really can't."

"That's okay. Maybe next time." The disappointment on his face is nearly my undoing. The words *I'll stay* are on the tip of my tongue, but they disappear with Brandon's next words. "When can I meet your roommate?"

I set our plates on the table and sit across from him before answering, "I don't know."

Natalie and I have gotten to be good friends, best friends, I'd like to say. But at the same time, I'm hiding a whole part of my life from her. I hate doing this, especially when she's been so open with me about everything in her life. This is different, though. I'm sure Natalie's never heard of the BDSM lifestyle, let alone was ever friends with someone involved in it. She clings to her conservative upbringing like it's a lifeline. Without it, she'll drown. The times I've suggested taking even a small step away from it and embracing different ideas, she's nearly shut down.

"She really doesn't know anything about your father or the lifestyle?" Brandon asks as he eats.

"Nothing. Natalie believes Papa's involved in the natural gas industry in Russia. She has no idea about his connections with the Bratva. And she definitely doesn't know anything about BDSM."

"Wow. It's hard to imagine being an adult with such a sheltered view of life."

"Natalie's lived a very sheltered life. Even though she's away for school, she's still very controlled by her parents and her boyfriend."

"Hopefully, you find a way because I'd really like to be a part of your life outside our little bubble."

Brandon's words have played on repeat in my head all afternoon. Even as Pyotr drops me off this evening, I can't stop thinking about it. I'd love to have him meet Natalie. To have him come to my apartment like a *regular* boyfriend, but I don't see how that could ever be possible.

When I get inside, Natalie's sitting on the couch with her textbooks and notebooks scattered around her. She looks up when I walk into the room. "I didn't think you'd be home today."

"I have a big paper due, and I forgot to bring my stuff with me." I quickly change the subject.

"What smells so good?"

"I'm making lasagna. It's my grandma's recipe." She smiles proudly.

"I'm glad I came home early because it smells divine."

Natalie giggles. "I made enough to freeze, so we'll have a few dinners pre-made for another night."

"You're amazing." I flop onto the loveseat and rest my head back. "I think I might take a nap. I'm exhausted."

"What do you do at your *close family friend's house* that you come home exhausted all the time?"

"What?" My head pops up.

"You always come home and say you're exhausted. Then, you go for a nap." Natalie tilts her head. "Don't you get any sleep wherever it is you disappear to?"

"We go out a lot. You know, and stay out late. Things you should be doing." I elbow her playfully.

"Things I shouldn't be doing because I have a boyfriend."

"Having a boyfriend doesn't mean you can't go out and have fun. It's not like you're going to cheat on him. You're just setting your schoolwork aside and going out with your girlfriends for a few hours. It's okay to take a break and have fun every now and then."

Natalie closes her tablet in her textbooks and quickly gathers her things. "I'm going to go to my room to study. I have an exam on Monday."

"I'm sorry, Nat. I didn't mean—"

"It's fine, really. I have a lot of schoolwork I need to get done," she says as she hurries out of the room.

I drop my head back again and groan. This is precisely why I try not to bring these things up. If Natalie and I can't even talk about these things, how could I ever initiate a conversation about the more taboo parts of my life? I don't see any possible way for her to meet Alex and Brandon.

Svetlana

"You don't have to drive me to the airport. I can take an Uber," Natalie says for the millionth time.

"It's not a problem. Pyotr doesn't mind." I was forced to tell Natalie about Pyotr a few months after we started rooming together.

Natalie and I were coming home from a TED Talk the school hosted. It was late, so we cut through Washington Square Park on the way back to our dorm when we were approached by a group of drunk guys who were coming back from a frat party. Pyotr allowed me the space to deal with them on my own, but when they wouldn't take no for an answer and were starting to get handsy with us, he stepped out of the shadows.

I still laugh when I think about the looks on their faces when my well-built and intimidating Russian bodyguard educated them on proper behavior around women. When he was through with his lesson, Pyotr forced them to apologize to us, which I don't think any of those guys had ever done. They thought they were off the hook, and then Pyotr issued a very up close and personal threat that had them shaking in their skin as they scurried away.

Of course, after that, I had to tell Natalie about Pyotr. It's a tried-and-true story based on truth that I've used for years. Papa's work in the natural gas industry has made him a great deal of money. With that also comes many enemies. Because of that, he insists I always have security with me. Natalie didn't question that rationale at all. She was just happy Pyotr was there to help us out.

Since then, Pyotr has been able to have a little more of an open presence in my life, which makes Papa and him happy. We even had him over for dinner a few times.

"Are you sure you don't want to come with me?" Natalie asks. "I hate knowing you're going to be alone for Thanksgiving."

"I've never celebrated Thanksgiving, so I'm not missing anything," I say, smiling. "I promise I'll be fine." I'll be more than fine. I have some very hot plans with a certain man I know.

"If we don't leave now, you'll miss your flight," Pyotr calls from the kitchen.

"We're coming." Natalie and I grab her luggage and hurry down the hall.

"I'll get those." Pyotr takes the bags from us, and we go outside to the car.

"I hate this," Natalie complains as we sit at a dead stop on the highway. "That's one nice thing about Northmeadow. There's never any traffic."

"No, but we have gotten stopped by cows standing in the middle of the road." We both laugh. "Honestly, I don't know how you go back to that after being here with all this."

"New York is only temporary. Northmeadow is home."

"I guess." I shrug. "I could never live in such a small town."

"It'd be different if you knew your future was there." Natalie smiles. "I have a job waiting for me, and after Thanksgiving break, I'll have a fiancé there, too."

"I can't believe you're getting engaged." I try my best to sound happy for her.

"Tommy hasn't said it for sure, but he's been giving lots of big hints."

"Don't you think you're too young to get married?"

"Most of my girlfriends are already married. Some even have children."

I don't have to fake my reaction because I'm honestly shocked. "You're kidding?"

"No. I told you, girls from Northmeadow don't go to college. After high school, we're expected to marry and stay home to raise our children."

"Wanting to get married and have children are wonderful things. I'm not arguing that. But why is getting an education not valued?" I ask, genuinely confused. "What if you want to work?"

"Because of my scholarship, I'll be working for at least a few years."

Natalie's road to NYU was even more difficult than mine. Her desire to attend university was a foreign concept to her parents. In their eyes, Natalie was expected to graduate high school, marry Tommy, pop out his babies, and live the same life her parents had. When she approached them with her desire to attend college, they were furious and refused to help her.

Natalie thought her dreams were over until Ms. Campbell, the head of her local school district, approached her with an offer she couldn't refuse. This woman knew Natalie was still recovering from her brother, Michael, and his boyfriend Evan's suicide. Ms. Campbell wasn't originally from Northmeadow and held a different view of the world outside the small town. She also realized that there would be more tragedies if something wasn't done to address the needs of the young people in town.

Ms. Campbell, on behalf of the school board, offered Natalie a full scholarship for both undergrad and graduate school. It paid for everything down to her books with the caveat that she returned to Northmeadow and remain employed by the school district for five years.

When Natalie first told me the terms of the scholarship, I was shocked. Signing up for a five-year employment commitment sounded insane to me. Natalie earned her bachelor's degree with a 4.0 GPA. She's already receiving job offers from agencies in the city, but she's had to turn them all down because of her restrictive scholarship.

I understand why she accepted it, though. Without it, she would've had no way to go to school, and that was something she couldn't live with. Making this move was the only act of rebellion she's ever done.

I'm surprised her mother didn't lock Natalie in her room until she saw *reason,* according to them.

"I'm glad about that. You deserve to do what you want with your life before and even after becoming a mom."

"Tommy's everything I want in life," she says dreamily. "I'm going to have the best life ever."

"I'm so excited for you." As much as I want to shake some sense into her, Natalie's going home to get engaged. Now's not the time to argue with her. If she's truly happy with the path she's on, then I'll be here cheering her on every step of the way. "You better send me pictures of your ring."

The JFK airport is like a city inside the city. Roads twist and turn, leading in so many directions. I'm thankful I don't have to figure out where we're going because we'd never get there. Pyotr doesn't have an issue navigating through the maze, bringing us to where we need to go with apparent ease.

He pulls into a parking spot and starts getting out of the car.

"You guys don't have to walk me in," Natalie says. "I'm sure you have better things to do."

"Don't be silly. I have nothing better to do," I say, linking my arm with hers. "I added some stuff to your wedding board on Pinterest."

"Thank you. I'll look at it after I'm home." We get to the terminal, and Natalie stops walking. Turning to me, she says, "I know you think I'm crazy for getting engaged so young, and it's no secret you aren't Tommy's biggest fan. Which makes me even more grateful for your support."

"I'll always be in your corner."

"Will you be my maid of honor?" Natalie asks.

"Of course," I squeal and wrap Natalie in a tight hug. "I love you, girly."

"Love you too, Lan."

"Have fun, and text me as soon as you're officially an engaged woman."

"I will."

"Have a safe flight," Pyotr adds.

"Thanks for the ride." Natalie stands on her toes and surprises Pyotr by kissing his cheek before she takes her bag.

We watch as she goes through the security checkpoint. She gives us a small wave before disappearing into the waiting area to board her flight.

"You did good, little butterfly," Pyotr says as we return to the car.

"What do you mean?"

"Her soon-to-be-fiancé is a prick, but for some reason, she loves him. I'm proud of you for being supportive rather than arguing with her."

"I've tried arguing. It doesn't work." I shrug. "All I can do is be her friend."

"Natalie's a genuinely sweet girl," Pyotr says with a smile. "She deserves so much better."

"I couldn't agree with you more."

When we first left for the airport, I texted Brandon.

Me: We're leaving now. I'll see you soon.

Brandon: I'll be waiting.

I knew Natalie would be out of town for the week, so I gave Brandon a set of keys to the apartment. Although I still haven't agreed to sign the contract, we're doing what I'm sure will be a hot scene. Brandon was apprehensive about doing a consensual, non-consensual role-play, but I really wanted to try it. It took a lot of negotiation and safeguards before he agreed.

My job was to let him know what we were leaving for the airport. After that, we won't have any more contact until the scene starts. We didn't put an exact time on when we're starting. Not knowing when it'll happen should keep the scene as authentic as possible.

The drive home doesn't take as long as it did to get to the airport. Pyotr pulls to a stop outside my apartment. "Do you want company, little butterfly?"

"No thanks. I'm going to get some studying done."

"You are going to use your break to study?" Pyotr raises an eyebrow. "Where are you really planning on going?"

"You can relax." I step out of the car. "I'm not going anywhere."

"You're up to no good."

"I'll call you if I need you." I close the door and wave goodbye.

Pyotr watches as I walk up to the door. Goosebumps run up and down my spine, and I get the feeling I'm being watched.

That's probably because I am.

Brandon

When Lana asked me about a CNC scene, my first instinct was to run screaming in the other direction. It brought up too many memories of that awful night with Celia. I didn't want to involve Alex, but I had to talk to someone about it.

He reminded me that what Lana and I are doing is consensual. What happened to Celia was non-consensual, and they are two very different things. Lana and I planned out everything that would happen tonight, including the element of surprise.

The other part of my hesitation is due to Lana's past. As a little girl, she experienced her sister being abducted from right next to her. She wasn't there to witness anything and still doesn't know the details. But given the circumstances, it's safe to say Jelena was raped and tortured. Even though this scene was her idea, I've been struggling with the possibility of doing something that will unknowingly trigger her.

I was less than thrilled when Lana told me she consulted her therapist, Grayson, about our scene. My jealous, irrational side doesn't want her confiding in another man about what we do together. Alex was the voice of reason that forced me to step back and try to look at things through her eyes. He also suggested the possibility of going to an appointment with her. It wasn't until I attended my first session that I became comfortable with the situation. Grayson is completely professional and has Lana's best interests at heart.

Since then, Lana and I have gone to several sessions together to discuss tonight's scene in more detail. It's been helpful for me to learn what to do if something triggers Lana. We talked about body cues Lana often gives before she's consciously aware that something's about to affect her. Those sessions, along with having safe words and signals built into every part of tonight, have given me the confidence to move forward.

While Lana was out, I went into her apartment to set up a few things, including two small wireless cameras to watch her movements. As soon as Svetlana gets home, there's no doubt she'll know someone's been in there.

I'm just getting home when I get a text.

Pyotr: Lana's up to something.

Me: What do you mean?

Pyotr: I just dropped her off and offered to keep her company, but she told me she's going to study. It's a school holiday. I KNOW she's not studying.

I'm trying to formulate a response when I get another text.

Pyotr: Maybe I should hang around, just in case.

Me: I don't think you need to do that.

Actually, that's the last thing I want.

Pyotr: What do you know that I don't?

Me: I'm going to her place tonight. I'll make sure she stays out of trouble.

Pyotr: Why didn't she tell me you were coming over? I don't have to worry about her if you're there.

Me: I'm sure she was embarrassed. Thanks for the heads up, though. I appreciate it.

Pyotr: Have a good night.

Now, I wait until I'm ready to make my next move.

Svetlana

With each step I take, I can't help but look over my shoulder. I know it's just Brandon stalking me, but that doesn't stop the anxiety I'm experiencing. As soon as I'm in my apartment, I lock the door behind me. Not that it will do much. He has a key.

As I walk through the living room, something on the fireplace mantle catches my eye. One of our picture frames is turned backward. I know it wasn't that way when I left. With cautious steps, I make my way across the room and right the frame. When I step into the kitchen, I find a vase with a red rose in the middle of the island. That wasn't there when I left. Is Brandon already here?

On the way to my room, I open the doors to the guest bathroom, extra bedroom, and Natalie's bedroom checking each one before closing the door and going to my room. My hand trembles as I turn the handle and push the door open. After a thorough search, I'm confident I'm still alone, but for how long?

Brandon

The cameras I placed allow me to watch Lana as she finds the things I left behind. She knows I've been in her apartment. She's on high alert right now, so I'm sitting back and biding my time. I don't plan to make another move until Lana's relaxed and lets her guard down.

It's late. Lana's beyond pacing and looking out the windows. She gave up on that hours ago. That's when I went back into the city to grab some dinner. After I ate, I came to Washington Square Park, where I've been enjoying a quiet evening of people-watching.

Lana has just finished watching a movie and is walking to her bedroom. I watch as she strips her clothes and walks into her bathroom for what I'm assuming is a shower. That's when I decide to make my move.

Once inside the apartment, I lock the door and quietly walk down the hall to her bedroom. The shower water's still running, so I hurry to set up a few things before she comes out. Then, I sit on the edge of her bed and wait.

The water shuts off, and my heart rate increases, knowing when Lana opens the door, I'm the first thing she'll see, and our scene will start. My intent is to catch her off guard and startle her. It's all part of the scene. It's also a fine line between CNC and true fear—a line I don't intend to cross.

The handle on the bathroom door turns, and Lana steps across the threshold. She's looking down at her phone as she pulls the door closed. Everything begins moving in slow motion as her blue eyes meet mine. She gasps and drops her phone. I stand and close the gap between us, caging her against the door with my arms.

"Do not make a sound." I keep my voice low. "Nod your head if you understand."

Her head lifts and lowers slowly.

Reaching out, I tug on the towel wrapped around her and watch it fall to the floor, puddling at her feet. Goosebumps cover her still-damp skin. I reach out and squeeze one of her already hard nipples. "I'm going to have fun with this hot little body tonight." I grab her arm and try to drag her to the bed.

"No, please. Don't hurt me," she cries. "I have money. I can get you as much as you want."

"I didn't come here for money. Be a good girl, and don't cause a scene." I tug harder, encouraging her to move. Lana stumbles into me. My hard cock presses against her toned abdomen. She inhales sharply, and I know she feels it. "You want some of this?" I thrust against her.

"No," she spits.

"Don't play hard to get, sweetheart."

"Let me go. If my bodyguard comes back here, he'll—"

"You sent him away hours ago." I move closer to her face. "Now listen to me closely. You need to close those pretty lips unless you want to find them wrapped around my cock." Her mouth snaps shut. "Now, get over here."

I drag her across the room and push her onto her bed. Lana fights hard, so I straddle her body to gain control. Taking her left arm, I pull it over her head. A loud click sounds as I snap the cuff around her wrist.

"No. Please let me go." I ignore her plea and cuff her other arm above her head. Then, I move to her legs. Lana doesn't make it easy. She fights me at every turn.

The fear I see in her eyes and hear in her voice feels too real. It takes all my self-control to stay in character—to remind myself this is all planned. Lana agreed to be fully restrained. We planned that she'd beg me to stop. That she'd fight back, and I'd ignore it. Other than the warning signs Grayson and I reviewed, this scene stops only if she says yellow or red.

Once her legs are secure, I step back. Lana's naked body is spread out. Every inch is on display for me, and she's bound to the bed. Her dark hair, still wet from her shower, fans out messily around her. She's never looked more beautiful than she does right now—completely powerless and at my mercy.

Rather than terrifying me, the knowledge that I'm solely responsible for her safety while she surrenders control turns me on. My dick strains inside my jeans.

"We're going to have so much fun tonight," I say and drag my finger through her wet pussy. She's enjoying this as much as I am.

"I don't want any of this."

"Your body tells another story, sweetheart."

"Go to hell," she snarls.

I pull my T-shirt off and toss it onto the floor. "I warned you what would happen if you didn't keep your mouth shut." Reaching into my bag, I pull out the open-mouth gag I brought and dangle it in front of Svetlana. "This is my insurance policy. I don't want you getting any ideas about using those teeth while I fuck your face."

"No, please," she whimpers. "I promise I'll be quiet."

"It's too late for that," I chuckle.

I lean over her to fit the gag around her head. Lana thrashes her head back and forth, causing me to struggle with the latch. "Hold your fucking head still," I say as the bedroom door flies open, banging off the wall, and a flashlight shines in our direction.

"Stop," a female voice yells. "The police are on their way."

"Natalie?" Lana shrieks as she lifts her head. "What are you doing here?"

Natalie? As in Natalie, her roommate, who has no idea that Lana's involved in the BDSM lifestyle or that she's dating me and has now walked in on a CNC scene. This isn't going to end well.

The ceiling light flips on. Natalie takes one look at Svetlana, splayed out and restrained on the bed, and she screams. Then, her focus shifts to me. "You. Don't move," she yells and points her phone at me. I drop the metal gag. It lands with a thud on the floor, and I put my hands up.

"Nat, this isn't what it looks like. Can you uncuff me?" Lana asks.

I look at Natalie and then back to Lana before quickly releasing her arms and legs.

"I thought you were in Missouri," Lana says as she jumps out of bed and grabs her robe. She ties the belt around her waist and hurries over to Natalie. "What are you doing home?"

"Are you okay?" She grabs Lana's arms and looks her up and down. "Did he hurt you?" Natalie asks and glares at me over Lana's shoulder.

Banging on the apartment door startles me. "NYPD, open up."

"Oh my God, you really called the police." Lana's voice is panicked.

"Of course, I called them."

There's pounding again. "NYPD, open the door."

"Come with me." Lana grabs Natalie's arm and drags her along. "We need to fix this."

Keeping a safe distance, I follow the girls out of the bedroom.

Lana heads straight to the door and unlocks it. "Good evening, officers. Please come in," she says calmly and steps aside, allowing them room to enter the apartment.

"We received a call of an assault in progress." The taller of the two male officers says.

I move to take a step closer when the other officer reaches for his gun. "You, put your hands up and don't move."

I freeze in place with my hands in the air.

Svetlana

"There's a very good explanation for all this," I say, hoping to find the right words to get us out of this mess without Brandon ending up in handcuffs. "Please put your weapons away." The police officer looks between Brandon and me. "That's my boyfriend. May I call him over?"

He doesn't take his hand off his weapon but says, "Yes."

I look behind me and see a confused Natalie sitting on the couch with her head in her hands. I'll take care of this with her later. Right now, I need to address the situation with law enforcement. I motion for Brandon to come over. He looks at me hesitantly before walking across the room.

"Officer, this is my boyfriend, Brandon Carpenter. My roommate was supposed to be out of town this week, so he and I planned some private couple's time."

"We got a call of an assault in progress," the office says.

"Brandon and I have very particular tastes when it pertains to intimate things." The officer looks between his partner and me. "We practice bondage and other more adventurous bedroom pursuits."

"I see." The man finally removes his hand from his weapon, replacing it into his holster.

"Natalie comes from a small mid-western town." I look over my shoulder at my roommate before continuing. "She's very sheltered and naïve. I haven't even told her I have a boyfriend."

"She was supposed to be gone home for the school holiday," Brandon adds. "We didn't expect her to walk in on us."

The officers separate Brandon and me and ask us more questions in their attempt to clarify what was going on and to be sure there was no crime in progress. It takes a bit of doing, but we finally convince them there was no wrongdoing.

"Thank you, and sorry for the confusion," I say, shaking the officers' hands before they leave the apartment. Then, I close the door and blow out a breath.

"Do you want me to stay?" Brandon asks, taking my hand in his. "I can help you explain."

"I don't think that's a good idea. I'll call you in the morning."

"Okay, talk to you tomorrow," he says, kissing my forehead before leaving.

I take my time locking up, knowing the conversation Natalie and I are about to have will be equally as difficult as dealing with the NYPD. After taking a deep breath, I turn on the lamp and sit beside Natalie on the couch. "I don't know where to start," I say and then turn to look at her. What I see concerns me. "You've been crying." She nods. "What's wrong? Why are you home?"

"Tommy," Natalie says, quickly changing the subject. "What was going on back there?"

I look down the hall toward my room before answering. "It wasn't what it looked like."

"Did he hurt you?"

"No. Well, not any more than I asked for." I can't help the giggle that slips out.

"What?" Natalie's clearly confused.

"I'm going to grab us a glass of wine. I think we're going to need it." I get up and go into the kitchen. While I get the glasses and open the bottle, I ask, "What happened with Tommy?"

"I got to his dorm and found him having sex with Ashlynn."

Holy shit. Forget about a glass. We may need the whole bottle. "Ashlynn, as in your best friend?" I ask as I hand Natalie her glass.

"The one and only."

"Wow."

"Right now, I'm more concerned about what was happening here," Natalie says, motioning around the room.

"I wasn't expecting you to be home." I take a sip of the red wine and then set my glass on the table. "What you saw wasn't what you thought. I mean, it was, but not like you think."

"You were handcuffed to the bed and begging him to stop. It looked like he was hurting you."

"Oh boy, I don't know where to start."

"How about the beginning?"

I don't think there's any way to do this, so I blurt out the question. "Have you ever heard of BDSM?"

Natalie nearly chokes on her wine. "I've read about it in some romance novels. It's all that kinky sex and stuff." Realization washes over her face the second the words are out. "Is that what was going on back there?" Her hands tremble as she sets her glass down.

"Yes," I say and slowly nod. "I grew up in the BDSM lifestyle. Papa's a Dominant, and Mama's his submissive."

Natalie's mouth hangs open. "You mean to tell me your dad goes all Christian Grey and ties your mom up in the bedroom?"

"Ha, ha. You're so funny." I can't help but laugh. "That's not exactly how it is in real life. My papa adores Mama, and she him. Their relationship has always been an example of what I hope to find someday."

Whenever I talk about my parent's relationship, I can't help but be filled with great pride. I've always loved watching the affection they showered on one another in words or actions. I never hid my eyes or pretended it was gross seeing Papa give Mama a chaste kiss or hug.

When I was young, I'd tug on Papa's leg, begging for my own kiss. He'd scoop me up and swing me around before placing a kiss on my cheek. As I grew older, I recognized the adoration in Papa's eyes when he'd quietly watch Mama demonstrate her love and respect for him through her actions. Whether or not I entered the lifestyle, I knew from a young age that I wanted to find a man who looked at me and loved me the way Papa does Mama.

"Why would you want to know what your parents get up to in their bedroom?" Natalie scrunches up her nose.

"Eww." I nearly vomit at the thought. "We didn't talk about any of that stuff. BDSM is about so much more than kinky sex."

Keeping Natalie's upbringing in mind, I explain that the kinky things in the bedroom are just the basics of everything BDSM encompasses. It's a lifestyle choice where the submissive, be they man or woman, cares for the daily wants and needs of their Dominant. The person willingly hands control of their life to another, trusting that person sometimes with their very life.

In return for their gift of submission, the Dominant challenges their submissive to grow, not only in their submission but as a person. They are the granters of pleasure and the administers of discipline. Dominants ensure their submissive is safe and cared for. More than that, they're adored and cherished by their Dominant.

"What you walked in on tonight." I pause, trying to find the right words. "That was a scene Brandon and I'd been planning for a while. You were supposed to be gone."

"Wait a minute. You do this BDSM thing, too?"

"I'm a submissive," I say without hesitation.

"How were we roommates for two years, and I never knew?" She turns to face me and sits cross-legged on the couch.

"It's not a topic that's easy to bring up. Hi," I say and extend my hand for a simulated greeting. "I'm your new dorm mate. I like to get tied up and whipped." We both laugh.

Part of the reason I kept this from Natalie was because I didn't know how to introduce someone who's had so few experiences to BDSM. It was easy for me. I've known about the lifestyle for as long as I can remember. My parents and I have a very open relationship. They didn't hide their involvement in the lifestyle, but they also didn't go into detail about their private sex life. I mean, why would they? Instead, they modeled a healthy Dominant/submissive relationship. Which really models a healthy, traditional husband and wife relationship.

"When I was about eighteen, I asked my parents more about the lifestyle," I explain. "We had many conversations where my parents emphasized the commitment required for this kind of relationship. From the beginning, I knew I was a submissive. Mama wasn't as easily convinced. She stressed the importance of being mature enough to put my needs second to someone else's. I know from experience it isn't as easy as it sounds."

I give Natalie a minute to digest what I said while I take a drink.

"Mama gave me some books to read and introduced me to a trusted friend who was an experienced submissive. I mentored under her until I went to Moscow to study. That's where I submitted to a Dominant for the first time."

"Do you still happen to have the books she gave you?" she asks, trying to sound nonchalant.

Natalie's question catches me off guard. "Why?"

"I figure reading them might come in handy when I graduate." She shrugs, feigning innocence.

"I've been to Northmeadow." I sit back and cross my arms. "I don't think your teen clients will be into BDSM."

"Maybe I'm curious."

The way she places emphasis on *I'm* makes my head spin. Never in a million years did I think that would be Natalie's reaction. "I'll be right back." If she wants to broaden her horizons and learn about something new, I won't stop her. I think it will be good for her to realize there's more to life than marrying young and having babies. I grab the e-reader from my bedroom and return to the living room. "They're loaded on here." I pass the tablet to her and return to sit. "Your turn. Tell me exactly what happened when you got to Mizzou."

"I was so excited to surprise Tommy." A stray tear trickles down her cheek. "But when the door to his dorm opened, and I saw them together, my perfectly constructed life fell apart. I've never felt so betrayed. That was my boyfriend and best friend." Natalie presses the heel of her palms against her eyes as she tries to stop the tears from falling. "Maybe my parents were right when they said I shouldn't leave town for school?"

I listen quietly, all the while seething inside. What kind of a person betrays their best friend like that? And Tommy, I'd love to see him alone in a room with Pyotr for a few minutes.

"Now I have to come up with an excuse to tell my parents," she says and yawns. "There's no way I'm going back there until I have to."

I grab our empty wine glasses and bring them to the kitchen. "Why don't you sleep on it first. We can come up with something later."

The sun's beginning to break through the dark night sky, and we're still awake. I know I'm tired, and Natalie must be past exhausted with everything she's been through tonight.

"You have to promise to tell me more about you being tied up by that hot guy." She smiles.

"I just hope he's still interested. Someone scared the shit out of him by calling the police." I link my arm through Natalie's as we walk to our rooms.

Natalie's room is before mine. "Thank you." She hugs me. "And I'm sorry I ruined your night."

"There's nothing to apologize for." I wipe a tear that drips down her cheek. "That's the last time you're allowed to cry over Tommy. You're far too good for him."

"Lana—"

"Don't Lana me. Tommy's a piece of shit, and I won't let you make excuses for him anymore," I say in my best bossy voice. "Tomorrow starts a whole new adventure. One where you get to determine your future."

"I love you."

"Love you more. Now get some sleep."

When I get to my room, I look around at the remnants of our interrupted scene. I'm disappointed that we didn't get to finish. Heck, we barely got started. Brandon left a key on the bedside table and use it to remove the cuffs from the bed. I pick up the gag from the floor and put it all in his bag.

After changing into soft pajamas, I grab my cell and climb into bed. I intend to text Brandon, but a wave of exhaustion washes over me, and I drift off to sleep before I hit send.

Brandon

Last night was insane. When I left Lana's, I went right home. But today, I need someone to help me process everything, so I shoot a text to Alex.

Me: Tell me you're not in the office.

Alex: I'm not in the office.

Me: Is that the truth, or are you just telling me what I want to hear?

Alex: I just got back from my run. How did everything go last night?

Me: I don't want to talk about it over text. Are you able to get together for lunch?

Alex: Sure. The regular place?

Me: Yeah. I'll meet you there in about an hour.

After a quick shower, I take the subway across town and walk the few blocks to the little bar. It's mid-afternoon, so the place is pretty quiet. I easily spot Alex in our usual booth in the back corner.

"You look awful," Alex smirks. "Must have been a pretty long night."

"You don't know the half of it." Our server comes to our table, and we place our orders. Once he's gone, I say, "Things were just starting to heat up when her roommate showed up."

"You're kidding, right?"

I shake my head. "I wish I was. You think I can make this shit up? I couldn't have written that if I tried." I rewind and give Alex a brief outline of the events leading up to the bedroom door flying open. "Another few seconds and, well, things would've been even more uncomfortable. As it was, while Lana was trying to figure out why Natalie came home early, the NYPD started banging on the door."

Alex bursts out laughing. "I wish I was there to see you two trying to talk your way out of that one."

"It's not funny."

"You're right. It's hysterical."

"You wouldn't be laughing if you were the one with your hands in the air and a policeman pointing his weapon at you."

"Damn. They took it seriously."

"They received a phone call about an assault in progress. You're fucking right they took it seriously."

"I'm glad no one got hurt," Alex says, no longer laughing. "Now what?"

"I offered to stay and help Lana explain what happened to Natalie, but she wanted to do it herself."

"From what I've heard about that girl, that's probably a good idea." We stop talking while our food is served. "How are things there today?"

"I don't know. Lana hasn't called. I'm assuming she has a lot of explaining to do with her roommate, and I don't want to interfere."

"You also don't want her assuming you're mad or worse," Alex says.

He has a point. I need her to know we're still good. That last night's demise didn't scare me away. So, I pull out my phone.

Me: How was Natalie after I left? Is everything okay?

Lana: It went better than expected.

Me: Good. Can I come over today and officially meet your roommate?

Lana: I don't think that's a good idea. Natalie's been extra quiet. She came home early because she caught Tommy in bed with her best friend. Then everything with us. I think she's still trying to process everything.

Me: Maybe it'll help if we're both there to answer her questions.

Lana: I appreciate the offer, but I don't think that's a good idea. I want to keep everything calm and quiet today. I'll call you in a few days, okay?

Me: Okay.

I set the phone on the table and rub my hands over my head.

"What's wrong?"

"She doesn't want me to come over. That she'll call me in a few days." My heart sinks.

"Don't freak out yet. I'm sure she's overwhelmed with everything that happened last night. You know Lana, she retreats inward while she works things through."

"I'm sure you're right." Alex starts laughing again. "What?" I ask, slightly annoyed at his inappropriate response.

"I can't believe her roommate called the cops on you."

As hard as I try not to laugh, I lose the battle and join him.

Svetlana

NATALIE'S BEEN QUIET AND SPENDING MOST OF HER TIME IN her room. I've been walking on eggshells, unsure of what to do. I know she's still heartbroken over what happened with her now ex-boyfriend. Add to that the shock of what she found the night she came home. It's a lot for anyone. At some point, she needs to talk about it—all of it. I'm just not sure how to bring any of it up.

I'm in the kitchen cooking when Natalie walks into the room. Without saying anything, she sits at the kitchen island, tapping her fingers on the granite counter.

I ignore the noise as long as I can before I spin around, spatula in hand. "You're driving me crazy with the nervous tapping. What's up?"

Her hand stills, but she doesn't speak for several long seconds. "I was wondering if I could ask you some more questions? You know, about the books I'm reading."

"Sure," I answer and turn back to the stove so my food doesn't burn.

"What're you making?" Natalie asks.

"Piroshki. It's kind of my mama's recipe, except I cheated and bought the dough," I say and smile. "But I don't think that's what you wanted to ask. Dinner's ready. We can eat and talk."

I set the table while Natalie pours the wine. With our plates full, I watch as she takes her first bite. "Oh my God, Lana. This is amazing," she says, closing her eyes.

"Thanks, but you're avoiding," I say, pointing my fork at her.

"I want to learn more," Natalie says quickly and then takes a bite.

I can't help but laugh. "That's what you were so nervous to say?"

She shrugs.

I swipe Natalie's phone and unlock the screen. Knowing each other's passwords comes in handy. "Here's the club I go to. It's called Fire and Ice." I pass the phone back to her so she can see the website. "They have classes for people who think they might be interested. You should take one."

"I'm not ready for anything like that," Natalie says, setting aside her phone. "Isn't there anything else I can read?"

"There are tons of books, but you'll learn more by taking the class and talking to real people."

"I'll think about it."

After we clean up, we settle on the couch with a bowl of popcorn. We've been watching popular American '80s movies. Tonight's flick is *The Breakfast Club*. I'm told it's a must-watch, and by the time the end credits roll, I totally understand why this movie is so loved. I didn't have to grow up in America to connect with the onscreen teenage struggles. They seem to transcend the boundaries of where a person is raised.

"Are you going to stay at your friend's house this weekend?" Natalie asks.

"I was thinking about it. Why? What's up?"

"I have Saturday off, and I was hoping to go shopping. I'm in need of a new wardrobe."

That's an offer I can't pass up. "I'll be ready bright and early."

"Thanks, Lana." Natalie smiles. "If we have a long day of shopping, I better get to sleep."

I haven't seen Natalie smile this much since she got back from her devastating trip home. Things were so bad after that she had to change her cell phone number because Tommy wouldn't stop harassing her. He obviously doesn't take hints very well.

She gave her parents her new number. As we figured, they haven't stopped bugging her about going home. She keeps giving them excuses about why she can't leave the city. I was afraid she'd cave and give in to their demands, but it seems like Natalie might be turning a corner with her independence.

I knew it was a big stretch asking Natalie to go to a club the other night, but I'd love for her to take the beginner class. It would put her in an environment with people who'll encourage her to stand up for herself and remind her that she has a voice in her life. For the first time in her life, she'd also be shown how she deserves to be treated by a man.

Since I don't think I can get her there, I'll have to talk to Gray and see if he has any other resources I can give Natalie. I don't want to push her too far out of her comfort zone. But if she wants to learn about the lifestyle and explore her developing sense of self, I plan to cheer her on.

Grayson

Today's the first time I've seen Svetlana since before the Thanksgiving holiday. She canceled her appointment last week because of illness.

The session started as per usual. Svetlana caught me up on the past several weeks, including the CNC scene she and Brandon did. Svetlana was not triggered in any way, which was a significant concern for her boyfriend. It was successful in many ways until her roommate, Natalie, unexpectedly showed up and called 911. According to Svetlana's account, she did a remarkable job handling the authorities and her traumatized roommate.

Of particular interest was the fact that she didn't mention anything about Brandon after that night. When I asked, she told me she texted him briefly the next day. He wanted to come over, and she refused. It appears she's kept him at arm's length ever since. She was not receptive to more questions about that subject, so I let it go. It is something I'm hoping to explore further in a future session.

After recapping recent events, I asked her what she wanted to discuss. Svetlana is always given the choice to lead the direction of our session.

Today, she was focused on her roommate, who has expressed curiosity about the BDSM lifestyle but is resistant to doing anything in person. Svetlana asked for more resources to give Natalie that would allow her to continue learning but in a more comfortable manner.

I provided Svetlana with several reputable websites to pass on to her roommate and an offer to speak with Natalie directly if she's interested.

My overall observations are that Svetlana remained guarded throughout today's session, preferring to shift the attention to Natalie rather than herself. Having worked with Svetlana for over a year, I know it's part of her pattern to have periods where she retreats. I've learned that where it may appear she's not making forward progress, she typically has a breakthrough in the weeks following a more reserved session.

Brandon

Christmas is this week. Before the craziness that happened over Thanksgiving break, Svetlana and I planned to spend the Christmas holiday together at her apartment. On Christmas Eve, we were to attend a Christmas party at Fire and Ice, where we were finally signing the contract, making our Dominant/submissive dynamic official. Afterward, we planned to drive to JFK, where Maxim's jet would be waiting to fly us to Russia to spend a few days with her family.

Everything changed after Natalie found her now ex-boyfriend with her now ex-best friend. Since then, Natalie refuses to go back to her hometown until she absolutely has to, which means she won't be out of town for the holiday. Svetlana's still not comfortable having Natalie and I interact. At first, I was upset and questioned if Svetlana was trying to push me away. When I expressed my concerns, Lana assured me she was not and asked me to try to put myself in Natalie's shoes.

When I did, I realized that this young woman was betrayed in the worst possible way by two of the people she cared about most. She returned to what was supposed to be the safety of her apartment to find what she thought was her other best friend being sexually assaulted. Then, she finds out that the same best friend is hiding a part of her life, and it's no small part. BDSM is still considered by many to be a deviant or taboo lifestyle. Needless to say, Natalie's struggling to process everything. As difficult as this is, Lana's being a good friend by not shoving me in Natalie's face.

Complicating things on our end is that Svetlana wants to hold off on signing the contract until she returns from Russia. I agreed, but I can't help the lingering disappointment that our dynamic is getting put on hold—again.

"What are you doing here still?" Alex asks when he walks by my office.

"Same thing you're doing here, I suppose."

"Lana's still refusing to leave her roommate?"

"I can't blame her. The girl was terrified."

"I get that," Alex says as he walks into my office and sits across from my desk. "But she's not a fragile flower that's going to wilt and die if she's left alone for a few hours."

"I don't know her roommate." I shrug. "So, I'm following Lana's lead."

"This is a hard time of the year for her."

"That's why I'm not pushing."

"Don't give up on her," Alex encourages me.

Falling for Lana was never in my plans. Little did I know that from the very beginning, my chances of resisting her were slim to none—I never stood a chance. From the first night, an inexplicable addiction took hold. I had to see her again.

While others describe Lana as a strong-willed woman, I see beyond the surface. She's a woman who's braved the darkest depths of what humanity offers. Lana endured horrors that would bring most of us to our knees. Instead of succumbing to hatred and resentment, her compassionate heart remains tender, yearning to alleviate the suffering of others. There is an undeniable feistiness about her, a fiery spirit that ignites my own passions. I wouldn't dare dream of extinguishing that flame because doing so means snuffing out part of what makes Lana so special.

I love Svetlana Solonik. Like the life-sustaining beat of my heart, she's a part of me that I need to survive. Without her, I'm nothing. Giving up on Svetlana is something I'll never do.

Grayson

DECEMBER 18 SESSION NOTES

Svetlana was visibly anxious when she arrived for her appointment this afternoon. She began the session by telling me about the changes to her upcoming trip to Russia to visit her family. Initially, Brandon was to accompany her, but now her roommate is traveling with her instead.

She expressed apprehension about returning home at this time of the year. Although she won't be there on the anniversary of her sister's abduction, it's still a somber time for her family. *Note- Natalie is not aware that Lana had a sister. Lana's concerned because Natalie lost her brother to suicide several years ago, and she doesn't want to trigger any unpleasant memories.

I suggested that if Svetlana opens up to Natalie about her past, it might be a time of healing for both young women. Svetlana is opposed to that because it will lead to revealing her father's career in the Bratva, which is something she's unwilling to do. I support her reasoning as this is a topic that falls out of the realm of typical.

Svetlana then shifted the conversation to the Dominant/submissive contract she's ready to sign with Brandon—something that was supposed to take place before she went to Russia. She informed me she needed more time, so she postponed this event. I asked how Brandon took the news. She explained he was rightfully disappointed but understanding. I reaffirmed that if she wasn't ready to move forward with the contract, she did the right thing by asking for more time. I also reminded her I'm here if/when she's ready to discuss her reasoning in more detail.

For most of her young adult life, this time of the year is when she chose to retreat both mentally and physically. Svetlana is a unique case and has the ability to disappear with her bodyguard, someone who's known her since childhood. He's always helped her avoid the traumatic memories associated with the anniversary of her sister's abduction. This is something Svetlana has not done for several years. The act of choosing to make a trip home so close to this date marks progress in her healing.

I will be available to her round the clock while she is away due to the increased risk of trauma responses.

Svetlana

ALL THE LAST-MINUTE CHANGES HAVE MADE THIS TRIP HOME a whirlwind experience. Since my trip no longer includes Brandon, I made plans with Natalie to fly home in time to celebrate Christmas on December 25th since we'll need to be back in New York before Orthodox Christmas.

"We're here," I say and elbow Natalie who fell asleep on the ride here.

Natalie opens her eyes and stretches. "I didn't realize I fell asleep."

The on-duty guard must've been tracking our car via its GPS locator because the gates are already opening before Misha makes it to the guard station.

"Svetlana," she says and grabs my arm. "I've never seen anything so beautiful."

Papa mentioned he was having the house decorated for Natalie so she wouldn't feel like she missed out on celebrating the holiday. But I had no idea he was doing all this.

A breathtaking scene unfolds before us. Luminary candles line the path, casting an inviting glow that dances in the gentle breeze. Each flickering flame creates a mesmerizing display that captures the enchantment of the holiday season. The surrounding trees are adorned with strings of clear twinkling lights that only add to the magic.

When our house comes into view, even my breath catches. Softly shimmering lights embellish every nook and cranny, delicately tracing the edges of our home with a whimsical radiance. In each window is a candle. Their warm glow illuminates each space with a cozy ambiance.

As if nature herself was in on Papa's plans, snow begins to fall. Each flake glistens in the glow of the lights. The air is filled with an undeniable aura of joy and anticipation, as if everything around us hums with excitement.

Misha pulls the car to a stop, and Natalie jumps out. She twirls around with her mittened hands outstretched. "I feel like I'm in a life-sized snow globe," she giggles.

"I think it's more like one of those Hallmark Christmas movies you girls force me to watch," Pyotr says.

"The ones that always make you teary," I joke.

Misha looks at him. "You cry at movies now? Has living abroad made you soft?"

"I'm afraid my little butterfly is so exhausted she has no idea what she's talking about." Pyotr looks at Natalie, who's watching the interaction cautiously, and winks. "Natalie will tell you. I watch them under duress."

"He hates them." She corroborates his story.

"Sure," Misha laughs as he walks past with some of our bags in tow.

"I knew I liked you," Pyotr says, making Natalie smile bigger. He grabs the rest of our bags while I explore some of the lights with Natalie.

"Did you know about this?"

"Kind of." I smile. "Papa mentioned he was going to do some decorating. I should've known he'd go all out."

"I thought I heard a car," Mama says as she steps outside. "How long have you been out here?"

"Only a few minutes." I walk over to her and give her a hug.

"It's so good to have you home. I've missed you so much."

"It's only been a few months."

"It feels like longer to me. Welcome home, Natalie," Mama says, wrapping her in a hug.

"Thank you, Irina," Natalie says hesitantly. "I was excited when Lana asked me to come home with her."

"I thought I heard my girls," Papa says, appearing in the doorway. "The three of you need to get inside before you catch a cold."

"Maxim," Natalie says quietly, "The decorations are beautiful."

"I was hoping you would like them." He smiles.

"They're perfect."

I was afraid that coming home this time of the year would feel suffocating with sorrow. Instead, the combination of holiday decorations and the softly falling snow transports us to a realm where dreams come true, and the spirit of the season fills our hearts with warmth and joy. And it doesn't stop outside.

Walking into the house feels like stepping foot inside a Christmas wonderland. The staircase inside the foyer is adorned with lighted evergreen garlands. Holiday trees decorate the entrance, and our antique nativity is on full display. I don't know where to look first.

"Are you girls hungry?" Mama asks. "I can have Olga prepare a snack."

I look at Natalie, who shakes her head. "I think we're going to get settled in and try to get some sleep."

"Your rooms are ready for you," Mama says. "It's so good to have you girls home."

We celebrate Christmas morning, exchanging gifts by a tree that's easily ten feet tall. It's something we've never done before, at least not like this. Despite being fully grown, I can't help the childlike excitement that takes over as I tear the paper off my presents.

Papa and Mama shower both Natalie and me with clothes, jewelry, and gift cards for our favorite stores in New York.

"Thank you both so very much," Natalie says when we've finished opening the gifts.

"You are very welcome, Natalia," Papa answers with a smile. "Having you and *moya babochka* here has been good for the heart."

"I wasn't looking forward to this holiday," she says sadly. "After everything that happened with Tommy."

"That young man was not deserving of you," Mama adds.

"We are not talking about him today," Papa says. "Today is for celebrating."

Unfortunately, our trip home is not long enough, and before I know it, we're back on Papa's jet, returning to New York.

I hate not being here with my family through this difficult time. Celebrating Christmas with Natalie took what's always been dreaded days and infused them with joy. It feels like a new beginning. Hopefully, this is a tradition we can continue.

Grayson

MAY 13 SESSION NOTES

Svetlana has regularly attended sessions every two weeks over the past few months. There were many difficult weeks as she faced the memory of the events leading up to her sister's murder. On the anniversary of Jelena's death, I accompanied her to Central Park, where we released a single white balloon that carried a note Svetlana wrote to her sister. It was an emotional moment for both of us. I'm proud of Svetlana for not running from her memories as she's done in the past.

She's still seeing Brandon but has yet to sign a Dom/sub contract with him. Svetlana is open about having feelings for Brandon outside of any dynamic. However, she refuses to address why she's putting off signing the contract. I suspect she fears the commitment that comes with a contractual relationship. Something Svetlana denies.

Svetlana expressed excitement about the completion of her first year of law school. Because she's in an accelerated program, she'll only have one more year of study to be eligible to sit for the bar exam. Her work ethic is second to none, and for that, I have to commend her.

We will be continuing sessions over the summer months as she plans to remain in the United States and will be interning at a law firm in Manhattan.

Grayson

September 7 Session Notes

This is the first in-person session Svetlana and I have had since July. She has kept in touch via text, but because of some last- minute travel during her summer break, she could not attend in-person sessions. Despite not meeting in the office, Svetlana continues working on her treatment goals.

School's back in full swing, and Svetlana reports being happy with her courses. She's said for some time that she's experiencing anxiety concerning school, interning, and her personal life. I've suggested different coping mechanisms I thought might be helpful. Despite her efforts, none of them seemed to be beneficial.

Given her history of running and secluding, I was concerned. I was pleasantly surprised when she informed me that while she was in Russia, she visited the school where she took ballet as a child.

I was unaware until this time that Svetlana took ballet lessons as a young girl. She reports that it was something she loved but gave up in her teens. Svetlana describes stepping into the studio as feeling like being home. When she returned to Manhattan, she found a ballet school and has attended several classes.

Svetlana explained dance has provided her with an outlet for the emotions she otherwise bottles up. I expressed how proud I am of her for admitting she was struggling and also for finding a coping mechanism that is healthy and effective.

My recent observations correlate with her self-reports. Svetlana's much more settled—at peace. I'm hopeful that this represents a turning point in her healing journey.

The subject of Brandon and their unsigned contract was revisited. Although they two have been seeing one another more over the summer, coupled with the fact that Natalie's expressed an interest in getting to know him, Svetlana still keeps them separate.

Svetlana explained she's been doing a great deal of soul-searching regarding the unsigned contract. She acknowledges that her fear of commitment has been a significant deterrent and reason for her not signing. I suggested the possibility of a shorter-term contract—baby steps, if you will. Svetlana was not opposed to that idea and said she'd consider bringing that idea to Brandon.

Once again, I reminded her about the importance of honest communication in the BDSM lifestyle. I encouraged her to talk to Brandon about her fears. Adding that if they're going to be a Dominant/submissive couple, she must allow herself to trust him. It's an idea she seems to be warming up to.

As it was time for our regular evaluation, I asked Svetlana for her opinion about our sessions. She feels therapy has been helpful and is beginning to see progress. We're in agreement to continue our therapeutic relationship.

Svetlana

Three years. That's how long it's taken to get to this moment, but we're finally here. Brandon's picking me up from Alex's apartment, and then we're going to Fire and Ice, where we'll sign our contract. It's been a lesson in patience and understanding for each of us as we waded through the murky waters of our pasts.

Brandon's already proved himself as a capable Dominant. He's been my safe place while I've been learning how to better regulate my emotions and face my insecurities. After this process, I have a better understanding of why a prospective couple shouldn't be intimately involved. It creates a messy and confusing situation—one I wouldn't suggest to anyone. However, I stand by the decision Brandon and I made for us.

While I do my make-up, I think back to that night in the private room at the club. I thought I was ready to submit to a Dominant and was sure Brandon would offer me a contract and suggest we start vetting. Instead, he asked for more time.

Initially, I was disappointed. I thought if I told him I was okay with going slow, it would only be a few weeks, a month or two tops, before we took the next step. Days turned into weeks, into months, into years.

And then the tables turned. This time, Brandon was ready, but it was me holding back. At times, it seemed we'd never get on the same page. But finally, after a lot of serious negotiations, we made it.

"Lana," Alex calls as he knocks on the door. "Brandon's here."

"I'll be right out." I twirl in front of the full-length mirror, ensuring everything is perfect. When I was shopping, I couldn't make up my mind. So, I bought three outfits for tonight. I've gone back and forth all day before settling on a simple white strapless mini-dress that dips slightly on my back. I've paired it with five-inch white stilettos that tie around my calves. Once I'm satisfied with my appearance, I shut the lights off and follow the sound of the guys' voices to the kitchen.

Alex stops speaking mid-sentence when he sees me standing in the doorway. He motions with his chin for Brandon, whose back is to me, to turn around.

"Holy—" He swipes his hand over his head. "You look fucking incredible."

"I think I'll leave you kids alone," Alex says.

"Aren't you coming to the club tonight?" I ask.

"No. I'm staying in."

"You really need to get out more," Brandon says.

"I get out plenty. You two have fun." Alex takes his bottle of water and leaves Brandon and me alone.

"I'm a little worried about him," Brandon says after Alex leaves the room. "All he does is work."

I've been concerned about Alex, too. But I didn't think it was my place to say anything because, let's face it, all my ducks aren't exactly lined up.

"I wish he'd be more open to a submissive. Star's had so many girls approach her asking about him, but he refuses to even consider it," Brandon explains.

"You don't have to tell me. I hear about it all the time. They think because we're friends, I can somehow get Alex to pay attention to them." I roll my eyes, annoyed at the thought.

"Hopefully, he'll come around." Brandon takes my hand. "We need to leave, or we'll be late."

"Late for what?"

"I made reservations for dinner," Brandon says on the elevator ride to the parking garage.

"I thought we were going to the club?"

"I changed the plan. Tonight's a special night."

"Do I get to know where we're going?" I ask as we walk to where he's parked.

"Nope." Brandon opens the car door and helps me in.

After a drive across town, Brandon pulls up to valet parking at Torch, an exclusive restaurant in Brooklyn.

"I'm afraid I didn't dress appropriately for a restaurant," I say as I get out of the car and link my hand with Brandon's.

"You look good to me." His hungry gaze travels up and down my body. "But you won't have to worry. No one will see you."

"What do you mean?"

"You'll see," Brandon smirks.

We're escorted into a dark room and seated at a table for two. I hear the soft murmurings of what I assume are other diners, but it takes my eyes a few seconds to adjust before I can make out the shapes.

"I'm going to put your blindfold on now," the server says before tying a piece of silk over my eyes.

"Brandon, what's going on?" I ask quietly when I'm certain the server is no longer at our table.

"This restaurant offers an immersive dining experience. We'll remain blindfolded while our meal is served."

I've never heard of such a thing, but over the next hour and a half, we're treated to a dining experience unlike anything I've ever had. A fruity wine that tastes like peach and apricot is served with an appetizer that's meant to be eaten with our hands. I find what feels like a small piece of toasted bread. I put it in my mouth, and an explosion of flavors assaults my senses. The toast had a subtle garlic flavor. Topping it is a sweet and creamy ricotta cheese and fiery honey. Together, this dish is divine.

The main course is set before us. With my vision restricted, my other senses are on high alert. The aroma is unfamiliar except for the smell of basil. Taking my fork, I try to get some of all the ingredients I feel in the bowl onto it. The food hits my tongue, and I'm overwhelmed by the unfamiliar flavors. The tomato sauce has a hint of spice, giving it a slight bit of heat, and the pasta is rich and nutty. The next bite contains another flavor I'm not accustomed to. It's tender and has earthy notes.

"What is this?"

"I think it might be eggplant," Brandon answers.

I'm familiar with eggplant from a dish, *Ikra*, lovingly known as Eggplant caviar. But in that dish, the eggplant is pureed with peppers, garlic, and tomatoes and served as a cold appetizer. I've never had it prepared like this.

"Do you like it?" he asks.

"It's yummy." I take another bite. "I'd love to learn how to cook eggplant like this."

"We can ask Tony if he can teach you this dish," Brandon suggests.

"Do you think he'd mind?"

"Not at all."

Paired with the main course is red wine. The fragrance has aromas of cherry and roses. The taste is earthy yet has fruity undertones. I hope after the meal, we get to know what everything we're trying is.

Dessert is served in what feels like a coffee cup. We're instructed to use our spoon for the dessert portion and then to drink the remainder, which I can already tell is coffee. When the spoon hits my tongue, I recognize it as ice cream with subtle hints of chocolate. After I finish the ice cream, I take a sip of what can only be a rich Italian espresso.

Just as I'd hoped, after the meal, we're instructed to remove the blindfolds. The lights in the room are turned to a dim setting. Our server hands us each a copy of the menu from this evening's meal.

"Thank you," I say to Brandon as we leave the restaurant. "That was the most unique dining experience I've ever had."

"I'm glad you enjoyed it."

"Where to now?"

"We're going to my house. There's a contract waiting to be signed."

A surge of excitement courses through my veins as my heart rate kicks into high gear, knowing tonight will not end before we're finally Dominant and submissive.

Brandon

I GRIP THE STEERING WHEEL TIGHTLY, TRYING TO MASK THE trembling in my hands. We've just had an incredible dining experience that far exceeded my expectations. Now, Lana and I are on our way back to my house, where we'll finally sign the contract. If all goes as planned, I'll have her gagged and tied to my bed shortly.

Luck is in my favor because we hit all green lights. I pull the Mustang into my driveway and kill the engine. Turning slightly in my seat, I say. "Are you ready?"

"I am."

Before I left the house, I set out the papers and pens on my dining room table. I didn't want to waste any time once we got here. I usher Lana into the room and pull the seat out for her. "Can I get you anything to drink?"

"A glass of ice water would be wonderful."

When my parents passed away, their house was left to me. The house is more traditional in style, with a formal dining area that's separate from the kitchen. My plan is to eventually knock out the walls and have a modern open floor plan. Because I work so much, I haven't had much time to do any updates.

I leave Lana and go get our drinks. My anxiety's out of control. So, I take my time, ensuring I'm calm and centered before returning to Lana and setting the glass on the table.

"Thank you." Svetlana looks up. Her blue eyes remind me of the sky on a cloudless day. If she's nervous, she's hiding it well.

I sit across from her and sip my water before setting it down. Pulling the papers closer to me, I look at Lana. "I'd like for us to review the contract a final time to ensure all the requested changes were made correctly and that we're both in agreement with moving forward."

Her mood shifts to serious and business-like. "I appreciate that."

We start on page one and take it line by line. It may be overkill, but this is important, and I want to be sure that every detail has been covered. Mistakes can be made too easily, and I'm not leaving anything to chance. Svetlana shows no signs of impatience as I read aloud.

"I added the time limit of one year as promised. With the agreement that we'll review the contract at that time," I add.

"That's perfect. Thank you."

Finally, we reach the last page. At the bottom are two blank lines where we'll sign our names, solidifying our agreement and the beginning of the contract.

"Before we sign, there's something I need to say."

"Okay," Lana says hesitantly.

"Contract or no contract, I've fallen for you." I get up and walk over to where she sits. "I'm excited about what's on those pages, but I want so much more. I love you, Svetlana."

She looks up, meeting my gaze. "I love you, too."

I lean down and brush my lips against hers. "We need to sign this because I don't want to wait another second to take you to bed."

Lana giggles and then picks up her pen, signing her name. She holds it out for me, and I do the same. With that one small move, the remaining walls between us finally crumble.

She rises from her chair and asks, "What now?" Lana bites her bottom lip.

The look on her face makes me lose the last shred of self-control. I swipe my hand across the table, causing papers to fly through the air. Our water glasses smash off the hardwood floor, but I don't care. Reaching behind her, I unzip her dress and watch as she shimmies it down her legs. She steps out of the pile of fabric, and I kick it aside. I'm not surprised to find her bare underneath.

"Lay on the table and open your legs." My voice is low and commanding. She obeys without hesitation. "You're so wet already," I say as I drag my finger along her slit.

Unzipping my pants, I free my hard cock. "Who do you belong to?"

"I belong to you, Sir."

I pull her to the edge of the table. My hands grip her hips as I tease her with the tip of my cock. Her hips lift from the table, and I stop. Lana groans at the loss of contact.

"I'm the only man who'll ever touch this pussy again."

"You're the only man I ever want to touch me. The only one I want to feel inside me. It'll always be you."

I didn't know how badly I needed to hear someone say that I'm their everything. Hearing Svetlana say those words healed fissures in my heart that I didn't realize were still there. For the first time in so long, I feel completely whole.

With one hand on her hip, I line myself up with her opening and enter her. Lana's breath catches. "You feel so fucking good. Like you were made for me."

"Mmm," she responds.

I start moving slowly at first. Her hands move to her breasts, kneading the flesh and twisting her nipples between her fingers. Gripping her hips, I increase my pace. One of my hands goes between her legs, rubbing fast, hard circles on her clit. I need her to come with me. To solidify our words with our bodies.

I don't have to ask. I know from her panting breaths and the tensing of her body that she's close. Her orgasm begins a second before mine. The quick pulsing of her body around my cock triggers my own pleasure. The significance of this shared moment, the joining of our bodies and the beginning of our dynamic, only makes me come harder.

Once our bodies still, I ask, "Are you okay?"

Lana pushes up on her elbows. "Yes, I am. But I don't think your dining room is."

"I don't give a fuck about my dining room." I pull out and help her up.

"Where do you keep your broom? I'll clean up the broken glass."

"I'll get it later."

"Don't be silly," she says. "It'll only take a minute."

"Are you arguing with me already?"

"Maybe," she says coyly.

"I have a cure for that."

"You do?"

"Yes." I toss her over my shoulder, earning a squeal. "There's a ball gag in my room with your name on it."

Svetlana

Since the night Natalie walked in on her ex-boyfriend in bed with her ex-best friend and then walked in on Brandon and me, she's been making a lot of changes in her life. No longer is she the timid girl from a small town who lets everyone walk all over her. She's much more confident and has even gone out with me on several weekends.

Still, I haven't figured out how to tell Natalie about tonight. I've tried so many times but backed out at the last second. Now, I'm out of time. What I'm about to ask will be a big stretch, though, and I'm terrified.

"Are you still studying?" I snatch the textbook from her hand and read the title aloud, "Love and Attachment: Adult Relationships." I do my best to hold in a laugh. "You need to get out of this apartment."

"I have a paper." Natalie jumps off the couch and swipes at the book. I'm several inches taller than her and easily hold it out of reach.

"You can study tomorrow. Tonight, I want you to come out with me."

"But—"

"Come on, Nat." I give in and return the book.

Natalie takes it and sits back on the sofa, quickly flipping through the pages to find her place. "I'll go out next weekend, I promise."

"I need you to come out tonight." I drop down on the sofa next to her.

"Why?"

Here goes nothing. "Well, you remember Brandon, the guy you called the cops on?" I hold back the laugh that's threatening to escape.

Natalie's cheeks turn bright red. "How could I forget."

"Thankfully, you didn't scare him away."

"That's good because he sure is hot."

"He is, isn't he." I can't help the smile that spreads across my face. "I've finally consented to be his submissive," I say and gauge Natalie's response before continuing, "We're doing a scene at the club tonight, and I really want you there."

Natalie's eyes widen, and she closes the book giving me her full attention.

"You're doing a scene? Like getting naked in front of an audience?"

I nod slowly, hoping I haven't totally freaked her out. I don't want her to lose all the ground she's gained.

"This is what you want?" she asks, uncertain.

I'm scared to admit how much I want this. "I'm so excited about it, but please, I need my best friend there."

"I wouldn't miss it for the world," Natalie squeals and pulls me in for a tight hug.

Her reaction is unexpected. "I'm so glad you said yes. You're going to have a great time."

The look on her face tells me she's not convinced, but I have a plan up my sleeve that will hopefully make this the best night of her life.

I'm even happier when Natalie puts her books aside and spends the day primping for tonight. We spend the rest of the afternoon giving each other mani/pedis before I shower. When I come out, Natalie's waiting to fix my hair.

Brandon and I are doing a very intense scene tonight, and I need my hair up and out of the way. Fortunately, Natalie is great at fixing hair, so I let her have free reign. She starts with a fishtail that transitions into a beautiful tight bun.

"There. All done," she says after putting in the last pin.

I hold up an extra mirror to see the back of my hair. "Thanks, I love it."

"I need to jump in the shower quick and find something to wear," Natalie says as she leaves my room. "What do you suggest I wear tonight?" she asks from my doorway, startling me.

"I was hoping you'd ask. I have the perfect outfit for you." I hurry into my closet to grab the dress I put aside for her.

Natalie lets out a huff. "You're kidding, right?"

I knew this part might be a fight, but I'm far more stubborn than she is. "Nat, you're gorgeous." I push the hanger into her hands. "You're going to turn heads tonight."

"Do I want to turn heads?"

"You never know who you might meet." I point Natalie in the direction of her room and give her an encouraging nudge forward. "Go shower and get dressed. Now."

"Are you sure you're not a Domme?" She laughs as she walks down the hall to her room. "You're awfully bossy." Several moments later, Natalie yells down the hall again. "How do I wear a bra with this thing?"

"You don't." It's my turn to laugh this time.

I get dressed and start my makeup when I get a text.

Brandon: Are you ready for tonight?

Me: I'm finishing up right now, Sir.

Brandon: Good. I'll be waiting for you at the club, *mon petit papillon.*

A shiver of excitement runs down my spine. I knew from the first time I met Brandon, when Alex brought him home for dinner, that if I was given the chance, I'd agree to submit to him. He's everything I've always wanted in a Dominant—even some things I didn't know I wanted. This is the first scene Brandon and I are doing as an official Dominant/submissive couple. We've been doing scenes for several years, but nothing like what we've planned for tonight and certainly nothing in public.

At first, Brandon wasn't sold on the idea of a public scene. Although he'd never admit it, what happened years ago with Celia still haunts him. One of the main sticking points in our contract is that he's unwilling to share me—ever. It's something I wasn't necessarily looking for, but I'm not opposed to it, either. It was so important to him, so I agreed to it. But I never agreed to not doing public scenes.

We've been going back and forth about it for a few weeks. He even brought Star into the conversations. Once he was confident there'd be no one else involved and that Star would have security on hand specifically for our scene, he agreed. I'm so excited he did.

I finish my makeup and go to Natalie's room to see if she's ready. I find her checking herself out in the mirror. "I knew it! You look amazing!" Natalie turns around and wraps her arms around my neck.

"What should I expect tonight?" she asks, suddenly looking nervous.

"The car's here. I'll tell you on the way."

"The car?"

"Brandon sent a car to pick us up. You ready?"

"Yep. Don't want to keep your man waiting."

Brandon

WHAT THE HELL DID I AGREE TO THIS FOR? HOW DID I LET Svetlana talk me into a public scene? I would never have agreed to this if it wasn't for Star's intervention.

But I know this club. It's not like Chains. The people here are strictly vetted. Star and Owen have detailed plans for every public scene in Fire and Ice. They'd never let what happened to Celia happen in their club. Although I know all this, I'm still nervous.

As if all that wasn't enough, Svetlana approached me earlier this week with another of her crazy ideas. She wants to set Alex and Natalie up. I have to admit at first, I wasn't on board. I mean, this is the same girl who called 911 on me last year. I haven't seen her since that night, but Lana says Natalie's different. She's opened up to a lot of new ideas and has even shown an interested in BDSM.

And then there's Alex. He's been single for more years than I can count. Alex says he's not interested in a relationship, but if things don't change, he's going to work himself into an early grave. So, I agreed to help Lana get them together.

I pull up Alex's contact on my cell and send him a text.

Me: Remember Lana's roommate?

Alex: Yes...

Me: She's coming to the club tonight. I need a favor.

Alex: No.

I'm choosing to ignore his protests.

Me: She needs an escort.

Alex: The same girl who called the cops on you last year?

Now, I kind of regret telling him about that because it's only going to make getting him to say yes more difficult.

Me: Yeah.

Alex: And you want me to escort her?

Me: Come on, bro.

There's a long pause, and I know it's because he's trying to find a way to get out of this.

Me: You know I'd do it for you.

Alex: I'm not feeling well. I don't think I can make it.

Me: The fuck you aren't. You're out running right now. Tell me I'm wrong.

Alex: Fine. But you owe me.

Me: Thanks, man.

Step one is complete. Now, we cross our fingers and hope they hit it off.

Svetlana

ON THE RIDE TO THE CLUB, I TRY TO TELL NATALIE AS MUCH as possible about what to expect at Fire and Ice tonight. She asks a lot of follow-up questions, and although I do my best to answer her, I know she won't fully understand until she sees it for herself. I think she's going to be surprised. The club isn't anything like what I know she's imagining it to be.

Brandon's driver pulls the car to a stop in front of the building. When we get out of the car, Natalie looks around. "Is Pyotr here?"

"I'm sure he's around somewhere." I know he's lurking in the shadows, keeping a watchful eye on me, but he's no longer a significant presence in my life. The closer Brandon and I get, the more distant Pyotr gets. When I asked him about it, he said it's because I don't need him as much now that I have Brandon. Part of me is thankful for the space and freedom, but the other part misses the man who's been by my side since I was a little girl.

The bouncer opens the club's door when he sees us approach. We step into the foyer, which is already busy. Master Kyoshi, a Shibari expert, will be doing a scene tonight. I'm sure that's why everyone's here so early. But unless they're helping set up or are in one of the scenes, they'll be waiting out here for a while.

There are several people in line ahead of us checking in. While we wait, Natalie tugs at her dress.

"Stop fidgeting," I say, and I feel like a mother hen.

"I'm so nervous, but I'm also excited. Is that normal?"

"It's perfectly normal. Don't worry." I squeeze her hand. "We're going to have a great time tonight. When we get to the desk, you'll be checked in as my guest. Mistress Star will give you a colored wristband."

"What's it for?"

"The colors represent a person's availability." I point to the sign on the wall that explains the color system. It's based on a rainbow where each color represents whether a guest is a Dominant or submissive, with a partner or alone, just watching or looking to play.

"You'll get a purple band. It means you're being sponsored by a Dominant, and no one can approach you without asking his permission first." It's our turn to check in, so I approach the counter. "Good evening, Lana."

"Good evening, Mistress. This is my friend, Natalie." I motion next to me. "She'll be our guest this evening."

"Brandon gave me her information." Mistress Star looks at Natalie. "Has Lana explained our color system?"

"Yes, she has."

"Do you have any questions?"

"No," Natalie says quietly.

"May I have your right arm?" Natalie holds it out, and Star puts the wristband on. "You understand you'll have a Dominant responsible for your comfort and safety tonight?"

"I do."

"Are you comfortable with that?" Star asks.

One of Natalie's concerns was if the club took consent seriously. She was online and read some horror stories. Natalie doesn't know about Brandon's past. It's not my story to tell. I assured her neither Brandon nor I would be members at a club where safe and consensual play wasn't enforced.

"Yes, ma'am."

"You ladies can go right in. Brandon is waiting for you by stage three," Mistress Star instructs. "Natalie, I hope you have a wonderful evening. I'll be around all night if you have any questions or concerns."

We're fully checked in. This is it. I grab Natalie by the arm and nearly drag her through the large medieval-looking doors that lead into the club. "Come on. I'm so excited for you to officially meet Brandon."

Natalie steps into the room before me and freezes as she looks around the room. She says nothing, leaving me to wonder what's going through her mind.

Fire and Ice is an upscale club with a modern industrial vibe. The main room, where we're standing, is where all the public scenes occur. Currently, the bright overhead lighting is on. Later, the professional stage lights will help to set the mood for each scene.

"Things don't start for a few hours. That's when the real fun happens." I wiggle my eyebrows, trying to break the tension. Feeling more confident that Natalie's okay, I look for Brandon and motion for Natalie to come with me. Without me saying anything, he turns around and gives me a look that makes my insides quiver. "Natalie, I'd like you to meet my Dominant, Brandon."

"It's nice to meet you." Brandon offers her a kind smile.

Natalie's cheeks turn pink as she says, "It's nice to meet you too. I'm sorry for calling the police."

"Already forgiven. It's good to know Lana has someone looking out for her."

The sound of creaky wheels steals Natalie's attention. On the stage, two of the club's members are moving a black walnut St. Andrew's cross onto the stage. Once it's in place, the only sound remaining is from the metal cuffs banging against the wood.

"What's that thing? It looks like a torture device."

Brandon laughs. "It's a Saint Andrew's Cross. I'll secure Lana to it and use my whip to pleasure her."

Natalie's brow furrows. "Your whip? Won't that hurt her?"

"I won't her hurt—much." He winks.

Natalie looks at me, her eyes full of concern. I don't have a chance to respond before Brandon explains, "Lana likes pain, and I know how to give her what she craves without hurting her." He attempts to reassure her, but she doesn't seem convinced.

"It's okay, Nat. Brandon and I have already talked about everything we'll do tonight. This is something I want."

"You're sure?" she asks, clearly not believing me.

"Positive."

Brandon looks over Natalie's shoulder, and a grin spreads across his face. Natalie spins around, and I know the exact second she sees him. Alex has just walked in and is standing across the room. He runs his hand through his dark hair and looks around. As soon as he sees Brandon, he smiles and starts walking our way.

It never ceases to amaze me how both men and women fall all over themselves when Alex enters a room. The other submissives always carry on about how hot he is. They think I'm crazy when I don't join them, making up fantasies about him. When I look at him, all I see is Alex, the guy I've known for years. The one who, most times, makes me want to scream and pull *his* hair out.

What's most important is that Natalie seems to have fallen under his spell. And Brandon didn't want me playing matchmaker.

"Glad you made it," Brandon says as he shakes Alex's hand.

"I wouldn't miss it." He turns to me, and from the amused look on his face, I know he realizes I'm behind this little setup. "How are you tonight, Svetlana?"

"I'm fine, thank you," I answer and, like a well-trained submissive, keep my gaze cast down. Well, that and I don't want to fight with Alex right now.

Thankfully, Brandon steps in. "Natalie. I want to introduce you to my best friend, Alex." She remains quiet, her eyes fixed on the man across from her. "Alex is also a Dominant here. I've asked him to be your escort in my absence tonight."

"Oh," she says. "I thought I'd be staying with you and Lana?" Natalie looks at me, and I shrug, feigning innocence. If all goes well, she'll thank me later.

"We won't be available for the entire evening, and because you're a first-time guest, you can't be alone in the club," Brandon explains. "You're in good hands with Alex."

"I've heard a lot about you." Alex tries to hold back a smirk.

"You have?" Natalie turns to me, but I slink behind Brandon.

"I have. You're the girl who called the police on my friend here." Alex smiles and slaps Brandon on the back.

"Oh, my God. I can't believe you told anyone about that." If I thought Natalie's cheeks were red when I introduced her to Brandon, I was wrong. Right now, they are flaming from a mix of embarrassment and fury.

"There's no reason to be embarrassed. I'm sure Brandon appreciated your desire to protect your roommate," Alex chuckles.

"Lana and I have to finish setting up our stage," Brandon interrupts. "We'll see you two later."

I give Nat a small wave as I walk away with Brandon, leaving Alex and her alone. "Do you think they're going to get along?"

"Maybe." Brandon shrugs.

"What do you mean, maybe? They're both unattached. And did you see how they couldn't take their eyes off each other?"

Without warning, Brandon stops, and I nearly collide with his back. "Svetlana, I do not like you playing matchmaker with our friends."

"But you agreed—"

"I agreed to ask Alex to come tonight to sit with Natalie because she's your friend, and I don't want her being paired with someone I don't know. But that's as far as I'm willing to go."

"But—"

"No more buts. After tonight, that's it. I won't be a part of trying to get them together." He starts walking again. "And neither will you."

"Yes, Sir."

If everything goes according to plan, they won't need our intervention after tonight.

Brandon and I spend a few minutes together before our scene. He reserved a private room, so we have a quiet place for aftercare. Providing aftercare is the responsible thing to do following BDSM play, but Brandon places extra focus on it because of my traumatic past.

With my permission, Brandon met with Gray several times to discuss his concerns. He wanted to be sure he had every resource on hand to help me recover physically and emotionally from a scene. Especially tonight's. It's going to be intense and will challenge each of us.

"Are you sure you're ready for this?" Brandon asks when I exit the ensuite in my black silk robe.

"I'm positive," I say, closing the distance between us. "Are you still on board with it?"

"I am." He pulls me against him.

His grey eyes have a faraway look. "What's wrong?"

"I know the damage a whip can do. I don't—"

"You aren't going to hurt me." Brandon doesn't react. "May I speak freely?"

"Of course."

"Celia was not injured by your hand. I know you don't like to hear it, but you both were victims that night. If you weren't drugged, you would've never let any harm come to Celia, just like you'll never allow me to be hurt." He tries to turn away, but I use my hand to direct him back to me. "I trust you, Sir."

"I'll protect you with my life, *mon petit papillon.*" His lips meet mine, and he kisses me. It starts slowly and gently. Then, he grabs the back of my neck and deepens the kiss. His other hand slides down my front. He fumbles with the belt, holding my robe closed. Brandon groans, "We need to stop before I decide to fuck you instead."

"We'll be back in here after the scene. We can pick up where we're leaving off then."

"Not at the club."

We've had sex at the club once—in the school role-playing room. That was the one and only time Brandon let his guard down. Since then, he has refused to have sex here.

"Can't blame a girl for trying." I smile.

He steps back, putting a few inches of space between us. "It's time to go."

Brandon

When I open the door, the music from the club's main room floods in. Part of me wishes I had the courage to pull Lana back inside to finish what we started. The other part thrums with excitement for what we're about to do.

I've spent years learning and practicing with a whip. I'm confident in my skills, but that doesn't stop memories from creeping into the forefront of my mind. But this time, I'm older and more experienced. We're in a reputable club. Star has extra security in place to help me feel more comfortable with a public scene. I've also worked closely with Grayson to ensure I can properly care for Lana when the scene ends.

With Lana's hand in mine, we step into the main room. The music stops, and the noise in the club lowers to a soft murmur as we step onto the platform. Lana turns and faces me. I nod, her cue to begin. With ease, she unties the belt, and her robe flutters open, exposing her breasts and neatly groomed pussy. Reaching out, I slide the silky fabric down her arms and set it on a table that's positioned off to the side.

When I return to Svetlana, I pause, needing to take a deep breath. Lana stands facing the club filled with people, most of whom are gathered in front of our stage. She's completely nude yet shows no signs of nerves or insecurity. Instead, her arms hang loosely at her sides, and her head is lowered. I'm in awe of the poise she's demonstrating.

I walk back to her and run my knuckles down her cheek. "What are your safe words?"

"Red and yellow," she answers.

"I know we agreed on a gag, but I'm eliminating that. I don't feel comfortable."

"Yes, Sir."

I hold my hand out, and she threads her fingers with mine. Together, we approach the X. Lana stands against it and raises her hands above her head. Taking one hand, I wrap the leather restraint around it and secure it tightly before doing the same to the next. "Do they feel okay?"

Lana gives them a tug before answering, "They feel good."

Lowering to my knees, I take her first ankle and secure it in the same fashion as her wrists. Then, I do the same with her left ankle. "Are they too tight?"

"No, Sir."

I take a deep breath and turn toward the main room. I raise my hand to let Jim, our tech person who controls the lighting and music, know I'm ready. The lights in the club dim, and "Cult of Personality" by Living Colour begins playing.

Movement in the crowd catches my attention. Alex and Natalie are taking their place to watch. I pause and look at my best friend, who nods, offering me his silent support. Then, I face Lana, ready to give my undivided attention to our scene.

I lift my bullwhip from its resting place and take several practice swings to warm up my arm. It only takes a few minutes before I hit my stride, and I crack my whip—my signature move signaling I'm starting.

With a flick of my wrist, the thong makes its first contact with Lana's body. My intent with these first few licks of the thong is to warm up her skin and get her used to the stinging sensation. Her body remains relaxed.

Carefully, I work her up to the next level. Each point of impact stings but is still well below where I know her pain threshold typically lies. The extra adrenaline coursing through her system makes tonight's scene more of a balancing act. Lana's less likely to feel pain in the same way she usually does. Because of that, I need to be more aware of any minute reactions she has.

My goal isn't to injure her or cause her any unpleasant pain. I'm turned on each time the leather caresses her skin. I take pleasure in seeing her pale skin turn a stunning shade of red. Her cries are a mix of pain and pleasure. As much as Lana craves pain, I ache to give it to her.

This scene goes beyond eroticism. Lana carries scars from her traumatic past. She's overcome so much, but what happened to Jelena will always be a part of her. As a way to compensate for the helplessness she felt when Jelena was ripped away from her, Lana takes control in every situation she can. That's a heavy weight for anyone to carry.

Tonight, Svetlana is willingly submitting to me. She trusts I'll give her the pain she craves without going too far.

I alternate the intensity and frequency of each lash, ensuring I don't fall into a predictable rhythm as I make a crisscross pattern across her back. When I see her tensing in anticipation, I know it's time to stop and check in with my sub.

Lana's dripping with sweat, and I suspect arousal. Reaching out, I tuck a loose strand of hair behind her ear. "What's your color, *mon petit papillon?*" I whisper.

She pauses before answering, "Green."

Using my thumbs, I tenderly wipe the tears cascading down her cheeks. "You look so fucking gorgeous right now." I feather kisses on her neck. "If we're going to keep going, you need to stop holding your breath. I want you to relax into each strike. Let everything else go. It's just you and me."

"Yes, Sir," she whispers.

"I'm going to start again now."

Lana closes her eyes and takes a deep breath, letting it out slowly. Her body relaxes, and I feel confident about continuing.

With the leather-covered handle firmly in my grasp, I resume the scene with three lashes in quick succession. The crack of the whip echoes in the expansive space. Lana's returned to a relaxed state, so I challenge her with the intensity of the strikes. I will not push her past the agreed-upon boundaries, but I will bring her to a place where she releases everything she clings to.

When Lana's hands relax in their restraints, I know she's nearing the end. I begin to bring down the intensity. As soon as her whimpers silence, I know she's reached subspace, and the scene is over.

I set the whip on the table and stand behind my submissive, running my fingers gently over the marks I left on her. None of them broke her skin, but when she looks at her back in the mirror, she'll have a visual reminder of tonight. Once her aftercare is done, I'll take pictures for her.

Then, I stoop down and begin unfastening her ankle restraints. "You did so well, *mon petit papillon,*" I say quietly as I stand and release her wrists. When Lana goes to subspace, she's unable to speak, but I know she hears me. "You were strong and so beautiful." I cradle her in my arms, and she curls against my chest.

This moment is one I'll cherish—my submissive finding solace and comfort in my embrace.

Svetlana

The cracking sound fills the air for a fraction of a second before I feel the sting of the braided leather against my skin. The first few strikes are painful, and I have to focus on relaxing and controlling my breathing. I crave this feeling—it silences my thoughts and allows me to be free.

Most people have the reaction Natalie did when she found out I was consenting to be whipped. They have visions of a bloody, battered body, but that's not what will happen—this is not abuse. Brandon and I negotiated every second of this scene. He's skilled with a whip and is able to bring me pleasure without bruising or cutting me.

My mind wanders, and I lose focus and start holding my breath. Without being fully relaxed, the impact of each lash is magnified. The scene is too intense. I brace for the next strike, but it doesn't come. Brandon is at my side checking on my color.

"What's your color, *mon petit papillon?*" he says, his breath cool against my sweat-drenched skin.

I stop and take a mental inventory before responding, "Green."

"You look so fucking gorgeous right now." Brandon rains kisses on my neck. "If we're going to keep going, you need to stop holding your breath. I want you to relax into each strike. Let everything else go. It's just you and me."

"Yes, Sir."

Why did I feel safe doing this scene with him? This right here. Brandon is so tuned into me that he sees those small changes, ones that will quickly put me at yellow, and knows to stop and check in. He breathes slowly and deeply with me until I'm back in a relaxed state of mind.

"I'm going to start again now."

"Thank you, Sir." I take a cleansing breath and ready myself to feel the whip make contact with my skin and penetrate deep inside. To the place where my darkest memories reside.

With each crack of the whip, the pressure gauge rises higher and higher until everything I've bottled up inside explodes. Tears stream down my face as I watch the memories, emotions, and nightmares rush away from me.

I'm free.

Light as a cloud drifting somewhere between wakefulness and sleep.

The scene is over. Although I can't talk, I can see, hear, and feel. The restraints around my ankles release. Brandon's speaking to me. He's telling me how proud he is of me. With each word, I soar higher. My wrists are released, and my arms fall limp by my sides. Strong arms lift me, and I rest my head on Brandon's chest as he holds me close, whispering words of devotion.

With the door to the suite closed, I can no longer hear the music from the club.

"I'm going to lie you down. I need you to roll onto your front," he instructs.

The bed dips as Brandon sits next to me. "This might sting a little." He squeezes Arnica gel from the tube and gently rubs it on my back. "Are your ankles or wrists sore?" I shake my head. "You did so well. I'm in awe of you, *papillon*." The breeze from the air conditioner vent overhead makes me shiver. "I'm going to cover you." Brandon pulls the lightweight blanket over me and lies beside me, holding me close.

Subspace is peaceful. There are no worries or pain, only softly spoken words of comfort and love. I want to stay here forever, but I have no control over what my mind chooses. Little by little, I become one with my physical body.

"Brandon," I whisper his name and reach for him.

"I'm right here." His arms tighten around me. "Welcome back. Do you need anything?"

"I'd love some cold water."

"I can do that." He smiles warmly. "I'll be right back."

I watch as he walks across the room to the mini fridge and marvel at how his muscles flex with every movement.

Brandon twists the cap off the plastic bottle. "Can you sit up?"

I push up onto my elbows and adjust to a sitting position. The cold water is refreshing on my dry throat.

"Take these." He passes me two acetaminophen from the little white bottle we left on the bedside table. "Are you ready to eat?"

"No, not yet." I screw the lid back onto the bottle. "I'm a bit sleepy."

Brandon climbs back into bed and lays down next to me. I rest my head on his chest, and he wraps his arm around me. "Sleep, *mon petit papillon.*"

"I don't want to miss the Shibari demonstration." A yawn escapes.

"There'll be others."

I don't have the energy to argue. My eyelids are heavy and close despite my futile protest. Sleep pulls me under its spell.

After a quick shower, I redress and meet Brandon back in the bedroom just as he's finishing cleaning up.

"Did we miss it?"

"I think so." My stomach growls loudly. "Hungry?" Brandon asks with a grin.

"Very."

"Come on. Let's go find Alex and Natalie and see if they want to get something to eat."

We emerge from the hallway and find the earlier crowd is beginning to disperse.

"Great scene tonight," Anthony approaches Brandon and gives him a congratulatory hug.

"Thank you. How did yours go?"

"It went very well." Anthony beams. He and his submissive, Leo, were scheduled to do a wax scene. I love watching them. Their chemistry is off the charts.

"Have you seen Alex?" Brandon asks.

"Yes, he and the girl are in the café."

I look in that direction and spot them. They appear engrossed in conversation.

Anthony glances over at them. "I haven't seen Alex that enamored by a woman in a very long time. Where's she from?"

"She's Lana's roommate."

"And she's a submissive?" he asks, surprised.

I can't help the laugh that escapes.

"No. My wayward sub is playing matchmaker tonight."

"I see." Anthony smiles. "It seems she's done an excellent job of it."

Brandon rolls his eyes. "Don't encourage her."

After saying our goodbyes, Brandon and I walk to the café.

I come up behind Natalie as she's saying, "I read all the books she gave me, but I still had a very different picture in my mind. Being here tonight, it's nothing at all like I imagined. Each couple we watched shared a genuine connection. There was nothing wrong about—"

"I'm so glad you liked it," I squeal and throw my arms around Natalie's neck.

I scare her, and she nearly jumps out of her seat.

"Great scene tonight." Alex stands and shakes Brandon's hand. "Grab some chairs and join us."

Brandon grabs chairs from an empty table and drags them over. "Are you enjoying your evening?" he asks Natalie.

"I've had a great time," she says, her eyes sparkling as she looks at Alex and then back to Brandon. "I think I'd like to learn more."

"The club has intro classes during the week. You should sign up," Brandon suggests.

When I got the idea of setting up my best friend with Brandon's best friend, I hoped they'd hit it off, but I never imagined it would actually happen. By the smiles on their faces, it looks like maybe they're headed in the right direction.

I hope it sticks. Alex and Natalie deserve to find happiness.

Brandon

We spend the next few hours with Alex and Natalie in the club's café. The two of them can't keep their eyes off one another. I'll be the first to admit I thought Svetlana was off her rocker trying to set up her innocent roommate with my broody best friend. By some miracle, they hit it off. I haven't seen Alex this happy in years. If there's anyone who deserves a happily ever after, it's him.

"Oh, wow, it's almost two a.m. I promised Cinderella here I'd have her home early," Lana says and looks at me. "Sir, do I have permission to leave?"

"You did great tonight." I run my knuckles down her cheek. As much as I want to take her home and finish what we started earlier, that was never the plan. Svetlana wasn't sure how Natalie would react to everything she saw tonight. We agreed it was more important for Lana to be home with her to address any questions she may have. Fortunately, it seems she had a good time. "Go, get your friend home."

"Thank you for the tour, Alex."

He stands and kisses Natalie's cheek. "It was my pleasure."

I kiss Lana goodnight, and the girls head for the door. Alex remains standing, watching them walk away.

"Go after her," I encourage him.

"I don't know if I can," he says without taking his eyes off Natalie.

I nudge him forward. "You can't just let her walk away."

"Natalie," he finally calls and hurries to catch up with them.

I don't know what the future has in store for them, but if they can make each other happy, even for a short time, it's all worth it.

Svetlana

I'M IN MY ROOM PACKING MY BAG TO SPEND THE WEEK AT Brandon's when Natalie appears in the doorway.

"Are you going to Alex's this week?" she asks, confused.

"No. I'm moving some of my stuff into Brandon's place."

"Moving in? You haven't been seeing him for that long," Natalie says, confused.

"Come in. We need to talk." Natalie sits on my bed, crisscross applesauce, she calls it. "Brandon and I have been together since right after I came to New York City."

"Why didn't you tell me?"

"At first, it was nothing serious." I try to explain. "Then, you were so freaked out by everything that happened that night. And all the BDSM stuff." I sigh loudly. "I was afraid of what you'd think, and I didn't want to lose your friendship."

I came to New York to escape being Maxim Solonik's daughter. It isn't that I'm not proud of Papa or that I'm ashamed of being his daughter. Actually, it's the opposite. I measure every man I meet by the example he's demonstrated with Mama. It can be suffocating, though. People judge me by how they judge him. Especially after Jelena was taken.

Despite being in the Bratva, Papa always kept a low profile. The people in our community respected him. I was a happy little girl with friends—a normal life.

Until the day she disappeared.

Papa was ruthless in his search for her. He tortured and killed anyone who had anything to do with her disappearance. He never laid a finger on an innocent person, but that didn't matter. Our neighbors and friends no longer wanted anything to do with us. They were scared.

It wasn't until I went to university in Moscow and met Mei that I had another close friend, but time and distance have caused us to grow apart. I treasure my friendship with Natalie and don't want to do anything to destroy it.

"I was shocked that night, but I would never let something like that come between us. I couldn't imagine my life without you in it."

I swipe at the tear that escapes. "I treasure my friendship with you."

"Me too," she says sadly. "I wish you would've shared it with me. I could've supported you and been happy for you."

"I'm sorry. It doesn't feel like enough. I hope you can forgive me."

"I already do."

I've never met anyone like Natalie. I don't know how she forgives so easily, and I know I'm undeserving, but I'm incredibly grateful.

"So, you and Brandon are serious?" she asks.

"We've been all over the board." I chuckle. "But I think we've finally figured *us* out and signed a contract. I really like him a lot, Nat."

"So do I." She smiles. "I hope you'll give me the chance to get to know him better."

"I will. I promise."

Brandon: I'm outside. There's no parking, but if we switch off, I can come up and get your stuff.

Me: I only have one bag I can manage. I'll be out in a minute.

"Brandon's here." I zip up my bag. "Are you seeing Alex this week?"

"I don't think so. I have a big paper due."

"It's okay to put schoolwork aside and go out every now and then."

"I have to keep my grades up for the scholarship."

"Really, Nat? It's our last term before graduation, and you have a 4.0. I don't think you're in any danger."

"Have a good week." She hugs me.

"We're continuing this conversation when I get home."

Brandon carries my bag into his house. The door barely closes before he orders me to take my clothes off. I knew I'd be spending most of the week naked, so I didn't bring much with me. He dims the lights while I remove my pants and shirt.

"Where do you want me, Sir?

He smiles, and I see a mischievous glint in his eyes. "In front of the window."

"Yes, Sir." The curtains are partially open, allowing anyone outside to glimpse what we're about to do. When I get to the window, I turn around and watch as Brandon unbuttons his dark grey shirt. He slides it off his arms, exposing his toned body.

His chest rises and falls with each breath, enhancing the cords of sculpted muscles. My eyes lower to his abdomen, and the defined muscle that leads to a sculpted-V then disappears beneath the waistband of his pants.

I stare unashamedly as Brandon's hands move to his belt. His biceps flex as he opens the leather and works at his button and zipper. He lowers his pants and steps out of them. His cock is hard and tents the black boxer briefs that sit low on his hips.

"Do you see what you do to me, *mon petit papillon*?" Brandon's dominance takes up every inch of the room. I nod. "You're going to have to do better than that."

"I do." I manage to say. He hasn't touched me, and I can already feel my insides clench in anticipation.

Brandon closes the distance between us, and his mouth crashes against mine. My back presses against the cold glass, sending shivers down my spine. His hands tangle in my hair, pulling my head back as his mouth travels down my neck and lower. He draws my nipple into his mouth, sucking and nipping it. My hands roam his shoulders and back as I bask in the attention he gives first to one breast and then the other.

"Put your hands on the window," he orders. I watch over my shoulder as he lowers his boxers. He positions himself behind me and thrusts inside, pushing my breasts against the window.

A moan slips from my lips as he pulls out. His hands go to my ass, and I feel the tip of him press against me. My head drops back on his chest as he pushes past the tight ring of muscle. He takes me this way as often as possible, so my body accepts him readily.

His arm snakes around my waist, splaying his hand on my flat stomach, holding me tightly against him. "You're so fucking tight," he says and starts moving, rocking his hips into me. He slides his hand lower, leaving a trail of fire along my skin. His fingers dip inside my pussy, matching the thrusts of his cock.

"Do you like knowing someone can come by at any second and see me fucking you?"

"Yes." The word comes out breathy. The curtains provide a thin barrier between us and the outside world. My heart races with the knowledge that someone might walk by and see what we're doing at any moment, but I don't care. Nothing else matters except for the exquisite sensations coursing through my body. Brandon spears two fingers into my center. My body squeezes them as pleasure radiates in ripples.

His fingers pump in and out at a feverish pace. "I can't, please." The feelings are too big.

"You can." His fingers move to my overly sensitive clit, rubbing circles. His cock grows impossibly hard inside me as he inches closer to his release. Brandon moves his free hand to my neck, putting the smallest amount of pressure against it. He thrusts harder and so incredibly deep. "Fucking come for me again, Svetlana."

An orgasm explodes, and my body shakes from the overwhelming crescendo. He thrusts one last time as his cock swells, spilling inside me. Brandon holds me against him, and our hearts beat in synchrony. I'm lost in the pure ecstasy of the moment.

When the last waves of pleasure have ceased, Brandon pulls out and steps back. Immediately, I miss the warmth of his body against mine.

"Let's go shower. I'm not through with you."

Svetlana

THE WEEK WENT BY FAR TOO QUICKLY. EVEN THOUGH IT'S Saturday, Brandon had to go into the office, and I have schoolwork I need to get done, so I had him drop me off early this morning. Natalie and I are sitting at the kitchen table having a cup of coffee while she tells me about her date.

"Last night was like a real-life fairy tale. Alex is amazing."

"I knew you two would get along." I just wish I had given her the benefit of the doubt and introduced them sooner.

"How long have you known Alex?"

"A little while."

"How long's a little while?"

This conversation cannot happen. Natalie may be able to handle the BDSM lifestyle, but I'm sure there's no way she'll be okay with Papa being in the Bratva. Thankfully, the doorbell rings. I don't know or care who it is. All that matters is it's a distraction. "I'll get it," I say, hurrying to the door.

"Saved by the bell," Natalie calls. "But this conversation isn't over."

"Alex," I say his name louder than necessary. "I didn't know you were coming over."

"Is Natalie here?"

"You bet. She's in the kitchen."

Natalie jumps up from her chair and tries to make a beeline for her room, but she's not fast enough.

"Good afternoon, Natalie." Alex's voice stops her in her tracks.

"Hi. Can you excuse me for a minute? I need to get changed."

"You look perfectly fine to me."

"I'm going to shower and study," I say in a sing-song voice. "I'll leave you two alone." As much as I'd love to stay and eavesdrop, it would infuriate Alex.

After a long hot shower, I blow dry my hair and throw on sweatpants and a T-shirt. The rest of my afternoon will be dedicated to preparing a closing argument for the mock criminal case my class is working on. I sit at my desk with my laptop and stare at the screen, but curiosity gets the best of me, and I crack the door to listen for voices. Natalie says goodbye to Alex, and the door closes.

"Is he gone?" I ask, peeking my head into the room.

"Yes, he just left. He had to work."

"And?" I walk into the living room and drop onto the sofa.

Natalie sits next to me and puts her head on my shoulder. "He brought a contract. Will you look it over with me?"

I want to squeal with excitement, but I school my features and keep my voice even. "I'd love to."

She grabs the papers from the kitchen table and returns to the sofa. I look through the four pages, making sure to read everything, which isn't difficult. It's a basic contract that reflects Natalie's newness to the lifestyle very well. It's reminiscent of the contract Slava offered me.

"What do you think?" she asks.

"I want to hear your thoughts first." I set the papers on my lap and look expectantly at Natalie.

"Alex and I went over each part, and I feel comfortable with it," she says hesitantly.

"But you're still worried about your scholarship and having to go back to Northmeadow."

"Alex said he was okay putting a time limit on it, but I don't think it'll be as cut and dry as he makes it seem."

Natalie was so desperate to go to NYU that she accepted a scholarship with a ridiculous work clause attached. At the time, she didn't think twice because she was planning to go back and marry Tommy. But everything's different now, and that scholarship is more like a ball and chain holding her hostage.

"Let me call Papa. He'll buy out your contract, so you don't have to go back."

"You're as bad as Alex." She blows out a frustrated breath.

"I'm just offering you a way out."

"And I appreciate it, but I can't accept it." She holds up the contract. "I want to sign this."

"Then, I think you should do it."

"I just don't know. It's not that simple."

"For once, don't overthink it. Just do it," I encourage her.

"I need to think about it. I don't want either of us to get hurt."

She hasn't said it yet, but I know she's going to do it. I'm happy for both of my friends. My only regret is that I didn't introduce them sooner, and because of that, their relationship will be short-lived.

Brandon

WHEN LANA AND I FIRST GOT TOGETHER, I HAD NO IDEA what our future might look like. Little by little, it's become clearer. After graduation, she agreed to move in with me. Typically, I work long hours, and although Lana's studying for the bar exam, she insists on keeping the house and doing all the cooking. I've become very spoiled coming home to a hot meal and a woman I love every night. Our lives have become very domestic, but that hasn't damped the flames of our relationship.

The past few months have been trying. Alex was in Russia working closely with Maxim and Nicholai Federov, one of Maxim's close associates. I worked even more than usual, keeping the company going with the actual marketing accounts and everything on the trafficking network end.

On top of work, Lana and I were helping Alex with his plan to propose to Natalie—which he did yesterday, Christmas Eve. I'm not entirely sure how he pulled it off, but he planned an entire day of surprises before the proposal in Central Park. It was no surprise that she said yes.

"Wake up," Lana says. "It's Christmas."

I don't bother opening my eyes. "The sun isn't even up yet."

"But other things are." She moves down my body and takes my hard length into her mouth. My eyes roll back in my head.

Lana's mouth feels exquisite. I let her control the pace as she gently runs her teeth along my dick before paying extra attention to the sensitive tip. She runs her tongue along my slit, blowing gently before slowly taking me into her mouth.

It's my turn to take over. I wrap her hair around my hand and lift my hips. Lana relaxes and lets me use her mouth. Over and over, I push her head to the root of my cock. She takes everything I give until I shoot ribbons of cum down her throat. I let her hair go, and she licks me clean.

"Merry Christmas, Sir," she says as she sits back on her knees.

After I give her pussy the same attention with my mouth, we shower and go downstairs to exchange presents. It's the perfect Christmas morning. Outside, the ground is already covered in white, while more fluffy snowflakes float on the cold breeze. We're in the middle of opening our gifts when my cell rings.

"Merry Christmas and congratulations," I answer the phone.

"Brand." Alex's voice is strained.

"Is everything okay?"

"No. We're on our way to Northmeadow. Natalie's father was shot."

"Shot?" I ask, certain I misheard.

I put the phone on speaker as Alex tells us that Natalie got a phone call around four a.m. informing her that her father had been shot in a robbery gone wrong. Tommy, her ex-boyfriend, broke into her family's pharmacy, looking for drugs. Stanley had recently installed a silent alarm system, and rather than calling the police, he decided to go to the store himself. During the confrontation, Tommy shot him.

"How bad is it?"

"He was shot in the chest and life-flighted to Branson for emergency surgery," Alex explains. "All the office could tell us is that things don't look good."

"Can I talk to Natalie?" Lana asks through her own tears.

"She's not up to talking right now."

"Tell her I love her, and we'll be praying for her father."

"Keep us updated when you can."

"I will. I have to go. We're pulling into the airport now."

Lana walks over to the window. "This isn't fair." Her body shakes from the force of her crying.

I wrap my arms around her, and she rests her head on my chest. "Life rarely is."

"This was supposed to be one of the happiest days of their life. Now, it'll forever be mixed with tragedy."

Stanley sustained a direct hit to his right lung. He was in surgery for nearly twelve hours to repair the damage. Even then, the odds weren't in his favor. It was a huge relief to everyone when Natalie texted Lana yesterday to tell her that her dad was awake and breathing on his own. There's still a lot of uncertainty, but things aren't as bleak as yesterday.

While Lana's out for a run with Pyotr, I check my work email. While I'm scrolling through my inbox, Alex calls.

"Hello?"

"I fucked up. Natalie safeworded." His voice cracks. "She left me."

I was expecting an update on Stanley, so it takes a beat for me to process what Alex just said. "What happened?"

"I bought out her contract and handed her resignation to the school district."

"Shit, Alex. I thought we talked about giving Natalie the freedom to make her own choices?"

From day one of their relationship, Alex begged Natalie to let him buy out her contract. As much as she dreaded having to return to Northmeadow, it was important to Natalie that she fulfill the promise she made.

He and I have had this conversation a million times, and each time, we come to the same conclusion. Natalie needed to be able to handle this on her terms.

"That was before her psycho ex almost killed her father." His voice cracks. "What do I do now? I can't go after her. My hands are tied."

"You really dug yourself a hole this time."

"I was terrified and reacted. I realize it was too far now, but I don't know how to fix it. I need to get her back. I don't want a life without Natalie in it."

"Where are you?"

"I'm in Branson. I can't leave."

"Let me talk to Lana, and I'll call you back. We'll figure this out."

After we hang up, I drop my head into my hands. The gravity of the situation weighs heavily on me. But as much as Alex wants me to swoop in and fix this, I don't know that it's my place to intervene. While I understand exactly why Alex did what he did, he also overstepped a boundary.

"Natalie just called," Svetlana says, bursting into my office. "She safe—"

"I know."

"You do?" she asks, surprised.

"Alex called."

"What are we going to do?" She sits in the chair across from my desk.

"Nothing."

"What do you mean nothing?" she asks, her voice growing louder. "We can't just sit by and watch this happen."

"Yes. We can." I try to sound more confident than I'm feeling. "I can't believe this. I'm going to shower." Lana storms out of the office.

The reality is that I have no idea what I'm supposed to do. They're our friends, but should we insert ourselves into a situation that doesn't involve us?

After going back and forth, I decide we need to stay out of it. Alex and Natalie need to work this out for themselves.

They'll get through this—I hope.

Svetlana

"Please don't keep shutting me out," I say on Natalie's voicemail for what has to be the hundredth time. "I'm here when you're ready to talk."

It's been nearly three weeks, and Natalie still won't take my calls.

"No luck?" Brandon asks when he walks into the kitchen.

"I left her another voicemail. Did you get Alex?"

"Yes. He's still in Branson." Brandon sits across from me at the table.

"I know you said we need to stay out of this, but—"

"I booked us a flight into Northmeadow tomorrow," Brandon says, and my jaw drops. "Natalie will be driving back to Northmeadow tomorrow to pick up some things for her mom. She'll be spending the night."

"Really?"

"Yes, really."

"How do you know this?" I ask.

"I know people in high places," he says, laughing at his joke. "Alex bought a cottage at that lake outside of Northmeadow. He had it renovated. It was supposed to be Natalie's Christmas present, but they never got that far."

"Why didn't you tell me?"

"Alex asked me not to." I grin. "He's on his way there today. Our job is to get Natalie to the cottage."

"And how do you propose we do that?"

"We have until tomorrow evening to figure that out."

Our plane landed at the small airport in Northmeadow in the late afternoon. We had enough time to rent a car and drive to Clarke's house, where we've been parked, waiting for Natalie to show up. It's been close to two hours, and the sun is just beginning to set.

"Are you sure she's coming?" I ask impatiently.

"I'm sure."

How do you— Never mind, there she is now." I spot the beat-up silver car she lovingly nicknamed Rhonda, the Honda. She pulls into the driveway and shuts the engine off but makes no move to get out. "Do you think she saw us?"

"I don't know," Brandon says as he watches in the rearview mirror. "There's no reason to wait here. Let's do this."

The words are barely out of his mouth when I open my door and jump out, running toward her car. I know the second she sees me because she throws her door open. She's barely to her feet when I wrap my arms around her.

"What are you guys doing here?" she asks, looking between me and Brandon, who's standing off to the side.

"We're here for an intervention. Can we come in?"

"An intervention?" Natalie asks hesitantly.

Brandon walks over and gives her a hug. "All we ask is that you hear us out. If it doesn't change your mind, we won't say another word about it."

"Okay." I can tell from the tone of her voice that she's not sold on the idea.

"I have to get the groceries." She opens the trunk and grabs a few bags. Brandon gets the rest, and we follow her into the house.

"Just put them on the table." Natalie puts them away quickly. "Can I get you guys something to drink?"

"Water would be great," Brandon says.

"Make yourself at home." Natalie motions to the sofa in the living room.

The mood is tense while I help her get the drinks. She doesn't say anything to me, which makes this even more awkward. With our ice waters in hand, we join Brandon. I sit next to him, and Natalie sits across from us in the old, worn chair that's her father's favorite.

That's when I get a good look at her. She's exhausted. Her eyes are puffy, and she has dark circles under them from not sleeping. On the ride here, Brandon told me that Viktor's been keeping an eye on Natalie from a distance. She's been driving back and forth trying to manage her parents' pharmacy and everything at the hospital. If something doesn't give, she's going to end up in the hospital, too.

"Alex is miserable. And you aren't much better," I blurt.

"It's been a rough few weeks. But it'll get better, eventually."

I've rehearsed this part in my head since Brandon told me the plan yesterday. Now's the time, but I'm terrified. I look at Brandon, who gives me an encouraging smile. I haven't even started speaking, and I'm already getting emotional. I swallow over the lump in my throat and start.

"I need to tell you a story. It's not something I like talking about, but you need to hear it." Natalie doesn't respond, but she watches me intently. "I'm not sure where to start. So, I guess I just say it. My papa is a *pakhan*, the boss of a group in the Bratva."

"You expect me to believe Maxim's in the Russian mafia?" she laughs.

"Yes." My answer is matter-of-fact.

"And I thought there wasn't anything more you could tell me about Maxim that'd surprise me. But what does that have to do with Alex?"

"I had a sister," I say, fighting back tears. "Jelena was five years older than me. She was smart and beautiful. I wanted to be just like her. I was ten years old when she was taken. We were walking down the street when two men jumped out of a van and grabbed her—we were holding hands, and they ripped her away. Jelena yelled at me to run and not look back." I swipe at the tears that are now falling.

"I had no idea. I'm so sorry."

"They were traffickers. Papa searched day and night, but even with all his connections, it was too late when he found her. She'd already been sold and killed. Since then, Papa's used his position in the Bratva to fight the traffickers. He couldn't save Jelena, but he has saved many others."

Silent tears slip down Natalie's cheeks as she listens to the secret I've kept for so many years.

"It's made him very overprotective of me. So, when I approached Papa and told him I wanted to come to America to study, he went crazy." I laugh. "He wouldn't be able to protect me here, which was unacceptable to him."

"I'm sure he was terrified something would happen to you. But I still don't see what this has to do—"

I put my finger up, stopping her. "Hang on. I'm getting to the part about Alex." She takes a sip of her water. "Papa didn't want to hold me back, so he arranged for me to stay with a business associate of his who lived in New York. This is where Alex comes in." I smile. "My parents and Alex's parents had been friends for many years. Which is how Papa started working with him in the first place."

That got Natalie's attention. She adjusts her position on the chair.

"Papa's responsible for reintroducing Alex to the lifestyle. He knew that after Alex's Mom passed away, he lost his focus—his direction. The first anniversary of his mom's passing was a particularly bad time for Alex. Papa found him drunk in his room. He was concerned about him and stayed with Alex the rest of the night. The following morning, he told Alex about his friendship with his parents and invited Alex to the club. Initially, Alex was resistant. He wasn't interested in having a sub. But my papa can be persuasive, and Alex finally gave in."

"That's how Alex got involved at Fire and Ice."

"It is. Fast forward a few years. The businessman Papa went to visit was Alex. Papa asked if he would step in and become my Dominant."

"You and Alex were a couple?"

"Alex and me?" I raise my eyebrows. "He's a great guy, but he's not my type. We were never a couple."

"What Lana's trying to explain." Brandon steps in to help. "Is that Maxim asked Alex if he'd be willing to be responsible for Lana's safety. To allow her to wear his collar of protection."

"Doesn't wearing a collar symbolize a relationship—ownership?" she asks, clearly confused.

"In some cases, yes, but there're other kinds of collars," Brandon explains. "Lana was young and would be alone in a big city—in a foreign country. She was also a submissive who would be playing at a new club. Maxim wanted to ensure Lana had someone willing to protect her in his absence. A protection collar doesn't represent a partnership but rather a Dominant's commitment to be responsible for another's safety. It also meant any Dominants interested in Lana couldn't approach her without getting Alex's permission."

"So, you and Alex were never together?" Natalie asks.

"Nope, never a couple. Never played together." I reach into my purse and pull out the collar with the locket. I hold it out to Natalie. At first, she doesn't move, but finally, she takes it and examines it closely. "That was my collar. On the charm, you can see Alex's initials and the lowercase p to show I was under his protection."

Recognition sweeps over her face. "You wore this when I first met you."

"I wore it for almost six months." The memories are bittersweet. "I was so lonely until Alex showed me the city and introduced me to his friends at the club. Without him, I probably would have packed up and gone back to Russia. But it wasn't always smooth sailing. Alex can be a bit overprotective. He made decisions for me that I didn't always agree with."

Brandon laughs a full belly laugh. "Alex and Svetlana became famous at the club for their very heated disagreements. Star and Owen had to step in on more than one occasion." Natalie cracks a small smile.

"The thing is, he saw things and knew things I didn't. It was hard, but I had to learn to trust his decisions. And in the end, he was always right."

She passes the collar back, and I drop it into my purse. "This isn't the same, Lana."

"It is, Nat. You may not see the big picture. Actually, I know you don't see it."

"When Alex lost his mother, he gave up. He closed himself off from everyone around him. He was afraid of caring about someone and losing them, too. Then you came into his life, and his carefully constructed walls crumbled," Brandon says. "All those fears rushed to the surface when your dad was shot. When you told him what Tommy did to you that night, it pushed him over the edge. I'll admit, he made some rash decisions."

"That's an understatement," she adds sarcastically. "Alex and I had an agreement, and he broke it."

"I agree with you, Natalie. Alex and I have discussed what happened. He knows he was wrong and understands that he should've approached things differently. Alex is a Dominant, a protector—sometimes to a fault." Brandon pauses. "He's also only human, and sometimes he screws up. But Alex is a good man. All he was thinking was that he couldn't risk losing you. I know you disagree—"

"Disagree? I more than disagree."

"That man loves you." Brandon's expression changes, and the Dominant emerges. "Do you love him?"

"Yes," she says softly.

"Do you trust him?"

"Brandon—"

"This lifestyle revolves around trust. Do you trust Alex as your future husband and, more importantly, as your Dominant?"

Natalie looks down at her hands, fidgeting with her fingers for several long seconds. Finally, she looks back up. "Yes, I trust him."

"Get your coats, girls," Brandon says. "We're going for a ride."

I jump up and grab my coat, but Natalie doesn't move.

"Where are we going?"

"This time, you have to trust me." Brandon has a playful grin on his face. "Get up. Let's go."

I grab Natalie's hand, and she reluctantly follows me.

When we're all seated in the car, Brandon turns around. "One more thing. You need to put this on." He holds out a blindfold.

"You're seriously crazy. You know that?"

She swipes the fabric from his hand and puts it over her eyes.

"Good girl. Sit back and relax."

Brandon looks at me, and we share a knowing smile. I can only imagine what Natalie's thinking as we drive to the lake. Finally, we're making the final turn onto a gravel road that leads to the cottage. Brandon puts the car in park and says, "You may remove the blindfold now."

Natalie slides it off, her eyes blinking a few times while they come into focus. She looks out the window at the enchanting stone cottage set amongst the trees. Luminaires line each side of a path leading to the front door.

"It's gorgeous. But what are we doing here?"

"Go knock on the door," Brandon says.

"But I don't—"

"Stop questioning, and just trust me." Brandon corrects her. "Get out and go knock on the door."

Natalie exits the car and takes a few tentative steps before looking back.

"Keep walking," Brandon encourages her through the open car window.

Reluctantly, she continues walking. Before she gets all the way to the door, it swings open. A nervous-looking Alex stands in the doorway. He says something to Natalie before giving us a small wave. That's our cue to leave.

"Do you think they'll be okay?" I ask.

"I do," Brandon reassures me.

Brandon

ALEX AND I HAVE BEEN IN ALMOST CONSTANT CONTACT THE
past week. There's been a series of security threats on the encrypted files
we hold for Maxim. Viktor's checked them out and assures us they're
coming from inside the office. That sets my mind at ease somewhat.
Since Alex is still in Missouri, it's up to me to find out what's going on.

My office phone rings.

"Hello?"

"Mr. Carpenter," Paul, our front desk attendant, says. "Ms. Solonik
is here to see you."

"Please send her back."

Lana's only come to the office a few times and never unscheduled.

"I hope I didn't interrupt anything," Lana says as she appears in the
doorway of my office.

"Nothing that can't wait. Is everything alright?"

"I wanted to discuss this guy I'm seeing." She closes and locks the
door. "He's been spending more and more time at his office. I'm afraid
he's having an affair with his receptionist."

"Given the fact that his receptionist is a man," I say and walk around
my desk, closing the distance between us. "And he's only interested in

women. One woman in particular. I don't think you have anything to worry about."

"I thought it was important I come to check things out for myself. You know, stake my claim and all." She smiles.

"And how do you propose to do that?"

Her hands go to my belt, opening it, and then move to my pants and boxers, sliding them down my legs as she lowers to her knees. I'm already hard with the anticipation of what she's about to do.

She drags her tongue from the base of my cock to the top and looks up at me for a second before opening her mouth and taking me in. I close my eyes, savoring the feel of her warm mouth wrapped around me.

Lana alternates between gently sucking and lightly dragging her teeth up my cock. Releasing it from her mouth, she uses her hand, pumping up and down before taking a finger and sliding it through the pre-cum that's gathering at the tip.

She looks up and gives me a wicked grin before taking me in until I hit the back of her throat. At the same time, she uses her lubricated finger to slide into my ass, earning a deep throaty groan. She massages the area gently at first while licking and sucking my cock. She adds more pressure with her finger as she takes me in her mouth deeper and faster.

I grab her hair and wrap it around my fist, needing to control the pace as my orgasm builds from deep inside. Her finger massages inside me harder and faster. "Fuck, Lana," I growl as my body convulses inside her mouth. Wave after wave of cum shoots down her throat. Lana doesn't stop massaging me as she swallows everything I give her. A moan escapes my lips, and my legs nearly give out from the force of the orgasm.

Finally, my body begins to come down from the high. Slowly, she pulls her finger out and circles the tip of my dick with her tongue before releasing me.

Without a word, she pulls my boxers and pants back up and closes them. I grab her neck and pull her to me, kissing her deeply.

"Will you be home on time tonight?" she asks, still breathless.

"I'm afraid not," I say, releasing her.

"Are you going to tell me what's going on yet?"

"Not here. I'll talk to you at home tonight." The office's walls tend to have ears, and I don't want anyone overhearing the information I've learned.

She kisses me. "I'll have dinner waiting."

"I'll text you when I'm leaving the office." Lana turns to leave, but I grab her waist, stopping her. "Be ready for reciprocation when I get home."

It's killing me to watch Lana walk out the door, especially after that, but Alex is flying in tomorrow, and I have information to put together that he'll find very interesting.

Alex and I met late last night to form a plan for today. When I looked into what was happening in the office, I found two employees venturing out on their own, a move Alex always supports—except this time. Rather than doing things in an honorable way, these two are trying to poach Alex's personal clients. They might've gotten away with it, except they tried to access Alex's encrypted files. I'm certain they thought they would access information about some secret clients. Unfortunately for them, they set off alarm bells that are about to expose their plan.

I meet Alex in the conference room after the last of the employees have filed in. Our security guards are coming this way. They'll be waiting outside until they're needed. I give them a nod before closing the door and joining Alex at the front of the room.

"If everyone can take their seats. I want to keep this short so we can start our weekend early," Alex says, waiting for everyone to turn their attention to him. "First, I'd like to congratulate Cameron and Morgan on signing two new clients to the agency this week." Applause and congratulations fill the room. When they die down, he continues, "I want to thank Brandon for steering the ship while I was out of town. Everyone's done a great job keeping the day-to-day operations running seamlessly. I appreciate you all. I'll open the floor for any questions."

Several employees ask questions about some outstanding accounts. Alex and I address them quickly. "Anyone else?" No other hands go up.

"I have one more thing, and then you can go. It's come to my attention that several of your colleagues are branching out from Montgomery Advertising to start their own company. Ben and Michelle, please make your way up here."

Alex and I step aside, allowing Ben and Michelle to bask in their short-lived success. The unsuspecting pair smile proudly, believing their secrets are safe. They're about to experience Alex's ruthlessness, something few ever experience.

"These two employees came to my company fresh out of college. Over the years, they've worked hard and achieved a remarkable amount of success." he pauses, giving them several more seconds of false security. "Typically, I support employees taking the next step and opening their own company. But that isn't going to happen." Their smiles disappear as they look at one another with confused expressions. "Ben and Michelle made the mistake of trying to steal my clients. Your personal belongings are waiting at reception. Security will escort you out of the building." Alex opens the door, and our security team steps in.

The room is shrouded in uncomfortable silence as Ben and Michelle take their walk of shame.

"Now that that's out of the way," I address the remaining employees. "Does anyone have anything to add before we wrap up?" When the shock of what just happened begins to wane, heads shake, indicating no questions. "In that case, have a great weekend."

Everyone grabs their things and says goodbye on the way out.

"That went well," I say.

Alex drops into a chair. The stress of the afternoon weighs heavily on him. "I'm just glad it's over."

I know Alex is in a hurry to get back to Natalie. "Lana's out with the girls tonight. I'll drive you to the airport."

With that pressure off at work, I'm free to put more time and attention back where it belongs—on Svetlana and me.

Svetlana

Brandon and I flew into Branson last night. Today, we're driving to Alex and Natalie's lake cottage. We'll be joining Anthony and Leo, Alex's dad and his sub, Luna, and Natalie's parents to celebrate the July Fourth holiday. There's very likely to be more fireworks than what's in the sky when Natalie's parents meet Anthony and Leo.

I haven't seen Natalie in seven months, which makes the hour-long ride feel like it'll never end.

"You're driving me nuts," Brandon says. "Stop tapping your fingers on the door."

"I didn't even realize I was doing it."

"We'll be there in a few minutes."

"I don't know if I can wait that long."

Brandon laughs. "You don't have a choice."

He turns the car onto the bumpy gravel road that leads to their cottage. It looks much different during the day. Brandon parks off to the side, and we get out of the car. We're getting our bags from the trunk when the sound of tires crunching the gravel draws our attention. Natalie's parents are right behind us.

"Go on ahead," Brandon says. "I'll get these."

"Are you sure?"

"Yes. Once Charlotte gets in there, neither of you will get a word in edgewise."

"Thank you." I plant a kiss on his cheek and hurry into the house. The front door is open, so I walk in. I spot Tony and Leo in the kitchen. "Something smells good in here."

"Hey, girl," Leo says.

"Do you know where Natalie is?"

"She's in her room getting dressed."

"Thanks." I hurry down the hall and stop at the only closed door. "You going to be in there all day?"

The door swings open. "I can't believe you're here!" Natalie squeals and throws her arms around my neck.

"I wouldn't miss this for anything in the world." I squeeze her back. "Your parents were just pulling up when we walked into the house."

"Lana, I'm so nervous. What if they hate everyone?"

"Not even Charlotte could hate Leo."

We both laugh.

"I hope you're right." She grabs my hand. "Come on, let's go say hi."

Brandon

TODAY HAS TURNED OUT TO BE A RELAXING DAY. ALEX AND
Natalie were worried about everyone getting along, but everyone's
gone smoothly. Dinner was a huge success, something that doesn't come
as a surprise to me. Tony's cooking is incredible. Now, everyone's gathered around the fire pit, enjoying a spectacular sunset that'll eventually
give way to tonight's fireworks display over the lake.

I have a surprise of my own for Svetlana. I've been waiting for the
perfect time which I've decided will be tonight during the fireworks.

While we're talking and enjoying one another's company, a tense-
looking Viktor appears in the doorway and motions for Alex to go
inside.

"I wonder what's going on," Lana whispers.

"I have no idea. I'm sure it's nothing, though."

A short time later, Alex emerges from the house just as the fireworks
light up the night sky. He takes his seat and pulls Natalie onto his lap.
I'm about to make my move when Lana's phone chimes. She pulls it out
and opens the text message. I read it over her shoulder.

PapaL There has been a development with the computer attacks at
Alex's office. You and Brandon are to stay at the lake tonight. Tomor-

row, you will all leave for JFK. My jet will meet you there. We will be staying at the compound until further notice.

Lana: I understand.

She schools her features and slides the phone back into her pocket. Lana and Alex exchange a tense glance before she settles against my chest and returns to watching the fireworks.

I'm not sure what's going on, but whatever it is, it must be important if Maxim's calling everyone to the compound. My plans for tonight are going to have to wait.

Stanley and Charlotte leave right after the fireworks conclude. We're all still gathered at the firepit when Alex and Natalie return from saying their goodbyes.

"Are you going to tell me what's going on now?" Natalie says, her hands on her hips.

"No. Sit down," Alex says quietly. "We have guests."

Natalie ignores him. "I saw the look between you and Lana earlier. What's going on?"

The mood shifts from relaxed to awkward.

"I think it's time we turn in," Anthony says with an exaggerated yawn.

"You don't have to. Don't let my wayward sub chase you away." Alex narrows his eyes at Natalie, issuing a silent warning.

"It's really okay," he says and motions to Leo, who's kneeling at his feet. "It's time for us to turn in anyway."

Lana pulls Natalie aside and whispers something. Hopefully, she's trying to talk some sense into her. Natalie doesn't break her stare down with Alex as she shrugs.

I decide it's time we make an exit and let Alex deal with this privately. "Lana, we should go too."

"No, you two need to stay."

"Oh?" I ask, hoping Alex gives us a hint as to what's going on.

"Dad, I need you to stay too."

"Luna, go to bed. I'll be in shortly," Sam Montgomery says to his submissive.

"Let's move this inside," Alex says. "I'll get Viktor and meet you in the living room."

It's only a few minutes before Alex and Viktor enter the room.

"There was another attempt at accessing the encrypted files earlier today." He takes a deep breath. "I was wrong from the beginning. The files weren't being accessed from within the company."

Lana takes my hand in hers, the only outward sign of her nerves.

"It wasn't the employees you fired?" Sam asks.

"No. The timing of everything was purely coincidental."

"Is Max aware?"

"Yes. He called earlier. His jet's enroute to JFK. We're leaving in the morning for an extended stay in Russia."

"We're what?" Natalie spins around. "We can't do that. My parents. Our bridal shower." Tears pour down her face.

Alex hurries to her and takes her by the shoulders. "We don't have a choice."

"I'm not going to Russia."

"Come with me." Alex struggles with keeping his temper under control. He takes Natalie by the arm and walks her outside.

"I'll get your things and move them into my cottage tonight," Viktor suggests. "I think these two are going to need some time alone."

While Alex was finalizing the purchase of their cottage, the one next door also became available. He bought it so Viktor could set up their security and have a private place to stay.

"That's a good idea. Do you want a hand?"

"No, I've got it." Viktor disappears down the hall to get our things.

Sam, Lana, and I exit through the front door and walk to the other cottage.

"I thought everything was taken care of," Lana says.

"So did I. This is a total shock."

"My heart aches for Natalie," Sam adds. "She's not handling this well."

"She's dealt with a lot the past few months," I say.

"I don't think she understood the full extent of what Alex's involvement with Max entailed."

Viktor catches up with us.

"Is Nat okay?" Lana asks him.

"I don't know. I didn't see them." Viktor sets us up in one of the guest rooms. "If you need anything, let me know." He leaves, closing the door behind him.

I sit on the bed and drop my head into my hands.

"What's wrong?" Lana asks, sitting next to me.

"Everything."

"It's not that bad. The compound's incredible. You'll love it there."

"That's not it." I sit up and turn to face her. "This is not how tonight was supposed to go."

"What are you talking about."

I reach into my pocket and pull out the small box I've been carrying all day. "I had everything planned. It was going to be perfect." I open the box, and Lana gasps.

Inside is a three-carat princess-cut diamond set on a platinum band with flowing ribbons of beaded milgrain and diamonds.

"Brandon," she says, bringing her hands to her mouth.

"Every time I go to do this, something else comes up. I'm done waiting for the perfect time." I drop to one knee. "The first time I met you, when you walked into Alex's kitchen, time stood still. You took my breath away. Since then, we've had our fair share of hurdles. Through every trial fate through our way, our connection was an unbreakable thread weaving our destiny together." I take one of her shaking hands into mine.

"I'm sure our trials aren't over, but I know that as long as we face them together, we're invincible." I wipe a tear from her face. "You're the sun that brings light to my darkest days and the compass that guides me through life's stormy seas. You breathed life back into me. Svetlana, I love you with all that I am. I can't imagine my life without you by my side. Will you do me the honor of becoming my wife?"

Silence hangs between us as I wait for her answer. "Yes," she whispers the one word, the only word I hoped she'd say.

I slide the ring onto her finger before standing. Leaning over, my lips meet hers as I push her softly onto her back. My hands go to the hem of her shirt and begin sliding it over her body when there's a knock on the door.

"Who is it?"

"It's me," Viktor says.

I get to my feet and open the door. "What's up?"

"I'm sorry to interrupt, but there are a few things we need to go over."

I look over my shoulder at Lana, who's sitting up, examining the ring.

"Give me a minute."

"No problem."

I close the door and walk back to the bed just as Lana slides the ring off.

"What's wrong? Don't you like it?" My stomach sinks.

"I love it."

"Then why did you take it off?"

"Our engagement should be a time of great joy. Whatever's going on is very serious, or Papa wouldn't make us all go to the compound. I don't want to start our forever with a dark cloud hanging over us." She places the ring in my palm and closes my fingers around it. "Will you ask me again when this is over, and we can celebrate?"

"You deserve no less than perfect, *mon petit papillon*. As soon as this storm passes, I'm putting this ring back where it belongs."

"There's nothing I want more."

I pull her to me and kiss her deeply. "I have to go see what Viktor needs. I expect you to be on your knees waiting for me when I return."

"Yes, Sir."

Our engagement is important enough to wait until nothing else overshadows it. I leave the room, both disappointed that she's not wearing a token of our promise and overjoyed with the knowledge that she's mine.

Maxim's men are highly skilled. We'll go to the safety of the compound while they figure out where the threat is coming from and eliminate it. The second they do, Lana and I will be free to share our good news.

Our happily ever after is just around the corner.

When Lana runs from Brandon to escape her pain, she discovers that the truth cannot be outrun. In the final chapter of their story, they face the ultimate test of love, forgiveness, and healing. Start reading *Mended Hearts* today and experience the powerful conclusion to their unforgettable journey.

Become one of Tara's VIP readers. Sign up for her newsletter today! https://subscribepage.io/FireandIceBooks

Mended Hearts

Dear Reader

I'd like to offer a gentle and thoughtful heads-up before you embark on the journey within the pages of this book. Within its storyline, you will encounter themes that revolve around the deeply sensitive and personal topics of pregnancy loss and infertility.

While using my personal experience with this topic, I've done my best to ensure the themes are handled with utmost care and respect, aiming to portray the emotional complexities that individuals and couples may experience. It's my intention to provide a realistic and empathetic portrayal, shedding light on the struggles and resilience of those who face such challenges. However, I understand these topics can evoke strong feelings, memories, and personal experiences for many readers.

If you find that these themes hit too close to home or may trigger difficult emotions, I urge you to consider your emotional well-being before proceeding. Should you decide to continue reading, I encourage you to reach out for support if needed. Remember that you are not alone, and seeking help from friends, family, or professionals is always a valid option.

My hope is that this fiction story provides a window into the lives of its characters, fostering insight, understanding, and a profound sense of connection for those who've experienced similar journeys, as well as for those who seek to empathize with these experiences. I wish to extend my deepest appreciation for your willingness and openness in exploring these themes with my characters and me.

With empathy and respect,

~Tara

Svetlana

PREGNANT.

I'm pregnant.

When everyone left for New York to welcome Alex and Natalie home, I was sure I had the flu and wasn't up to traveling. Brandon and I stayed in Russia so I could recover. Our visit became extended when *Dandekar* Konstantin, Mama's older brother, surprised us with a visit.

Konstantin is a high-ranking general in the Russian army and is stationed in Novosibirsk. The Russian military is the opposite of most other countries in that the higher your rank, the less leave you get. We hadn't seen him in several years, and I was excited to introduce him to Brandon and spend time visiting with him.

I thought my period was late because of all the stress I'd been under. Knowing my pregnant best friend and her husband were abducted by one of the most notorious traffickers in the world was a living, breathing nightmare. But my doctor's visit earlier today and the ultrasound picture I now hold say otherwise.

Although Brandon and I have been back in New York for almost two weeks, I've only spoken to Natalie on video chat. I wanted to tell her about Brandon's proposal and my newest secret, but she and Alex have literally been to hell and back the past month. She was malnourished and had some complications that kept her on bed rest for a few weeks. I wanted to visit her, but Alex insisted on no visitors while they healed both mentally and physically. Thankfully, she and the baby survived their harrowing ordeal and have made a full recovery.

Standing in front of my mirror, I pull up my shirt and place my hands on my still-flat stomach. "Hi, *kroshechnaya babochka,*" I say to my unborn child—my tiny butterfly. "I can't wait to tell your daddy about you. He's going to be so happy."

I tuck the ultrasound photo in the hidden pocket of my purse and go into the bathroom for a quick shower. Alex planned a surprise collaring ceremony for Natalie tonight. Something that's become quite the habit with him. Natalie's none the wiser and thinks it's a farewell dinner for my parents. I can't wait to see the look on her face when she realizes what's actually happening. After everything they've endured, they deserve happiness.

As much as I believe that to be true, I'm still struggling with jealousy. I want to be celebrating our engagement and pregnancy. Instead, I'm sitting on the sidelines, watching and waiting. After I put my clothes in the laundry basket, I step into the shower. With my eyes closed, I stand under the stream of hot water, using it to wash away the unwanted envy.

Arms wrap around my waist, and I scream.

"It's just me," Brandon says, laughing.

"You scared the shit out of me." I turn around and slap his chest.

"I'm sorry," he says with a mischievous grin. Pulling me against him, he leans down to kiss me. "When I saw you naked, I couldn't help myself."

The way Brandon looks at me, a mix of desire and tenderness in his gaze, sends a shiver of anticipation down my spine. Brandon traces my jawline with his thumb, causing my heart to skip a beat. His hands slide lower until they cup my ass. He lifts me, and I wrap my legs around his waist as he kisses me. The sensation of water droplets caressing my skin, combined with my heightened arousal, is exhilarating.

This feels so different. Brandon's taking his time as though he's savoring the intimacy of the moment. With my back against the smooth tile of the shower, he slides his hard length inside me. With every touch, every gentle stroke, he's exploring my contours as though it's our first time. Brandon's worshipping of my body extends beyond purely physical, as though he's deepening an emotional and spiritual connection between us.

I love the feel of his muscles flexing beneath my hands as he moves his body with fluid motions alternating between teasing my opening with the tip of his cock and thrusting deeply. The circling of his hips creates beautiful friction against my clitoris.

"You're so tight," Brandon says between kisses. "It feels so good."

"Mhm."

We're entwined in an intimate dance. The mingling of our breaths creates a symphony of desire. We move in harmony as we build toward a shared crescendo. I cry out as pleasure explodes in rippling waves. Brandon follows me as we float freely through the melody of euphoria.

He puts his forehead against mine as the water flows over us, washing away everything, leaving only the profound connection we share. Time stands still as we hold tightly to each other, savoring the moment of being lost in one another.

Brandon

Svetlana looks regal in her flowing white dress that shimmers beneath the glow of the twinkling lights. Right now, she's talking with Star's current submissive, Zayne. The two are laughing and having a good time. As though she senses me watching her, Lana looks over her shoulder. A radiant smile spreads across her face.

The buzzing of the phone in my pocket steals my attention.

Alex: We're pulling up now.

Me: Thanks for the heads up. We're ready for you.

"Excuse me," I call, and everyone turns my way. "They're pulling up now. Please take your places, and then we'll turn the lights off."

There's a hushed murmur as the Dominants take their places around the edge of the circular garden. The submissives, all dressed in white, kneel before their Dominants. After Maxim and Irina arrive and take their place, they'll complete the circle surrounding Alex as he collars Natalie.

The clang and groan of the tall gate opening fill the darkness.

"Are you ready?" Alex asks.

"Ready for what?" The words barely leave Natalie's mouth when the lights turn on. "What's going on, Sir?" she asks, looking around in disbelief.

"No more talking, baby girl." Alex steps away from her to stand in the center of the circle.

Maxim takes his place next to me as Irina gracefully kneels at his feet.

"Natalie, please join your Dominant," I instruct.

Lana reaches out and grabs Natalie's hand as she walks by. The girls exchange a smile.

Alex motions toward a black silk blanket laid on the ground in front of him. "Kneel." He holds Natalie's hand to steady her as she takes her place. "Look at me."

I walk to the center, stand beside Alex, and hand him the velvet box containing Natalie's collar. Alex removes the lid and angles it to show Natalie. Her breath catches when she sees the silver chain with the heart-shaped lock next to it.

Alex clears his throat before he addresses his guests. "I'm thankful for each of you who came tonight to share this special evening with us. The last few weeks have been the scariest of my life. Not only was I unsure if I'd live to see another day, but my submissive, the most precious person in my life, was in grave danger. Even though we're back safely, we're both still healing." His voice cracks, and he struggles to maintain his composure. "I had this collar made before all that happened. Since we've been back, I've struggled with how to proceed. I wasn't sure if I should let more time pass before offering a collar to my submissive, fearing it would trigger her."

The Dominants and submissives gathered here tonight are our closest friends. They know Maxim works to stop human trafficking, but they don't know the full extent of what he does or how deeply Alex and I are involved. However, they all know about Alex and Natalie's abduction—how close we all came to losing them.

"I sought the advice of a wise friend." He looks toward Star, and the corners of his mouth turn up. "Who explained to me that the piece of leather Natalie was forced to wear was meaningless—it held no significance in our lifestyle or relationship. This collar in my hand is the one that holds meaning and commitment, the only one that matters. I decided to take a chance and seize the moment because no one is guaranteed a tomorrow. I didn't want to let another day go by without my submissive knowing how much I treasure her. How much it will mean to me if she accepts my collar."

Alex lifts the collar and hands me the empty box. I clasp his shoulder before returning to my place in front of Svetlana.

"Natalie, as your Dominant, your heart, your safety, your life are mine to care for. I'm honored that you've chosen to submit to me. I cherish that submission. Tonight, I'm asking you to take your commitment to us one step further. I'm asking you to wear my collar." He stops to clear his throat. "By accepting this collar, you demonstrate your commitment to our relationship and your willingness to submit to me both physically and emotionally. You promise to obey me and accept my guidance, knowing I will care for and protect you in every way. Moreover, this collar represents my commitment to continue to train and support you, always respecting your boundaries and helping you grow in your submission. Above all, I promise to cherish and protect you for as long as we live. So, Natalie, I ask you now. Will you accept this collar and all the promises it symbolizes?"

"Yes, Sir. I will," Natalie replies, her commitment evident in her words.

Natalie holds her hair up as Alex places the silver chain around her neck and attaches the lock. "Thank you for your gift of submission, baby girl."

As I look around the circle, I notice there isn't a dry eye. We've all been privileged to witness this intimate exchange as Alex and Natalie take their dynamic to the next level.

After the ceremony concludes, Anthony escorts us to a separate area that's set for a meal. Each couple has a private table where we enjoy a seven-course dinner. Lana's uncharacteristically quiet while we eat. "What's wrong?"

Lana's eyes widen. "What do you mean?"

"You haven't said two words since we sat down," I observe.

"I'm taking everything in." She scans the surroundings. "This is all a lot."

"Collaring is a serious step in any dynamic," I state, setting my fork down. "I'm hoping we take this step. Soon."

Lana takes a sip of her ice water. "That sounds wonderful."

"What is it you aren't saying?" I press gently.

"We have our engagement to announce," she whispers. "And you'd like to have a collaring. I don't want anyone to think we're copying whatever Alex and Natalie are doing."

"I get it, but I don't think anyone would feel that way," I remark skeptically.

"What if," she says thoughtfully. "When we get married, we have a dual ceremony?"

"I'm not sure I'm following," I admit, intrigued.

"A wedding and collaring. Something kinky and fun," Lana proposes with a mischievous smile.

"I like the way you think," I reply, a grin spreading across my face.

Svetlana

I MORE THAN LIKE THE IDEA. I LOVE THE IDEA OF NOT ONLY becoming Brandon's wife but also being collared by him. As much as I loved the idea of a Dom/sub dynamic, a part of me feared I'd feel trapped or voiceless. I dreamt of having a Dominant of my own, but at the same time, I couldn't see myself finding contentment or freedom. Until Brandon, I never fully understood how freeing submission truly is.

I finally understand what Masha said to me all those years ago. That when I found the right Dominant, my submission would be a gift I'd willingly give. She doesn't like this lifestyle, so I blew her off. I wish I could tell her how right she was and how wrong I was.

My life and heart are safe with Brandon. Gifting him my submission has been the best decision I've ever made. Brandon's my anchor amidst the tumultuous storms of life. He's my rock when I'm weak and ready to give up. Knowing I'm going to spend forever with him is a wonderful secret to have, but I'm aching to slip my engagement ring back on my finger and announce to the world that I said yes. Brandon keeps saying that Natalie and Alex won't be upset if we announce our engagement, too. I'm sure he's right, but I don't want to take any of the attention from them. It just doesn't seem right.

"Svetlana," Papa says and waves his hand in front of my face.

"Yes?"

"What is on your mind, *moya babochka*?" He sits in the chair next to me.

"Nothing, really." I shrug.

"You were a million miles away."

"I guess I was daydreaming a bit." My gaze drifts across the courtyard to where Brandon and Owen are talking.

"That man is very much in love with you," Papa says softly. "I believe you will get your happily ever after one day very soon."

"Do you really think so?" I turn my attention to Papa.

"I do." He leans over and kisses my cheek. "We are getting ready to leave. Mama wants to say goodbye."

"I wish you could stay longer." My heart breaks a little each time they leave.

"Brandon will be flying out in a few weeks. You should come with him."

"I wish I could. The law firm I'm interning with is in the middle of a big criminal case. I can't leave right now."

"You'll be very proud of her, Max," Brandon says as he walks up next to me. "She was chosen over fifty other applicants."

"I have always known the potential that Svetlana has. It is about time the rest of the world also sees it." Papa beams with pride.

"Alright, you two." I push my chair out and get to my feet. "I'm going to say goodbye to Mama."

On the way inside the restaurant, Papa and Brandon get stopped by Alex. I leave them behind and go find her. Mama's standing off to the side, talking on her cell phone. She doesn't see me coming, which gives me a minute to watch her.

She's beginning to show signs of aging. Her dark hair is peppered with grey. I think it looks stunning, but Mama's unsure if she wants to color it or keep it natural. Fine lines extend from the corners of her eyes. We call them *linii kharaktera* or character lines. She's insecure about the physical changes that come with her age, but I think she's only growing more beautiful. Her head turns, and a smile spreads across her face. She holds a finger up, letting me know she's almost done with her phone call.

I nod and walk over to the windows overlooking the street, giving her privacy to finish her call. Outside, Misha stands against their black car. Although he's talking with Viktor and Pyotr, his eyes continually scan the area.

"I wish those boys would find a woman. Or a man," Mama adds.

"Pyotr and Viktor?" I ask, surprised.

Misha is married and has a few children, but Pyotr and Viktor are single. I've never considered Pyotr's personal life—or lack thereof. Something very selfish on my part. And Viktor, I honestly don't know how any woman could tolerate his overprotectiveness. I see how he is with Natalie, and they're not even in a relationship. I can only imagine how much worse he'd be if he were with someone.

"They've been loyal to our family for so long. I would love to see them find love. I have friends with single daughters," Mama says and sighs loudly. "But your papa doesn't want me meddling in their lives. Enough of that." She turns to me. "When will we see you again?"

"I'm not sure. My internship is taking up more time than I thought it would. And I have my bar exam scheduled for November."

"I can't believe my little girl is all grown up."

"There you are," Papa says as he walks toward us. "Are you ready to leave, *moya vozlyublenny*?"

"I'm never ready to say goodbye."

Papa wraps his arm around Mama. "We will see her again soon."

After we say our goodbyes, they leave the restaurant and get into the car. Tears run down my face as I watch them drive away.

"Hey," Brandon says, wiping the moisture from my cheeks. "Why are you crying?"

"It's been hard watching from the sidelines and wishing it was us."

"We don't have to wait. Alex and Natalie won't be mad if we announce our engagement."

"I know." I thread my fingers with Brandon's. "But it's important to let them have this time. I know we'll get our turn."

"We will, *mon petite papillon*."

Svetlana

BRANDON: I NEED YOU IN THE OFFICE.

Me: Can I have ten minutes, Sir?

I'm in the middle of putting dinner together and need to get it into the oven if we're going to eat at a decent time.

Brandon: Put aside whatever you're doing and come up.

I roll my eyes but turn the burner off and set the pan aside. In a display of annoyance, I walk up the stairs, ensuring my footsteps are a little louder than they should be. When I get to the office doorway, I nearly collide with Brandon.

"Put this on," he says, handing me one of his T-shirts.

"You want me to get dressed?" I ask in confusion. Brandon prefers to keep me naked at home.

"Yes. Max and Irina are on video chat."

"Why?" In a panic, I hurry to pull the shirt over my head. "Is there something wrong?"

"They didn't say, but I don't think so." I follow Brandon to the desk and see my parents' images on the screen. "She's here," he says as he takes his seat.

"What's wrong?" I grab Brandon's hand, preparing myself for some unknown awful news.

"Hello to you, too." Papa laughs.

"Hi. What's wrong?"

"There is nothing wrong. Your Mama and I have news we want to share."

"Okay," I say hesitantly. Brandon tugs my hand gently, and I sit on his lap.

"You remember that young Australian girl Natalie met at Moreno's compound?" Mama asks.

"Amelia?"

"Yes, Amelia." Mama smiles warmly. "We promised Natalie we would personally oversee her treatment, so we brought her to Jelena's Hope."

My parents see Natalie as another daughter, so it doesn't surprise me that they made that promise. "How is she?"

"She's doing as well as to be expected," Irina states.

"Amelia is strong. She will do well," Papa adds.

"You've met her?"

Early in their recovery, most of the girls distrust men. Despite his kind and caring disposition, Papa's appearance is intimidating. For that reason, he typically doesn't interact with the girls until much later in their treatment.

"I have. Amelia is an exception." Papa and Mama exchange a smile. "We have decided to adopt her."

"Congratulations," Brandon says without missing a beat.

Certain I misheard, I ask, "Can you repeat that?"

"Amelia and I have been working closely at the center," Mama explains. "She's an exceptional young lady. We've bonded rather quickly."

"Your mama introduced us a few weeks ago, and although it has been a little rocky, we are slowly getting to know one another," Papa adds with a smile on his face. "Your Mama and I already love the girl and wish to legally adopt her."

My parents are the most loving and giving people I know. The fact that they're opening not only their home but their hearts to another child doesn't surprise me at all.

"We've talked to her therapist about how best to approach the subject and will ask Amelia very soon. We wanted to tell you before we brought it up to her. We weren't sure how you'd feel about it," Mama says hesitantly.

Excitement bubbles inside. I feel like a little kid on Christmas morning. "I'm going to have a little sister?"

"Yes, *moya babochka*." He takes Mama's hand in his. "Your mama and I hope you will be okay with this."

"Of course, I'm okay with it. I'm thrilled."

"Congratulations, big sis," Brandon says and kisses my cheek. "When do we get to meet her?"

"She's here now if you'd like to talk to her. Please don't bring up the adoption," Mama says.

"I won't." I bounce on Brandon's lap from sheer excitement. He grabs my hips, stilling me.

Mama leaves the view of the camera to get Amelia.

"How old is she?" I inquire.

"Fifteen," Papa replies, and a dark shadow crosses his face.

"The same age as Jelena," I mumble.

Papa lowers his voice. "Amelia is still very timid."

It isn't lost on me that he ignored my comment.

"She'll come around." Brandon tries to encourage him.

"Come on, sweetheart. It's okay." I hear Mama before I see her.

When Amelia comes into view, concern overtakes me, and I struggle to keep a smile on my face. She's tiny and so very thin—far too thin for her age. Her long red hair is dull and lifeless. Amelia's hazel eyes dart back and forth between Papa and Mama.

"Amelia," Papa says. "I would like to introduce you to our daughter, Svetlana, and her boyfriend, Brandon."

"Hello," she whispers.

"It's very nice to meet you," I say as cheerfully as possible. "I've heard a lot about you."

"You have?" she asks without looking up.

My heart aches. I feel her terror from here and can only imagine the hell she lived through at Moreno's hands.

"Will you ladies excuse me for a minute?" Papa stands, causing

Amelia to startle. "I have to attend to something. I will be back in a few minutes."

"Natalie told me about you."

"You know Natalie?" She glances at the screen, her eyes wide.

"Brandon and I both do. Natalie's my best friend."

"Really?" The corners of her mouth turn up in a smile.

"Cross my heart." I grin.

"Mr. Max," she says, looking over her shoulder. "He said I'll get to talk to Natalie."

"I'm sure you will."

"Amelia has been a guest in our home the past two nights," Mama says. "She's staying in your room."

"Miss Irina said you wouldn't be mad." She wrings her hands. Her body is still on high alert. "I haven't touched any of your stuff."

"I'm not mad at all. And you're more than welcome to touch anything in there," I say, keeping my voice soft, hoping to ease her nerves. "There's a bunch of clothes in my closet. You can look through them and take anything you want."

"Really?"

"Really," I giggle.

"You were right," she whispers to Mama. "She's very nice."

"I'm glad you think so." Mama pats Amelia's hand.

"May I be excused now?" she asks cautiously.

"Sweetheart, you don't have to ask."

"I forgot. I'm sorry." Amelia turns back to me. "It was nice to meet you. If you talk to Natalie, can you please tell her I miss her?"

"I will. I promise."

Amelia gives a small wave before turning and leaving.

Mama waits until she's out of the room before speaking. "She's not comfortable around your papa."

"I see that."

"That's the thing that worries me most." Mama's eyebrows pinch together. "I'm hoping they can work through it."

The door cracks open, and Papa peeks in. "Is she gone already?"

"Amelia was having a snack with Olga when I got her. I think she wanted to finish." Mama turns back to me. "She and Olga get along very well."

"I am envious," Papa says as he sits. "The child is terrified of me."

"You're a good man, Max," Brandon says, leaning closer to the screen. "Once she sees that, she'll come around."

"I hope you are right."

"Are you sure it's still a good time for me to come out?" Brandon asks.

"That is one of the reasons I called. It is best if we hold off on your trip for a few weeks. We are hoping to have Amelia stay here a little longer. It is hard enough with my men and me. I do not want to scare her more than she already is."

"My schedule's wide open. When you're ready, let me know."

"I knew you would understand," Papa says, then turns his attention to me. "I hope you will consider coming with Brandon and meeting the child."

"I'll see what I can do."

"I will be in touch."

We say our goodbyes, and the screen goes black.

"How are you really feeling?" Brandon asks.

"I'm shocked. But I'm so happy." I shift on his lap so I can see him. "I can't believe I'm going to have a little sister."

"Your parents have so much to offer a child. Amelia's a lucky little girl."

I can't help but think Jelena had a hand in this. That somehow, she brought Amelia to our family.

"Now, about what you did to me by bouncing all over my lap like you did," Brandon says with a mischievous smile.

"Surely, I don't know what you mean." I bite my lower lip.

Brandon takes my hand and puts it over his hard cock. "Does this give you any hints?"

"Maybe."

With his hands on my hips, he removes me from his lap and pushes his chair back.

My hands go to his belt, undoing it, and then work on his button and zipper. He lifts his hips, allowing me to slide his pants and boxer briefs down his muscular legs. I lower to my knees between his spread thighs.

I run my thumb along the slit, already glistening with pre-cum, and then lean forward and do the same with my tongue. My lips feather kisses along the soft skin at the head of his dick, and my tongue makes gentle swirls. Without warning, I take him all the way in until he hits the back of my throat. Brandon takes a deep breath and drops his head back.

Taking my time, I worship his body with languid movements that alternate between shallow and deep. My hand plays with his balls while I suck and nip at him. His breathing turns shallower, and I know at any minute, he'll fuck my mouth roughly. It's a powerful game of cat and mouse, seeing how far I can push him before he loses control.

I let the tip slip out of my mouth and trail kisses down his length until I reach the base. Then I take him back in, allowing him to feel the tightness of my throat around his cock. He moans as I continue to lick and suck. Slowly, I move my hand up and down his shaft in time with my mouth. He lifts his hips up, encouraging me to give him more. I pull away and look up at him.

He's so sexy with his eyes closed and his chest rising and falling. Knowing it's me doing this to him is arousing. I consider sliding my hand through my wet folds and bringing myself to orgasm with him, but I stop myself and focus all my energy on Brandon.

Needing to taste him again, I let my tongue trace the ridges of his cock, and then I take him deeper. The tip hits the back of my throat again. I hold myself there for a moment and then slowly pull back. Brandon's had enough of my teasing. He grabs my hair and thrusts himself all the way into my mouth. His move catches me off guard, and I gag, but he doesn't let go.

"Relax and take my cock," he growls.

He fucks my face hard and fast. It takes all my concentration to relax my throat and take it all. Brandon pulls my head back and then lifts his hips, ensuring I take all of him. He swells even bigger, and I know he's close.

"Do you feel what you do to me?" he asks. I nod. "Do you like sucking my cock, *papillon*? Tell me you love sucking my cock."

He loosens his hold so I can answer him. "I love sucking your cock, Sir."

Those words make him lose all control. With both hands on my head, he slams his cock into my mouth.

"Fuck," he roars, and I moan against his dick.

I feel the first pulses of his orgasm hitting the back of my throat. I swallow everything he has to give me before licking him clean.

"You're going to be the death of me," he says as he pulls me from my knees so I straddle him, and he kisses me deeply. I rub my pussy back and forth on his still-hard dick. "I need to be inside you now."

I line him up with my opening and lower myself onto him. My head drops back, and I moan loudly.

"Fuck me," he commands, and I oblige, riding him hard and fast.

I grind my clit against him, driving myself closer to orgasm. Closing my eyes, I lose myself in the rhythm of our bodies. Brandon wraps his hands around my waist and pulls me up and down on his cock faster and harder. I scream out his name as my body squeezes his cock. He follows me over the edge, and I feel him explode inside me. My orgasm seems to go on forever as I milk every last drop of cum from him before I collapse onto his chest.

Wrapped in each other's embrace, the rest of the world fades away. It's only him and me. I wish we could stay in this moment forever.

Svetlana

ONE DAY FADES INTO THE NEXT UNTIL THEY'RE NOTHING BUT a jumbled blur. My mind is fuzzy. The information I'm studying feels like it's going through my head like a siphon. I can't seem to remember anything, which is frustrating me to no end. The bar exam is coming up quickly, and I feel more unprepared now than ever.

I'm sitting on the couch, rereading the same paragraph for the millionth time as I desperately try to keep my eyelids from closing.

"Why don't you go take a nap?" Brandon suggests.

"I can't. I need to finish this chapter, and then I have to fold the laundry."

"You can barely hold your head up." Brandon reaches over and pulls the book off my lap. "I think you should make an appointment at the doctor."

"Why?" I ask, my voice coming out too high-pitched.

"You haven't been feeling well since we were in Russia."

"It's just the stress of Alex and Natalie's kidnapping and the bar exam. I'll be okay once all this is over," I say, hoping my answer sounds convincing.

"I don't think—"

My phone rings. I answer it quickly, thankful for the distraction. "Hey, girlfriend. How did your appointment go?"

Natalie had her check-up with the obstetrician this afternoon. I've been waiting all day to hear if the issues with her placenta have been resolved.

"Everything's great. I got the all-clear." Natalie breathes an audible sigh of relief.

"That's awesome." I put my hand over the phone to tell Brandon the good news. "Does that mean you'll be leaving us to visit your parents?"

"Alex is booking the flight now. Are you and Brandon free to come over for dinner tonight?"

"Hang on, let me ask." I turn to Brandon. "They want to know if we're available to have dinner with them tonight."

"Are you up to it?"

"I am," I smile reassuringly.

Brandon hesitates for a long second before answering, "Yes, we can be there."

"We're free. What time?"

"About seven-ish," Natalie suggests.

"We'll be there." Quickly, I add, "Have you talked to my parents?"

"No, why?"

"I was just curious."

"Can we pick this up later? We have a few errands to run before dinner."

"Sounds like a plan to me. Talk to you later."

After we hang up, I set my phone aside and turn to Brandon. "May I have my book back, please?"

He keeps a hold on it. "I'm concerned about you, Svetlana."

"Bran—"

"No." He stands. His dominant presence looms over me. "You don't ever stop. If you aren't cleaning, you're cooking. If you aren't cooking, you're studying. You need a break, *papillon*." Brandon tosses the book onto the sofa and takes my hands, pulling me up from the couch. "I want you to go and rest."

"But—"

"Don't *but* me." He points to the steps. "You will go lay down. I'll finish the laundry."

"Yes, Sir." I relent, knowing he's not going to budge on this. "Will you come with me?"

"If I come to bed with you, you won't get any rest." He leans in and kisses my forehead. "Go. I'll wake you in a bit."

Brandon

Lana pouts as she slowly walks up the steps. It seems whatever she picked up in Russia is still hanging on, and I'm getting concerned. Staying behind was supposed to be so she could rest, but then her uncle showed up, and any idea of rest went right out the window.

Svetlana was determined to be the perfect hostess. When she explained how long it'd been since she last saw her uncle, I took a step back and allowed it. But it's time to put my foot down before she collapses from exhaustion. While she rests, I fold the laundry and unload the dishwasher.

Alex: Do you have a minute?

Me: Yeah, what's up?

Alex: Are you alone?

Me: I am.

He's being oddly cryptic, especially since I'll see him in a few hours.

Alex: I'm planning a surprise wedding for Natalie while we're in Northmeadow.

Me: How can I help?

Alex: Don't tell Lana until after tonight. I'll get you more info as soon as I have it. Just make sure you both will be there.

Me: I wouldn't miss it for the world.

Maybe I should be more surprised by Alex's text, but I'm not. I knew that after how close he came to losing her in Mexico, he wouldn't want to wait to get married. However, it's another thing that'll get in our way. I hoped to talk Lana into telling Alex and Natalie about our engagement tonight. But in light of this news, she wouldn't agree to it.

Knowing I proposed and Lana said yes, but being unable to tell anyone is hard. Selfishly, I want to put the ring back on her finger and tell the world she's agreed to be my wife. But I get why she wants to hold off. Alex and Natalie lived through hell at Moreno's hands. It's only fair that all the attention should be on them right now.

After booking our flight to Missouri, I go into our bedroom. Svetlana's curled up on my side of the bed. Her hair is splayed out on my pillow, and her hands are tucked under her cheek as she snores softly—something I'll never tell her about. She looks so peaceful that I hate to wake her. But if I know her, she'll want some time to get ready before we have to leave.

Sitting on the edge of the bed, I gently shake her shoulder. "Lana. It's time to wake up."

"I don't want to." She swats my hand away.

"Says the girl who argued about napping," I chuckle.

Lana rolls onto her back, and her eyes flutter open. Her hands wrap around my neck, pulling me to her. "Do we have time before we leave?"

I look at my wrist, pretending there's a watch. "We should be fine," I say as I pull the sheet down and find her nude underneath. I swirl my tongue around her nipple, and she moans softly.

With my free hand, I open my pants and shrug them down my legs. I crawl up between her legs, kissing my way as I go. Then, I bury my face in her pussy and lick her clit gently. She moans louder and grinds against my face. I put my arms under her thighs and lift her ass to get better access.

I bite her clit lightly, and she cries out in pleasure. "You're dripping for me," I say as I slide two fingers inside her fucking her hard and fast.

She bucks her hips against my face. "Oh God, Brandon. That feels so good. Please don't stop," she begs.

I keep up my pace and feel her pussy tighten around my fingers. I push them deeper inside, hooking them to hit the spot that drives her wild. I move my tongue faster and suck her clit harder.

She cries out, and her back arches as she explodes in my arms. I continue sucking her clit and pumping my fingers, drawing out her orgasm. I don't stop until every last ripple has stopped, and she lies panting on the bed.

I pull my fingers out and sit back on my knees. Lana watches with lust-filled eyes as I lick her juices from my fingers.

"Turn over and get on your knees," I command.

I rub the head of my dick through her pussy, teasing her overly sensitive clit. She wiggles her ass, trying to get me to hurry. My hand lands with a crack, and she yelps. Without warning, I slide my cock into her pussy and my finger into her ass and begin to move. With my other hand on her hips, fuck her hard and fast.

Reaching around, I pinch a nipple as I thrust into her. Lana moans loudly. I slam my cock deep inside and hold it there.

"I'm so close. Don't stop, Sir."

I chuckle. "Your wish is my command."

Pulling my finger out of her ass, I grab her hips and pound my cock into her as fast as I can. Her pussy tightens around my cock, and I explode deep inside her. When I pull out, cum drips from between her legs, and fuck me, my cock twitches in arousal. But we're out of time. If we don't get dressed now, we won't leave the house tonight.

I watch Lana as she and Natalie ooh and ahh while looking at the ultrasound photos.

"It's hard to believe you're going to be a father in a few months."

"You're telling me. Fatherhood was never in my plans, but I wouldn't change a thing," Alex says, not taking his eyes off his soon-to-be wife. "The second Natalie told me she was pregnant, everything shifted."

"I can't even imagine."

"Just wait. Lana will get the baby bug now. We'll be raising our kids together," he chuckles.

Raising children together? Alex and I have been through many things, but much like him, I never envisioned us having kids. Now that he's said it, I can't wait to put a baby inside Lana and watch her body grow and change as she gives our future child life. A little girl with light brown skin and long curly hair. Or perhaps a little boy with Lana's blue eyes.

"This is so good." Natalie groans after taking a mouthful of noodles and vegetables.

Lana laughs. "I've never seen you enjoy food so much."

"I am eating for two." She smiles and places her hand on her little round tummy.

"Lana said you two are leaving for Missouri this weekend. How long are you staying?" I ask.

"Only a few weeks," Alex answers. "We promised Charlotte she could have a small bridal shower while we're there."

"Has she settled down about the baby yet?" Lana asks, rolling her eyes.

"Kind of." Natalie gestures with her chopsticks while she talks. "Mainly, she avoids the topic, and that's fine. Right now, I don't need any more stress."

"Do I get to throw you a proper Russian shower before your wedding?" Lana asks.

"Of course." Natalie pauses and looks between us. "Can you two come to Northmeadow? You're my maid of honor. You should be at the shower."

Lana looks at me for permission. "The bar is coming up fast. Are you sure you can take the time away from studying?" I ask, raising an eyebrow. I don't give her a chance to respond before answering, "We'll talk about it and get back to you."

"Are you done?" Natalie asks Alex before taking his plate.

"Yes, baby girl," he says before turning to me. "How about we move to the living room while the girls clean up?"

I follow Alex into the other room. "Did Max call you guys yet?" I ask quietly.

"He called earlier this evening."

"So, you know about them adopting that Amelia kid?"

"We do. Natalie was ecstatic." He glances into the kitchen where the girls are whispering and giggling. "She's really attached to her. I think it'll be good for them," Alex says thoughtfully. "Amelia's not a replacement for Jelena, but it might help to fill the hole left in their hearts."

"I think you might be right."

"What did Lana think about it?" he asks.

"She was thrilled. Once she's more settled, I'm hoping we can fly home and spend some time getting to know her."

The girls come into the living room, chatting about bridal showers, babies, and weddings. Alex excuses himself.

When he comes back, he's holding up a manilla folder. "This is the real reason I asked you over tonight." He takes his seat next to Natalie.

"What is it?" Alex pulls some papers from the folder and passes them to me. He and Natalie are silent while I quickly skim them. "You're kidding, right?" I ask, looking up in complete disbelief. With shaky hands, I set the papers on the glass coffee table.

"I'm dead serious."

"What is it?" Lana asks.

"Alex wants to step down from his company, and he wants me to take over as the CEO," I say in disbelief.

"Are you kidding?" Lana looks between Alex and Natalie.

"I'm not kidding," Alex says, taking Natalie's hand in his. "We're planning to start a new venture together."

I don't know what to make of any of this. Alex is routine and patterned. It's completely out of character for him to make rash decisions or to change course abruptly. I'm concerned that what happened in Mexico messed with his head more than anyone realized. "Care to elaborate?"

Alex takes a deep breath before announcing, "We're opening Jelena's Hope NYC."

I don't know what I expected, but that wasn't it. "I don't know what to say."

"All you have to say is yes and sign the contract." Alex pulls out a pen and slides it across the table.

"Aren't you afraid this might put a target on your back?" Lana asks, concerned.

"Judging by recent events, I think the target is already there. But for this, there'll be state-of-the-art security in place." I pick up the pen and click it nervously, listening to Alex explain. "Dimitri's already on it. So, I have no doubts about our safety." He pauses and looks at me expectantly. "The new position comes with a raise. If that helps sweeten the deal."

Lifting the papers from the table, I make a big show of flipping through each page until I reach the last one with the blank line waiting for my signature. Putting pen to paper, I sign my name and then look up. "I would have signed either way."

We all share a laugh.

"What does the timetable look like?" I ask, curious to hear his vision for the transition.

"I plan to speak to the employees and contact my personal clients over the next few weeks." Alex leans forward to sign the contract. It isn't until he's done that his body visibly relaxes. "By the six-week mark, the transition will be complete."

I didn't see this coming, but given the circumstances, it makes perfect sense. We've been involved with Maxim and his fight against trafficking for years, but it's always been more of a passive involvement. Everything we did was from the safety of our New York office or Max's home. We were removed from the true horror of trafficking.

Moreno taking Alex and Natalie has been life-altering for everyone, especially for Alex. He hasn't said much about what they endured, but I've heard about the ruthless nature of Moreno and his men. I also know Alex had a hand in Moreno's demise. It goes without saying that their lives are irrevocably changed.

Unfortunately, trafficking will never go away. As long as that sad reality remains, places like Jelena's Hope will be necessary. Having a facility like this in New York City will be a great resource. Alex walking away from the company he worked so hard to build is a significant life change. Doing so to open Jelena's Hope here in the city is an even bigger leap toward being more actively involved in Maxim's business.

"That sounds doable."

"Are you planning on working at the center, Nat?" Lana asks.

"We haven't talked about all the details." Natalie looks at Alex. "But yes, I plan to be on the staff as much as I'm able."

"I'm so proud of you. You could've let your experience in Mexico ruin you, but instead, you're going to change so many lives because of it," Lana says, clearly in awe of her best friend's bravery.

"It hasn't been easy," Natalie says quietly. "I know Silverio's dead, but the memories can be so vivid—so real. Every day, sometimes more than once a day, I have to make a conscious decision not to let the memories get the best of me." Alex wraps an arm around his wife as she wipes a tear from her cheek. "I have to be stronger than the memories."

"I know a little about that," Lana says. "Obviously, not in the same way, but if you want to talk about it, I'm here."

Natalie gives a slight nod and rests her head against Alex's shoulder.

The web of human trafficking is a sinister force that preys on the vulnerable and has mercilessly robbed countless people of their dreams and aspirations. Svetlana's life was completely changed by this dark reality, leaving scars that will never fully heal. Max and Irina faced a heart-wrenching tragedy when Jelena was forcefully taken away, erasing all their plans for her future. Yet, a twist of fate granted them the chance to restore a young girl's stolen life.

My gaze drifts across the room, settling on Alex and Natalie, knowing how close they almost came to losing everything. Their story reminds me that not everyone is as lucky. Although invisible scars may forever mark their hearts, they've chosen not to let anger consume them, choosing resilience over resignation. Instead, they've embraced their roles as champions against the very forces that once sought to crush them.

Alex embodies courage in its purest form. He's the bravest man I know and someone I strive to be more like. And Natalie, I'm in awe of the personal growth she's experienced in such a short time. They refuse to turn their heads and assume someone else will deal with the problem. Because of people like them, I believe in the promise of a better future.

Svetlana

When Brandon told me Alex was planning a surprise wedding for Natalie, I assumed a small, understated ceremony at the local courthouse. I was wrong. He wants the whole experience. I've spent hours texting back and forth with him, Anthony, and Charlotte.

"Yes, Mrs. Clarke. I'm certain Natalie wanted the dark purple orchids," I say patiently. "I can send you the pictures again."

"I'm sorry to be such a pain, dear. Since Natalie isn't getting a say in all this, I want to be sure everything is perfect."

Natalie's mother has never been my favorite person. I don't think that's a secret. She was downright awful to Natalie with the whole Tommy thing. Natalie forgives far easier than I do, but I'm biting my tongue and trying to keep my personal feelings out of it. This is my best friend's wedding. I only care that it's everything she's ever dreamt about.

"I understand."

Charlotte continues complaining. "Leo's been sending me pictures." Charlotte continues complaining. "But Stanley and I haven't been able to be at the lake to oversee anything."

"He's sending them to me too. Natalie's going to love it."

"How long until you get there?"

"We're pulling in now."

"Natalie's coming. I have to go," Charlotte whispers.

"See you later." I chuckle and disconnect the call.

"You're being very patient with her," Brandon says as we exit the car.

"I'm not going to lie. Charlotte's a lot." I follow him up the path to the house. "But she's Natalie's mother, so I'm trying to behave."

"Can you zip my dress, Sir?" I ask Brandon when he comes out of the bathroom.

"I can." He steps closer to me, his warm breath on my neck as he slides the zipper up. "I already can't wait to unzip it."

"Unfortunately, that won't be tonight. You'll be staying in Viktor's cottage with the other guys."

Brandon groans. "Don't remind me."

"Are you two ready?" Alex calls from outside the door. "They'll be here any minute."

Brandon opens the door while I slide my shoes on. "We're good to go."

"Am I doing the right thing?" Alex asks nervously. "Maybe this is too much?"

"It's too late to be asking that."

Alex's eyes widen as he looks at me over Brandon's shoulder.

"They're pulling in now," Tony calls from the kitchen.

"She's going to love it," Brandon says and clasps his shoulder. "Let's go get you to your girl."

We part ways when we get to the main area of the house. While Alex hurries to the front door to intercept Natalie, we go out the back door to join the rest of the guests who are having drinks and hors d'oeuvres.

"For you, *papillon*." Brandon offers me a glass of Chardonnay.

If I decline, he's going to question my actions. "Thank you." I accept the drink and bring it to my lips, only taking a tiny sip.

It's only a few minutes before Alex and Natalie step out onto the patio. Although I can't hear what they're saying, I can see the confused look on Natalie's face. Finally, Alex takes Natalie by the hand and leads her to where we're all waiting.

I set my drink down and hurry over, wrapping my arms around the bride-to-be. "Can you believe he did this?"

"I'm still trying to process everything," she says as she hugs me. "Were you in on this too?"

"I was," I answer proudly.

"Before we start our meal," Alex says, getting everyone's attention. "I want to take a moment to express my gratitude. I would never have pulled this off on my own. Even with such short notice, you've all helped create something incredible. Without each one of you, none of this would be possible. From the bottom of my heart, I thank you."

"Please take your seats, and the meal will be served," Anthony instructs.

We enjoy a leisurely al fresco dinner. The mood is light and carefree as the sun gracefully begins to dip below the horizon. Despite the idyllic evening, memories of the last time we were all here threaten to intrude on the present moment. I make a conscious effort to push those thoughts aside. This is about the present and the future. I refuse to allow the horrible events of the past to overshadow this celebration.

As the evening winds down, the number of remaining guests grows smaller.

"Excuse us, please," Alex says as he and Natalie walk her parents to their car.

Once they're out of earshot, Luna asks, "How exactly did they meet?"

Brandon and I look at each other and laugh. "Who gets to tell the story?"

"You can," Brandon says, shaking his head. "I told it last time."

"Good." I rub my hands together. It wasn't funny the night it all happened, but it's since become one of my favorite stories to tell. "When I first met Natalie, she was a shy, backward girl who could barely utter the word sex."

"You're not serious, are you?" Luna asks in disbelief.

"She's dead serious." Brandon jumps in. "Lana and I had dated for a few years before I met Natalie."

"So, Brandon and I planned this CNC scene a weekend when Natalie was supposed to be out of town. I was naked and cuffed to the bed when she came home unexpectedly and walked in on what she thought was an assault. She called the NYPD—"

"What did we miss?" Alex asks as he and Natalie appear from around the corner of the cottage.

"Lana's just telling us how Natalie first learned about the lifestyle," Luna says, trying to hold back a laugh.

Natalie looks at me with her best angry face. "I was hoping she would've forgotten that by now,"

"How could we ever forget that?" Brandon chuckles, then turns back to Luna. "I thought for sure I'd be calling Alex to bail me out."

After I finish telling everyone about Brandon's brush with the law, we fast-forward to the night I invited Natalie to the club for the first time. I skip the parts about the private room and the flogger—Sam doesn't need to know the details.

When I'm done, Sam tells us some childhood stories about Alex. It seems he was always a serious, detail-oriented person.

Natalie yawns and snuggles up next to Alex for a second before he announces, "We're going inside. My bride-to-be is ready for bed."

"We should all turn in." Sam yawns and stretches. "Tomorrow's going to be a big day."

"Girls in one house, boys in the other." I jump from my seat.

"Says who?" Alex asks, laughing.

The original plan was to have a traditional wedding shower. Mama and I were going to make Russian *korovai*. We were going to have Alex take part in the tradition of *vykup nevesty*—paying a ransom for his bride. Since he decided to have a surprise wedding, all those plans went out the window. But I'm getting my way with this. The bride and groom *will* spend tonight apart.

I put my hand on my hips and cock one out to the side. "You can't see the bride on her wedding day until the ceremony."

"You have a bossy little sub there, Brand."

"She can be bratty at times." Brandon smacks my ass, and I shriek. "But she's right. Time to say goodnight. You can't see Natalie until the wedding."

"Some friends you are." Alex makes a show of rolling his eyes and takes Natalie by the hand. "Come on, baby girl. I'll walk you to our bedroom door, and we'll say our goodnights."

"Viktor, maybe you should stand guard in case he tries to sneak into her room," Brandon jokes.

Alex flips Brandon off as he and Natalie disappear inside the house, leaving the rest of us laughing.

While they say their goodnights, the rest of us start cleaning up.

"Do you think you and Brandon will walk down the aisle next?" Luna sidles up to me as I collect the empty drinks.

"Us? Oh, I don't know." I feign innocence.

"I know love when I see it," she says. "That boy is in love with you."

"What about you and Sam? You've been together for a long time."

Luna watches Sam, who's talking to Anthony and Leo. "Sam is my Dominant, but there will never be anything else. He made that clear when we first met."

"Never say never." I smile, hoping to encourage her.

Sam motions to her. "I'll be back," she says and walks away.

While Anthony extinguishes the fire, Leo comes to help me finish cleaning up the last of the cups that are strewn around the sitting area. When we're done, we sit down and go over some details for the morning. Our heads swing to the house where Alex has just shut the patio doors rather forcefully.

"He looks like a lost puppy," I whisper, and Leo laughs.

"Night, everyone. Come along, kids," Luna says, motioning for Leo and me to follow her. "Let's go find the bride."

"He gets to stay in the house?" Alex whines.

"He's just one of the girls," Tony jokes.

I thread my arm through Leo's and grin at Alex as we walk past him. Even though he's acting like a spoiled toddler, he's a big boy. It's only one night without Natalie.

Svetlana

It's Natalie's wedding day. We're just getting our gowns on, and I'm already exhausted. We've been going nonstop since we got up this morning.

Me: I think I want to elope.

Brandon: Why?

Me: This is insanity. I want it to be just you and me. We can tell everyone after it's done.

Brandon: *Papillon*, I'll gladly marry you in whatever kind of ceremony you wish.

Me: I'll see you at the end of the aisle.

After I hit send, I realize what I said and how much I wish it were Brandon and me getting married today. And once again, I find myself pushing unwanted thoughts back down where they belong so I can focus on the present.

My dress is stunning. It's a floor-length dark purple chiffon gown that sits off the shoulder. I step into it and reach behind me to zip it, but I can't quite get it. Holding it against me, I open the bathroom door.

"Can you help me with my dress, Mrs. Clarke?"

"Sure, honey. Turn around." She zips up my dress and says, "You look stunning."

"Brandon's going to go crazy. You'll be walking down the aisle next," Natalie says, and I see the dreamy look in her eyes.

"I don't think so. Marriage is not in my plans." What? Why in the world did I say that? I want to marry Brandon.

"Not in your plans? What do you mean, dear?" Charlotte asks.

"Natalie, can you help me with my bowtie?" Leo gives me a questioning look.

"Let's see what I can do. Sit down."

Thankfully, there's a knock on the door, and Charlotte's attention is shifted away from me.

"Luna, don't you look beautiful," she says, stepping aside to let her in.

"And you are a gorgeous mother of the bride."

"Speaking of the bride, I think it's time we get her dressed." I get the hanger with Natalie's vintage dress and lay it on the bed.

"I'll step outside while you change," Leo says, earning an approving smile from Charlotte.

Carefully, I unzip the gown and hold it as Natalie steps in. She unties her robe and tosses it onto the bed. "Those pearls are so hot. It's a good thing Alex won't know what's underneath until later," I say when I see her lingerie.

"Svetlana," Charlotte scolds me.

"Sorry, Mrs. C." I shrug. "But it's the truth. He's going to go crazy when he undresses her tonight."

Charlotte's cheeks turn a deep red. Luna slaps my arm, making me laugh.

"Saved by the bell," I say in a sing-song voice when my phone starts ringing. Mrs. Clarke steps into my place, helping Natalie get dressed while I grab my phone.

My eyes fill with tears when I see Papa's picture on the screen. One minute I'm happy. The next, I'm crying and saying ridiculous things. These darn hormones. I blink them away and answer the call, putting it on speaker.

"How is my little girl today?" Papa's voice is warm and affectionate.

"I'm good, Papa," I reply with a smile.

"Turn on your camera. Mama and I want to see your dress," Papa insists eagerly.

"Svetlana. You look beautiful," Mama remarks with pride.

"Thanks, Mama." I turn the camera around. "Say hi to everyone."

A chorus of hellos fills the room, adding to the excitement.

"Natalia. You are a most stunning bride. I wish we could be there to celebrate with you today," Papa expresses wistfully.

"So do I," Natalie responds.

"I'll have them on video the whole time. They won't miss a second."

"Hi, Natalie." Amelia pops into view. She looks so much happier than the last time I spoke to her.

"Hi, sweetheart." Natalie's face lights up. "How's everything going?"

"I'm starting to get used to it here. Miss Irina is teaching me Russian, or at least trying to." She scrunches her face.

"I hope you do better than I have." Russian is not an easy language to learn. I can manage a few words to get by, but mostly I rely on Alex to do the talking for me.

"You look like a princess, Natalie."

"Thank you."

"When will I get to see you?"

"I'm not sure. We'll talk to Max and Irina and see what they can do, okay?"

"Yep. Gotta go."

"I have to finish getting ready. I don't want to be late for my own wedding." Natalie laughs nervously.

"*Pozdravlyayem vas oboikh I nadeyemsya, chto u vas budet mnogo schastlivykh let vmeste,*" Papa says.

Natalie looks at me to translate.

"He said congratulations to both of you. And they hope you have many happy years together."

"Thank you, both."

I promise to call them when the ceremony starts and hang up.

"I can't believe I'm about to marry Alex."

"And it's all thanks to me," I say proudly.

Natalie takes my hands in hers. "I'm so grateful you asked me to go to Fire and Ice with you that night," she whispers, her eyes filling with tears.

"We just spent hours getting our makeup done. There will be no tears yet." I wave her off, not because I'm not equally as thankful but because I don't want to start crying, too.

"It's time to put your veil on. Come sit down." Charlotte directs Natalie to a chair, where she sets the exquisite crystal tiara on her head, pinning it so it doesn't fall off. The photographer's camera clicks furiously, capturing every second.

"It's exactly what I wanted. How did you know?"

"Aren't you glad I know your Pinterest password?" Natalie and I both laugh.

After exchanging the traditional old, new, borrowed, and blue treasures, it's time to go. I hold the train of Natalie's dress over my arm so it doesn't catch on the floor as we walk through the cottage.

We're still posing for pictures when the front door opens, and Viktor walks in. Everyone else is oblivious, but I watch Natalie turn around. Viktor freezes mid-step and swipes his hand over his shiny bald head before he catches himself. "You're the most perfect bride. Alex is a lucky man." He leans in and kisses her cheek before clearing his throat. "We're ready to start."

"We're ready, too," I say a little too loudly after witnessing the oddly tender interaction.

"I'll see you out there." Viktor studies Natalie a minute longer before walking outside.

I step up next to Natalie. "If I didn't know better—"

"Don't," she says, not letting me finish my thought. "We've been through a lot together, that's all."

"Whatever." I roll my eyes. Viktor never lets his feelings slip, but this time, he did, and I saw. He's in love with Natalie.

Before I can think about it anymore, Leo throws open the French doors. "Time to go, ladies."

Brandon

Maxim called several weeks after the wedding and asked me to fly out to Russia. There was business that needed to be done in person and couldn't wait any longer. Amelia was living with them full-time and eagerly anticipated her adoption. Since she and Lana were introduced, they video chat every night and have been looking forward to spending time together.

Lana was all set to travel, but the firm she was interning with assigned her to another criminal case. She's competing against other highly qualified candidates for a full-time position with this firm. So, at the last minute, she had to back out of the trip. As disappointed as I was, I understand Lana's just starting her career and can't afford to let opportunities like this pass her by.

While I'm in Russia, I'm also planning to take the opportunity to speak to Maxim. I want to do this right and ask for his blessing to marry Svetlana. Now that Alex and Natalie are happily married, it's time for Lana and me to move forward with announcing our engagement.

With the ring box in my pocket, I walk through the sprawling estate and find Misha at his post. The office doors closed. "Is the boss busy?" I ask.

"He's going through some emails he received this morning."

"Can you see if he has a few minutes? I want to talk to him about something."

"Go right in," Misha says and opens the door.

"Brandon." Maxim looks over his laptop screen at me. "I was not expecting you."

"There's something I need to discuss with you."

He closes his computer. "Please, have a seat."

My legs are wobbly as I take tentative steps into the room, and my voice comes out shaky as I say, "Yes, sir."

"What is wrong?" he asks, alarmed.

"Nothing's wrong." I sit on the edge of one of the antique wing-backed chairs across from his desk. I've sat here many times before and never felt fear—even at times I probably should've. But today, I'm terrified.

"What can I do for you?" He folds his hands on the desk in front of him.

"I'd like to speak with you about Svetlana."

"Go on."

"As you know, we've been dating for several years." I practiced this speech in my room all morning to ensure I didn't screw up any of the details. I knew exactly how many years it had been, but now that it's happening, my thoughts are scattered. My mind is blank. Everything I'd so carefully rehearsed is gone. It's a struggle to get coherent words out of my mouth. "I care about her very much."

"Care about her?" he asks, raising an eyebrow.

"I... I more than care." I stumble over my words. "I love her."

Maxim studies me with a discerning gaze. He stays quiet for a long moment, and I'm unsure if it's to process my declaration or to give me time to relax. When I don't say anything, he nods and gestures with his hand for me to continue.

I take a deep breath and wipe my sweaty palms on my pants, trying to summon the courage to speak. And hoping when I do, that I sound more like a grown man than a bumbling teenage boy.

The room seems to shrink around me as I search for the right words to convey the depth of my emotions. "You know my history." Maxim nods. "For most of my adult life, I punished myself for my past sins. I didn't believe I was worthy to have another submissive. Deserving the love of a woman wasn't even a consideration. I was prepared to go through life alone until the night Svetlana walked into Alex's kitchen," I say, finally finding my stride. "Svetlana's brought purpose to my life. I've worked hard to be deserving of her love."

Maxim's expression softens, his stern demeanor giving way to a glimmer of understanding. He may be a tough Bratva boss and a strict Dominant, but he's also a man who, after nearly forty years of marriage, is still very much in love with his wife. When I speak of the meaning Lana's brought to my life, I know Max understands exactly what I'm talking about.

"Svetlana's shown me the true meaning of love. Together, we've built a foundation of trust and respect. She completes me in ways I never thought possible." My voice cracks with emotion. "I can't imagine a future without her. I want to spend the rest of my life with Svetlana." I stop and swallow over the lump in my throat. "I'm asking for your blessing to ask Svetlana to be my wife."

A moment of silence hangs in the air as Maxim seems to be absorbing what I've asked. "Russian tradition is that the male suitor brings gifts to the prospective young lady's family," he says, watching me expectantly.

Oh shit. I didn't research what traditions there might be. "I'm afraid I didn't come prepared." I move to stand, ready to leave the office, knowing I've lost my chance.

"Sit." Max's voice booms, and I drop back onto the chair. Then, a smile spreads across his face, "Love is a powerful force. It can bring both immense joy and formidable challenge." He leans forward, his expression revealing a mixture of emotions—pride, concern, and a flicker of paternal warmth. "I have witnessed the love you have for my daughter. You have remained by her side, supporting her through triumph and trial. You have my blessing to marry *moya babochka*."

Relief washes over me, knowing I have his approval. "Thank you, sir."

Maxim stands and rounds his desk. "Let us go find Irina to tell her the joyous news, *moy syn*."

My heart's full of gratitude, knowing this moment marks the beginning of a new chapter in my life—a chapter that will be filled with love and happiness for Svetlana and me.

It's early evening in Russian, about midnight in New York, when I sneak away to call Lana. We talk this time every night, so she'll be expecting my call. I bring up her contact and tap the green connect button. There's a slight delay before the line rings. Instead of Svetlana answering, it goes to voicemail. I try again and get the same result.

Me: Are you there?

With my phone in hand, I wait to see the text switch from *delivered* to *read,* but it doesn't happen. It's not like her to be unreachable. For a moment, I panic, anticipating the worst. Then, it dawns on me—she must've fallen asleep early. I told her she was working herself into exhaustion.

Me: It seems you're sleeping. I'm glad to know you're finally taking my advice. Rest up, *mon papillon.* I'll be on a plane back to you tomorrow morning. We have three weeks apart to make up for.

I slide the phone into my pocket and return to Maxim's office to finish up the file I'm working on. This unnamed contact in Yemen and their group are working to crack a child trafficking ring, something not uncommon in that region, that's said to have nearly one hundred children—boys and girls.

They're planning to intercept what's supposed to be an outbound shipment heading for Saudi Arabia. It's a complicated and dangerous mission, but with so many children's lives on the line, there's no room for failure. If they make a mistake and the traffickers get the children out of Yemen, we may never be able to find them.

While Maxim coordinates the details of the rescue mission, I'm making calls to secure beds in treatment centers for the children. Once they're safe, the work begins to find out who they are and if they have families searching for them or if their families are responsible for their current situation.

As I round the corner, I nearly collide with Misha. "I was just coming to find you. The boss needs you in the situation room." We hurry down the hall as he explains, "There was a leak. The *ublyudoks* discovered the plan and attempted to move the *deti* early."

"Fuck. How far did they get?"

"They made it through three checkpoints. They're within a half hour of the border."

If they make it across the border, the children will disappear. "Do we still have a chance?" I ask as we arrive at the room. But Misha doesn't have a chance to answer. As we step across the threshold, I see what looks like a small war playing out on the large screen hanging on the wall. Shots ring out. Men are yelling in languages I don't understand. "What the hell happened?"

"There was a traitor in the group. The traffickers moved early," Dimitri explains without taking his eyes off the monitors.

A child's piercing scream silences everyone in the room. We watch in horror as a little body falls lifeless to the ground. My stomach roils, and I fight the urge to vomit.

We're silent for the duration of the fight. I don't know how long it is before the gunshots cease and the dust begins to clear. On the ground are several men lying in pools of blood. In the background are the sounds of terrified children crying.

Max's phone rings. "*Zdravstvuyte. Day mne podrobnosti. Chert voz'mi.*"

"What's he saying?"

"He's asking for the details," Dimitri explains and listens. He continues to translate for me. "The leak was caught and is being dealt with. Five children were injured but not seriously." His shoulders fall. "Two children lost their lives."

A heaviness settles in the room.

Maxim finishes his phone call. Without a word, he stands, pushing his chair out so forcefully it falls over. With heavy strides, he leaves the room, slamming the door behind him.

I turn to follow him, but Timur grabs my arm. "You're best to give him space. He won't be in a good head space right now."

I look between Timur and the closed door. "I'll take my chances. I don't think he should be alone."

The office door is cracked open. Max is standing with his hand on the window. His shoulders are hunched, and his head is down. Quietly, I step into his space, closing the door behind me.

"Tell Misha to call and have my jet ready. It's time for you to return to New York," he says without turning around.

"I'm sorry," I say quietly, but I know my words do little to quell the anger and helplessness Max is experiencing right now. The same helplessness we're all feeling.

"What happened is unacceptable. We must do better." His arm drops to his side, and he turns to face me. "We cannot lose another child."

"I'll let Svetlana know my trip has been extended." My declaration leaves no room for argument. "Where do we start in tightening up our forces and ensuring there are no more traitors among us? Tell me what to do and where to go."

"I appreciate you making yourself available for a longer time," Maxim says. "However, your work begins and ends in this room. I cannot have you directly involved. Svetlana's life has already been tainted by too much danger."

"I want to take a bigger role," I argue. "I can do that while ensuring she's safe."

"No." Maxim slices his hand through the air. "I appreciate your eagerness to do more, but I will not allow it. I cannot let you take any greater risks."

"But—"

"There are no buts. If you wish to maintain my blessing over your union with Svetlana, you will respect my decision."

I want to continue to argue. To make him see things my way, but the resolute look on his face makes it clear no matter what I say, he won't budge. "I understand and will respect your authority."

"Thank you. Now, we must get busy. There is much work to be done."

It's going to be a long and busy night. Before we get to work, I text Lana, letting her know my trip home has been delayed and that I won't be leaving Russia for a few more days. Then, I rejoin Max and Dimitri in the tech room. Misha and Timur have already begun arranging safe transport for the children to treatment facilities.

Predatels, traitors, will be dealt with in the harshest of ways. Death will not be swift. The men responsible for tonight's events are in the custody of our Yemen contact. Their fate is being spread throughout the various channels. Hopefully, the message is loud enough and strong enough to discourage anyone else from double-crossing us.

This job is mentally and emotionally draining. By the time we wrap up for the night, I'm barely able to drag myself to my room, where I collapse in bed. I check my phone again, but there's still nothing from Lana. I lose the fight to stay awake. My eyes close, and I drift off into a restless sleep.

Svetlana

"Do you want me to stay with you?" Pyotr asks as we exit the hospital elevator.

"It's my yearly gynecology appointment. I think I can manage on my own."

"I'll wait downstairs in the main lobby then. Text me when you're done."

"Will do." I smile and walk through the glass doors leading to the doctor's office.

I'm actually here for my first pregnancy visit, but Pyotr doesn't know about the baby yet. It felt wrong to tell anyone before Brandon knew. I held off on telling him before he left for Russia, knowing that if I did, he wouldn't have gone, and Papa needed him. He was supposed to be home a few nights ago, but unfortunately, the rescue mission went terribly wrong.

I'm disappointed that he's not here with me today to hear the baby's heartbeat. I plan to record it and play it for him when I tell him I'm pregnant.

"Can I help you?" the receptionist asks.

"I have an appointment with Dr. Young."

"Your name?"

"Svetlana Solonik."

The keys on her keyboard click as she types in my information. "It looks like I have everything I need." She looks up and smiles. "If you have a seat, he'll be right with you."

The waiting room is cozy, with only about ten seats. There are two other visibly pregnant women there. One of them is engrossed in her phone. The other is flipping through the pages of a magazine. She looks up, and we exchange smiles as I take a seat. I'm suffering from a mix of nerves and excitement. Trying to keep myself busy while I wait, I pick up a magazine with a picture of a mother cradling her newborn. It's a tender interaction and one I can't wait to share with my own baby. I flip through the glossy pages, but I'm unable to concentrate long enough to read any of the articles.

The door to the patient rooms opens, and a woman wearing light blue scrubs steps out. "Svetlana?"

My legs tremble as I walk across the room to meet her. "That's me."

"My name's Jill. I'll be taking your vitals today," she says as we walk to the triage area. "How have you been feeling?"

"Actually, I'm feeling quite well."

"No morning sickness?"

"It seems to have gone away," I answer, thankful I'm no longer vomiting.

She takes my weight and blood pressure before escorting me to an exam room. "Dr. Young's finishing with another patient. He'll be with you shortly."

While I wait, I pull out my phone and scroll my secret Baby Carpenter board on Pinterest. The day I learned I was pregnant, I started searching for baby shower decorations and nursery ideas. I can't wait to convert the guest bedroom across from our room into our baby's nursery. I'm hoping Brandon will be okay with it being traditional in style with elements of Russian design.

There's a quick knock before the door opens. "Good afternoon, Lana. How are you today?"

"I'm doing well."

"Are you ready to have a listen?"

"I am," I say excitedly. "Do you mind if I record the baby's heartbeat for my fiancé? He couldn't be here today."

"That's perfectly fine with me." Dr. Young smiles kindly. "Can I have you lie back and pull your shirt up?"

While he gets the doppler ready, I do as he requests and move my shirt to expose my stomach. Then, I open the recording app on my phone. Dr. Young squirts some warm gel on my lower abdomen and places the probe against my skin. There's staticky noise as he moves it around, but nothing that sounds like a heartbeat.

"Sometimes, these little ones can be tricky to find."

"Is everything okay?" I ask nervously.

"Early in pregnancy, locating the heartbeat with the doppler can be difficult." He removes the instrument. "I'm going to get the ultrasound machine for a better look. Excuse me for a minute."

The doctor leaves the room, and for the first time, I wish I asked Pyotr to stay with me. Dr. Young has been my physician since I moved to New York City. However, being here for an obstetrician visit feels intimidating. Rather than being excited, I'm feeling scared.

"Alrighty," the doctor says when he returns, wheeling a big machine in front of him. "This should do the trick."

He puts more gel directly onto my stomach, and the machine flickers to life. A tiny bean-shaped image appears on the screen. "Is that my baby?"

"Mhm," he mumbles as he moves the probe around and clicks buttons on the machine. The look on his face makes me uneasy.

"What's wrong?" There's a long pause before he removes the probe and wipes the gel from my stomach. I push up to a sitting position. "Dr. Young?"

"I'm so sorry, Svetlana. Your baby doesn't have a heartbeat."

"What? No, that can't be." Tears well up in my eyes. "You need to look again."

"According to your dates and the results of the blood work, you should be at twelve, almost thirteen weeks gestation. But the fetus is measuring at what I'd expect for the beginning of the tenth week. There's no movement and no heartbeat."

I hear all his words, but they don't make sense. "What does that mean?"

"Your baby stopped developing about three weeks ago," he explains patiently. "I know from our phone calls that you were experiencing nausea and fatigue. Did those things happen to go away?"

"I've been feeling much better. Everything I read said that's normal for starting the second trimester."

"That's true, but a loss of pregnancy symptoms can also indicate early pregnancy loss. Have you had any cramping or spotting?"

"No, nothing." Which is why he has to be wrong.

"Sometimes a woman's body misses the cues that the baby is no longer growing."

"Can you fix it?"

"No, sweetheart. There's nothing I can do." Dr. Young takes my hand in his. "We need to talk about what happens next. Is there anyone you want to be here with you?"

"No." Brandon's the only person I want, and he's on the other side of the world. "What happens now?"

"Ordinarily, I'd offer you the choice of waiting for the miscarriage to happen naturally or offering a D&C. However, there's another issue that's of concern to me." When I don't speak, he continues. "The ultrasound showed that your placenta is at the top of your cervix and looks to be something called placenta accreta."

"What does that mean?"

"It's when the placenta grows too deeply into the uterine wall."

"Is that what caused this?" I can't say the word because then this will be real.

"No. This is a completely separate diagnosis. Unfortunately, we probably will never know the exact cause of the miscarriage."

I want to slap my hands over my ears and run like I did when Papa tried to tell me Jelena was gone, but I force myself to remain rooted in place.

"You're my last patient this afternoon. I'd prefer to take you to the operating room immediately for the D&C procedure."

"Can't it wait?"

"The longer we wait, the greater the chance for complications. It's much safer if I operate today," Dr. Young says. "I know how difficult this is. My wife and I lost our first baby, too." I nod as tears begin to fall. "Who can I call to be here with you?"

"Pyotr," I whisper and hand the doctor my phone with his contact pulled up.

He offers me a kind smile and presses the green call button. While the doctor explains what's going on to Pyotr, I lie down and curl into a ball on my side.

"He's on his way," he says softly. "Do you want me to stay with you until he comes?" I shake my head. "I'll send him back as soon as he gets here." The door opens and closes, leaving me alone.

My mind is a whirlwind of thoughts and emotions, a tumultuous mix that's hard to untangle. It's only been a few weeks, but I had so many dreams for my baby's future—everything Brandon and I would share and teach our child, the places we'd explore together.

I had this image of Brandon's face lighting up with joy when he came home, and I told him we were going to be parents. I can still vividly picture him cradling our tiny newborn in his arms, a look of tenderness on his face. We were going to be a family with so many possibilities for our future.

But now, in a matter of minutes, it's all slipped away. My hopes and dreams shattered, leaving nothing but an empty space within me. My chest aches as I attempt to wrap my head around the reality of what's happening.

This is my fault. This wouldn't have happened if I'd listened to Brandon and not pushed myself the past few months. Three weeks ago. That was right around Alex and Natalie's wedding, and it's when I started to feel better. A pang of guilt washes over me for mistaking it as something good, a progression of my pregnancy rather than the death of my baby.

Amidst the sadness and confusion, my thoughts drift to the impending procedure. Dr. Young seemed very concerned about the placenta accreta. Fear seeps into my thoughts as I grapple with the uncertainty of what lies ahead. Once again, I wish Brandon was here.

My fingers move to call him, but I freeze. There's no way to tell him that I was pregnant and never told him. I can't call him and tell him I've lost a baby he didn't know existed. As the room envelops me in silence, my mind fluctuates between the pain of loss and the longing for support. Pyotr will be here soon. I keep reminding myself. He'll help me get through this.

I don't know how long I lay here before the door opens, and Pyotr rushes to my side. "I'm here, little butterfly." As soon as I hear his voice, the dam breaks, and my heartache pours out. Pyotr scoops me into his arms and holds me close as I cry. "Did you call Brandon yet?"

"No." My voice quivers as I hold back a strangled sob.

"I'll call him." Pyotr reaches for his phone, but I grab his hand.

"You can't. He doesn't know."

"What do you mean?"

"I didn't tell him I was pregnant. Please don't call him."

"Lana, he should know." Pyotr gently urges me.

"Not like this. Not when he's so far away," I beg. "Please, Pyotr."

"Okay." He kisses my forehead. "We can wait."

The door cracks open, and Dr. Young returns. "You must be Pyotr?"

"I am."

"I'm sorry to meet under these circumstances. We're ready to take Lana up to pre-op."

"Can I stay with her?"

"Until she's ready to go into surgery, yes." Pyotr stands with me in his arms. "There's a wheelchair outside the door," Dr. Young says. Pyotr carefully lowers me into the chair and moves to the handles. Dr. Young walks with us and explains, "The procedure should take about thirty minutes," he explains. "I'll come and speak to you when I'm done. Then, when Svetlana's awake, they'll bring you to her."

"I need to be outside of whatever room she's in at all times."

"I'm afraid that's not possible in the surgery suite."

"This is non-negotiable. It's a matter of safety. You are familiar with Alexander Montgomery?" Pyotr asks, lowering his voice.

"I am."

"We work for the same employer. My presence is a requirement."

"I see. I'll make the necessary arrangements."

"Thank you."

When we arrive at the pre-op area, we're introduced to an older nurse. "This is Esperanza. She'll take over from here." Dr. Young places his hand on my shoulder. "I'm going to scrub in. I'll see you in the operating room."

"Right this way." The woman leads us to a small private room. "I need you to put this on." She hands me a hospital gown. "I'll be back in a few minutes."

Pyotr leaves my side only long enough for me to change.

"I'm scared, Pyotr."

"I know, butterfly." He sits next to me. "I'll be here the whole time."

"Excuse me," Esperanza says. "I know this is all happening quite quickly. Are there any questions you have?"

"This procedure," Pyotr says. "Is it safe?"

"A D&C is a standard procedure. As with any surgery, there are risks, but overall, it's safe." Her voice is kind. "Svetlana's in good hands." She turns to me. "I'm going to get your IV started."

"Okay," I say with a shaky voice.

Esperanza places my IV with expertise and then prepares a syringe.

"What's that?" Pyotr asks, putting himself between the nurse and me.

"It's just a sedative," she explains. "Something to help Lana relax before the procedure."

I watch as she inserts the needle into the IV tubing. "Don't leave me, Pyotr." I cling to his hand.

"I'm right here, little butterfly." His voice sounds far away. "I'm not going anywhere."

Svetlana

Lights.

Smells.

Pain.

Beep. Beep. Beep.

Slowly, my eyes open. "Where am I?" My voice is gravelly.

I move to sit and groan in pain.

"Don't try to sit up yet," Pyotr says, placing his hand gently on my shoulder. "I'll call for the doctor now that you're awake."

"I'm so thirsty."

"Let me help you." He carefully lifts my head and holds a straw to my lips. "Just take a small sip, okay?"

The cold liquid soothes my sandpaper throat.

The door opens, allowing bright light from the hallway to creep into the dimly lit room. "She's awake?" Dr. Young asks quietly.

"She is." Pyotr gently lays my head on the pillow before setting the plastic cup on the bedside tray.

"Can you help me sit up?" Pyotr looks to Dr. Young, who nods before pushing the button that raises the head of my bed. I wince and wrap my arms around my abdomen and realize there's an incision. "I thought the procedure was done through my cervix?"

"We need to talk, butterfly," Pyotr says and sits on the edge of my bed.

Dr. Young pulls a chair closer and takes a seat. "Do you remember we discussed the placenta accreta I saw on the ultrasound?"

"Yes," I say hesitantly.

"When I got in there, it was worse than I anticipated. You had a rare condition called placenta percreta. Instead of the placenta being adhered too deeply in the uterine walls, it grew through them and attached to your bladder." The doctor pauses, giving me a moment to digest the information. "I called in a urology specialist to assist me in the surgery. While we were attempting to separate the two, your uterus ruptured, and you began hemorrhaging. I did everything I could to save your uterus, but we couldn't get the bleeding under control."

I cover my ears, desperately trying to block out the truth that threatens to suffocate me. "Stop," I plead, my voice trembling with anguish. "I don't want to hear anymore."

"Svetlana, please try to calm down." The doctor attempts to console me as if relaxation is possible in the wake of such devastation.

"Can you please leave us?" Pyotr asks, his voice laced with quiet authority.

"I think it's best I stay and explain to her—" Dr. Young attempts to argue, but Pyotr's unwavering stance demands compliance.

"I'm no longer asking." Pyotr stands. "You need to leave. I'll take care of her."

"Do you want me to order a sedative?" he asks as he stands.

"No." Pyotr turns back to me.

"I understand," the older man says softly. "I'll be back later to check on Lana. In the meantime, if you need anything, have me paged." He walks away with his shoulders hunched. As the door closes behind him, Pyotr moves closer, his presence a balm for my shattered soul.

I lower my hands, my vision blurred by tears. I meet his gaze, searching for solace amidst the wreckage of my hopes and dreams. "I can't have another baby, can I?" I ask, my voice choked with a pain that threatens to consume me.

"No, little butterfly. You can't," Pyotr replies, his voice filled with tenderness. Tears stream down my face. Each drop represents a piece of my irreparable loss. "They tried everything to stop the bleeding, but it came down to a hysterectomy or your life. Dr. Young rightfully chose your life."

The weight of his words crashes down on me, the finality of the decision forcing me to confront a reality I never expected to face.

A hysterectomy.

My ability to bear life was stolen by the ruthless hands of fate.

Bile rises in the back of my throat, and I begin retching and gasping for air, the agony of the truth leaving me breathless. My body's wracked with pain that mirrors the anguish in my heart.

Pyotr's arms envelop me, his embrace my lifeline in this storm. "Svetlana," he whispers, his voice thick with sorrow. "We need to call Brandon."

"No, Pyotr, please," I beg, my voice quivering with fear.

"He deserves to know. You need to allow him to grieve with you."

"I can't... I can't tell him. Brandon can't know."

Pyotr's hold on me tightens. "Butterfly, Brandon needs to be told."

I shake my head, my tears mixing with the ache in my heart. "No, Pyotr, you can't tell him." I look up, begging him to understand. "You have to promise me you won't say anything."

He softens his voice. "You know I'll support whatever decision you make."

Pyotr's been there for me since I was a little girl. Throughout my life, he's been my anchor when the storms rage around me. Every trial I've endured, it's always been him I could run to, knowing he'd provide unwavering support. "I'm so scared, Pyotr," I whisper, my voice laced with vulnerability.

His touch is familiar, soothing. "No matter what happens, I'll always be here for you."

At that moment, with Pyotr's arms wrapped around me, I allow myself to grieve. To shatter in the arms of my bodyguard, knowing he'll be there to help me pick up the pieces.

Brandon

Per Charlotte Clarke's orders, we arrive at the Montgomery's early on Thanksgiving morning. When we walk into the apartment, everyone's already hard at work.

"There you are," Charlotte says when she sees Lana. "How are you feeling, sweetheart?" She goes to hug Lana, but Lana flinches away.

"I'm still sore but getting better every day." Lana forces a smile.

I stand back as the two ladies talk for a few minutes, wishing Lana's words were true. She hasn't been the same since I got back from Russia. At first, I thought it was that she still wasn't feeling well from the burst appendix or that maybe she was overly drowsy from the pain meds. She's no longer on pain meds, and nothing's improving. Lana's becoming more withdrawn every day.

Our conversation the other night about our contract convinced me that something serious is going on. She asked for things that were out of character for her. Things she knows I can never give her. The whole time, she acted as though our dynamic was nothing more than an annoyance, something she was trying to get rid of.

Desperate for answers, I texted Pyotr, but he said Lana seemed fine to him. I'm at a loss for what else to do.

"What do you think, Brandon?" Charlotte asks and motions to Lana, who's wearing her new apron.

"Wow." Lana stands beside Natalie's mom, covered in pumpkins and turkeys. "She's never looked more beautiful."

Lana rolls her eyes, a move that would get her ass smacked if she wasn't still recovering.

"I told you he'd love it." Charlotte turns and grabs a glass baking dish filled with sweet potatoes. "Brandon, come and take this for her. You two are going to make my famous sweet potato casserole." She hands Lana a note card. "Here's the recipe. Everything's in the tray."

Svetlana looks down at the card in her hand. Charlotte looks between us, seemingly as confused by Lana's silence as I am.

"We'll get right on it," I say and give Charlotte a big smile.

"If you get stuck, let me know."

We find an empty spot at the kitchen island. I set the baking dish down and pull out one of the tall stools for Lana to sit. "Are you comfortable? I can get a pillow for your back."

"I'm okay." Lana's answer is quiet.

"Are you going to join us or just keep watching?" Charlotte asks, and I turn around to see Natalie standing outside the kitchen.

"I was just watching everyone together." She walks over and puts her arm around her mom. "You have no idea how happy this makes me."

"I think I do, sweetheart. Alex was kind enough to buy breakfast for everyone. Grab yourself a bagel, and then get over there and help your husband set the table."

On her way to get breakfast, Natalie comes over to Lana. "I'm so glad to see you. Brandon said you weren't feeling well. I was afraid you weren't going to make it today."

"I'm fine." Lana doesn't look up from peeling her potato.

Natalie glances at me, and I shrug. I was hopeful being around everyone would pull her out of whatever funk she's been in, but so far, that isn't happening. Which worries me even more.

Several hours later, everyone's gathered around Alex and Natalie's dining room table that's overflowing with a plethora of steaming dishes.

"Before we eat, we always go around the table and say something we're thankful for," Stanley says. "I'll start. I'm thankful to be here, in this crazy city, celebrating with my daughter and son-in-law."

"This is the first time I'm celebrating an American Thanksgiving," Amelia says, beaming. "I'm thankful for being safe, for having food to eat." She looks at Max and Irina. "And for having a new family."

"Our family has much to be thankful for," Maxim adds. "Amelia's adoption was finalized last week. She is now legally Amelia Solonik, our daughter." He smiles proudly.

"You didn't tell me the adoption was finalized," I whisper to Lana.

"I didn't? It must have slipped my mind."

Slipped her mind? I'm puzzled by her odd answer. Lana was so ecstatic about having a little sister. I don't buy that the finalizing of Amelia's adoption slipped her mind, but now's not the time to get into it.

"I'm thankful that Svetlana is on the road to recovery after her surgery scare," I say when it's my turn.

"I second that," Natalie says, smiling at her best friend.

"I'm thankful for that, too," Lana says quickly.

Alex goes next. "This amazing woman sitting beside me has made me the happiest man in the world. She's given me so much more than I ever thought I'd have. Thankful doesn't come close to expressing my feelings today." He leans over to kiss his wife. They exchange quiet whispers.

Stanley clears his throat. "Let's hold hands and say grace."

I haven't had a big family Thanksgiving since my parents passed away. Being here with my new family is wonderful but bittersweet at the same time. I wish my own Mom and Dad were here. They would've loved Lana as much as I do. And maybe Mom would've been able to give me advice on what to do about the distance that's growing between us.

Svetlana

AFTER DINNER, NATALIE GOES DOWNSTAIRS WITH VIKTOR
while we transform the apartment for Natalie's baby shower. It's the one
part of the day I've been dreading since Charlotte called and asked for
my help.

*My phone rings, and I see Charlotte Clarke's name pop up. She's never
called me before.*

"Hello?"

"Svetlana? It's Charlotte, Natalie's mom."

"How are you?"

*"I'm doing well. Natalie told me about your health scare. I hope you're
on the mend."*

*"I'm getting a little better every day," I tell a half-truth. Physically,
I'm recovering, but emotionally, the pain only grows worse.*

"I'm glad to hear that. Listen, I have a favor to ask."

"What is it?"

*"I want to throw a baby shower for Natalie while we're in town. I'm
thinking after Thanksgiving dinner," she says. "It won't be as lavish as one
of Alexander's surprise affairs, but it'll be lovely nonetheless."*

"I'm sure Natalie will love that."

"I know you're still recovering," she says hesitantly, "But you and Natalie are so close, I don't want to leave you out of the planning."

"Thank you for thinking of me, but you're right. I'm not really up to doing much."

"As long as you're going to be there. That's the most important."

"I'll be there."

"You look exhausted," Alex says, coming over to where I'm standing out of the way watching.

"I am."

"Charlotte and Irina have everything under control here. Why don't you go lie down while they get everything ready? I'll send Brandon to wake you up before we start."

"That is a good idea, *moya babochka*," Papa adds. "You are too pale."

"I'm just tired, Papa. I think I'll take Alex up on his suggestion and take a short nap."

"You can use the bed in the room Mama and I are staying in."

"Thank you." I kiss his cheek.

"Svetlana." An unfamiliar voice calls my name and gently shakes my shoulder. "Svetlana, it's time to wake up."

I open my eyes and see Amelia looking over me.

"It's time for the baby shower," she says with a big smile.

I push myself up and flinch. My stomach still hurts when I try to use the muscles.

"Do you need help?" She offers her hand.

"No, thank you."

Amelia looks toward the door. "I'll leave you alone."

"Amelia, wait," I say, reaching out for her hand and making her jump.

"I'm sorry. You startled me."

"I shouldn't have grabbed at you." I give her a small smile. "I wanted to apologize for not coming home for your adoption."

I'd grown to love the video chats Amelia and I had every night. She's sixteen and mature beyond her years in some respects, but in others, she's still a little girl. We spent hours pouring over virtual paint samples and décor to redecorate her new room and planned all the things we were going to do together when I came home to visit. But that hasn't happened.

"You don't have to do that. You're recovering."

"I know, but I should've been there. Can you keep a secret?" She nods. "I'm flying home with you guys after Thanksgiving. I'm planning to stay for a while, so we'll be able to get to know each other."

It's an idea I came up with while I showered this morning. Things between Brandon and I are tense, too tense. He's accepted my excuse of recovering. But I know it's wearing thin. He's going to start asking questions. Ones I can't answer. Going home for a while will give me the space I desperately need to clear my head and think. To figure out what to do next.

"Really? That'll be so much fun. Is Brandon coming with you?"

"No," I say sadly. "He has to stay here to work. He doesn't know yet, so please don't say anything."

"You have my word." She pretends to zip her lips and throw away the key.

I put a fake smile on my face. "We better get out there before we miss all the fun."

When I step out of the hallway into the main living area, I gasp. Star, Anthony, and Leo have arrived for the shower. The apartment is now bathed in pink and elephants.

"How did you do all this?" Natalie asks as she steps off the elevator with Viktor.

"Your mother's a very efficient party planner," Mama says.

"I've missed seeing you." Star gives Natalie a big hug.

"Look at you, girl." Leo rubs her tummy. "How's my little niece?"

"She's very active today."

"I feel that." He laughs.

"You look terrific, Natalie." Tony hugs her. "Pregnancy suits you."

This hurts so damn much. I love my best friend, but I can't stop the pain and resentment festering inside, seeing how happy everyone is for

Natalie. Brandon and I were supposed to be engaged right now. He was supposed to be standing proudly by my side, like Alex is with Natalie, knowing he was going to be a father. Natalie and I would be pregnant together. Maybe we'd be sharing this baby shower? But now all that's gone.

"Let's have dessert, shall we?" Alex leads Natalie to the table, and we all take our seats.

Charlotte, Mama, and Amelia carry in pies and a two-tiered pink and grey baby cake.

"Look at that cake," Natalie squeals. "It's adorable. How did you manage to get this on a holiday?"

"I told you Maxim is bossy," Charlotte chuckles. "He's responsible for that."

"Thank you so much, *dedushka*."

"Nothing will stop me from giving you and *moya vnuchka* everything."

His words are like a punch to the gut. He's my baby's *dedushka*— was. I'm reminded that Papa will never have a biological grandchild.

"Mrs. Clarke. You must give me your recipe for this pecan pie. My customers will love it," Tony gushes.

"You want to use my recipe for your restaurant?"

"Of course, I'll compensate you for it."

"There's no need for that, Anthony." Charlotte waves her hand at him. "I'd be honored for you to have it."

I pick at a piece of pumpkin pie while everyone else chatters about all things baby. I do my best to smile when I'm supposed to and pretend I'm having a good time. I'm struggling with self-hatred, but I don't want to ruin today for Natalie. This will probably be the last time I see her, so I take a deep breath and, with as much cheerfulness as I can muster, say, "Let's get to the presents."

"That sounds like a great idea. I can't wait to open them." Natalie returns my smile.

Alex helps Natalie get comfortable in an armchair next to the stack of presents. Charlotte had already asked me to help with the gifts. Carefully, I cut the ribbons from each package and pass them to Amelia.

Charlotte said something about making a hat that Natalie has to wear. I think it's bizarre, but I do as I've been instructed.

"Oh, Mom. It's stunning." Natalie holds up a baby quilt with elephants on it.

"The ladies from church worked on it with me. I was hoping you'd like it."

"I don't just like it. I love it."

"It's exquisite, Charlotte," Alex says as he inspects the stitching. "This was truly a labor of love, and we'll cherish it."

Next are Brandon and my gifts. She opens the first one, a designer baby pram. It's the same one I have on my secret Pinterest board.

"I read it's all the rage with high society in the city," I say, waving my hand.

"It's stunning," Natalie says.

Our other gift is something else from *my* wish list. It's a bassinet that rocks in different patterns and can mimic how a mama rocks their baby. My heart aches.

"The lady at the store said this thing is magic," Brandon adds and shrugs.

"It's a smart bassinet," Alex says as he reads the box. "It'll sense if the baby is fussing and gently rock her."

"I figured if it works, I'll get the award for best uncle."

Everyone shares a laugh. I smile and pretend all the while I'm dying inside.

I've been passing gifts for what feels like forever, but finally, we get to the last one. Beautiful hand-painted pictures for the nursery wall.

"Thank you all so very much. This is more than we could've asked for," Natalie says, wiping the tears from her eyes.

"You've made today extra special for my family." Alex lovingly caresses Natalie's tummy. "Thank you all so much."

"We're not done yet," Charlotte says and stands with a mound of ribbons.

While they do whatever they're doing, I excuse myself before I lose it in front of everyone. Quietly, I slip back into the room my parents are staying in and sit on the bed.

Several minutes later, there's a knock on the door. I stay quiet, hoping whoever it is goes away. Instead, the door opens, and Natalie peeks in, "Do you mind some company?"

"It's fine. Just close the door, please."

She sits next to me. "Are you going to tell me what's going on?"

I turn my head, not wanting to have this conversation but knowing there's no way to avoid it. "Things aren't okay between Brandon and me."

"I know."

"Is it that obvious?"

"To me, yes. What's going on?"

"He wants more," I say, pulling my legs onto the bed.

"What's wrong with that?"

"I don't."

Lies. I'm burying myself in so many lies.

"What do you mean you don't? I thought you loved him?" she asks, clearly confused.

"He's a great Dominant, and I care about him." I do my best to sound flippant.

"I sense a but coming."

"He's ready to settle down. He wants what you and Alex have—the husband/wife thing." I wave my hand and sigh loudly. "He wants to be a father."

"And what do you want?" she asks softly.

"I love the club and public scenes. I might want to try adding other people." Natalie's eyes go wide. "I'm not ready for marriage, and having kids isn't possible." I stop quickly, realizing what I just said and hoping she doesn't catch on.

"Have you talked to him? Told him how you're feeling?"

"I told him what I want and what I don't want. We've been trying to renegotiate our contract but haven't reached any agreements."

"What does that mean?" I hear the worry in her tone.

"We're not on the same page anymore. So, we're putting our dynamic on hold." Pain grips my insides, tearing me apart.

"Don't do anything you'll regret. Give it some more time. Keep trying to work it out."

The door opens, and Brandon steps in. "There you two are. Alex is looking for you, Nat."

Natalie squeezes my hand. "Please give what I said some thought."

I nod but say nothing for fear if I do, everything I'm hiding will spill out, and the fractured pieces I'm barely holding together will shatter, and I'll never recover.

Svetlana

"Good morning, sleepyhead," Brandon says when I walk into the kitchen. "I made breakfast." He places a soft kiss against my lips. "Sit down, and I'll make your plate."

I pull out a chair and quietly sit as Brandon puts scrambled eggs and toast on my plate.

"Here you go."

"Thank you." I pick up my fork and take a small bite.

"How do you feel today?"

"Okay." I shrug and play with the food on my plate.

Brandon's eyes search mine. Worry is etched across his face. "I don't understand why Pyotr didn't call me.

"You and Papa were busy," I reply, my voice softening. "I didn't want to worry you unnecessarily."

"You come first," Brandon says, his voice filled with sincerity, as he cups my cheek tenderly. "Always."

His touch sends a shiver down my spine, and I feel the weight of my guilt pressing upon me. My heart aches as he leans in and kisses me, a gesture filled with affection. Affection I don't deserve.

As our lips part, a heavy silence hangs in the air. I intended to tell Brandon the truth when he got home, but then he told me about the child trafficking ring. He was still devastated, knowing two children died during the shootout. When Brandon expressed his hope that the work Papa and his network of heroes do today will make the world a better place for our future children, I knew I couldn't do it.

I made a split-second decision to tell him I had an emergency appendectomy. It was wrong, I know. It's a lie I'll never be able to come back from—I'm aware of that, too. But what's done is done. Nothing good lasts forever.

"Alex called this morning," Brandon says, a smile playing on his face. "He's invited everyone to their house for Thanksgiving next week."

"Who's everyone?"

"His dad and Luna. Max, Irina, and Amelia." He pauses. "And Stanley and Charlotte."

"All at the same time?"

"That's how the holiday works," Brandon chuckles nervously, trying to disperse some of the tension. "They want us to come over for Pie Day, too. I told him we'll be there."

A mix of joy and dread washes over me. Joy because I love spending time with our families, and dread because I know my guilt will only intensify in their presence.

Brandon reaches out and takes my hand. "What's wrong, *papillon*?" he asks softly, his voice laced with concern.

I take another deep breath, gathering my thoughts. Once again, the truth sits on the tip of my tongue. If I tell it now, I can mitigate the damage. But if I tell him I'm unable to carry his child, he'll stay with me out of pity and his sense of honor. Brandon will never have the child he's always wanted. I search for the strength to speak the words that have been haunting me, but it's not there. I'm too weak. "I don't know if I'll be up to going out two days in a row." The lie drips from my lips, and I lose what little appetite I have.

"I didn't even think about that. I can call and cancel."

"No, don't do that." I might not have grown up celebrating Thanksgiving, but I know it's an important celebration here. One that revolves around gathering with family and friends. It's a holiday

Brandon loves. I refuse to take this away from him. "If you don't mind, maybe I'll stay home from Pie Day so I have the energy to go on Thanksgiving."

"Whatever you need to do while you're recovering." He looks at the nearly full plate I've pushed away. "You've barely touched your breakfast."

"I'm not hungry," I mutter, my voice low and lacking in energy.

"Go lie down. I'll do the dishes, then come up, and we can watch a movie," he suggests, his tone gentle but carrying a sense of determination.

"Actually, we need to talk," I interject, my voice sounding weary.

"About our engagement?" he asks hopefully, his tone rising slightly.

"That and our contract," I confirm, my voice heavy with the weight of the conversation.

"Oh yeah. I almost forgot about that," he replies casually, his tone not fully grasping the seriousness of the situation.

When we originally signed our contract, I requested that we set a date to renegotiate. I almost didn't ask, but given the circumstances now, I'm glad I did.

"Are you sure you're up to that?" Brandon asks with genuine concern.

"I am."

"Okay. I'll be up in a few minutes."

While I wait for Brandon, I find myself rehearsing my words repeatedly. I know he won't take it well, but I have to do something to start putting some space between us.

"I grabbed a copy of the contract," Brandon says, waving the papers in his hand. "Are you sure you want to do this now?"

"Yes."

Brandon, I'm so sorry for what I'm about to do.

Svetlana

"Wʜᴀᴛ ᴛʜᴇ ʜᴇʟʟ ᴅᴏ ʏᴏᴜ ᴍᴇᴀɴ ʏᴏᴜ'ʀᴇ ɢᴏɪɴɢ ʙᴀᴄᴋ ᴛᴏ Russia?" Brandon yells as I'm packing.

"I want to spend some time with Amelia. Get to know my new sister," I say while trying to fold a shirt. My hands are shaking so badly that the task is impossible, so I ball it up and toss it into the suitcase.

"What about the bar exam?" he asks.

"I'll reschedule it for another time." I throw more clothes in.

"What about us?" Brandon asks quietly.

I freeze and look into his stormy grey eyes. Eyes that I'm going to miss so damn much. "I think the distance will do us some good while we figure everything out."

"You're fucking kidding, right? The last thing we need is distance."

"I'm not kidding. We—" I motion between us. "We need some space. Time to figure out what we want."

"I thought we already knew what we wanted." Brandon grabs my arms, holding me tight. "What's going on with you, *papillon*?"

"What do you mean?"

"First, you didn't call me to tell me you were sick or to let me know you were having surgery. You haven't been the same since I got back from Russia." His eyes plead with me to confide in him. "And now you tell me you're leaving me."

"I feel like I'm drowning. There's too much on my plate," I say quickly. "I need to take a step back. I need to go home."

"I'll go with you." He turns to go to the closet, undoubtedly to grab his suitcase.

"No," I say, and he stops moving. "Alex is giving you his company. You can't just walk away from that."

"How long are you going to be gone?"

"I don't know."

"What can I do to get you to change your mind?" he asks, desperation written all over him.

"Please don't make this any harder than it already is." I close my suitcase, lock it, and drag it off the bed. "I need to do this for me. Please try to understand."

"I'd love to understand, but how do you expect me to do that if you won't talk to me? If you refuse to tell me what's really happening."

"I told you why. I want to get to know—"

"Yes. I know. You want to get to know Amelia." He throws his hands up. "But I also know that's not the truth. That's nothing more than your excuse for whatever's really going on."

My phone buzzes.

Pyotr: Maxim's outside. Are you ready to go?

Me: I'll be down in a minute.

"You're really leaving." Brandon's shoulders sag in defeat.

"I have to," I say sadly.

He grabs the handle of my suitcase and storms out of the room. I follow a few steps behind, watching him walk down the steps and head straight for the door. Wordlessly, he passes Pyotr, who's waiting for me in the foyer.

"I take it you didn't tell him?" I shake my head. "Svetlana..."

I can count on one hand the times Pyotr referred to me by my given name. None of them were good. "This is hard enough as it is. Please don't start on me, too."

"This wouldn't be nearly as hard if you'd tell him the truth."

"Your bag is in the car," Brandon says, interrupting us. "I take it you're not going to tell me what the hell's going on either." He glares at Pyotr.

"I'm sorry," Pyotr says softly. "I'll be outside."

When Brandon looks at me, the betrayal in his eyes nearly brings me to my knees. This mess is all my fault, and although leaving is tearing me in two, it's the best option. The hurt Brandon's experiencing by my leaving is nothing compared to what he'd feel knowing I lost our baby and kept it from him. That I can never give him the child he wants.

Once I'm gone, he'll heal. He'll move on and be happy with someone else.

"Please, Svetlana. I'm begging you not to do this."

I reach out and cup his cheek. "I love you, Brandon." My lips touch his for the briefest of seconds before I hurry from the house.

Brandon

My hand shoots out, grabbing the doorframe as I watch the woman who's my world slide into the back seat of her father's rented car. The door closes, and they drive away. I watch until the vehicle is out of sight.

How am I supposed to go on without her here? Why does it feel like she was saying goodbye—for good? Tears flow in rivulets down my face, and my lungs struggle for my next breath.

I close my door and drag myself to the living room, where I drop onto the sofa. Nothing makes sense right now.

It's been days since I went to work. I don't know when I ate last. I'm still in the clothes I was wearing when Svetlana left me. Nothing in my world is right.

I'm drifting in and out of a restless sleep when my cell rings. I don't bother looking at the screen.

"Hello?"

"Brandon?" Viktor asks.

"Yeah."

"I don't know how to tell you this."

"Tell me what?" I sit up. What else can possibly go wrong?

"It's Alex." Viktor's voice cracks. "He's dead."

Everything that happened with Svetlana has my head screwed up to the point that I'm hallucinating. "Can you repeat that, please?"

"There was an explosion at the new building. Alex didn't make it out." I hold the phone to my ear but don't say anything. I can't. There's no way this is really happening. "Brandon? Are you there?"

"I'm here. What the hell happened?" I listen carefully as Viktor explains that Alex was getting into his car in the parking garage when the car exploded with him in it. "Who's behind it?"

"I don't know. I don't fucking know," Viktor says, his voice full of pain.

Natalie. Oh my God. She's just recovered after their ordeal in Mexico. Now this. "Are Natalie and the baby okay?" I ask as I drag myself off the couch. I need to take a shower and find some clean clothes. I have to get over there.

"She's devastated."

"Give me an hour, and I'll be there." I hang up and take the steps two at a time. Without thinking, I bring up Svetlana's contact and hit the green call button. Her voicemail picks up. "Lana, I need to talk to you. It's important. Please call me."

I don't wait for her to return my call. I turn the hot water on and allow the steam to fill the bathroom, clouding my reflection in the mirror. After I shed my clothes, I step under the hot spray. The water cascades over me, soothing my weary body but failing to wash away the chaos within. Thoughts of Svetlana, Alex, and Natalie swirl in my mind, mingling with regret, grief, and a desperate longing for things to be different.

The water pounds against my skin, almost as if trying to wake me from this nightmare. But reality is just as harsh and unforgiving. Alex, my best friend, is gone. Ripped away from everyone who cares about him in an explosion that's been made to look like a tragic accident. Even without all the details, I'm certain that's not the truth. Someone is behind this. The shock of his loss shakes me to the core, a reminder of the fragility of life and the pain that often accompanies it.

With trembling hands, I turn off the shower and step out, wrapping a towel around my waist. Water drips from my hair, mingling with the tears I've been holding back for too long. I glance at myself in the mirror, seeing the reflection of a broken man, haunted by his past and uncertain of his future.

I dry myself off quickly and put on fresh clothes. Right now, my mind is fixated on one thing—being there for Natalie. She's pregnant and has just lost her husband. I can't imagine the depth of her sorrow. Despite my own struggles, I have to be strong for her, for both of us.

As I reach for my phone to check the time, I notice a missed text.

Svetlana: Papa told me.

I call her back, hoping against hope that she'll answer. My heart sinks when her voicemail picks up again, but I don't leave another message. As much as I need to hear her voice, it's clear she doesn't want to speak to me. My hands shake as I put down the phone and take a deep breath, trying to steady myself. The weight of the world rests on my shoulders, but there's no time for self-pity. Natalie's going to need all of us to get through the horrific tragedy.

As I drive toward Alex and Natalie's house, rain begins to fall, adding to the somberness of the day. The windshield wipers move rhythmically. Their sound doing nothing to drown out the thoughts rapidly running through my mind.

While I navigate the congested New York City streets, I do my best to put aside my own heartache and prepare to be the pillar of strength Natalie's going to need. I'll be by her side as we find a way to navigate the storm that has engulfed our lives.

Brandon

"Where is she?" I ask as the elevator doors open, and I burst out.

"Excuse me." Charlotte Clarke appears in the foyer with her hands on her hips. "May I ask what you think you're doing?"

"I'm sorry, Mrs. Clarke." I take a deep breath, trying to remember they've all just experienced an unexpected loss. "Viktor called and told me what happened. I'm here to see Natalie."

"The doctor said she needs to rest."

"I understand. I just—"

"Brandon," Viktor interrupts our exchange. In an uncharacteristic move, he steps around Charlotte and embraces me. "I'm so sorry."

"I was hoping to get here, and it would be a bad joke," I say, clearing my throat.

Charlotte quietly excuses herself.

"I still can't believe it's real." Viktor quickly wipes his eyes.

"Have you heard anything yet?" I ask, lowering my voice.

"Maxim's been apprised of the situation. He has Dimitri working all the angles, but there's been no information so far."

"Where's Natalie?"

"She's in the kitchen. Her mom's trying to get her to eat."

I follow Viktor and find Natalie sitting at the kitchen table, a bowl of soup in front of her. Instead of eating, she's playing with the spoon, circling it in the broth. Natalie doesn't look up when we step into the room. It's as if she's lost in her own little world. She's so pale, her skin is almost translucent, and her eyes are red-rimmed and swollen.

"I'm pretty sure she's in shock," Viktor whispers. "Dr. Young was here to check on her and the baby. He said they're doing okay but wants her to rest as much as possible."

"When is she going to catch a break?"

"Brandon?" Natalie's voice is barely audible.

"I'm here, sweetheart." I hurry over and wrap my arms around her. She slumps against me and begins to cry. "I've got you, Nat," I murmur repeatedly until her weeping subsides. Viktor slides a chair over for me, and I settle in beside her. "You should try to eat some."

"I'm not hungry."

"I know, but you have to think about the baby." I push the bowl to her. "You can do it. Just a few spoonfuls."

Natalie picks up the spoon and sips some broth from it. "Does Lana know?"

"She does. Maxim told her."

"Is she coming home?"

"I don't think so."

"What happened?" Natalie asks as a lone tear slides down her cheek. I wipe it with my thumb. "She told me you guys needed a break, and she was going home for a while."

"You know as much as I do." I sigh. "We were renegotiating our contract like we'd agreed when she blindsided me with all kinds of crazy requests." I guide her hand back to her bowl, hoping she'll take another spoonful of soup.

"I'll try to talk to her," Natalie offers.

"Thank you, but right now, you need to focus on yourself and the baby."

"I don't know how to do any of this without him," she says, her eyes filling with tears once again. "Alex was my world. He was the other part of my heart, and now he's gone."

"I'm here, and Viktor's here." I rub her back and exchange a worried glance with Viktor. "We'll be by your side for every step. You won't have to do this on your own."

Even as I say the words, I know we have big shoes to fill. Alex is a good man—*was* a good man. He always put himself and his needs behind those of others. Not only did he run a successful company, but he was also about to open a treatment center for rescued victims of human trafficking. As a husband, he treasured Natalie, and I know he would've been an incredible father to baby Rose. No one will ever replace him, but I'll do everything in my power to be sure Rose knows exactly who her father was and that Natalie will never be alone.

We aren't family by blood but family by choice. Somehow, we'll take the pieces of our fractured lives and learn how to live again.

Svetlana

"Natalie's your best friend. Her husband was just killed. She's going to need everyone who cares about her to get through this," Mama reprimands me. "I don't understand how you can refuse to fly back with us."

"I just can't." I walk away and turn toward the window, unable to face her.

At first, I didn't believe Papa when he told me Alex had been killed. I couldn't imagine why he would joke about something so awful. It wasn't a joke, though. Once the initial shock wore off, I found myself struggling to wrap my head around the fact that Alex was dead.

I've been in Papa's world long enough to know that things like car explosions usually aren't an accident. Someone set out to kill him. Papa has all his men working the case. Whoever did this can run, but they can't hide. Papa will find the responsible people, and he'll make them pay.

"I don't understand what's going on with you, Svetlana." Mama comes to stand next to me. Softening her voice, she says, "Please help me to understand."

"There's nothing to understand. I came home to spend time with

Amelia. She's devastated about what happened. I'm not going to leave her here alone."

When Mama told Amelia about the explosion and that Alex was gone, she fell apart. She couldn't understand why someone would want to hurt him. We were concerned it would set back her recovery, but right now, she seems to be holding her own. She only asked if Papa would find out who did it and take care of them.

Papa didn't want Amelia to know what he did outside of Jelena's Hope. When they were getting ready to enroll her in school, I suggested he tell her. She would hear it from the kids at school, which would've been more of a shock than Papa telling her. Amelia is very perceptive, and I suspect she already has an idea. Either way, it seemed to help her feel more secure both at home and with Papa.

They asked if she wanted to go to New York with them, but she said no. She didn't think she could handle attending the funeral.

My parents left yesterday. It'll be a quick trip to New York for the funeral and back home. Papa has been very hands-on with searching for who's behind the explosion. I haven't seen him this distraught since Jelena was taken.

This evening is Alex's memorial service. Natalie and I have been on a video call for the past two hours. She's spent most of the time going from tears to silence. I assure her she doesn't have to talk but that I'll be here if she wants to.

"I don't know how I'm going to get through tonight," Natalie says as she tries to do her make-up. "How do I say goodbye to him?"

"I hate that I'm not there with you." Fate has been cruel lately. We've both lost people who we loved very much. One a husband and soon-to-be-father and one an innocent baby who didn't get the chance to be born.

"I wish you were here too." Natalie sets her make-up brush down as a fresh wave of tears falls. "I don't think I can do this, Lana."

"I know this is hard, honey." I move the camera closer. "But you have to be strong. For Alex."

My words are weak. If she only knew what a cowardly hypocrite I am right now. I'm preaching to her to be strong while she's facing life without her husband. In comparison, my loss was nothing, and instead of being strong, I lied and ran.

In the background, Natalie's bedroom door opens, and Charlotte steps into the room. "Sam and Luna just got here. He'd like to see you."

"You can send him in." Natalie turns back to the camera. "I have to go. We'll talk soon?"

"I don't care what time it is. If you need me, just call. I love you, Nat."

"Love you too, Lan."

The screen goes black, and I break down. Just a few months ago, everything was perfect. Our best friends were married and getting ready to welcome their first baby. Brandon and I were about to announce our engagement, and I would surprise him with the news of our pregnancy. And now, we're here. Alex is dead. Natalie is a young widow who's facing giving birth and raising a child on her own. Our baby is gone, and Brandon and I are no longer together.

I want to stomp my feet and scream at just how unfair life is. But what good will that do? It won't bring back what we lost.

"Svetlana?" Amelia says my name, startling me.

I swipe at the wetness on my face and turn around. "What's up?"

"I heard you crying and wanted to be sure you're okay." Her voice is small and quiet.

"I'm good," I say, hoping she accepts my answer, but she doesn't.

"You don't have to hide your sadness from me," Amelia says, coming closer. "I won't break if you tell me the truth."

"I was just talking to Natalie." I pat the couch, inviting Amelia to join me. "She's getting ready for the memorial service."

Amelia sits and tucks her legs up under her. "Is she doing alright?"

"Not really. But Natalie's strong. She'll get through this."

"I should've gone with Max and Irina," she says, and her lip quivers. "Natalie's my friend. She's probably going to hate me now."

"Natalie would never hate you. She understands that you're still getting adjusted. When you're ready, you can call and talk to her."

"Are you sure she isn't going to be mad?"

"I'm positive." I smile at the girl—my sister. "What do you say we get dressed and go out for some dinner?"

It may seem callous to go out and do something fun while Natalie is going through hell, but I'm trying to think of Amelia. She's struggling in so many ways. The last thing she needs to worry about is whether Natalie will be mad at her or not. The only thing I can think of doing is trying to distract her.

"Um." She looks uncertain, and I think she's about to say no, but she surprises me by asking, "Will Pyotr be coming too?"

"He will, but he'll stay out of our way."

"But he'll be there, right?"

"Yes. Would it help if I asked Timur to come, too?"

"It would."

"How long will it take you to get ready?" I ask.

"Ten minutes." The corners of her mouth tip up in a small smile.

"Perfect." I smile.

We go our separate ways to change. Then, I search for the guys to let them know we're going out.

Brandon

THE SUN IS BEGINNING TO SET AS I ARRIVE AT THE STONE chapel for Alex's memorial service. I left early, ensuring I was the first to arrive. I wanted the opportunity to say a few words to him before anyone else got here.

Stepping inside, I find the room lit by hundreds of flickering candles. The urn holding Alex's remains sits on a table beside a picture of Natalie and him holding one of the baby's ultrasound photos in front of her round tummy.

We were just together a few days ago for Natalie's shower. Alex was alive. There was so much to look forward to. Everyone was happy. I've reached for my phone to call him so many times over the past few days only to remind myself that he's gone.

"Max will search every corner of the earth to find whoever did this. Your death will not go unpunished." I swallow over the lump in my throat. "Don't worry about Natalie and the baby. I'll be there for her."

A hand lands on my shoulder. "You are a good friend, Brandon," Maxim says.

I drop my head. "We have to find who did this."

"We will," Maxim assures me. "Whoever is responsible will answer directly to me." I nod, satisfied with Maxim's response. "Natalie and

Viktor are pulling in now. I thought you would want to be with them."

"Thanks, Max." I turn and start walking away.

"Brandon," Max calls, and I turn to face him. "Everything will work out with Svetlana as well."

Hearing her name is painful. I wish she was here, by my side, helping me say goodbye to my best friend. I can't speak. My emotions are running too high. So, I say nothing and continue making my way to Natalie.

I find her standing next to Viktor, who's on high alert, as they greet the mourners who've come to pay their final respects.

"Is there anything you need?" I ask as I put my hand on Natalie's elbow.

"No, thank you."

"I'll be inside."

Maxim motions for me to sit by him and Irina. It's hard to be with them. It makes Lana's absence all the more painful, a void that deepens in their presence.

Alex should be here. He'd know what to do. He and Svetlana were close. If there was anyone who could get her to talk, to open up, it would be him. Instead, we're all here floundering without him and preparing to say our final goodbyes to a man none of us are ready to let go of.

Although we're in a chapel, the ceremony is not being led by a member of the clergy. Alex wasn't a fan of organized religion. Instead, Natalie asked me to deliver the eulogy. When she and Viktor take their seats, I rise and walk to the front of the room, unsure how to get through the words I wrote.

"Today, we gather to remember and honor a dear friend who left us too soon. We're all shocked and heartbroken by the suddenness of Alex's passing. Alex was a wonderful person who impacted the lives of all those he encountered. He had a unique ability to bring joy and laughter to any situation. Many of you know I dated Natalie's college roommate. Little did she know her arrival home one night would mark the beginning of an unforgettable tale. Natalie and I hadn't had the privilege of meeting one another yet. Actually, I don't think she knew I existed until late one night when she mistook me for an intruder. Natalie, armed with her cell phone flashlight, promptly declared that the NYPD was en route."

Laughter erupts, relieving some of the heaviness in the air.

"Thankfully, we were able to clear up the misunderstanding, sparing me a close encounter with handcuffs." It's a story that became a cherished part of our shared history and one we recount with endless amusement. "A year later, with a spark of inspiration, Svetlana and I orchestrated a blind date between Alex and Natalie. We didn't know that we were setting the stage for a love story that would forever be etched in our hearts."

I look at Natalie, who's wiping tears from her face and am reminded of the incredible journey she and Alex embarked on. Alex's presence in Natalie's life brought love, happiness, and countless cherished memories. They shared laughter, tears, and unwavering support for one another. Together, they wove a tapestry of love that will forever endure.

"Though we mourn our shared loss, we must also be grateful for the unforgettable chapters Alex authored in our lives. Alex's kindness knew no bounds, and although he's no longer with us, we can take comfort in knowing he's left a lasting impact on our lives. His spirit will continue to live on through the love he shared, the laughter he gifted us, and the immeasurable impact he made on our hearts. As we say our final goodbyes, I ask everyone to honor Alex's memory by embracing the love and laughter he so effortlessly brought into our lives. May his legacy serve as a reminder that the bonds we form and the moments we share are precious treasures to be cherished."

My voice cracks as the emotions I've been holding back break free. Tears fall unbidden as I look up and speak directly to the man whose untimely departure has left an undeniable void in my life. "I always admired you, Alex. Until we meet again, brother."

I step off the platform and walk over to Natalie, taking her trembling hand in mine. "You were his world, Natalie. Thank you for loving him." Her shoulders shudder as sobs wrack her body. I wrap my arms around her, hoping to offer her even a small measure of comfort.

How do we do this? Where the hell do we go from here?

Svetlana

"Svetlana," Papa calls as he rushes into the indoor swimming pool room. "Natalia is in labor."

"She's early," I say as I climb out of the pool.

"That is all you have to say?"

I wrap the towel around my dripping body. "I'm sure Viktor's with her."

"But Alexander is not."

Crossing my arms over my chest, I stare at Papa, neither of us backing down. I want to tell him everything. Open up about my heartache and loss, but I can't force the words to come out. The emotions remain locked deep inside. "People die. It's a part of life."

Papa takes a step closer. His presence is imposing, and I drop my arms. "When did you become so cold-hearted?" he asks, narrowing his eyes.

"I'm not cold-hearted, just realistic." I grab my bathing suit cover. "I need to get to the center. I'm volunteering there today."

"You will be well served to remember why Jelena's Hope was started."

I ignore Papa's last statement and hurry away.

As soon as I get inside the safety of my bedroom, the tears I was struggling to hold back can no longer be contained. I slide down the door and pull my knees up to my chest. The last time I spoke to Natalie was before Alex's memorial service. She's texted me several times, sending me ultrasound pictures and recordings of the baby's heartbeat. Each time I open one, my heart shatters a little more. I've taken the time to delete her texts without opening them.

It's not Natalie's fault. She has no idea. I've picked up my phone so many times and pulled her contact information up, intending to tell her everything, but each time, I stopped myself. She's had enough heartache the past few months. She doesn't need me tossing my problems into her lap.

And now she's in labor. I'm concerned because the baby is early. Viktor is by her side, so he'll take care of her, and I trust Dr. Young will ensure Rose arrives safely. If things were different, I'd be by her side, holding her hand through each contraction and celebrating the birth of her daughter. Instead, I'm drowning in my own pool of grief from losing both my baby and the ability to conceive again. I should be happy for Natalie, but I don't know how. Let's face it, I'm a shitty excuse for a friend.

After my tears stop falling, I drag myself into the shower to rinse off the chlorine before getting dressed and going to find Pyotr for a ride to Jelena's Hope. I pop my head into the command room, and instead of Pyotr, I see Dimitri.

"Hey, kid. What's up?" he asks, smiling.

"I'm looking for Pyotr. Have you seen him?"

"He's out training with some of the other guys."

"Thanks. I'll go find him."

"Not so fast." I stop mid-step. "Come in here and sit down."

"I really need to go." I motion toward the door.

"You're not going anywhere without Pyotr, and he's going to be tied up for a little longer," Dimitri says while he's typing. "So, have a seat, and let's catch up."

I pull my phone out to text Pyotr.

Me: Please let me know when you're done. I need a ride to the center.

The legs of the chair squeak on the tiled floor. Dimitri turns to face me as I sit down.

"What's up with you?"

"Is it so hard to believe I wanted to come home?" I snap. "I wish everyone would stop giving me a hard time."

"Woah." Dimitri holds his hands up. "What's that all about?"

"I'm sorry." I take a deep breath. "No one seems to understand that I just wanted to come home. They all seem to think there's another reason. Something I won't tell them."

"Is there another reason?"

"Not you, too." I roll my eyes and cross my arms.

"I'm not jumping on any bandwagon." Dimitri chuckles. "You have to look at it from their point of view. You fought so hard to go to New York. Over the past few years, you've made a life there. Then, out of the blue, you come back here. It's understandable that the people who care about you want to be sure there's nothing else going on."

Dimitri's always held a special place in my heart. For a few seconds, I consider telling him. I know he wouldn't betray my trust, but I also know he won't have a clue what to do. Still, it makes it hard to keep things from him. "I get it, and I'm glad I have so many people who care about me. But there isn't any big conspiracy. I got my degree, and now I want to put it to good use at the center."

He studies me carefully, and I do everything possible not to break eye contact with him. Dimitri may be a computer geek, but he's as well trained as any of Papa's men. If I'm not careful, he'll see right through me. "I don't know that I buy that completely," he says with a raised eyebrow. "But I'll let you get away with that answer for now."

My phone dings with an incoming text.

Pyotr: I'm out front with the car.

"Pyotr's ready. I have to run." I jump up from my seat and attempt to make a quick exit.

"Lana," Dimitri says, softening his voice. "When you're ready to talk, I'm here."

I don't react. Instead, I turn my back on another person I love, all in the name of protecting them.

When I get outside, Pyotr's leaning against the car, waiting for me.

"I'm sorry if I interrupted your training."

"We were finishing up when you texted," he says as I slide into the car and he closes the door.

Pyotr drives slowly down the meandering driveway that leads to the main road. "What are your plans for this afternoon?"

"I'm meeting with the legal team. They're putting together their case against Damian Nox, that trafficker they caught last month." After I returned home, Papa used some of his government contacts to get me registered with the Ministry of Justice so I could practice criminal law with the attorneys he employs at Jelena's Hope. "Unfortunately, no matter what we do, the punishment will never fit the crime."

"I keep telling Maxim to forgo the justice system and let us take things into our own hands."

"It would probably be more effective, but you know Papa. He wants to keep anything that goes through Jelena's Hope within the law's boundaries."

"That's why your father has kept his position for so long. He's a good and honorable man."

We've had that argument before. I believe every trafficker they catch should be forced to endure every ounce of torture they inflicted on their victims. Then, instead of putting them out of their misery, they should be left to die a slow, painful death.

But Papa isn't a *killing machine*. If he doesn't have to, he won't take a life. Instead, he strives to strengthen the laws and punishments for these animals. "It's a noble effort, but I still think torture and death are the better options."

"And that, little butterfly, is why Maxim is the boss and not you." Pyotr chuckles as he pulls into the parking lot at Jelena's Hope. "Text me when you're done. I have a few errands to run for your father."

"Will do. See you later."

I step inside the familiar building. Standing in the foyer, I look around at what we've created. To the professionals and survivors alike who are strolling through the halls. My mind drifts back to the heartbroken ten-year-old version of myself. To the day I dressed in my sister's clothes and marched into Papa's office.

"Is Papa busy?"

"He's on a phone call. Is there something I can help you with?" he asks.

"No. I need to talk to Papa about it."

"Misha, I—" Papa says, opening the door startling me. "Moya babochka, you look like you are ready to go to work."

"I am." I nod. "Do you have some time to talk?"

"For you, any time." Papa smiles and steps aside, allowing me to enter. "Please excuse me, Misha. I have an important meeting with Ms. Solonik. Can you make sure we're not interrupted?"

"Sure thing, boss."

Papa sits in his big, comfy chair with his hands folded. "What can I help you with today?"

I open my notebook and clear my throat. "I made a promise to Jelena that I wouldn't let her be forgotten."

"That will not happen."

"I know we won't forget her, but other people might. They'll forget how good she was." I pull my feet under my legs. "I don't want that to happen."

"I see. What do you have in mind?"

"I don't know for sure." I bite my lip while I look at the notes I made. "I know Jelena wasn't the only person who's ever been trafficked and that it happens to lots of people." I look at Papa. "Pyotr said many of the people that are taken don't have anyone who loves them or looks for them."

"That is very true."

"There has to be something we can do to help."

"You are a remarkable young lady. Do you know that moya babochka?" I shrug, not thinking I'm anything other than normal. "I have been thinking precisely the same thing."

"You have?" I ask, surprised.

"Yes. I've been busy getting some colleagues together to form a network to go after people like Rudolf Sergin and Farouk El Alami. I want to make sure no one else ever has to lose a loved one."

"I like that very much. But what about helping the people that were stolen? I want to help them."

"How so?" Papa tilts his head.

"When I was talking to Pyotr, he told me your men found other people, even kids, who'd been taken from their families."

"Yes. That is true."

"And that when they're rescued, they are usually sick or hurt." Papa nods. "Who helps them?"

"I would like to get your mama. She should be here for this conversation, don't you think?"

"Yes." I smile.

Papa texts Mama, and a few minutes later, she joins us in the office. Papa catches her up on what we've talked about so far.

"I'm on board. How can I help?" Mama asks.

"Well, you're a doctor. You can help fix whatever's hurt, right?"

"I can fix a lot, yes. But often, there are things in the mind that have been hurt. I can't fix those."

"Who can?"

"Doctors called psychiatrists and therapists."

"Can we get some of them, Papa?"

He grabs a pen and starts writing notes of his own. "Yes, I will look into hiring some mental health professionals."

"And some more doctors. I'm only one person," Mama adds. "And where are we going to do all this?"

"We are going to need a building," Papa says. "And a name."

"Yelena Nadezhda," I say.

"Jelena's Hope," Mama whispers. "I love it."

"It is perfect," Papa says. "Svetlana, you have done something truly remarkable here. It is not often that adults even consider helping trafficking victims. You have created something special that will provide care and support for so many people. It shows what a tender and caring young lady you are. I am incredibly proud of you."

"As am I."

At the time, I had no idea what I was suggesting. Losing Jelena opened my eyes to the true evil that exists, and I wanted to do something to help the people Papa saved. I never imagined it would grow into what it is today.

Jelena's Hope is a lifeline, a beacon of hope, to so many people—myself included.

Brandon

I STOP BY THE FLORIST AND THE BABY BOUTIQUE BEFORE making my way to Alex's, I mean, Natalie's house. God, saying that feels like losing him all over again. My heart's heavy with a mix of bittersweet memories and anticipation. I'm about to meet my niece for the first time. The excitement of holding a miraculous new life in my arms is tempered by the realization that this moment will forever be entwined with my memories of Alex.

During the elevator ride up to her apartment, my mind wanders back to the many times over the years that I took this same elevator ride. So many of the memories I made with Alex rush through my mind. It still doesn't feel real that he's gone. But fate dealt us a cruel blow, cutting Alex's life short and leaving Natalie to raise their child alone.

Guilt at my excitement gnaws at me, and I'm reminded that Alex should be here with us celebrating the birth of his daughter. I'm not sure how to reconcile the two opposite emotions. It's a demonstration of the harsh realities of life's unfairness. Of the dreams that are destined to remain unrealized.

I also feel a deep sense of responsibility for Natalie and little Rose. I made a promise to Alex that I'd do everything in my power to take care of them the way he would. To ensure that although his daughter will never meet her father, she'll know him through the stories she's told.

The elevator doors open, interrupting my inner turmoil, and I'm greeted by Natalie's warm smile. Her eyes reflect a mix of joy and exhaustion, evidence of the sleepless nights she's endured since Rose's arrival. "Congratulations," I say and kiss her cheek."

"I'm so glad you're here," she says, her voice tinged with both relief and happiness.

"These are for you." I hand her the bouquet of pink roses along with a small bag. "This is for the baby."

"Thank you. They're beautiful." She smiles. "Do you want me to open this now?"

"Sure."

I follow her to the kitchen, where she sets the flowers on the island and opens the bag. She pulls out a pale pink sleeper that reads, *Hi, I'm new here.* "It's adorable. Thank you."

"I didn't know we had company," Viktor says as he walks into the room carrying a tiny bundle swaddled in a blanket.

"Brandon just got here." Natalie holds up the sleeper. "Look what he got us."

Viktor glances from the sleeper to the roses and back to me. "Thank you."

"You're welcome?" Viktor's reaction to my presence and my gifts is puzzling.

Natalie delicately takes the peacefully dozing baby from Viktor's arms and steps closer to me. "Uncle Brandon, I'd like you to meet your niece, Rose." Her words carry a tender resonance.

Time stands still as a surge of love and affection like I've never experienced before envelops me as I fixate on the precious baby cradled in Natalie's embrace. The soft contours of the infant's features, the innocence conveyed by closed eyes, and the gentle rise and fall of her chest all combine to form a portrait of purity and innocence.

"She's beautiful," my hushed voice escapes in an awe-filled whisper, reflecting my profound amazement for this new life before me.

"She has Alex's blue eyes," Natalie says softly, tears glistening. "Looking into them reminds me that he should be here."

"We have a little piece of him." My hands tremble slightly as I reach out to stroke Rose's delicate cheek.

"There are a few things I have to get done," Viktor says, clearing his throat. "I'll be in the office if you need me."

Natalie watches as he walks down the hall, disappearing into Alex's office. Turning back to me, she asks, "Would you like to hold her?"

"I'd love to."

"Why don't we go sit down."

She leads us into the living room that's decorated for the upcoming holiday.

"The tree is beautiful," I say as I sit on the sofa. "I wasn't sure—"

"I wanted to forget all about Christmas. The tree and decorations were Viktor's idea." She shrugs. "He insisted that we decorate because it's Rose's first Christmas."

"He's right," I say, and Natalie carefully passes the baby to me. "What's up, little one? I'm your Uncle Brandon." I gaze at the precious little girl in my arms. Her features are the perfect mix of Alex and Natalie. "I want you to know I'm here for you and that I'll do everything I can to be the best uncle to Rose."

Natalie's eyes lock with mine, and a flicker of gratitude dances across her face. "Thank you, Brand. Rose and I are lucky to have you." She rests her head on my shoulder, and I slip my arm around her. We sit quietly, lost in our thoughts until Rose's eyelids flutter. Her tiny mouth opens, and a loud wail comes out. "I think someone's hungry."

"She needs a diaper change first."

"I can do it. If that's okay." I lift the baby against my chest and rub her back softly. Her crying stops.

"Have you ever changed a diaper before?"

"No. But how hard can it be?"

"How about I go with you? Just in case." She smiles.

We walk down the hall past the baby's nursery. For a second, I'm confused, but then I think about it. Rose is a newborn. She must be in her bassinet in Natalie's room. I turn to step into the primary bedroom but freeze when Natalie says, "No. Not in there." Her eyes are wide with fear.

"I'm sorry, I thought."

"We sleep in here." She motions into the guest room. "I can't go into the other room. Not without Alex."

After my mom passed away, Dad couldn't step foot into the bedroom they'd shared for over forty years. He always said there were too many memories he wasn't ready to face in their room.

"It's okay, Nat. I understand."

I follow her into the guest room, where she's hurrying to pick up a pair of men's boxers from the floor.

"Viktor must've dropped these when he was carrying out the laundry," she says as she puts them in the hamper. "It's a wonder anything is getting done. We're running on fumes right now." She motions to the bed. "We haven't brought the changing table in yet. You can put her on the bed to change her." I lay the baby down while Natalie grabs a diaper and wipes.

Natalie looks nervous. I'm not sure what's going on between her and Viktor or if I should even ask.

"I know what you're thinking. Why are Viktor's clothes in the room I'm sleeping in?"

"It's really none of my business."

"He's been staying up here to help me with the baby overnight. I don't think I could do this without his help."

"I can always come over, too," I offer.

"Thank you for offering, but I think we're doing okay." The baby starts crying again. "Miss Rose is getting impatient."

Natalie walks me through changing her diaper, a task that's a little more difficult than I imagined. She's using cloth diapers that have more snaps in one place than I've ever seen. But, with a bit of patience, I successfully complete my mission. Then, Natalie lifts her from the bed.

"I'll give you some privacy to feed her."

"Thank you."

I leave the girls alone and go to the office to speak with Viktor. The door's open, so I walk in unannounced and find Viktor behind Alex's desk. He's concentrating on whatever's on the laptop in front of him.

"Have you made any progress?"

"No." He doesn't take his eyes off the screen. "Dimitri's working day and night, but there's no leads." Viktor stops and looks up. "We won't stop until every bastard involved is caught."

"I have no doubt about that."

"Where's Natalie?"

"She's in your bedroom feeding the baby." I raise an eyebrow.

"For something so small, she eats an awful lot." He chuckles but doesn't fall for my bait. "But God, she's perfect."

He can't hide the awe in his voice when he talks about the baby.

"Is there anything I can do to help?"

"It's been a huge adjustment, but we're slowly finding our routine." He stands and walks around the desk. "It's been hard without Alex. He should be here," Viktor says quietly.

I can't speak over the lump in my throat, so I settle for a nod.

We leave the office and walk by the guest room. "She's exhausted," Viktor whispers and motions into the room.

Natalie's sound asleep, her arms draped over the baby sleeping on her chest. Viktor quietly walks into the room. I watch as he leans down and whispers something I can't hear. Natalie's eyes open for the briefest of seconds. Viktor places a tender kiss on her forehead before lifting the baby. It's a loving interaction. One that leaves me with even more unanswered questions.

Viktor leaves the room with Rose held protectively against his chest. "Do you want to stay for dinner?"

"No thanks. I have to go into the office for a bit and catch up on a few things."

"You sure?"

We walk toward the elevator, an odd tension between us. Viktor watches me as though he's expecting me to ask about what I just witnessed, but I say nothing. I'm unsure if my questions would be overstepping the boundaries of our friendship.

It's no secret Viktor's cared about Natalie for a long time. While Alex was alive, he would've never acted on his feelings. He has far too much integrity for that. But now, everything's changed. Alex is dead, and Natalie's alone. There's no reason for them not to find happiness with one another. But that's not a conversation for today. Instead, I say, "Tell Natalie I'll call her tomorrow.

Brandon

My concerns about Natalie have been growing over the past few weeks. She's steadily closing herself off from everyone who cares about her. Viktor and I are the only people she lets anywhere near her. When I spoke to Viktor, he said he tried reaching out to Svetlana. He left several voicemails begging her to call Natalie, explaining that she needed her best friend. Unfortunately, it did no good. She refuses to take his calls, and his texts sit unread.

Lana's shut me out completely as well. Pyotr checks in every few days, but he won't give up Lana's secrets despite my repeated requests. His loyalty to Lana is a quality I both admire and despise. If I knew what went wrong, I could fix it or at least try. Being kept in the dark isn't helping anyone, but I refuse to give up.

Love doesn't come without its challenges. Sometimes, it's messy and complicated as it leads us through intricate webs of emotions and labyrinths of complexities. At times, the path seems dark and endless, causing many to give up. However, for those who choose the virtue of patience and are willing to embrace the journey wholeheartedly, the rewards of love are endless.

Svetlana may have chosen to walk away, but I recognize her chosen defense mechanism. She always tries to push her emotions deep inside, retreating from everyone and everything. It's because I know she hasn't stopped loving me, but rather, she's struggling with something that I won't allow her actions to break us. What we share is real. I'll continue loving and trusting enough for both of us, knowing that same love will guide us through the darkness back to each other.

But today, my focus is on another woman I care about, Natalie. My gut tells me she's isolating herself because something is developing between her and Viktor. I think she's afraid to tell anyone because Alex has only been gone for a few months. Knowing Natalie, she feels guilty for moving on and fears what people will think. Yes, everyone will have their opinions, and not all of those opinions will be supportive. But that's not a decision for anyone other than her and Viktor. I hope to get some time alone with her today to discuss it.

"Are you sure you're okay if I go downstairs?" Viktor asks Natalie for the tenth time.

"Brandon will keep me company while you're gone," Natalie reassures him.

Viktor looks back and forth between us, still uncertain if he should leave or not. He and Natalie decided that any work involving Maxim was to be done downstairs rather than in their apartment. They don't want Rose to be exposed to it while she's so young. The major flaw with their plan is Viktor hates leaving Natalie's side.

"I think we'll manage while you're gone," I joke, but as usual, Viktor doesn't even crack a smile.

"Call me if you need anything, and I'll come right up."

Finally, we're alone, but when I go to open my mouth, Rose wakes up. Her baby noises come through the monitor app on Natalie's phone.

"I'll get her," I say, jumping up.

"She's going to need a diaper change," Natalie calls after me laughing.

"I can handle that," I call as I head to get the little girl I'm crazy in love with. "Wassup? Wassup, my precious little Rose?" I'm rewarded with a toothless grin. Lifting Rose from her crib, her big blue eyes study me. "Uncle Brandon's going to give you a dry diaper. Then we'll go find Mama."

There were a few mishaps along the way with the cloth diapers, but

I've finally reached a level of proficiency that makes diaper changes a breeze. I return to the kitchen with a happy and dry baby in my arms.

Although Natalie's breastfeeding, she pumps in between, so I ask, "Can I give her a bottle?" She turns around with a small bottle in her hand and a smile on her face. "Thank you, Mommy." I kiss her cheek and take Rose to the couch to sit and feed her. Natalie stays in the kitchen to load the dishwasher. It takes a few minutes for me to work up the courage to start the conversation. "Can I ask you a question?"

"Sure. What's up?" Natalie shuts the water off and leans against the counter.

"What's going on between you and your Russian?"

Her eyes open wide, and her words come out hurried. "He's only half Russian and nothing. Why?"

"Nothing?" I ask, trying to keep my tone soft. I don't want Natalie to get defensive and shut down. "He moved in with you, and I see how he looks at you. The man's in love with you." I hold Rose over my shoulder so I can burp her. "It's okay to move on, you know?"

"Why don't you put Rose in her swing? We need to talk."

Rose's eyes are already beginning to close as I buckle her in and turn on the gentle rocking motion I know she loves. Natalie's waiting for me at the kitchen island, where I sit beside her.

"You have to promise to keep an open mind," she says hesitantly.

"Okay."

"Alex always told me if anything happened to him, there were documents in his office that I'd need. I didn't want to go through them while my parents were still here, so I waited until the day they left. I'm so glad I did." She pauses.

"There were all the papers I expected, but then I found a handwritten note. Alex wrote it after we were rescued from Mexico. In it, he said he knew Viktor had feelings for me, and he'd already spoken to him. Alex's request was if anything ever happened to him, he wanted me to move on with Viktor."

It takes a few seconds to process what Natalie just revealed. I can't imagine how painful it was for Alex to not only write that letter to Natalie but also to speak with Viktor and give him permission to be with his wife in the event of his untimely demise. I don't know if I would have that kind of courage. "So, you and Viktor are a couple?"

"Yes. No. I don't know. I care about Viktor and know how he feels about me, but it's too soon. I'm not ready to move on yet."

I take her hand in mine, and her eyes fill with tears. "You have my support with whatever you choose." I can see how difficult this conversation is for her, so I attempt to change the subject, hoping to lighten the mood. "Everyone at Fire and Ice has been asking about you. Any chance I can get you to visit? Maybe bring your half-Russian with you?"

"Bring me where?" Viktor asks, coming up behind us.

"I didn't hear you come in." Natalie looks up at him and smiles.

"I was just asking Natalie if there's any chance she'd come down to the club. Of course, you can tag along, too." I smirk.

Viktor locks eyes with Natalie. "Is that something you want?"

"Thanks again for the invite," Natalie says, giving me a small smile. "But I don't think so."

"Suit yourself." Everyone's been asking about her. Going out for an evening would do her a world of good. The invitation is out there. Hopefully, she'll change her mind after she has some time to consider it. "How are things coming with Jelena's Hope-NYC?"

"Everything's a mess." Natalie sighs loudly. "We've had a hard time getting a contractor willing to fix the damage caused by the explosion. That's put everything behind with permits and licensing—I don't know all the details. Viktor's been handling it all." She motions to the man who's stepped away and is picking up the baby, who just started fussing.

"Sounds like a headache."

"It is," Viktor agrees. "Needless to say, the grand opening's been postponed indefinitely."

"I'm sorry. I know how much this project means to you." My phone's alarm goes off, and I check the time. "Shit. I'm going to be late. I have a meeting in an hour." I get up and give Natalie a peck on the cheek. "Hang in there. I'll see you soon."

"I'll walk you out." Viktor passes Rose to Natalie and follows me to the elevator. Once we're out of earshot, he says, "She told you."

"How did you know?"

"I can tell from the way you're looking at me. I'm sure you disapprove."

"That's where you're wrong." I look over his shoulder at Natalie, sitting at the island, rocking the baby. She seems so lonely. I hope to God Alex knew what he was doing when he set this arrangement up. "You love her almost as much as Alex did." Viktor raises an eyebrow. "If he trusted you with hers and the baby's life, then so do I."

"You can be a pain in the ass sometimes, but I think we'll keep you around." Viktor chuckles.

I step inside the elevator, shaking my head. "I'll see you next week."

"I'll count on that." Viktor gives me a reassuring smile as the elevator's doors close.

Svetlana

BRANDON: I'M NOT GOING AWAY. WE NEED TO TALK.

Every day for the past nine months, Brandon texts or calls, and every day, I ignore him. He wants to get back together. But as much as I want that, it can never be. Today, he's being more persistent than usual. I'm guessing he found out I'm not on the plane with my parents to celebrate the grand opening of Jelena's Hope-NYC.

Brandon: This has gone on long enough. You have to stop shutting me out.

He's right. For both our sakes, this needs to stop.

My hands tremble as I bring up Brandon's contact and tap the screen. The line rings once, and he picks up.

"Svetlana?"

"Yes."

"It's so good to hear your voice. I've missed you," he says, his voice deep and soft.

I want to tell him how badly I miss him, too. "You're right. We do need to talk."

"Why didn't you come to New York with Maxim and Irina?"

"The legal team I'm on is in the middle of a trial. I'm unable to get time off."

"It's the weekend. Even in Russia, courts aren't in session." He calls me out on my poor excuse. "Now, tell me the truth."

I take a deep breath and say, "I want to be released from the contract."

"What do you mean?"

"Before I came home, we tried to renegotiate our contract, and it didn't work." I squeeze my eyes shut and swallow over the lump in my throat. "It's time to accept that we've grown apart. We need to move on."

"You packed your things and left with no explanation. That's not growing apart," he says, raising his voice. "Lana, talk to me. Tell me what the hell went wrong so we can work through it."

"We had a good run, but we want different things." Tears pool in my eyes, but I keep fighting the urge to break down. I can't let him hear me cry. He needs to hate me so he can move on. "The sooner you accept what I already know, the better."

"So, that's it? After everything we've been through, everything I thought we meant to each other, you're done?"

"Yes." I bring a fist to my mouth, trying to hold back the sob that threatens to escape. "I'm asking you to end our contract and release me."

There's a long pause. "You're released," Brandon says softly.

"Goodbye, Brandon." I disconnect the call and double over from the force of the physical pain. A piece of my soul will forever remain with him.

Svetlana

My world is nothing but a dark abyss of self-hatred and loneliness. I was the one who asked to be released, but part of me thought, hoped, that Brandon didn't mean it. That the next day he'd leave me a voicemail and a text like he has for months. Or he'd show up at our door one day to fight for us. But each day, the sun rises and sets without any calls. My texts have been silent.

It's really over.

This was what I forced to happen. I needed Brandon to leave me. To move past us. What I didn't anticipate was the bone-aching sadness I'd feel. I don't think my heart will ever heal.

The sky is dark and full of millions of twinkling stars as I walk our estate tonight. While I stroll, my phone rings. Hope sparks inside that maybe it's Brandon. I pull it from my pocket and am shocked to see who the caller is. I accept the call without thinking.

"Hello?" I answer, my voice cautious.

"Svetlana?" A woman's voice asks, her tone carrying a sense of urgency.

"Yes," I reply, my voice wary.

"It's Charlotte Clarke," she announces, her tone firm.

"Hi. Mrs. Clarke." She hasn't called since she wanted help planning the baby shower, and I assume the worst. "Is everything okay?"

"No." I hear the unmistakable sound of crying over the line. "I messed up and fear I've lost Natalie for good."

"I doubt that." Natalie is good. She's the most kindhearted, forgiving person I know.

"Have you spoken to her recently?" she probes, her tone edged with concern.

"No. I haven't," I admit, my voice tinged with regret.

"Is she refusing to speak to you, too? It's that bodyguard. He's poisoning her mind—" she accuses, her voice rising with frustration.

"Mrs. Clarke," I interject firmly, cutting off her rant. "What are you talking about?" My tone demands clarification.

"Natalie's been refusing to answer my calls, so I ended up calling that Viktor. He agreed to bring her home so we could finally meet our granddaughter." She stops to blow her nose. The sound mimics a foghorn, and I have to hold back a chuckle. "We were sitting talking when he came waltzing into Natalie's cottage with a suitcase. He announced that he was going to put it in *their* bedroom. They proceeded to tell us that they're a couple now. Were you aware of this?" she asks.

Even though Natalie and I haven't spoken in months, I'm not at all surprised. Given Viktor and Natalie's shared history, which Charlotte can't know, it's only natural they'd be drawn to one another.

"No, I wasn't," I answer.

"I was horrified. I'm still horrified. It's been less than a year since her husband died, and she's shacking up with *him*," Charlotte says with disgust. "Natalie should be home with us. When the time is right, she can meet a nice boy from town. Someone that will be good for her and Rose."

And now we're back to this again. I roll my eyes, regretting taking her call. "With all due respect, Mrs. Clarke, I've known Viktor since I was a little girl. He's a good man. Natalie lost her husband, the father of her baby. If she's choosing to move forward with Viktor, I promise she and Rose will be well taken care of."

"I don't trust him. He's not like us."

"No, he isn't. But neither was Alex, and you learned to love him." My words come out harsh. "You asked, and Viktor brought Natalie and Rose to you. At least you got a chance to meet the baby." My voice cracks, and I'm forced to stop to compose myself. "It's more than some of us will ever get."

"Svetlana, honey. Is there something wrong?" Charlotte asks softly.

"No. It's Nothing," I reply.

"Don't give me that nothing silliness," she chides me. "I'm a mother. I know when something is wrong."

"Brandon and I broke up," I confess, my voice heavy with emotion.

"Why? You two seemed happy," she responds, her tone filled with surprise.

"We were," I acknowledge, a hint of sadness in my voice.

"And?" she presses, her tone expectant.

"Things happen," I reply tersely, my voice betraying the complexity of emotions beneath the surface.

"Yes, dear, they do," she says, her entire demeanor calm as if she's forgotten how upset she was when she first called. "That's when you should be relying on each other rather than going your separate ways."

"I wish it was that easy," I murmur softly, my words laden with longing.

"Relationships aren't always easy. Stanley and I have had our share of hard times," she confesses. "But there's no mistake that can't be overcome."

"What if it's not a mistake but something awful that's out of my control?" I'm not sure why I'm considering confiding in this woman. She called to complain and judge, but there's something in her voice that sounds understanding.

"If you're willing to share your burden with me, perhaps I can lend some experience."

"I appreciate the offer, but it's too late. There's nothing to fix," I say quietly.

"I don't believe it's ever too late. If you change your mind and want to talk, you can always call me," Charlotte offers.

I thank her and end the call.

Looking out across our property, fireflies dot the landscape, and katydids call back and forth. Charlotte's call unsettled me, and I'm not ready to go inside. I need space to think, so I take the path toward my old treehouse. It's a place I haven't visited in years.

When I get to it, I'm surprised to see the ladder still in place. I climb up the rickety rungs and pop my head through the opening in the floor. The bright moonlight streams in through the window that's framed by tiny green shutters. The walls are a patchwork of weathered wood that has acquired a warm, honeyed hue.

I crawl inside and lean against one of the walls. With my eyes closed, I reminisce about the crayon pictures Jelena and I drew of fantastical creatures and magic castles. We spent hours up here telling make-believe stories and then tacked our masterpieces to the walls. Today, only small pieces of torn, yellowed paper remain. If I concentrate hard enough, I can hear her whispered secrets of all the adventures we'd one day take together.

"Here you are, little butterfly." Pyotr's voice startles me. "Your father was worried and sent me to look for you."

He sits next to me and puts his arm out. I move closer and rest my head on his chest. Instantly, I'm enveloped in familiar feelings of safety and peace.

"Jelena and I made so many memories in this treehouse," I say, wiping a stray tear. "When I found out I was pregnant, I couldn't wait to bring my baby here. Now, I'll never have that chance."

"How much longer are you going to keep trying to do this alone?" Pyotr asks quietly. "You need to tell Brandon."

"We aren't together anymore," I declare, my voice steady but tinged with sadness.

"What do you mean?" Pyotr asks, her tone filled with confusion.

"I broke things off with Brandon and never plan on telling him," I admit, my voice firm but troubled.

"That's not right. The man has a right to know he had a child," he insists, his tone stern and unwavering.

"It's not that easy. You don't understand," I argue, frustration creeping into my voice.

"You're right. I don't." Pyotr's voice grows stern. "You asked for time, and I gave that to you, hoping that after you healed some, you'd see reason. But the more time that passes, the more distant you become. Now, you're saying you broke up and have no intention of ever telling him. Help me understand, butterfly." I push off his chest, trying to escape, but he tightens his hold. "No. You're not running. It's time to tell me what's really going on.

"Pyotr." He gives me a look that says I'm not getting out of this without confessing everything. I lower my voice and explain, "Years ago, Brandon had a submissive." I tell him the story of that terrible night at the club. "He didn't know she was pregnant until it was too late. I can't put him through that again."

"That's unfortunate, but it doesn't change anything between you and him. You don't get to unilaterally decide what information Brandon's allowed to know." Pyotr's reprimand takes me back. He must notice because he takes my hand in his. "The man loves you. Whether or not you can give him children isn't going to change his feelings for you."

"What if he stays with me out of pity and never gets to have a child of his own?" I express, my voice laden with worry.

"I don't think you're giving him enough credit," Pyotr counters, his tone firm and reassuring.

"What if knowing the truth changes how he feels about me?" I ask quietly, my voice barely audible.

"That's a bridge you can cross if you get there. But either way, Brandon needs to know," Pyotr insists, his voice steady.

"I can't," I protest, my voice breaking with emotion.

"I know you can, little butterfly," Pyotr reassures me, his tone gentle yet firm.

Papa: Where are you *moya babochka*?

It's Papa. I hold up my phone.

"Shit. I didn't call him," Pyotr mutters.

Me: I just met up with Pyotr, and we're on our way home now.

The walk back is quiet while I ponder what Pyotr said. As much as I want to believe him, I think he's wrong. If Brandon knew I had been pregnant and lost not only our child but also the ability to give him another, there's no way he'd forgive me. Not after all this time.

Svetlana

I'M SITTING ON THE TERRACE DRINKING A CUP OF COFFEE, A habit I picked up from living with Natalie when Misha and several of the other guards come rushing toward the house. They have their bags in hand and are so deep in conversation that they don't notice me sitting there.

"What's going on?"

"We're leaving for New York," Misha answers without stopping.

"Why? What's going on?

"I don't have time right now, Lan. We have to hurry." I trail behind them into the foyer, where they meet up with Papa. "The jet is fueled and ready to go."

"Good," Papa says, worry etched on his features.

"Dimitri's right behind us," Misha reports.

"The car is out front. He can meet us there." Papa looks my way but says nothing before he turns and walks out the front door.

"Dimitri." I grab his arm as he walks by. "What's going on?"

"When's the last time you spoke to Natalie?"

"I don't know." I shrug.

"You need to speak to her. I have to go." He hurries out the front door.

Natalie did everything to get me to keep in touch, but I blew her off at every turn. I let her down when she needed me the most. I know I have no right to text her just to satisfy my curiosity, but in my selfishness, I find myself taking my phone out to text her.

Me: What's going on that the guys all left in such a hurry?

I don't expect a return text, but my message switches to read, and the chat bubbles dance on my screen.

Natalie: Didn't your dad fill you in?

Me: He and I aren't exactly on speaking terms right now.

Natalie: Why? What's going on?

Me: He disapproves of the way I left things with Brandon. But stop changing the subject.

Natalie: Tommy's behind the explosion. They're coming to help Viktor find him.

Me: Holy shit!! Tommy? I thought he was in prison.

Natalie: Yeah, me too. It's a long story. One that I'm not even sure I understand. Now, back to you and Brandon. When are you coming back?

Me: I don't think I am. We both want very different things.

My message says *read,* but Natalie hasn't texted back. I'm just about to give up hope when my phone lights up.

Natalie: It's Viktor. It's late, and we're in bed sleeping, or at least we were until you texted. Natalie will call you tomorrow. Goodnight, Svetlana.

Viktor? What the hell is going on? My fingers fly furiously over my phone screen, texting my reply.

Me: What's Viktor doing in your bed?

Natalie: That's another long story, but not for tonight. I do need to get some sleep. Love ya.

Me: You better call me in the morning. Love you too.

Natalie is sleeping with Viktor?

Tommy killed Alex?

My head is spinning, and my heart aches to be with my friend.

While I swim laps, I replay the events of the past few months over and over. It's something I find myself doing almost every day.

I don't know why I expected Natalie to call me the following morning as though everything between us was okay. Needless to say, morning came and went with no call. It was several weeks before I heard from her again.

When she finally called, it was a tear-filled conversation as she told me how Tommy, her sleazy ex who was supposed to be in prison, somehow got parole and was behind the explosion that supposedly killed Alex.

What really happened was Tommy orchestrated the whole explosion and manipulated the building's security footage so it appeared as though Alex had died. All the while, Tommy held Alex in an old panic room in his apartment.

Instead of allowing Papa's men to handle it on their own, Natalie insisted on letting them use her as bait to draw Tommy out of hiding. Then, she put herself in further danger when, on a hunch, she insisted Viktor let her go with Tommy. That's when she found Alex.

Tommy was high and totally unhinged. He'd concocted some ludicrous plan to get Natalie back by killing Alex in front of her. And he came close to succeeding. Tommy injected Alex with a fatal dose of heroin. What he didn't count on was that Natalie had a gun. She shot and killed him.

Thankfully, Viktor had the foresight to put a tracker on her and swooped in to save the day. He administered an antidote for the drugs and saved Alex's life. That selfless act gave Natalie back her husband but left him alone. And from everything Natalie described, Viktor's devastated.

A wave of jealousy rushes through me. How does Natalie end up with not one but two men who are in love with her? Why does she always get a happily ever after?

What the hell, Svetlana? I mentally chastise myself. What kind of person have you become that you're not ridiculously happy for your best friend?

I've spent every day since grappling with that question. In an attempt to make amends, I shoved those feelings as far down as possible. As hard as it is to see Natalie and the baby, I've kept in touch. With one condition—talking about Brandon or why I left is off-limits.

I'm just climbing out of the indoor pool, my daily exercise of choice, when Papa comes into the room. "There you are. I have been looking all over for you."

"What's up?"

"Have you heard from Viktor recently?"

"No. We aren't exactly friends."

"Have you spoken to Natalie or Alex?" he asks impatiently

"I talked to Natalie yesterday." I grab my towel and wrap it around me. "Why?"

"Did she say anything about him?"

"Why the inquisition about Viktor?"

"He has been out of touch for quite a while."

"Viktor's a big boy. He can take care of himself." I roll my eyes. I know I shouldn't do it because it aggravates him, but I can't help it.

"When will you tell us the real reason you came home?"

Oh my God, not this again. "Because Brandon and I broke up. I had my fun in the States and decided it was time to come home." I rattle off the same answer I've been giving him for over a year. Maybe one of these days, he'll give this line of questioning a rest. Either that, or I'll make a recording he can play whenever he feels compelled to ask again.

Papa doesn't respond, but he doesn't have to. The look on his face tells me he isn't pleased with my answer. I'm so over this.

"Why is it so hard to believe I wanted to come home?"

"Things were going so well with you and Brandon," Papa says, exasperated. "Then, one day, you decide to come home without explanation to him or us."

"Everyone's always taking his side," I yell. "No one cares about what I want or how I feel. Forget it. I can't do this again." I toss my towel onto the chair and storm out of the room.

I'm beginning to think that coming back home was a mistake.

Maybe I should've disappeared and started a new life somewhere no one would find me. When I get to my bedroom, I slam the door and lock it.

Who am I kidding? I don't have the luxury of disappearing. Papa has eyes and ears in every corner of the globe. He wouldn't stop until he found me and dragged me back, kicking and screaming.

I need to get out of the house. The walls are starting to close in on me. Where can I go to get some space? The answer comes to me quickly. I know just the place to go to be alone and forget about my problems for a while.

Brandon

Two Years Later...

Owen and I have just finished teaching an impact play class at Fire and Ice. Everyone's gathering their things to leave when Andrea, one of the submissives who took the course, comes over to me.

"You taught a great class today, Sir." Andrea, my volunteer submissive for the class, says. "Thank you for volunteering," I reply, trying not to pay her too much attention.

"You're very welcome, Sir." She bats her big green eyes at me. "If you're ever doing a real scene—"

"I'm not looking for a submissive." I cut her off.

I've lost count of the number of submissives who've asked Star and Owen if they could scene with me. The answer is always no.

"Yes, Sir."

"The class is over. You can call me Brandon." I smile politely.

"I had fun today, Brandon." She makes a point of emphasizing my name.

"Thank you again for volunteering, Andrea." Owen steps in. "Have a good rest of your afternoon."

"You, too." With a defeated posture, she turns and walks toward the exit.

I sink onto the chair and lean my elbows onto my spread legs.

"Want to talk about it?" Owen sits next to me.

"It's Svetlana."

It doesn't matter where I am or what I'm doing. It's always Svetlana. Being at Fire and Ice is especially difficult. There are memories of her and me in every inch of this place.

"Have you heard from her?" he asks, a hopeful tone in his voice.

"Not since the day she asked to be released."

Owen has been my mentor for many years. He knows everything that's happened between Svetlana and me. After she asked to be released, he reached out to her, hoping to get her to open up, but she gave him the same line she gave everyone else.

"It's been almost two years." He states the fact I know all too well. "Maybe it's time you let her go and move on."

"No." The word comes out too harsh. "I'll never give up hope. She owns every part of me."

"What are you going to do?"

"I don't know." I scrub my hands over my head. "The only thing I can do is change. I need to be able to give Svetlana the things she wants—needs."

"Is that fair to you, though?"

"It doesn't matter."

"That's where you're wrong," Owen says. "I know what you're thinking. Relationships require compromise."

"Exactly," I agree.

"But one person can't be doing all the compromising. What was Svetlana willing to change?"

I think back to the night we started to renegotiate our contract. Svetlana was still recovering from her appendectomy. She was so pale and weak. I didn't think it was a good time to start something so serious, but Lana insisted. I gave in, figuring maybe she needed to get her mind off her recovery.

At first, everything was okay. There weren't many changes. Then we got to some of the more serious parts of the contract, our hard limits. That's when things started to go downhill, fast. She was asking for things I couldn't give her.

Between my concern for her health and my surprise at her requests, I think I was in shock. Saying yes to anything she was proposing wasn't in my vocabulary.

"I didn't even try to compromise. I said no to everything."

"Why?"

"What do you mean, why?" I don't know what Owen's trying to get at.

"Why did you say no? Were you on a power trip?"

"No." My answer is clipped, and I get defensive. "Everything she was demanding was a hard limit. Do you remember what happened with Celia? I'm not having sex in public, and I sure as fuck will not share Svetlana with anyone."

"Did she ever mention an interest in any of that before, or was it all of a sudden?" Owen asks.

"Lana was always interested in public scenes. The compromise was no sex in public. She was good with that. Not sharing was a hard limit for both of us." I stand and start pacing. "Did you know I proposed to her?"

"I did not." Owen sits back and crosses his arms, watching me. "When?"

"Before Alex and Natalie's wedding. Svetlana said yes, but after everything that happened in Mexico, Lana wanted to let them have the spotlight. So, we kept our engagement a secret. I was okay with that. While I was in Russia, Maxim gave me his blessing to marry her. I was so fucking excited to come home and make everything official." I stop moving and take a quick breath before I resume my pacing. "It was our time. Our fucking time. Except, when I got back, something was different. She'd changed. She grew cold."

"Lana's always been strong-willed, but all this is out of character for her," he says thoughtfully.

"I know." I drop back onto my chair. "That's what I've spent the past few years trying to figure out."

"What does Maxim say about her?"

"He's as perplexed as everyone else." I sigh. "Pyotr's just as concerned. He said she's spiraling out of control." I turn to face Owen.

"The problem there is he knows what's going on, but he refuses to betray her confidence to tell me."

"I'm glad she has someone like him, but that doesn't help the people who are trying to help her." That's been my point all this time. "So, what are you going to do about it?"

"What can I do? She asked to be released." I throw my hands up. "I have no right to insist she breaks her silence and speaks to me."

"This is about much more than a contract." Owen pins me with his intense stare. "You were more than just a Dom and his sub."

"Yes, we were," I confirm, my tone heavy with nostalgia.

"Are you serious about wanting her back?" Owen probes, his voice laced with curiosity.

"Of course I am," I assert, my determination evident in my tone.

"Then, you'll need a solid plan and some help executing it," Owen suggests, his smile conspiratorial.

"What are you proposing?" I inquire eagerly, my interest piqued.

Over the next hour, we devise a plan that includes taking a little trip to Russia to pay Svetlana a visit.

Svetlana

THE RIDE TO NOIRE HAS BEEN TENSE. PYOTR HASN'T SAID more than two words to me since we left the house. It isn't until we're only a few blocks away that he finally speaks to me.

"Are you sure this is a good idea?"

"Why wouldn't it be?"

"I don't think you're in the best headspace right now," he says, glancing at me. "I'm worried about your decision-making ability."

"Wow. Thanks a lot." I cross my arms and stare out the window.

"Stop being like that, butterfly." He nudges my elbow. "I'm only trying to look out for you."

"I appreciate it," I say, dropping my arms. "But I'm a big girl. I can take care of myself."

Pyotr slows the car to a stop in front of Noire. "Text me when you're ready to leave."

"I will."

"Please be careful."

"See you later," I say and exit the car.

It's been so long since I stepped foot in Noire. I thought it would feel familiar, like coming home, but as I open the door and step inside, it feels foreign. The sounds and smells are all wrong. Shaking off my uncertainty, I get in line at the check-in.

"Svetlana Solonik." Artyom, a Dominant and one of Noire's owners, says. "Maxim told me you were home. How are you?"

"I'm well, thank you."

"It's nice to see you out this evening. Are you here to watch or play?"

"I'm here to play tonight."

Artyom secures a green identifying bracelet on my wrist. "Have a great evening."

Noire is a more progressive club than Fire and Ice. Sexual acts are permitted anywhere in the club, not just on the main stages or in private rooms. Tonight does not disappoint. Moans of pleasure and desire fill the space. In one corner, a woman is being taken by three men. On the opposite side of the room, a male Dominant is being pleasured by his male submissive. In another section of the room, several Dominants are sitting at a table talking. Their submissives kneel on the floor next to them. The energy in the room crackles with a mixture of desire and curiosity.

Off to the right, a bondage demonstration catches my attention. I wander to the area to join the group, watching as the Domme skillfully maneuvers the ropes around her submissive. Her movements are fluid and deliberate. The demonstration is an intricate dance of power unfolding before me. At this moment, I'm acutely aware of how deeply I miss the visceral sensation of Brandon binding me. Of knowing I'm completely at his mercy.

"Svetlana?" A male voice asks, dragging me from my thoughts.

I turn my head, and our gazes meet. A smile tugs at the corners of his perfectly sculpted lips. "Slava." It's been several years since I saw him last. My eyes take in the tailored suit accentuating his strong, well-maintained physique. His mahogany brown hair now has hints of grey woven through it, and his deep brown eyes radiate genuine warmth.

"I heard you were in town." He looks at my wrist, and I know the second he sees the green bracelet. "You're here to play tonight?"

"I am," I say, my eyes never leaving his intense gaze.

"Where's your Dominant?"

"We parted ways."

"I'm sorry to hear that." A knowing smile plays on his lips. "Would you be interested in going to The Dungeon with me?"

A shiver of excitement rushes down my spine. "I'd love to."

Slava places his hand on my lower back and escorts me away from the crowded area. My heart races with a mixture of excitement and anticipation. "Our previous limits and safe words will be in effect tonight. Is that okay with you?"

"Yes, Sir."

It's been years since we've last seen each other, but the memory of our connection still lingers between us. Together, we navigate the club, the sounds of erotic energy surrounding us enhancing my arousal as we head down the steps toward The Dungeon.

We're stopped by a member of the Noire staff at the entrance to The Dungeon. "May I have your names?" the man asks. Slava gives our information as the man types on a laptop on the desk in front of him. "Please answer the questions." He hands a tablet to Slava.

Slava takes a few minutes to go through the questions. When he's finished, he passes it to me.

The Dungeon is a new addition to Noire, so I've never gone through this process. I hit the start button for the questionnaire.

Are you coming to The Dungeon of your own free will? Yes

The Dominant/Top you are about to enter with has indicated they will be engaging in bondage, whipping, and sensory play. Do you consent to these activities? Yes

The Dominant/Top you are about to enter with has indicated your safewords will be Yellow and Red. Do you understand what your safewords are and how to use them? Yes

Each room in The Dungeon is equipped with closed-circuit cameras. Monitoring of the cameras is done while rooms are in use. The Dungeon staff holds master keys to each room and will enter unannounced in the event of an emergency. Do you agree to be recorded while in The Dungeon? Yes

I come to the end of the questionnaire and hand the tablet back to the man.

He checks the screen. "Here's your keycard. You'll be in room three. Play safe."

My senses heighten as we cross the threshold into the dimly lit space. Slava leads me further down the hall, and I find myself feeling more vulnerable in his presence.

When we come to the black door with the small silver number three on it, we stop. Slava turns to me, his voice low and commanding. "Are you ready, Svetlana?"

With a mixture of nervousness and excitement, I meet his gaze, my voice barely a whisper. "Yes, Sir. I'm ready."

Slava swipes his keycard and opens the door, entering before me.

The air in the room carries a brisk chill reminiscent of what one might expect in an authentic dungeon setting. Stone walls amplify this sensation, fully immersing me in its atmosphere. Adorning the walls, flameless candles flicker, casting an eerie yet captivating glow. As my gaze sweeps the surroundings, I fixate upon a rugged wooden Saint Andrews cross securely affixed to the wall. Brandon. I'm here to get over him. I shake my head, willing all thoughts of him to disappear. Continuing my observation, I spot a standing cage and a pillory thoughtfully placed within the space.

I glance over my shoulder at Slava, who's leaning with his foot up against the wall and his arms crossed. He makes no move to come toward me.

Redirecting my attention to the room, I resume absorbing every detail. Positioned on the left wall is a Catherine Wheel, a legendary contraption of which I've only heard tales. Adjacent to it rests a spanking bench. An array of crops, whips, floggers, and canes is suspended on the wall above it. Each implement appears more ominous than the preceding one.

The door shuts behind me, and I jump.

"Feeling nervous, Svetlana?" Slava inquires, his warm breath caressing my neck.

"No." My voice cracks, betraying my nerves.

"Where shall we begin?" His question lingers as I take in my surroundings. "My favorite is the suspension rack."

My eyes trail up and see the medieval-looking device suspended from the ceiling.

"Whatever will please you, Sir."

"Turn around and strip. Leave your bra and panties on."

It's an unusual demand. Slava typically preferred me completely nude. Nevertheless, I'll oblige his wishes.

Stepping back, I pivot to meet his gaze. My hands move to the zipper of my skirt.

Slava

Svetlana's hands visibly tremble as she unzips her short leather skirt. It slides down her long, lean legs, landing by her feet. She steps out of it and brings her hands to the hem of her crop top, pulling it over her head. Leaning over, she picks up her skirt and looks around for a place to put her clothes. I hold my hand out, and she passes them to me.

Turning my back to her, I set her clothes on the spanking bench. We won't be using it tonight. Then, I go to a panel on the wall and hit a button. The chains holding the suspension rack make a clanging noise as the device lowers.

I watch Lana's eyes grow wide. She's afraid.

"Go to the rack and lift your arms."

Silently, she walks across the hardwood floor. For the briefest of seconds, she pauses in front of the apparatus, and I wonder if she's going to safeword before we even get started. I'm pleasantly surprised when she approaches it and places her hands in the still-open shackles.

I quickly secure her wrists before walking over to the wall and grabbing my favorite whip. Svetlana bites her lower lip as I set it on the table across from where she stands. Then I reach into my pocket and pull out a silk blindfold.

"Do you remember how much more acutely you experience everything when your sight is restricted?" I ask, keeping my voice low and seductive.

"I do, Sir."

Securing the blindfold over her eyes, I tie it behind her head. After I'm certain her entire vision is restricted, I step away and pick up my whip.

I treasure the memories of our time together. Svetlana used to love being on the receiving end of my whip. She'd hold herself regally as I'd redden her skin. Her mewls of pleasure would make my cock harden. Tonight, as I allow the leather to soar and their crack to fill the room, she startles. She's intimidated being in this dungeon-inspired room, which is exactly what I was hoping for. But tonight is not all as it seems.

Shortly after Svetlana came back home, I saw Maxim and Irina. At that time, Maxim told me she was in St. Petersburg for a few weeks to spend time with her new sibling. Several months later, we ran into one another again. When I asked how Svetlana was getting along, he expressed concern.

"Svetlana is still here. She left her Dominant," Maxim confesses. "He had just asked for my consent to marry her. Irina and I were getting ready for a wedding. Then, she left him."

"Did she say what happened?"

"Only that she missed home." He shakes his head. "I called Brandon, but he did not have information. He was just as confused as the rest of us."

I understand why Maxim isn't buying her excuse. The last place Svetlana ever wanted to stay was St. Petersburg. However, I doubt it's anything serious. "Give her some space. Svetlana is a strong girl. She'll find her way."

"Yes. I suppose you are correct."

I felt for him and wished there was something more I could do to ease his mind, but I hadn't heard from Lana since she left New York years ago.

Then, earlier this evening, I got a text from the last person I ever expected to hear from.

Pyotr: Svetlana's at Noire tonight.

Me: What does that have to do with me?

Pyotr: She's on a self-destructive path.

Me: Again, I don't know what any of this has to do with me.

Pyotr: You were important to her once, and she trusts you. I need you to step in.

It took me a few minutes to wrap my head around his messages. When Lana and I were together, Pyotr didn't approve, and he wasn't shy about telling me as much. What I also know is that man cares about her. If he's reaching out to me, something serious is going on.

Me: What's going on with her?

Pyotr: I can't tell you that. Only she can. I need you to get her to talk—to see reason.

Me: And how do you suggest I do that when I have no idea what's going on?

Pyotr: That's up to you. I just dropped her off. I'm trusting you to get there before she gets herself into trouble.

Lucky for him, I was already at the club and saw her walk in. I kept myself out of her view until I considered his request. Once upon a time, I meant something to her. That was a very long time ago. Would her feelings toward me be the same? If I approached her, would she go with me? Should I even get involved? None of this has anything to do with me. I came here tonight with a plan that didn't involve Svetlana Solonik. Yet, even as I silently war with myself, my legs carried me across the room, stopping behind her.

I crack the whip again. More to relieve my frustration than anything else. If it were anyone other than Svetlana, I would have told Pyotr to go to hell. Maybe I should've. But it's *moya nevinnyy malysh*. If there's something wrong, I can't turn my back on her.

After a few more measured swings, I carefully set the whip aside and take deliberate steps toward Svetlana. Over the years, Svetlana's only grown more beautiful. Her silhouette tells a story of elegance, accentuated by the play of shadows in the room. I long to run my hands over her, reacquainting myself with her soft curves. To see if my touch elicits the same moans of pleasure it once did. It takes all of my practiced self-discipline not to give in and touch her.

As much as I'd love to scene with her, to step back into the role of her Dominant, that isn't possible. Svetlana is not mine to have. Her heart and mind are with another man. I'm here because *moya nevinnyy malysh* is in trouble.

I didn't fully believe it until I saw her reactions for myself. Something's clearly off with her, but how the hell am I supposed to even know where to start?

I circle her, taking in every inch of her body, hoping to gain some clarity. That's when I notice a scar across her lower abdomen. Running my fingers along the raised skin, I ask, "What's this from?"

"My appendix ruptured."

That's an odd placement for an appendectomy scar. "Tell me what happened."

"I got sick and went to the hospital. They told me it was my appendix, and I had surgery."

"When?"

"It was a few years ago. I'm fully healed if that's what you're worried about," she says impatiently.

"What I'm more worried about is the competency of the physician who operated since your appendix is over here." I touch the right side of her abdomen. "So, either your surgeon was incompetent or—" I stop myself. Maybe this scar has something to do with why Svetlana ran away to Russia. "Or you aren't being honest with me right now."

She sucks in a breath, her voice tight with frustration. "Why would I lie about it?"

"I don't know. You tell me. Why would you lie about the surgery?" I challenge, my tone sharp.

"We didn't come in here to talk about my surgery," she retorts, her voice tinged with irritation.

"What did we come in here for?" I ask, lowering my voice, a hint of desire creeping into my tone.

"I thought you wanted to fuck me, Sir," she responds boldly, her words laced with both defiance and invitation.

"Is that what you want? Do you want me to shove my cock inside you? Do you think that will erase your memories of him?" I ask accusingly.

Her body stiffens.

"Why are you here, Svetlana?" I ask, my tone probing.

"I was looking to play tonight," she responds casually, but I sense she's avoiding the real question.

"I don't mean at Noire. Why are you in Russia?" I press, my voice firm.

"It's my home," she replies simply, but there's a hint of evasion in her tone.

"What happened to wanting to live in New York?" I inquire, noting the change in her plans.

"I did the whole New York thing," she says flippantly, her tone dismissive. "It got old, so I came home."

Oh, *moya nevinnyy malysh.* I know you so much better than that.

Svetlana's spent most of her life hiding her thoughts and feelings. She doesn't do it with malicious intent. Svetlana wholeheartedly believes she's protecting those she cares about. What ends up happening is that she alienates the same people she should be trusting and relying on to hold her up through whatever trial she's facing. That stops tonight. Without warning, I reach for the whip and crack it loudly. Svetlana gasps.

"Let's get one thing straight," I say, leaning close to her. "I will not tolerate anything less than the whole truth. Do you understand?"

"Slava," she says my name. "I don't want to discuss a silly surgery or why I came home."

"You will address me as Sir," I assert firmly, my voice carrying an air of authority. "I will not repeat myself again. When I ask you a question, I expect nothing less than honesty in your response. Do you understand?"

"Yes, Sir. I understand," she says in a clipped tone.

When Maxim first mentioned he was concerned, I blew it off. He's nothing, if not overprotective, where Svetlana is concerned. I don't have children of my own, but I can't blame him, especially after what happened to Jelena. Now, after spending a small amount of time with her tonight, I'm not so sure her behavior is *nothing*.

The scar and her reluctance to tell me the truth about the nature of her surgery, combined with her sudden departure from the United States, point to something bigger. I stand back and study her as I consider how to move forward.

The longer I remain quiet, the more Lana's nervousness grows. She's fidgeting in her restraints and straining to listen for where I am. Lana usually exudes poise. I've never seen her like this. Rather than continue with my questioning, I stay where I am and continue to observe her body language. The silence takes on a role of its own, aiding me in unraveling the intricate nuances beneath the surface.

After several long moments, she asks, "Are you still there?" I don't respond. "Sir? Where are you?"

"I'm here." She lets out the breath she was holding. "Are you ready to talk?"

"I didn't think I was here to talk," she says coyly.

"You thought I invited you in here to pleasure me all the while you were keeping secrets from me. Did you not learn your lesson last time?" I ask, my voice low and threatening.

"Red."

Fuck. I knew she was going to try to safeword. God help me. My next move is walking a dangerous line, but it's a risk I'm willing to take. I care too much about this woman to allow her to continue down this destructive path.

"Your safeword isn't going to work tonight, *moya nevinnyy malysh.* We're not leaving this room until all of your secrets have been brought to life."

Svetlana

SOMETHING ABOUT THIS DOESN'T SIT RIGHT WITH ME. THIS whole scene feels dangerous. Slava would never hurt me, right? If that's true, why are all my nerve endings firing at once? Everything's telling me to run.

"Are you still there?" I listen for any sign that he's still in the room. I didn't hear the door, but with how loudly my heart is thudding, I might've missed it. "Sir? Where are you?"

"I'm here," he finally answers. "Are you ready to talk?"

"I didn't think I was here to talk." I attempt to seduce him with the tone in my voice, but the words hang in the air.

"You thought I invited you in here to pleasure me all the while you were keeping secrets from me. Did you not learn your lesson last time?"

No. No. No.

I have to get out of here.

"Red."

Once again, I feel the heat from Slava's body and know he's close. "Your safeword isn't going to work tonight, moya nevinnyy malysh. We're not leaving this room until all of your secrets have been brought to life."

"You can't do this." I tug at my restraints in a futile attempt to get away. "I said red. The scene is supposed to stop."

"There's no scene to stop. I will not lay a finger on you. The second you tell me what you're hiding, I'll release you."

"What makes you think I'm hiding something?" I challenge, my voice defensive.

"Let's start with the placement of the scar. That's not from an appendectomy. What is it from?"

Slava's tone is sharp, cutting through my defenses.

"I told you. I had surgery," I insist, but my voice wavers with uncertainty.

"What kind of surgery?" His questions come rapid-fire, leaving me no time to think.

"My appen—" I begin, but he cuts me off.

"Don't lie to me, Svetlana," Slava's voice is tense, demanding the truth.

"I can't," I admit, my voice trembling with fear.

"You can and you will," he commands, his voice firm and unwavering. The crack of his whip startles me.

"No," I plead, shaking my head. "I can't. Please, Slava. I don't want to do this anymore."

Slava cups my cheeks in his hands. "Whatever you're hiding is too heavy to carry alone. You have so many people who care for you. Why do you insist on shutting everyone out?"

I raise my chin in a show of defiance. "I can handle it myself."

"I'm sure you can, but that's not the point."

"Release me so I can go home." Slava chuckles. "Why are you laughing at me?"

"*Moya nevinnyy malysh*, when will you learn that we weren't made to go through life alone? Do you remember when we were together?" he asks, softening his voice. "You were so young, yet so brave. When I met you, I knew I'd found the other half of my soul. I saw a long and happy future together. I didn't realize until it was too late that you were keeping things from me—things I needed to know. Things that would've allowed us to continue our relationship."

"My secrets aren't important," I say quietly, my voice barely above a whisper.

"You're going through a lot of trouble to hide something that's not important," Slava remarks, his tone tinged with skepticism.

Physical exhaustion's beginning to set in, and I drop my head, my energy waning.

"As soon as you tell me, I'll release you and send you on your way," Slava offers, his voice firm yet reassuring.

"It's not that simple," I murmur, my voice trembling with uncertainty.

"What's not that simple?" Slava presses, his presence looming over me.

"I can't," I reply, my voice strained with emotion.

"You can." He's standing so close it feels suffocating. "Tell me, Svetlana," he urges, his tone intense.

"No," I refuse, my voice growing weaker.

"You don't have to do this alone," Slava assures me, his words gentle yet insistent. "I'm right here. Allow me to help you."

"You can't help me," I protest, tears slipping down my cheeks. "Nobody can help me."

"The hardest part is saying the words," Slava notes, his voice softening.

"I'm scared," I confess, my vulnerability laid bare in my trembling voice.

"I'll keep you safe," Slava croons, his voice soothing. "All you need to do is trust me."

"I was pregnant and miscarried," I admit, my words strained with the weight of sorrow. The damn holding back my emotions bursts, and I struggle through the rest of my confession. "There were complications. When I woke from the surgery, I was told I couldn't conceive another child."

Slava quickly releases my arms, and I collapse into his embrace. We sink to the floor as I continue to cry.

"I'm so sorry, *moya nevinnyy malysh*. I'm so very sorry." He kisses my forehead. "This is something you should not have to face alone. Why isn't your Dominant by your side?"

"He doesn't know."

"What do you mean he doesn't know?"

Even though I feel as though I'm betraying Brandon's trust by telling Slava about his past, I have to do it. Revealing this hidden chapter is the only way to explain my silence and why I left him. Slava rubs gentle circles on my back. I struggle with sobs that hitch my breath as I try to tell the rest of the story. "I thought after all this time it would stop hurting, but it hasn't. It hurts worse."

"Loving someone, truly loving them, is never easy," Slava says, his voice soft and comforting. "Opening your heart and allowing yourself to be vulnerable is frightening. It means you might get hurt."

"Knowing what we lost was hard enough on me. I can't do that to Brandon. He deserves to find a woman who can make him a father. Someone—"

"Stop," he admonishes me. "What gives you the right to make decisions for this man about his future?" I open my mouth to speak but Slava holds up a finger, stopping me. "As his submissive, you were out of line taking matters into your own hands and choosing what information he was allowed to have. And as a woman in love with a man, you were wrong to keep something as serious as a child's existence from him."

"I was only trying to protect him." Even as I say the words, I know my methods are not the best.

"I don't know this man, but if it were me, I would want to know we created a child. I would want to know that our child did not get the chance to be born."

"If it were just the miscarriage, that would've been bad enough. Telling Brandon that I can never carry his child. That's too much, Slava. I can't hurt him like that."

"You have no right to make these decisions for him."

"I know," I whisper, looking down as my tears splash onto my lap.

"You must allow him as a Dominant and a man—a father, to know the truth. You must tell him about the life you created together and that tragically, that little life ended. You need to allow him to decide who he wishes to spend his forever with."

"Even if that's true. It's too late. It's been too long. I'm sure Brandon's moved on and has forgotten about me."

"*Moya nevinnyy malysh*, if this man loves you the way you love him, he's hurting as much as you are right now." He tucks some loose hair behind my ear. "You must find the courage to contact him."

"I don't know if I can."

"You, Svetlana Solonik, are one of the strongest women I've ever had the pleasure of knowing. You can do anything you set out to do. But if you need help, I will do anything you need to support you until you regain your confidence."

"Why are you being so kind to me after I hurt you?"

"Because love never goes away." His words, although uttered quietly, echo loudly. As though he can sense the questions I'm silently asking, he says, "Yes, Svetlana. I still love you. I'll always love you."

I rest my head on Slava's chest. He wraps his arms around me and kisses the top of my head. There's nothing sexual about this moment, yet it feels more intimate than any of the times we've shared.

"What do I do now?"

"You take the first step to make this right."

Svetlana

Rm

After my breakdown with Slava last night, he made me promise that I would do whatever was necessary to get in touch with Brandon and tell him the truth. After I got home, I knew what I needed to do. With the time difference, I had to wait until morning to implement my plan.

I spent the entire night awake, watching the time pass with aching slowness, all the while questioning my sanity. But I gave Slava my word, and for the first time in my life, I'm choosing to be deserving of the trust he's giving me.

I can't wait any longer. With my phone in my hand, I bring up a contact I never thought I'd use. My stomach turns as the line rings.

"Hello?" Mrs. Clarke's voice greets me warmly over the phone.

"Mrs. Clarke, it's Svetlana. I hope it isn't too early to call," I begin, my tone carrying a sense of urgency.

"Not at all, dear. I'm up with the sun," she responds, her voice gentle yet concerned. She hesitates before asking, "Is everything alright?"

"No, it isn't," I confess, my voice heavy with emotion. "Nothing's okay."

"How can I help?" she asks, genuine concern evident in her tone.

"I need to get away for a little while. Would it be okay if I came to stay with you in Northmeadow for a bit?" I request, my voice tinged with desperation.

"Of course, honey," she answers without hesitation, her tone comforting.

"May I ask another big favor?" I continue.

"Sure," she replies, her voice encouraging.

"Please don't tell anyone about this. Not even Natalie. I promise I'll explain when I'm there," I plead, my voice trembling with urgency.

"I can do that," Mrs. Clarke reassures me, her tone understanding.

After we hang up, I move on to the next part of my plan—getting to Northmeadow without raising any undue suspicion. Thankfully, my parents' attention is focused on Amelia, giving me some breathing room. They're currently in the States, visiting her wherever she happens to be on her cross-country tour.

When Amelia was younger, she was easy-going and compliant. Mama and Papa were thankful to finally have a daughter who didn't challenge them at every turn. When she told them she wanted to study music in California, I thought Papa would lose his shit, and he kind of did. He let her go on one condition, Viktor would accompany her as her bodyguard. That was nothing compared to what happened when they showed up for a surprise visit.

It was her first year of college, and the holidays were quickly approaching. Our parents were eagerly anticipating Amelia coming home for the school holiday. They were beside themselves when she informed them she wouldn't be flying home. So, they hopped on Papa's jet and decided to surprise her.

Everything exploded when they walked into her beach house and found her and Viktor kissing. Needless to say, Papa went ballistic and forbade them from seeing each other. He went so far as to threaten to kill Viktor if he went near Amelia again. I attempted to step in and rally for Amelia, but since Papa and I were barely speaking, that didn't go over very well, either.

I'm convinced Viktor has a death wish because he showed up here to tell Papa he was in love with Amelia. I don't know what he thought would happen, but I'm sure it wasn't that Papa would beat him within an inch of his life. Several of the guards were forced to step in to literally stop Papa from killing him. Dimitri got him back out of the country before Papa could go back for round two.

It was a tense few months before Alex and Natalie stepped in. In the end, it was Natalie who convinced Papa to allow them to continue to see one another. Since then, Viktor has been on the road with her and her band, Beautiful Division, as they tour the country.

Fortunately, the timing of their trip is working in my favor. Now, I have to get Pyotr on board, and I'll be in the clear.

Me: Are you busy?

Pyotr: Not at the current second. Why?

Me: Are you in the main house?

Pyotr: I'm in the command room.

Me: Are you alone?

Pyotr: Yes.

Me: I'll be down in a minute.

I hurry downstairs, hoping I can get Pyotr to go along with my plan. Skidding to a stop outside the door, I poke my head into the room, making sure he's still alone.

"It's just me," he says without turning around, his tone casual yet guarded.

"How do you do that?" I inquire as I walk in and sit next to him, my curiosity piqued.

"Your father pays me good money to be aware of everything," he explains matter-of-factly, his voice tinged with a hint of pride.

"Right." I fidget with my phone, trying to figure out what I'm going to say, my nerves getting the best of me.

"You're going to drive me crazy," Pyotr remarks, his hand shooting out to stop mine. "What's wrong?"

"Nothing," I reply automatically, but his penetrating gaze makes me reconsider.

"Mhm." He stops what he's doing and turns to face me, his expression serious. "The truth this time."

I take a deep breath, steeling myself. "I need you to bring me to Northmeadow."

"Missouri?" he clarifies, sounding surprised.

"Unless you know of another Northmeadow," I retort with a chuckle, trying to lighten the mood.

"Are you going to visit Natalie?" he asks, his voice tinged with relief.

"No. I'm going to stay with Charlotte and Stanley for a little while." Pyotr looks at me like I've gone mad. "It's a long story, and I can fill you in on the plane. I need you to go with me, but you can't tell Papa or anyone where we are."

"I have a lot of questions. Let's start with the bit about the plane. What plane might you be referring to because your father's jet is not in Russia."

"I have two first-class seats on Horizon Airlines for—" I check the time on my phone. "Eight hours from now."

"What the absolute fuck have you gone and done?" Pyotr demands, his voice filled with disbelief, shaking his head in frustration.

"Can I tell you something without you freaking out on me?" I ask cautiously, bracing myself for his reaction.

"Do I ever freak out on you?" he deadpans, his expression unreadable.

"Slava was at the club last night," I confess, my voice trembling slightly.

He sits back and crosses his arms, his demeanor tense. "Go on."

"He brought me to The Dungeon for a scene," I continue, my words rushed.

"That motherfu—" Pyotr starts, but I cut him off before he can say more.

"Nothing happened," I interject quickly, desperation evident in my tone. "We just talked."

"And?" Pyotr prompts, his expression expectant, waiting for me to continue.

"I told him about the baby. And the surgery." Pyotr doesn't react, so I continue, "I know that I need to deal with what happened and that I have to tell Brandon. That's why I'm going to Northmeadow. I need time to heal, and for some reason, I feel drawn to Charlotte to do that."

"That woman is the most judgmental person I've ever met. And you want to go to her for help?"

"I can't explain it. It's just a feeling I have in here." I place my palm over my heart. "Will you take me?"

"And cover for you?"

"Yes." I don't break eye contact with him.

"Fine." He stands and walks toward the door. "Little butterfly, if you try to run, I'll call Brandon and tell him myself."

"I won't run. You have my word."

Nearly twenty-four hours later, Pyotr's pulling the rental car into Charlotte and Stanley's driveway. He turns the engine off and moves to open the door.

"Wait," I say and grab his arm. "Before we go in, I want to apologize."

"For what?"

"Ever since I was a little girl, I used you to keep my secrets and protect me from facing anything I didn't want to deal with." I let my hand drop. "I know how wrong I was to continually put you in that position. I'm giving you my word that this trip represents the end of using you as my shield. When we leave here, it'll be to first come clean with Brandon and then with everyone else."

For so many years, I complained and acted like a spoiled brat because of Pyotr's presence in my life. He's been there for every significant moment—good and bad. We've shared laughs, fought with one another, and I've cried in his arms more times than I can count. He's seen me at my very worst, yet he's never turned his back on me. He's never betrayed my trust. Pyotr's so much more than a bodyguard Papa pays. He's one of my best friends.

"I've never been more proud of you, little butterfly." Pyotr leans over and places a gentle kiss on my forehead.

This moment, right now, him looking at me with pure pride in his eyes, is one I'll cherish forever.

Svetlana

"You didn't have to go through all this trouble for us," I say as I take another bite of the delicious tomato sandwich.

"It's no trouble," Charlotte says as she fills my glass of sweet tea.

It's clear where Natalie gets her love of hosting from.

"Where can I put these?" Pyotr asks as he comes into the kitchen carrying our bags.

"Svetlana will be in Natalie's room, first door on the left. You can stay in Michael's room. It's the last door on the right." She turns to look at me and lowers her voice. "Call me old fashioned, but I don't allow sharing a bed under our roof before marriage."

"There's nothing to worry about," I giggle. "Pyotr and I aren't a couple."

"He's always with you, so I just assumed."

"Pyotr's my bodyguard. Has been since I was a little girl."

Charlotte pulls out the worn wooden chair next to me and sits. "I don't understand why everyone has bodyguards."

I came here on a mission to tell the truth, so I'll be as honest with Charlotte as I'm able. "Papa works with a large network of people who are fighting against human trafficking." I study her reaction carefully before continuing. "When I was ten years old, my sister, Jelena, was kidnapped and sold to traffickers." She gasps and covers her mouth with her hands. "Papa did everything in his power to find her, but it was too late when he did. She'd already been killed."

"I'm so very sorry," Charlotte says. She pauses, and I can visibly see her making the connection. "Jelena. As in Jelena's Hope?"

I nod. "Yes. We started *Nadezhda Yeleny,* Jelena's Hope, as a way for our family to heal."

"By helping others." Charlotte wipes her eyes. "That's a beautiful way to honor your sister's memory. And it explains more about what Alex and Natalie are doing in New York."

"Yes, it does." I smile.

"I still don't understand the need for a bodyguard, though."

"There's a lot of money in trafficking. When these people find out Papa and his associates are after them, they're quite unhappy. Papa has had people try to come after him because of it," I explain. "So, to keep everyone he loves safe, he insists we always have security with us."

"I wish someone would've explained this to me years ago instead of keeping me in the dark."

"None of us were certain how you'd feel about Papa's job. But you're right. Instead of keeping the truth from you, we should've allowed you to form your own opinions. I'm sorry for my part in that."

"I appreciate that, sweetheart." Charlotte pats my hand.

"Can I help you clean up?"

"We can leave the dishes in the sink for now," she says and stands. "Would you care to help me gather vegetables from the garden for tonight's dinner?"

"I've never done that before, but I'd love to."

I've been in Northmeadow for about a week. This time, I'm allowing myself to relax and breathe. To embrace small-town life. And I'm finding I quite like it.

The Clarkes have retired from working at their pharmacy. Stanley drives into town once or twice a week to check on the store. I think he misses the job he used to do.

A few days a week, Charlotte disappears to some unknown location, but mostly, she busies herself at home, something I thought would be mundane, but I was wrong. Each day starts early with a cooked breakfast followed by a two-mile walk. It isn't the daily run I'm used to, but it's surprisingly invigorating just the same.

After our walk, Charlotte spends a few hours housecleaning. Although I'm not exactly sure what she's cleaning because everything's already spotless. Today, I'm hanging the bed linens on a clothesline. She assures me I've smelled nothing as wonderful as line-dried laundry. I'm finishing the last few clothespins when Charlotte, colander in hand, appears outside.

"What are we picking today?" I ask. I've quickly learned to love working in the garden with her.

"The green beans are ready. We need to harvest them and prepare them for tonight's dinner."

"Okay." I follow her into her expansive garden and start picking the green vegetables. "You should come to Russia with me and help me start a garden."

"I've never been out of the country," she says while she works.

"Even more reason to take a trip. It's beautiful there." Mindlessly, I pick a bean and take a bite.

"Natalie used to do the same thing when she was a little girl," Charlotte chuckles.

"I'm sorry. I didn't even think."

"You're fine." She smiles kindly. "I used to love gardening with the kids when they were little. Maybe I'll come and teach you so you can garden with your future little ones."

"That isn't a possibility," I reply firmly, my tone leaving no room for argument.

"Surely there are gardens in Russia," she counters, her voice filled with curiosity.

"Yes, there are. That's not the problem," I clarify, my tone indicating there's more to the issue.

"Don't you want children?" she asks, her question hanging in the air.

Her question opens the dam I've been holding back, and my tears begin to flow. "I can't— I can't have children."

"I didn't know. I'm so sorry." She sets the silver strainer on the ground and takes my hand. "Come with me. Let's go sit." She leads me to the black wrought iron chairs on their patio. She doesn't let go of my hand as we sit. "Do you want to talk about it?"

"No, but I need to." I use my free hand to swipe at my tears.

"Take your time. There's no rush."

"Where do I start?" I mumble. "About two years ago, I found out I was pregnant. I'm sure you aren't going to approve because Brandon and I weren't married, but—"

"I need to stop you right there," Charlotte interrupts. "I know I have a long history of being overly judgmental. I've made plenty of mistakes I'm not proud of, and I've paid the worst price imaginable." I know she's referring to Michael. "I'm far from perfect, but I'm learning and growing." She gives my hand a small reassuring squeeze. "How and when your child was conceived is not of any concern. Every baby is a miracle." Her eyes reflect kindness and compassion.

"I was so excited. Brandon was going to be an amazing father, and I was going to be pregnant at the same time as my best friend. Our children would've grown up together. Everything was perfect." I take a deep breath, steeling myself for the next bit. "Brandon was in Russia working with Papa at the time. I was going to tell him about our baby when he got home. While he was away, I had an ultrasound appointment. It was supposed to be a happy thing. I was going to record the baby's heartbeat for Brandon."

Recounting the memory makes it feel like it just happened yesterday. The pain is so sharp it's difficult to breathe.

"There was no heartbeat. The doctor told me my baby died. But that wasn't the worst of it. There were complications during the D&C surgery. I hemorrhaged severely. The doctor did everything he could to control the bleeding, but he wasn't successful. In order to save my life, he performed a hysterectomy." My throat tightens as a sob threatens to escape. "I'm never going to be able to carry a child."

Charlotte wraps her arms around me while I cry. She says nothing while I purge the sorrow from deep within.

It isn't until my tears stop that she speaks. "May I tell you a story?" I nod. "Stanley and I wanted more children after Natalie. We tried for years. I conceived several times but kept having early miscarriages." I sit stunned, listening to her story. "It was heartbreaking, but it ended up being a blessing in disguise. After my last miscarriage, I suffered from abnormal bleeding. The doctor found very early uterine cancer. The best course of treatment was a full hysterectomy."

"Natalie never told me you had cancer."

"She doesn't know any of this. Other than Stanley, I've never told anyone." She wipes at the moisture pooling in the corners of her eyes. "For many years, I struggled with the fact that I could no longer bear a child. I hid what I believed was something shameful. I felt like I was less of a woman or that perhaps God was punishing me." I open my mouth, but she holds her hand up and shakes her head. "Even though I don't believe in divorce, I silently believed Stanley was better off without me. Then, he could find a woman to give him more children. I even contemplated ending my life."

My tears continue to fall, but now they're less about me and more about Charlotte and the heartache she experienced.

"One day, when the kids were at school, Stanley came home unexpectedly. He recognized I was in a dark place and felt compelled to check on me. It's nothing short of a miracle that he chose that day at that time," she says and takes a shuddered breath. "I confessed everything to him. Instead of walking away, he embraced me and told me how precious I was to him. He, too, was also hurting from the loss of the babies we'd created and the knowledge we'd never have another child. But what mattered more to him was that I was alive and healthy. And that we were together."

"It's different. You already had two children."

"Yes, we were blessed with two children. There's nothing I can say that will take away your pain at not being able to have a biological child. What I can tell you is that you don't have to suffer alone. You created that child with Brandon. She takes my hand in hers once again. "Svetlana honey, you must tell Brandon about the child you *both* lost. You need to allow him the opportunity to grieve with you."

"He's going to hate me for keeping it from him."

"He'll be hurt and possibly angry, yes. But your path forward, whether together or not, depends on this. As long as you're keeping this secret and carrying around such a heavy burden, your heart will never heal."

"I'm so scared, Charlotte. I've let everyone I love down. How can anyone ever forgive me?" I drop my head, the weight of my situation weighing heavily on me.

"You're going to have to face the reactions of everyone affected. Unfortunately, there's no way around that, but I trust forgiveness will come. Once you're free of this secret, you'll be able to feel how very treasured you are."

"Do you really believe that?"

"With all my heart." She smiles kindly.

"There you two are," Stanley says as he walks out the back door. "I thought you ran away."

"You silly man," Charlotte says. "We were just having a chat."

Stanley looks between us. "I'm sorry. I didn't mean to interrupt. I'll just go back inside," he says awkwardly and turns to walk away.

"Please stay." I look at Charlotte, and she nods in encouragement. "I'd like to tell you the truth about why I came."

"Are you sure?"

"Yes." He sits beside his wife.

Stanley listens quietly as I tell him everything that's happened. Surprisingly, this time, it's a little easier to get the words out. When I finish, he stands. I'm confident he'll leave in disgust, but he surprises me by walking over to me.

"Sweet girl, thank you for sharing your pain with me," he says and wraps me in a fatherly hug. "I'm very sorry for your loss."

I'm speechless. Charlotte and Stanley Clarke are the last places I would've imagined finding unconditional support. Yet, even as I've borne my soul to them, they've surrounded me with only love and understanding—so much more than I deserve.

Through their love, a tiny piece of my broken heart has been mended.

Brandon

After my conversation with Owen the other night, I left Fire and Ice confident and with a solid plan. The first thing I did when I got home was purchase a one-way ticket to St. Petersburg, Russia. I intended to get Svetlana back, no matter what the sacrifice.

That's the only part I didn't tell Owen about. If Svetlana wants to remain in Russia, I'll leave New York behind and relocate. I can do most of what I need for the company remotely and fly back as required. The goal that's most important to me is for Svetlana and me to be together. Everything else is secondary.

While I'm packing, I call Maxim to let him know my plans.

"Brandon. What a pleasant surprise," he answers, his tone cordial yet guarded.

"I won't keep you long. I'm getting ready to leave for the airport. I'll be flying into St. Petersburg," I explain urgently. "I'm coming to get Svetlana back."

"I am delighted to hear that. However, *moya babochka* is not in Russia," he responds, his tone serious.

"Where is she?" I demand, a hint of desperation creeping into my voice.

"I am unsure of her whereabouts," he admits, his tone tinged with concern.

"She's missing? Are you searching for her?" I inquire, panic rising within me. The thought of Svetlana being in danger sends chills down my spine.

"She is with Pyotr," he reveals, his tone somewhat reassuring.

"Where?" I press, my voice urgent.

"I do not know. Neither Pyotr nor my daughter will say. He has reassured me she is safe and well," he explains, his tone steady.

"When will she be back?" I ask, my anxiety evident in my voice. I can't believe Max is allowing this uncertainty to persist.

"I am not sure," He sighs. "If she were with anyone other than Pyotr, I would be concerned. But he will not allow harm to come to her. I am hopeful this separation is what she needs to heal whatever has been broken inside."

"Thanks for letting me know," I reply, my tone grateful but tinged with concern.

"Brandon," Max calls out.

"Yes?" I respond, turning my attention back to him.

"Do not give up hope," he advises his tone firm and reassuring.

"Thanks again, Max," I acknowledge, my voice sincere as I appreciate his words of encouragement.

I disconnect the call and sit on the bed next to my packed suitcase.

I can't believe Maxim's allowing Lana to essentially drop off the face of the earth. It speaks to his level of trust in Pyotr. But it does nothing to help me.

"Hello?" Pyotr's voice answers.

"Hey. It's me," I say, attempting to keep my tone casual despite the urgency in my chest.

"What's up?" Pyotr responds, his tone neutral.

"I want to see Lana," I admit, my voice betraying my anxiety.

"I have to take this," Pyotr says suddenly, his voice becoming muffled as he presumably covers the phone.

"Who is it?" Lana's voice can be heard in the background.

"It's business. I'll be back in a minute," Pyotr reassures her before returning to our conversation. "I don't think that's possible."

"I know she's with you," I assert, frustration creeping into my tone.

"Yes, she is," Pyotr confirms.

"Where are you?" I demand, my voice growing more urgent.

"I'm sorry, *droog*. I can't tell you that," Pyotr replies, his tone regretful.

"What the hell? I thought you wanted me to help?" I raise my voice, my patience wearing thin.

"I do. But I can't tell you where she is," Pyotr explains, his tone apologetic.

"Pyotr, we're ready to go," Lana calls out.

"I'll be right there," Pyotr responds to Lana, then returns to me. "Who's we?"

"What the fuck is going on?" I explode, my frustration boiling over.

"She's safe and doing well. That's all I can tell you. I'm sorry," Pyotr says, his voice firm yet sympathetic.

As much as I want to argue with him, it won't do me any good.

"Tell her I called and need to talk to her," I instruct, my tone resigned.

"I'll do my best," Pyotr promises before ending the call.

I feel more helpless now than I did before our phone call. All this time, Pyotr's been on my side, or so I thought. I drop my head into my hands. I'm at a total loss for what to do next.

My phone rings a few minutes later. It's face down on the bed, so I can't see who's calling. Could it be Lana?

I pick it up, and my hope falls. It's not her.

"Hello?"

"Hello *wassup wassup*? Alex laughs.

After he came back to life, he thought Rose's name for me was ridiculous. Alex did everything he could to get her to call me *Uncle* Brandon, but my sweet little niece would have none of it. Finally, he gave in and started calling me by my lovingly earned nickname.

"How's my precious niece and nephew?"

Their children are the light of my life. They've kept me from being swallowed by the darkness surrounding me without Lana.

"Rose is the best big sister ever, and Michael is the most perfect newborn," Alex gushes. "I'm having a hard time, though."

"With what?"

"I've been here for every second of Michael's life from the moment he was conceived. I missed so much time with Rose. Time I'll never get back. I feel so guilty."

Alex was gone for almost the entire first year of Rose's life, but to see them together, you'd never know. They're as close as a daddy and his little girl could be.

"You can't beat yourself up for things that were out of your control. You fought hard to get back to Rose and Natalie. You're home now, and that's the most important thing." I do my best to encourage him. "How's Natalie feeling?"

"She's tired, but she's amazing. Being a mother comes so naturally to her. Natalie's the reason I'm calling. We're flying out to Missouri tomorrow," he explains. "Charlotte's planning a surprise birthday party for her, and we want you there."

"I don't know if I'm up to a party."

"Amelia and Viktor are going to be in town. I may have overheard that Amelia invited Lana."

"Is she going to be there?" I ask with renewed hope.

"I'm not sure. She didn't give Amelia a definite answer."

It's better than nothing. "I'll book my flight."

"We can't wait to see you."

"Thanks, Alex. You have no idea how much this means to me."

"I think I know."

This might be the break I need. If there's any chance of being in the same place as Svetlana at the same time, I have to be there.

Svetlana

THE SAYING THAT TIME HEALS ALL WOUNDS IS SIMPLY NOT true. Actually, it's the furthest thing from the truth. Some days, I'm able to get up and go about my day in a typical fashion. But then, unexpected triggers like a sight or sound instantaneously unearth all the emotions I've fought so hard to suppress, bringing me to my knees. The pain is visceral. It engulfs me in its grasp, threatening to suffocate me.

Charlotte has been the biggest source of support. Somehow, she knows exactly what I need, whether it be quiet support or a heart-to-heart conversation. She seems to know when I need space and when I need the company of others. On days when I'm content to stay in bed and feel sorry for myself, she marches into the bedroom and throws open the drapes. She ignores me when I grumble about the sun being too bright and that I want to sleep. Charlotte doesn't take no for an answer.

Today's an example of one of those times. It's the anniversary of the day I found out I was pregnant. My plan is to hide in my room, well, Natalie's room, and wait for the day to be over. But right on time, footsteps sound in the hall.

"Svetlana," Charlotte calls from outside the closed door. "Are you up?" I don't answer, hoping she'll think I'm sleeping and leave me alone. "I'm coming in," she says a second before the door opens.

I roll over, ignoring her.

"I know you're awake," she says as she opens the curtains. "Stanley and I had breakfast with Pyotr. Your plate is in the oven keeping warm." She walks around the bed to the side I'm facing and stands with her hands on her hips. "Haven't you learned that rolling over and ignoring me doesn't work?"

I groan. "Can I just have today?" She knows what today is.

"Give me a good reason why," she says gently.

"Today's the anniversary of the day I found out I was pregnant. I want to lie here and pretend it doesn't exist."

Charlotte sits on the edge of the bed. "Today's going to be a hard day. It's inevitable that you'll relive the happiness you felt at being pregnant. Then, the immense sadness of learning your baby no longer had a heartbeat will creep in and attempt to overshadow your joy."

"That's already happened."

"Hiding and wishing away the day won't stop the memories. It will ensure whatever you feel is experienced alone. And alone is the worst place to be."

"Alone is how I prefer to do this," I assert, my voice firm and resolute.

"Prefer or are used to?" she challenges, her tone curious as she cocks her head to the side.

"Either. Both," I admit, my voice tinged with frustration. "Does it really matter?"

"How has your way worked for you in the past?" she presses, her tone gentle yet probing.

"Not great," I confess with a shrug, my tone resigned.

"If your way isn't great, is there any harm in trying it my way?" she suggests, her tone hopeful.

I said I was healing, not that I was all the way there. Whatever *all the way* means. But do I want to abandon my plan of avoiding everyone and everything today? What if Charlotte's wrong? What if I crawl out of bed and do things her way, and it makes everything worse?

"But what if it makes it easier—better?" she proposes, her voice soft but insistent, her gaze searching mine for a response.

I'm frozen from my indecision. This day will happen once a year for the rest of my life; truthfully, I don't know how I'm supposed to feel. Last year, I treated it as a day of mourning. If I'm honest, until recently, I've treated every day that way. As if my life ended the day I was told my baby was no longer growing inside me.

"What will it say about me if I don't grieve today?" I ask, my voice trembling with uncertainty.

"It will say that you're a strong young woman who's choosing to live," Charlotte responds, her tone gentle yet firm, as she sits on the edge of the bed. "You don't have to sentence yourself to a life of grief. It's okay to be happy again."

"I'm scared that I'll forget my baby existed," I admit, my voice barely above a whisper, my fears laid bare.

"Sweetheart," Charlotte says softly, reaching out to tuck my hair behind my ear, a comforting gesture reminiscent of Mama when I was a little girl. "You'll never forget your child."

I pause, her words sinking in as I consider them carefully.

She stands and holds her hand out to me. "What do you say?"

I bite my lower lip, grappling with my indecision. "Okay," I say finally, hesitantly putting my hand in hers.

When I get to my feet, she smiles reassuringly. "I'll have your plate on the table in ten minutes. There's a lot to do today," she says, her voice filled with gentle encouragement.

After my later-than-usual breakfast, we put on our sneakers and set out for our daily walk.

"Natalie and Alex will be coming into town this weekend," Charlotte informs me.

"I haven't told Natalie I'm here."

"I'm aware." Charlotte smiles. "It's her birthday next week, and I've planned a surprise party."

"I know. Amelia called last night and told me about it. Alex had already called her."

"You and Pyotr have become part of our family," she says without missing a beat. "I would like you both there."

What do I say? I can't just show up at Natalie's party, all friendly with her parents. I'd have to tell her I'm here and why. It won't be easy, but I realize I can't hide in Northmeadow forever.

"Do you think I can talk to her first? I want to tell her everything before I just show up at her party."

"Yes." Charlotte offers me a kind smile. "I'm sure we can arrange that. One more thing."

"Okay," I say hesitantly.

"Alex is inviting Brandon." I freeze. "If you would like, we can arrange for you and him to have some time alone to talk." My heart hammers and I'm certain it's about to burst from my chest. "You don't have to have an answer right now. Take some time to think about it."

"I will."

We walk in companionable silence for the next few blocks. My mind is distracted by thoughts of seeing Brandon and attempting to convey everything to him, causing me to be distracted. Only when Charlotte veers off from our usual path does my attention return to the present moment.

"Where are we going?" I inquire, my voice tinged with curiosity as we walk down the street.

"There's a park down this way that I want to show you," Charlotte explains, her tone calm and reassuring.

"A park? With children?" I ask, a hint of apprehension creeping into my voice.

"There might be children," Charlotte confirms, her tone casual.

My feet remain glued to the sidewalk, and reluctance is evident in my posture. "I really don't want to—"

"I need you to trust me," Charlotte implores, her voice gentle yet firm, her eyes pleading for my cooperation.

I nod and follow a step behind her. If I'm being honest, though, the thought of turning and running back to the house has crossed my mind.

We round the corner, and I spot Stanley and Pyotr up ahead. They're outside of what appears to be a beautiful park filled with trees and flowers.

"What is this?"

"As we get closer," Charlotte explains, "This is Forever in Our Hearts Park. This place has been an enduring part of Northmeadow for generations. Anyone who's experienced the loss of a loved one can plant a perennial flower or a tree here. It's a way to create a living symbol, ensuring that the memory of your loved one will go on."

"I was beginning to get worried," Stanley says when we get closer.

"I'm sorry." Charlotte kisses his cheek. "We took our time getting here."

"It's nice to see you out today, little butterfly," Pyotr smiles.

"Come on, let me show you around." Charlotte leads us into the beautiful garden.

She points out the trees planted in both her and Stanley's parents' memory and the white roses for Michael.

"Over here," Charlotte says, bringing us to a fenced-off area. "Is a special garden for parents who've lost a child to miscarriage. They're Forget-me-Nots."

Within this area must be hundreds of beautiful blue flowers. Butterflies flutter about, bouncing from one to the next. I'm struck by the number of flowers, each representing someone's child.

"There's so many," I whisper.

"We brought one for you." Pyotr picks up a small pot with a plant in it. "I'd like to help you plant it for your baby."

Tears pool in my eyes as I look between Pyotr and the flower. "Would you be okay if I chose to wait a few days until Brandon's here? I want to plant it with him."

"I think that's the perfect way to honor your child, little butterfly."

We spend some time in the garden, sharing laughter and tears while Charlotte and Stanley tell us storiesabout Michael and Natalie when they were children.

The heat of the afternoon has given way to a cool evening breeze. Pyotr and I are sitting outside relaxing after a difficult day.

The wooden frame from the screen door emits a gentle scraping sound accompanied by the faint jingle of the metal latch as Charlotte steps outside.

"I'm sorry. I didn't realize you were both out here," Charlotte says. "I can talk to you later."

"I was just heading inside." Pyotr stands.

"Pyotr," Charlotte says, catching his arm as he walks by. "I'll be the first to admit that for many years, I didn't understand your place in Lana's life, and I have no idea how a bodyguard is supposed to act." She laughs softly. "The way you care for Lana is admirable. She's blessed to have someone as genuine as you by her side, and we're equally blessed to have this opportunity to get to know you."

"Thank you, Charlotte. That means a lot to me." Pyotr looks back at me. "Good night, little butterfly." Then he disappears inside the house.

"He's a good man," Charlotte says as she sits next to me. "Do you think he'd mind if I tried to find him a nice girl from town?"

"I've known him my entire life, and to my knowledge, he's never had a girlfriend."

"Does he prefer men?" Charlotte asks quietly.

Now it's my turn to laugh. "I don't think so."

"You never know these days," she says. "And I'm trying to be more open-minded."

"Papa's men are dedicated to their work. Although he doesn't ask for or require it, many of them sacrifice their personal lives for their job."

"Your father, although loud and often overwhelming, is a good man. The loyalty of his *men*—" Charlotte tries out the word. "Speaks to his character."

"He is a good man." I smile with pride.

"That's not what I wanted to speak to you about, though." Charlotte wrings her hands in her lap the exact same way Natalie does. "Stanley and I have talked about this. It's time I told Natalie about my miscarriages and the cancer—actually, it's long past time. I know it's the right thing to do, but I'm scared," Charlotte confesses.

If anyone can empathize with her right now, it's me. "I understand that fear."

"I know you do," she says quietly. "You're probably wondering, why now?" I nod. "Over the past few weeks, I've watched you grow through your trials. Today, at the garden, spoke to my heart." Tears pool in my eyes. "I've made so many mistakes raising my children. But I've learned that I have a responsibility as Natalie's mother to share my story with her. I pray she never has to feel the heartache of losing a child or hearing the word cancer, but it's part of my history, and she deserves to know. For too long, I believed she wasn't strong enough to handle the information. That's another thing I was wrong about. My daughter is strong and capable."

Charlotte's countenance brightens. A serene light fills her eyes, a mix of determination and hope. She takes a deep breath, gathering her strength for what lies ahead. "I want to be the one to tell her, to share my journey and let her know that no matter what life throws at us, we can find a way to overcome."

I reach out and place my hand over Charlotte's, offering a reassuring squeeze. "You're right, Charlotte. Sharing your experiences, especially the difficult ones, with Natalie is a gift, one that will strengthen your bond."

Charlotte smiles through her tears, a mixture of vulnerability and relief. "Thank you for helping me to see this truth."

"Me? I didn't do anything."

"You've done so much more than you'll ever know, sweet girl." Charlotte reaches over and hugs me. "It's a comfort to know I'm not alone in this."

"You're never alone, Charlotte. We're family now, and we'll face these moments together," I assure her.

As the night comes to a close, I reflect on my thankfulness at Charlotte's insistence that I get out of bed and spend it with people who care about me. She was right. It didn't keep the memories away, but in those moments when my emotions clawed their way to the surface, I wasn't alone. I was surrounded by people who allowed me to express my feelings. Who listened without judgment as I shared my regret for keeping Brandon in the dark and promised they'd be by my side for the next part of my healing journey.

Brandon

I booked a last-minute flight to Missouri. Unfortunately, I couldn't get a direct flight and have a layover at Charlotte Douglas Airport. There's another before my next flight, so I don't have to rush. While I'm standing in line at Starbucks waiting for my latte, I power on my cell. The voicemail notification pops up, and I see a phone number I don't recognize.

"Brandon," the barista calls my name.

I grab my cup and take it to a table in the corner, where I sit and listen to the message.

"Hello, Brandon. My name is Slava Olenev. We have a certain young woman in common. I need to speak to you about an urgent matter. Please call me as soon as you get this message. I don't care what time it is."

Why is Svetlana's ex-Dominant calling me? For a brief moment, I consider deleting his message and not returning his call. However, curiosity gets the best of me. I check the time on my phone. It's eight pm here, which means it's three am in Russia. He did say to call anytime. So, I hit the green call button.

The line rings three times before he answers, "*Allo?*"

"I'm looking for Slava," I respond, unsure what exactly I'm supposed to say.

"Brandon," Slava says. "Thank you for returning my call."

"You're welcome." I swallow a drink of my coffee. "What's the urgent matter we need to discuss?"

"Svetlana. Have you heard from her recently?"

"No. She's disappeared with Pyotr. I have no idea where she is."

"That's what I was afraid of. I warned her what would happen if she ran."

"You've seen her?"

"I have," Slava explains that she showed up at Noire a few weeks ago and agreed to do a scene with him. I ball my free hand into a fist, not wanting to hear the details of their night together. "I warned her what would happen if she ran."

"What are you talking about?"

"She promised me she was going to tell you. I didn't want you to find out this way," he says, regret lacing his tone.

"Find out what exactly?" If he tells me they're back together, so help me.

"Why she broke up with you and came back to Russia."

"She told you?" I raise my voice, attracting the attention of several others in the café. I force myself to lower my volume and ask, "Why did she come to you?"

"It wasn't by choice. Pyotr contacted me with concern about his charge being at Noire. He asked me to intervene before she did something stupid. It took some creative questioning skills, but, in the end, she broke her silence."

"What the hell did you do to her?" My blood boils.

"I did not lay a finger on her. You have my word." He pauses. "I wish she didn't put either of us in this situation. I'm not sure how to tell you."

"Tell me what? Just say it."

"Several years ago, Svetlana had a miscarriage."

My heart slams to a stop, and I fight to take my next breath.

"Svetlana was pregnant," I murmur. "With my baby?"

"Yes," he says quietly. "She had surgery while you were in Russia with Maxim."

"The appendectomy?"

"That's the story she told everyone, yes. It was a D&C for the miscarriage. But there were grave complications." Bile rises in my throat. "The procedure left her unable to conceive a child," he says softly.

I'm forced to hold onto the table's edge to keep myself upright. "Why didn't she come to me?"

"Svetlana convinced herself it was for your own good," he explains. "She didn't want you to feel stuck with her."

"Stuck with her?" I run my hand over my head as I try to make sense of everything. "I deserved to know we—" I can't finish the sentence.

"I knew I shouldn't have let her go, but she promised she'd tell you. I'm so sorry you had to find out this way."

"Me too."

"Can I offer you a small piece of advice?" When I don't answer, he continues. "Don't be too hard on her. She's already put herself through hell."

"I'll keep that in mind."

After we hang up, I text Maxim. I know he's in the States and will be at Natalie's party.

Me: I need to ask your permission to do something.

Maxim: What is it you want to do?

Me: I'm coming to Missouri for the party. I know Svetlana might be there. She's no longer my submissive, and I may be overstepping, but I need to get her alone and force her to speak to me.

Maxim: You have my permission.

I keep myself together long enough to board the plane. Once I'm in my seat, I put my earbuds in and pull up my playlist. Over the next two hours, every emotion possible floods my mind.

Svetlana was pregnant with my child and hid it from me. She

fucking knows how badly I want a child and how I blamed myself for what happened with Celia. She didn't want me to go through that pain again. This was different, though. Neither of us did anything wrong.

Grief washes over me, and I have to force myself not to break down on the plane.

A baby.

Svetlana and I created a child together. That child was growing inside her, and I didn't know. Our child's heart ceased to beat when I wasn't there. She's carried that grief for the past two years alone.

I don't know how to deal with my warring emotions.

Papillon, you better be prepared because you and I have a few things to discuss. This time, you aren't leaving without telling me everything.

Svetlana

I'M PACING BACK AND FORTH IN NATALIE'S CHILDHOOD bedroom. She, Alex, and the kids got into town yesterday. According to Charlotte, they were exhausted last night and stayed at the lake house. Right now, they're on their way here for a late lunch.

Charlotte encouraged me to call or text Natalie and tell her I was here. But I couldn't do it. I wish I had listened to Charlotte because I'm terrified of Natalie's reaction when she sees me at her parents' house. My time to worry is over because they've just pulled up.

I stand out of view of the window and move the curtains slightly to watch. Alex unbuckles Rose from her car seat, and she jumps out. Her curly blonde ponytails bounce as she runs into her Papa's arms. While Charlotte and Stanley dote on Rose, Natalie lifts their newest addition from his car seat. Michael's only two months old and is about to meet his grandparents for the first time. They've been beside themselves waiting.

Alex places his hand on the small of Natalie's back, a possessive and loving gesture, as they walk toward her parents. Charlotte reaches out and gently strokes the baby's cheek before hugging Natalie. Stanley, who's holding Rose, looks to be asking her about her brother because she's pointing and smiling at the baby. Stanley leans over and kisses Natalie on the cheek. Then, they disappear inside the house.

When Charlotte told me Alex and Natalie were on their way, Pyotr left for the lake. He gave me some excuse about helping Misha update the security software. I think it was just his way to ensure Natalie and I had privacy for the conversation that we are about to have.

I open the bedroom door and listen to the sounds of happiness coming from downstairs. The proud grandparents are oohing and aahing over their new grandson. Rose is talking nonstop about her brother *Mikhel* as she switches between English and a mix of Russian and Ukrainian. They're having such a wonderful family time. I hate that I'm about to walk down the steps and interrupt it.

Step by step, my feet carry me closer. I remain hidden until I hit the creak on the fourth step. Natalie's head snaps up. Her eyes open wide when she sees me.

"Svetlana?" She jumps up and rushes over to me. "What are you doing here?" She throws her arms around my neck, squeezing me so tightly that I fear she'll cut off my oxygen supply.

"I've been here for a few weeks," I say hesitantly.

"You have?" Natalie looks between her parents and me.

"*Tyotya* Lana," Rose squeals and runs over to me.

I lift her and kiss her chubby little cheeks. "*Kak moya milaya malen'kaya devochka?*"

"*Ya starshaya sestra,*" she says proudly.

"I bet you're the best big sister ever."

"I invited Svetlana to stay with us," Charlotte explains. "Why don't you two girls go outside and catch up? Alex and the kids will be fine with us."

I put Rose down and follow Natalie out the front door. We sit on the porch swing. An awkward silence hangs between us. The words I practiced swirl around all garbled in my head. None of them are willing to be said.

"How did you end up staying with my parents?" Natalie asks, confused but not the least bit judgmental.

"I don't know where to start." I turn sideways, sliding one leg up under me. "Can you do one thing for me?"

"Sure."

"Please don't stop me while I'm telling you this, or I won't be able to do it."

She scrunches her eyebrows. "Okay."

"It was shortly after the whole Mexico nightmare. I found out I was pregnant." Natalie gasps. "We were going to have our babies together. Brandon was going to be such a wonderful father. I was so excited and planned on telling Brandon about the baby when he returned from Russia." I take a deep breath. "While he was gone, I had an ultrasound appointment. I was supposed to record the heartbeat to play for Brandon when I told him I was pregnant, but there was nothing to record. The baby didn't have a heartbeat." Tears drip down Natalie's face as I tell my story. "I needed a D&C. The doctor said it was supposed to be straightforward and easy—routine. Except it wasn't. There were complications." My voice cracks. "Dr. Young couldn't stop the bleeding and had to do a hysterectomy. When I woke up, Pyotr told me I couldn't have children."

"I'm so sorry. Why didn't you tell me?" she asks, her voice filled with concern.

"I didn't tell anyone," I admit, my tone heavy with regret.

"Brandon doesn't know?" she asks quietly, her words barely above a whisper.

"No," I reply, shaking my head. "I couldn't tell him."

"That's why you left," she concludes, understanding dawning in her voice.

"Yes. I couldn't break his heart like that." My old reasoning sounds weak. "That's part of how I ended up here. Your mom contacted me back when Alex was dead, and you came here with Viktor. She was totally freaking out."

"Oh my gosh, that trip was a nightmare." Natalie chuckles. "I can laugh now, but it was anything but funny then."

"Charlotte wanted me to intervene, but, at the time, you and I weren't speaking. She picked up on something being wrong and offered to help. At first, I said no. But for some reason, I couldn't get her off my mind. Long story short. I reached out and asked if I could stay with them for a while." I pause, searching her face for a reaction but finding none. "Do you hate me for keeping this from you?"

"Hate you? No, of course not." Natalie wipes the tears from her face. "You had your reasons for making the choices you did, and I respect that. But I'm also thankful you told me so I can be here for you."

This time, it's me that embraces her, and we cry together. It's as much a release of what might have been and what will never be combined with an honest rekindling of a friendship.

"I feel awful that I brought the kids here—" Lana begins, her voice heavy with guilt.

"There's no reason to feel that way. You came to visit your parents. You had no idea I was here," Natalie reassures her, her tone comforting.

"What about Brandon? Are you going to tell him?" Lana asks, her voice tinged with concern.

"Yes. Being here with your parents has helped me heal. I feel much stronger and am ready to tell him. I'm planning to speak to him soon," Natalie confirms, her tone determined.

"Is there anything I can do to help?" Lana offers, her voice sincere.

"Just be my friend," Natalie replies, her voice filled with gratitude.

"That I can manage," Lana says with a smile.

"And introduce me to my nephew," Lana adds, her voice eager.

We return to the family room, where a beaming Charlotte is holding her grandson. Natalie walks over to her mom and takes the baby before turning to Lana.

"Aunt Lana, meet your nephew Michael Alexander Montgomery," Natalie introduces proudly.

She passes the tiny bundle to Lana. He's wide awake and looks at her with big hazel eyes. "Look at his hair."

"I know," Alex laughs. "We try to keep it covered up, but he was too hot with his hat on, so I took it off."

"Why would you cover it up?" Lana marvels, running her hand over his curly blond hair that pokes out in all directions. "It's absolutely perfect."

I have vivid memories of staying here with Natalie during our college days. Back then, the environment was judgmental and suffocating—toxic. Today, you'd never believe this is the same house with the same people. Love and acceptance are overflowing.

Northmeadow, this home, has served as a place of safety and respite. I can never repay Charlotte and Stanley for all they've done to help me mend my broken heart.

Brandon

I arrive at the Water's Edge Bed and Breakfast and am greeted on the expansive front porch by Anthony.

"This place is stunning," I say and shake his hand, but he pulls me in for a hug instead.

"Thank you. We've put a lot of work into updating the plumbing and electrical. Things Mrs. Wilson wasn't able to do," he explains. "She ran a solid business here for many years. We wanted to honor what she put into this place while also putting our mark on it."

"From the outside, it seems you've done just that."

Although I've never been here, I have seen pictures. The original part of the building was a log cabin façade that had fallen into disrepair. Tony replaced it with gorgeous cedar plank siding. He also had a large natural stone addition attached to the main structure. The once gravel parking area has been paved and lined with Flowering Dogwood Trees.

The front porch is a stunning stone masterpiece that wraps around the side of the main building. New rockers, tables, and padded loveseats are situated under the oversized ceiling fans. Giant flowerpots, each with exquisite flowers, decorate the space. I move closer to get a better look at the flower display.

Elegant lilies add regal color, while tower-like spires of foxgloves offer bursts of enchantment with their tubular bells of pastel purples and pinks. Interspersed among them are pansies and primroses, creating a captivating contrast and a touch of whimsy. Amidst the array, cascading vines of vibrant bougainvillea drape the rim. The display is a living canvas, a masterpiece painted by the brushstrokes of nature.

"I need you to design the flowers for my place."

"We'll talk after we get through this weekend." He opens the door. "Come on inside. We'll get you settled in your room before everyone arrives."

After checking me in, Tony leads me to an elevator, and we step inside. "This was one of the first things we had installed. It was important to Leo and I to make the entire space accessible." The doors open. "This floor caters to our guests with more particular tastes," he chuckles. "Originally, there were six rooms up here. We gutted the entire floor to reinforce the supports and fully soundproof each room. I didn't have the heart to modernize the locks." He holds up a key before unlocking the door. "Each of the rooms is identical in their setup and features."

The space is elegant. Somehow, he's spectacularly blended his modern aesthetic with the historic feel of the inn. The walls are pale grey, and combined with the large windows, the room feels airy and bright. "The view is stunning," I say as my attention is drawn to the glistening lake.

"I know what you're thinking." Tony grins. "The windows are tinted from the outside, making it impossible to see in."

"That's good to know." I chuckle.

Tony gives me a tour of the room, pointing out all the room's features. There are hooks in the ceiling for suspension play, and the bed has multiple spots for restraints. A deep red leather tantra chair is situated diagonally in the far-left corner.

"Inside here," Tony says, opening the doors to a large antique wardrobe. "Are various impact tools."

I'm impressed with the quality of everything. Not that I expected anything less from Tony and Leo. "It's stunning and will be perfect for later."

"I hope you make some headway with her." Tony clasps my shoulder.

"We're not leaving here until I do."

The party guests are beginning to gather in the yard behind the inn. I've gotten confirmation that Svetlana will be here. Everything is ready in my room for later, so I start downstairs.

"Brandon," Charlotte Clarke says when we nearly collide on my way outside. "It's wonderful to see you."

"You too," I say, confused at her overly friendly reaction. "I thought you'd be coming later with Natalie."

"Charlotte is an important part of Water's Edge," Leo says as he comes over and stands beside her.

"She is? I mean, you are?" I quickly correct myself.

"Leo's being too kind." Charlotte beams at him. "I'll be helping Tony with the baking and the front desk." A timer sounds from the kitchen. "That's the cookies. I'll see you later." She hurries back into the kitchen.

"What's that all about?"

"Mama C has been a huge help for Tony with the business and has become very dear to me." Leo smiles. The sound of Maxim's voice interrupts my next thought. "Why don't you go say hi to everyone. I have to get back to work."

When I step outside, I find a large group has already gathered. Many familiar faces are mixed in with those I don't know. Scanning them, I see the only one I care about, Svetlana. She's sitting off to the side, talking with Dimitri and Jessica.

On my way to see Maxim, I walk by the trio. Jessica stands and hugs me. "It's so nice to see you again, Brandon."

"You too. I hope this one's paying you more attention than his electronics," I joke and elbow Dimitri.

"Jessica appreciates a computer as much as I do." Dimitri smiles and snakes his arm around Jessica's waist.

"Hello, Svetlana." I force myself to stop at a greeting and not what I came to do.

"Hi," she says, not making eye contact.

Jessica and Dimitri look between us. Not wanting to make the moment any more awkward, I politely excuse myself and make my way to Maxim and Irina.

"It's good to see you, Max." We shake hands. "You as well, Irina."

"I am glad you could make it," Maxim says, glancing at his daughter.

"I wouldn't miss this opportunity for the world."

"I trust after tonight, everything will once again be right."

"I'll do my best."

Our conversation is cut short when a puppy dragging a pink leash lunges herself at Maxim. He laughs and picks up the dog, who excitedly licks his face. "Have you met Nadiya?"

"I haven't." I scratch the adorable puppy behind her ear.

"She is Viktor and Amelia's little girl." He sets the puppy down on the grass.

It still sounds odd to hear Viktor and Amelia spoken about as a couple. But as I see the two walking our way hand-in-hand, I realize just how perfect they are together. Viktor's smiling and, I dare say, happy, and Amelia's radiant.

"Congratulations on the tour and the record deal." I hug Amelia when they get close.

"Thank you," she says, looking at something over my shoulder. I turn and see Lana watching us. "Has she spoken to you at all?"

"A curt hello. But I'm not letting her leave without getting to the bottom of this."

"Let me know if there's anything I can do to help."

"I will."

"Alex and Natalie are pulling in," Leo announces.

Everyone's conversations come to an end while we wait for them to appear. As soon as they come around the building, there's a shout of "Happy Birthday."

Charlotte did a good job of keeping the party a surprise because Natalie is clearly shocked. "I don't know what to say."

Leo gives Natalie a big hug. "Your mom is responsible for all of this."

Charlotte smiles proudly.

"Thank you both. I can't believe everyone's here. How did you do this?"

"Leo and I have an announcement to make." Anthony takes his place beside his husband. "We'd like to tell everyone that we're now the proud owners of Water's Edge Bed and Breakfast." The gathered guests applaud. "We thought it very fitting for our first event to be a birthday party for Natalie. Especially since we would've never found this place without her."

"You guys bought it?" Natalie asks.

"We did," Tony says proudly. "To be fair, it was Leo and Charlotte who brought the idea up."

"We fell in love with the area when we were here for your wedding," Leo adds. "Mrs. Wilson let us know she was looking to sell the place so she could retire, and we were looking at getting out of the city and slowing down. So, we took the leap and purchased it." Leo motions to Natalie's mom. "Charlotte has been instrumental in helping us get it up and running."

"I can't believe you didn't tell me," Natalie says to her mom.

"Tony and Leo wanted to wait until today to make the big announcement."

"Let's sit and eat," Anthony suggests.

Everyone appears to be having a good time eating, talking, and laughing. But my attention remains fixed on Lana, who's at the far side of the yard. She's managed to avoid me all afternoon, but it seems her time is just about up. She excuses herself from the group she's talking with and walks toward the house, disappearing inside. I wait a few minutes, so I don't draw attention to myself before following behind her.

"She's in the hallway restroom," Tony says as he walks past me with some more pastries for the party outside.

"Thanks."

I lean against the wall, waiting for her. When she opens the door, she shrieks and attempts to close it, but I put my hand out, stopping her.

"We need to talk."

Svetlana

"THIS ISN'T THE TIME OR PLACE."

"That's where you're very wrong, Svetlana. This is the perfect time and place." He steps toward me, caging me against the wall. "You left me without an explanation."

"I told you. We had different visions for our future." I wasn't prepared to be confronted and don't know what to say. I can't do this here.

"I don't believe that. We had the exact same vision for our future. But something happened. You shut down and wouldn't let anyone in. That stops today."

"What are you going to do? Hold me hostage?"

He smiles and laughs. "If that's what it takes." My feet leave the floor as he tosses me over his shoulder.

"Brandon, put me down." I try to wiggle out of his hold. Brandon slaps my ass, making me yelp. "You can't do this," I yell.

"Who's going to stop me?" Brandon challenges, his voice filled with defiance.

"My father will come looking for me," I counter, my tone confident.

Brandon laughs. "Maxim's well aware I'm here and has given me permission to make you talk."

I growl and punch his back.

"If you don't stop fighting, you'll find yourself over my knee," Brandon warns as he carries me into the elevator.

"I dare you," I retort, my tone daring.

"Are you sure you want to do that?" Brandon questions, his voice laced with amusement.

"Yes," I reply firmly, my resolve evident.

The elevator dings as we arrive at a room. Brandon walks in and kicks the door shut. Then, he tosses me on the bed.

"Now, my darling, we're going to talk. You're going to tell me why you walked away from us," Brandon demands, his tone commanding.

"If you'd just been patient, I was planning on talking to you," I retort, sitting up and crossing my arms.

"Patient. You're going to lecture me on being patient?" Brandon argues, his tone incredulous.

"I didn't want to do this in the middle of Natalie's party," I explain, my tone defensive.

"Well, you're here now, and you're not leaving until we talk," Brandon insists, his tone firm.

"Not here. Not like this," I protest.

"You're crazy if you think I'm letting you out of this room without getting my answers," Brandon declares, his tone determined.

"I've been staying with Charlotte and Stanley." Brandon wrinkles his forehead, confused. "I'll be at their house tonight. You have my word that I'll meet you at that address tomorrow." I stand and take a step toward the door. "I know I don't have a right to ask you to trust me, but I'm asking anyway."

Brandon studies me but finally answers, "Fine. But don't even consider trying to run."

He steps aside and lets me leave. I hurry back outside to find Pyotr.

"Where did you disappear to?" he asks.

"I'm not feeling well."

He looks over my shoulder. "What did he do?"

I turn around and see Brandon coming out of the same door I just walked through. "He didn't do anything. Can you please take me back to the house?"

"Let's go." Pyotr takes my hand and leads me away from the party.

Restless hours of tossing and turning have been my companions tonight. Anxiety about my conversation with Brandon later today has rendered sleep impossible. The impending sunrise nudges me, a silent call to venture outside. Draping myself in a robe, I knot the belt and tread softly down the steps, slipping out through the front door.

"I'm sorry, I didn't realize you were already up," I murmur to Stanley, who occupies the porch swing.

He lifts his head, his expression soft and understanding. "You couldn't sleep either?"

"No," I confess.

"Come on and have a seat," he says, gesturing to the empty space beside him. "What's eating at you?"

I sit beside him, the coolness of the morning air a soothing balm against my restlessness. "I'm meeting Brandon at the memorial garden later today. "I'm scared thinking about how it might turn out."

"He's likely to be upset, maybe even angry, for being kept in the dark," Stanley speaks with measured calmness. "But I saw the way that young man was watching you yesterday. He still loves you."

"Will he still love me after he finds out I lied to him?" The turmoil within me echoes through my words.

"That's an answer only Brandon can provide. Only Brandon can decide the road forward."

"And that's what terrifies me," I admit, my gaze fixed on the horizon where the sun tentatively breaches the dark sky, casting gentle hues of orange and yellow. "Why couldn't you sleep?"

A shadow of pain crosses Stanley's face. "I had a dream about Michael. It was so vivid. I woke expecting him to be there until the weight of reality settled in. You'd think after all these years, my mind would accept that he's gone and would stop looking for him outside of my dreams." Stanley looks at me. "He deserved to become an uncle, maybe even a father himself."

The weight of his words sinks in. "I can't imagine the agony of losing a child you've raised. My own experience of losing an unborn child was heartbreaking enough."

"The pain is indescribable. Living with the guilt of knowing I played a part in his passing only intensifies it," Stanley admits, his gaze drifting away from me. "When the police arrived that night, I knew. Something in here—" He places his closed fist by his heart. "Already felt the loss. That night, I tried to bargain with God for Michael's return. I begged him to take me instead. I'm the one who doesn't deserve to be here. My existence held no worth."

"Stanley," I gently squeeze his hand, wanting to convey comfort. "You can't think like that. We're human, and errors are woven into our existence. Which of us hasn't screwed things up at least once?" I exhale softly. "You're a good man, one deserving of being here."

His response is a pat on my hand, but his eyes reflect gratitude. "I appreciate your kind words."

"They're not just words. They're my truth. Without you and Charlotte, I don't know where I'd be right now." I take a moment to collect my thoughts. "I've come to believe that our experiences are interconnected, shaping us to help those who may cross our path in the future."

"I meant everything I said. If it wasn't for you and Charlotte, I don't know where I'd be right now." I pause. "I think we all go through things for a reason. Maybe it's to help someone in our future." I rest my head on his shoulder.

His arm envelops me in a fatherly embrace, cocooning me in understanding. "Michael was a good boy," he reminisces, his voice tinged with wistfulness. "He wanted to study medicine. Did you know that?"

"He would've gotten along with Jelena. She wanted to be a pediatrician like Mama." I smile at the thought.

"Why couldn't I see how good he was back then? Who he loved didn't change the man he was or that he was my son." Stanley's voice quivers as he confesses, raw emotions painting his words.

"I don't claim to understand why bad things happen, especially to good people. And I don't believe in God the same way you and Charlotte do, but the image of a heaven where Michael, Evan, Jelena, and my unborn child find happiness is one I cherish." I lift my head and look up at him. "It's time to forgive yourself, Stanley. If there's one thing I've learned being here with you and Charlotte, it's the value of forgiveness."

"And the student becomes the teacher," he says, his lips curving into a smile.

"You and Charlotte have left an indelible mark on my life. For that, I'm endlessly grateful." My stomach growls loudly, and I giggle. "Well, that's embarrassing."

"How about we head inside and whip up some breakfast?" Stanley suggests, warmth in his eyes. "It'll be a surprise for Charlotte."

"Thank you, Stanley." I plant a soft kiss on his cheek.

"Thank you, Lana girl."

As the sun's rays dance across the landscape, a quiet acknowledgment passes between us. In the essence of dawn, we find strength, connection, and unwavering gratitude for the bonds woven through shared trials and compassion.

Brandon

I FIND MYSELF WAITING AT THE ADDRESS SHE PROVIDED, Forever in Our Hearts Memory Garden. The connection between this place and us escapes me. Unless it's some kind of symbolic reflection of what we used to be. A part of me wonders if letting Svetlana walk out of my room yesterday was the biggest mistake of my life.

I keep checking the time on my phone. The minutes seem to be dragging on for hours. It's eleven fifty-eight, and there's no sign of Svetlana. Impatience gnaws at me as I pace back and forth. Finally, I see her emerge from around the corner, a brown bag in her hands.

"Thank you for meeting me here," Svetlana says, her voice a mixture of gratitude and trepidation.

"Why are we here?" My question comes out with more impatience than I intended.

"Can we sit?" Her voice holds a delicate plea as she gestures toward a bench within the garden.

I follow her to the teak bench, the unease between us palpable. She places the bag on the ground and takes a seat beside me.

"Charlotte brought me here the other day," Svetlana begins, her gaze resting on a white rose bush nearby. "They planted that rose in Michael's memory."

"It's beautiful," I acknowledge, trying to mask my frustration at her for stalling. "Why did you leave me?" The question hangs heavy, my heart yearning for her to open up on her own terms.

"I thought it was the right thing to do," she answers, her voice tinged with uncertainty.

"The right thing for whom?" I press gently, my curiosity and confusion intertwining. "We were in love, or I believed we were."

"It was because I loved you," she admits, her eyes carrying the weight of unspoken truths.

"You don't leave someone you love." My frustration emerges, and I ball my hands into fists, fighting my anger at being kept in the dark for so long.

"God, I don't know how to do this," Svetlana's head drops into her hands, her vulnerability breaking through her defenses. "I was trying to protect you."

"Protect me? From what?" The distance between us now feels like a chasm.

"From finding out I was pregnant."

Her words settle like a lead weight on my chest, an anchor of heaviness that presses down on my heart and lungs. Hearing Svetlana utter the words makes what happened undeniably real. The emotional barrier I'd erected crumbles, allowing the profound weight of the revelation to flood in. I struggle to maintain my composure while she continues to speak.

"I found out shortly after Alex and Natalie were rescued from Moreno. I was planning to tell you when you came home from Russia, but while you were gone, I miscarried and had surgery."

"You didn't have an appendectomy." My voice trembles.

"It was a D&C," Lana confesses, her voice carrying the burden of pain and guilt.

"Why didn't you tell me?" My frustration dissipates, leaving behind a hollow ache.

"I knew how hurt you were after Celia's miscarriage and how much you wanted a baby," she says as tears slide down her cheeks.

"Creating life with you wasn't enough of a reason to tell me?" I take a deep breath, wrestling to control my emotions.

"There's more," her voice softens, and I brace myself for what's to come. "The surgery didn't go as planned. There were major complications." Her breath catches on a sob. "I started hemorrhaging, and the doctor couldn't stop it. He had to do an emergency hysterectomy." Her cerulean eyes lock with mine, revealing her hidden torment. "I can't give you a child."

Her words land like a hammer blow to my heart. An ache reverberates through every fiber of my being.

Svetlana's gaze remains fixed on mine, her tears revealing the pain she's carried for so long. "I understand if you're angry and can't forgive me. I'll accept whatever punishment you deem fit."

Speechless, I stare at her, a whirlwind of emotions stirring within me. The revelation she's laid bare hangs between us. The thought that she believes her confession will be met with punishment tugs at my heartstrings. Still, I feel anger at her choices. "Leaving was easier than the truth?" My voice is a whisper.

"I believed you deserved a chance at a life with someone who could give you children."

"Did I not deserve to know about our child? To make my own choices about our future?" My voice quivers with the weight of my emotions, and I'm forced to look away.

"Yes, you did. And I took that from you," Lana admits. "It isn't enough to say I'm sorry, but that's all I have." She wipes at the tears pouring down her face.

"*Papillon*, I'm hurt that you didn't tell me. That we didn't have the chance to mourn our loss together," my voice trembles with the pain of untold sorrow. She tries to turn away from me, but I grasp her shoulders, not letting her. "It wasn't just your loss. It's our loss, Svetlana."

Svetlana has carried the burden of this heart-wrenching secret alone. The isolation she must have felt, grappling with the unimaginable loss of our child. The agony of her fertility being ripped away from her—she battled it alone. It's a pain that cuts deep, and the realization of it gnaws at my heart.

"I never wanted you to feel this kind of pain," Svetlana's voice quivers. She falls against my chest as she breaks. I wrap my arms around her, holding her to me as she cries. "It hurts so much, Brandon."

"I'm here now. Let it all out," I offer a shaky reassurance. My own tears flow, a mingling of grief and acceptance as the reality of our loss takes root.

"I thought you'd hate me for not being able to give our baby life." She whispers, her voice strained. "And for not being able to give you another child."

"How could I hate you for something that was beyond your control?" The idea that I'd be angry over a miscarriage pierces me, casting a shadow over my heart. "I do feel an overwhelming sorrow for the life that slipped away and the weight of the secret you carried alone for all these years. You denied me the chance to stand by you."

"I'm so sorry, Brandon. I wish I did things differently." She pulls back to look at me. "Pyotr wanted to call you when it happened, but I made him swear never to tell you." Svetlana must sense my anger toward him for keeping this from me because she says, "Please don't be mad at him. He's never stopped encouraging me to tell you."

"Pyotr and I will talk, but not now."

"It was actually Slava who convinced me to come forward," she continues her admission as if to reveal the layers of deception one by one.

"Go on," I prompt, my hope swelling that this signifies a change to embrace honesty over secrecy.

"I went to Noire looking to play. Hoping it would numb the pain. Slava showed up and asked me to do a scene with him. It wasn't until later that I found out that Pyotr had called him, concerned about my well-being, and asked him to intervene. Slava restrained me and wouldn't let me go until I told him what I was hiding." Her voice falters, and she wipes at the tears streaming down her cheeks. "That's when I reached out to Charlotte. I didn't come here to escape but to heal."

Lana shares how instrumental Charlotte and Stanley have been in her journey toward healing. Her words shift the lens through which I see Natalie's parents.

"A few days ago, Charlotte brought me here." She reaches into the brown bag and carefully lifts a delicate plant out. "These are forget-me-nots. They're used as a symbol of miscarriage and fertility loss."

I look beyond where we're sitting, taking in an area filled with a sea of vibrant blue flowers. "That's why you brought me here?" I ask, my voice filled with a mixture of emotions.

"Yes," Lana says, her gaze unwavering. "Pyotr suggested planting them together, but I chose to wait—to plant them with you."

Guiding Lana by the hand, we step into the garden. An array of flowers surrounds us, each one a testament to the brief existence that was never realized. The weight of this sight engulfs me, and my legs buckle beneath the emotional tide. Collapsing to my knees, an avalanche of feelings overcomes me, and I double over as my body trembles from the force of my tears.

Lana sinks next to me and wraps her arms around me. "I'm so sorry, Brandon. So very sorry." Her pain echoes in every tear that falls.

Our shared heartache is a relentless torrent, and we surrender to its waves, allowing grief to consume us. In each other's arms, we find peace that binds us together.

Eventually, our tears run dry, and we stand together. Our entwined fingers outward signify our unity as we make our way to a place that resonates with our grief. With trembling hands, we cradle a remembrance flower, a delicate testament to love that endures beyond tragic loss. One that reminds us that enduring love transcends even the darkest of losses.

"Where do we go from here?" Lana asks quietly as she rests in my embrace.

"I want us, *papillon*. That's all I've ever wanted."

Her eyes search mine, uncertainty lingering in their depths. "But how can you want me when you've always wanted to be a father, and I can't give you children?"

"That doesn't change anything." I run my knuckles gently down her cheek. "Whether we have children or not is irrelevant. You are who I want to spend my forever with."

"But—"

I silence her protest with a gentle kiss. "I. Choose. You," I say, punctuating each word with a kiss. "I choose us."

That night, I bring Svetlana back to the bed and breakfast, where I slide my engagement ring back on her finger. "This time, you will not be removing it."

"Never again," she promises as her lips meet mine and her hands drift down to the button on my pants.

I grab her wrist, stopping her. "We're doing this the right way this time. We won't be having sex until our contract is negotiated and signed."

"You're kidding, right?"

"I'm dead serious," I say, stepping back.

The first time we did this, we ignored every rule regarding negotiating. We continued our physical relationship, which did, at times, influence things we agreed or didn't agree to. We've been lucky enough to get a second chance. I'm not leaving anything to chance.

"So, where do you plan to sleep tonight?" she asks, cocking her head to the side.

"In another room." I grin and hold up my key card.

"Well," she says, stepping closer to me. "In that case, let me kiss my fiancé goodnight."

Lana doesn't kiss me soft or sweet. It's heated and desperate. One of my hands tangles in her hair as the other pulls her body against mine. I said we weren't going to sleep together. I never said it would be easy. It takes every ounce of willpower to pull away from her and end the kiss.

"It looks like you have a little problem there," Lana says, pointing to the erection straining my pants.

"Little?" I raise an eyebrow.

"Can I take care of it for you?" She bites her bottom lip.

I give her a quick peck on the cheek. "Goodnight, *papillon*."

Her beautiful laugh follows me as I walk down the hall to the staircase. I insisted on having a room on a separate floor to help eliminate any temptation.

After I'm in my room, I strip my clothes and step under the hot spray of the shower. I wrap my hand around my cock as it grows hard. I close my eyes and picture Lana and how she looks at me when she's on her knees before me. I imagine her tongue licking up my swollen length. My finger slides over my head, stimulating the sensitive skin.

The hot water from the shower surrounds me. My body's on fire. I can feel my orgasm building and moan out loud. Putting a hand against the wall for support, I thrust into my hand faster and harder. My knees begin to shake, and I feel my balls tighten.

"Fuck." My orgasm hits me hard and fast. Rippling waves pulse through my body, and my breath comes in short gasps, and I shoot streams of cum onto my stomach. I rest my forehead against the cool tile, trying to catch my breath.

After my shower, I dry my body and put on a clean pair of boxers. I lay down on the bed and try to calm myself. Despite my release, my body wants more. It craves the woman upstairs.

Svetlana

THE NEXT DAY, BRANDON AND I ASK MY PARENTS, AMELIA, and Viktor, to meet us at the gazebo. It's time to tell my family, who's already there waiting for us.

"They're probably expecting us to announce our engagement," I say. "Why did I think this was a good idea?"

"Because they deserve to know," Brandon responds. "Your family is strong. They'll be able to handle it. I'm more concerned with how you are."

"I think I'm numb right now." I slide my hand into his and interlace our fingers.

"Lean on me, *papillon*. Let me be your strength." He rubs my hand with his thumb. "You're not alone anymore."

"Thank you for meeting us," I say as we sit down.

"Why do you look so grim?" Papa asks. "I was certain this was a happy occasion."

I look to Brandon and will my tears not to fall.

"We have something rather difficult to tell you all," Brandon says. "Two years ago, Svetlana and I lost our unborn child."

"Is that why you came home so suddenly?" Mama asks.

"It was more than that." I swallow over the lump in my throat. "I lied when I told everyone I had an appendectomy. I had a D&C. It was supposed to be routine, but things went horribly wrong." I make the mistake of looking at Papa and spotting silent tears streaming down his face. I can't hold my emotions back any longer and break down.

Brandon wraps his arm around me. "The doctor performed a hysterectomy to save her life."

"I'm so sorry. I'll never be able to give you a grandchild."

"*Moya babochka*, I would not trade your life…" He's overcome with emotion.

I walk over to where Papa sits. He opens his arms, and I crawl onto his lap like I did when I was a little girl.

"I do not need a grandchild." Papa holds me tight. "You are so very precious to me, Svetlana. I do not know what I would do if anything ever happened to you."

Mama tucks my tear-soaked hair behind my ear. "I'm so sorry, my sweet daughter. I only wish you'd told us sooner. Allowed us to support you when you were hurting."

"I thought I was protecting everyone." I cling to Papa.

In this moment of shared vulnerability, the bonds of family, forged in fire, anchor us against the turbulent winds of life. Through the years of joys and tribulations, our connection has only grown stronger. Each obstacle and challenge has merely added another layer of resilience to the unbreakable chain that links us. Our love for each other isn't simply a force that shelters us from the storm. It's a beacon that guides us through the darkest nights.

On my way back to Brandon's side, I stop to hug Amelia. "Is that an engagement ring?" she asks, grabbing my left hand.

"That's the other thing we wanted to tell you all," Brandon says, snaking his arm around my waist. "I've asked Svetlana to marry me, and she said yes."

There are more tears, but this time, they are tears of joy.

I allowed myself to believe my own lie that I had to protect my family—that I had to suffer alone. This moment is a testament to the enduring power of family, a reminder that no matter how rough the seas are, we sail through them together.

Brandon and I left Northmeadow together and flew back to New York. But we didn't go back to his house in Brooklyn, at least not right away. Instead, Brandon took me to his new penthouse in the Upper West Side, not too far from where Alex and Natalie live. It's a stunning three-bedroom home in the iconic Eldorado building. The inside is sleek and modern, but my favorite part is the large terrace overlooking the lake in Central Park. It'll be the perfect spot for my small vegetable garden next summer.

I was shocked that he no longer lived in his family home. He explained that he moved out about a year after we broke up. He toyed with the idea of selling it, but after rekindling his relationship with his sister, he opted for a short-term rental. Kendric, his brother-in-law, will be retiring from the Army next year, and they'll be moving back to Brooklyn. The house is undergoing extensive renovations, so when his family returns, they'll have a home waiting for them.

We've spent the past few weeks renegotiating our contract. Brandon and I are on the same page about everything except for sex in public, specifically at the club. He nearly went feral when I brought it up, but he heard me out about my comfort level with being naked and my desire to have sex in front of a crowd.

When it was Brandon's turn to state his case, he spoke about how much what happened at Chains still haunts him. I don't know if he'll ever fully get past it. Although I don't see the harm, I understand the trauma he endured that night and decided to withdraw my request. It's not an activity I feel comfortable pushing for.

That was the remaining area of contention, so with that out of the way, we're ready to sign our new contract, making our dynamic official.

To celebrate, we're going to Fire and Ice tonight. It's the first time we'll be there since we got back together. I'm a little disappointed that it's mid-week and there won't be a huge crowd. But there's plenty of time for reunions with friends.

Brandon: I'm stuck with a client at the office. Have Pyotr drop you off. I'll meet you there.

That's a text I've gotten used to. Brandon is not only the acting CEO of Montgomery Advertising but also has taken over Alex's position in Papa's network. The added responsibilities mean he often works long hours during the week. I have drawn the line at going into the office on a weekend unless it's an emergency with the trafficking operations.

His demanding schedule means I have plenty of time to study for the bar. Once I pass, I'll officially be joining the legal counsel at Jelena's Hope NYC. Until then, I volunteer several days a week in the children's unit.

It's difficult to see the damage done to innocent lives. Every day, I witness firsthand the profound damage inflicted upon innocent souls. The scars etched across their spirits are a painful testament to their unimaginable ordeals. The haunted look in their young eyes serves as a stark reminder of the urgent need for change. Every interaction reinforces the importance of our collective efforts to dismantle the networks of exploitation.

My role in restoring their stolen childhoods is minimal, but I'm grateful to be a small part of their healing journey. Every moment spent in their company, each effort to provide a glimmer of normalcy, is a step toward helping them reclaim their shattered innocence. The bond that forms between us, a blend of trust and shared understanding, fuels my determination to advocate fiercely on their behalf.

The path to healing is long and often full of setbacks. But the strength and determination these children show as they scratch and claw their way back to mental, physical, and emotional health is nothing short of awe-inspiring. Witnessing even the faintest spark of hope ignite within their eyes reinforces the unwavering truth that light and love will always triumph in the face of darkness.

Me: Yes, Sir.

I finish my makeup and slide my feet into my favorite black heels.

"You look beautiful, butterfly," Pyotr says when I step into the kitchen. "More than beautiful, you look at peace."

"I am. I should've listened to you from the beginning."

"Say that again?" he jokes, putting his hand up to his ear.

"Once is all you get," I chuckle.

My relationships with everyone in my life have all been more effort-less since embracing the truth. However, the most important relation-ship, the one I share with myself, has undergone the biggest transformation. No longer burdened by the weight of secrets, I've gained confidence in my authentic self. I can now look in the mirror and recognize my reflection. This inner harmony is a treasure that has paved the way for stronger connections with others and a brighter path forward.

Brandon

"You have the keys and remember how to work the alarm?" Owen asks.

"I do."

"What time are you expecting Lana?"

I check the clock on my phone. "She should be here any minute."

"Then, I'm going to make myself scarce. Enjoy your evening."

"I plan to."

Svetlana's expecting to come to the club to sign the contract and be collared. Both of those things are going to happen, just not like she's thinking.

While we were renegotiating, Svetlana asked for something I couldn't give her—sex at the club. Our very first scene together, having her naked in front of everyone, was a stretch. There's no way in hell I'm fucking her in front of anyone. Even the thought of having sex in a private room while others are outside was enough to send terror coursing through my veins. In the end, she agreed that it wasn't necessary to move forward.

I knew I wanted to sign our contract and collar her at Fire and Ice. When I was making arrangements with Owen, I came up with an idea. One that's going to play out tonight.

I double-check my surroundings, making sure everything is perfect. In the center of the room is a small table with two chairs. Our contract and a silver pen are on it. In the center is the jewelry box containing Lana's collar. Once we sign, I'll lock the chains around her neck, and then the real fun begins.

The front door chimes, alerting me that Lana's arrived.

"Good evening," I say as she walks into the club's main room.

"Where is everyone?" she asks, looking around.

"It's just you and me tonight, *papillon*." I pull out a chair.

Her heels click as she walks to the table and gracefully sits. I take the seat across from her. "The first order of business tonight is reviewing the contract to ensure everything is as agreed."

She nods and lifts the papers. Svetlana never looks up. Her attention focused on reading each page. When she comes to the end, she sets them in front of her on the table. "May I have the pen, Sir?"

I hand her the fountain pen I purchased specifically for this occasion. Lana smiles appreciatively and signs her name. She slides the papers across the table, and I take the pen from her outstretched hand and sign my name above hers.

With the contract signed, I pick up the jewelry box and step away from the table.

"Come here." Lana walks over and stands before me. "Take off your clothes and kneel."

I catch a fleeting glimpse of her confusion in the depths of her eyes. Then, with graceful determination, she begins to disrobe, the fabric of her clothing whispering softly as it falls away. Her posture exudes a blend of reverence and quiet strength, as if she's stepping into a role she was always meant to embody.

Her breathtaking beauty captivates my senses and takes my breath away. The soft glow of ambient light embraces her form, casting gentle shadows that contour her every curve. As she lowers to her knees, a cascade of thoughts and emotions tumbles through me, a symphony of admiration, affection, and respect. In this suspended moment, time seems to slow, and the world narrows down to her and me, two souls converging at the crossroads of understanding and desire.

"I've waited for so long to put my collar on you. To show the world you're mine, wholly and without reservation." My voice trembles, revealing the layers of anticipation that have been woven into this moment. "Our journey together has traversed the deepest valleys and scaled the tallest peaks. The road we've walked has been etched with trials that would have shattered lesser bonds. For a time, we waivered, but like a phoenix rising from the ashes, our relationship has emerged with renewed strength. Our relationship, our love, has been tempered by fire, refined by challenge, and burns brighter for all we've endured." I pause and take a deep breath, trying to keep my emotions under control.

"Tonight, I'm offering you my collar not as a simple physical object but as an embodiment of my unwavering dedication to you. It's my promise to be the best Dominant I'm capable of today and to endeavor to be better tomorrow. It's my vow to stand by your side, not just in moments of joy and celebration but also during the trials and tribulations that life may bring. Our love is not confined to the sunniest of days. Rather, it's an anchor that remains steady even in the fiercest storms. With this collar, I pledge to be your rock, shelter, and unyielding support through every chapter of our journey."

I blink away the tears that threaten to escape.

"The promise to respect your boundaries is etched into the very fabric of this commitment. Just as the moon respects the ebb and flow of the tides, I will honor the limits we've set. Yet, hand in hand with this respect, I promise to gently challenge your boundaries, encourage you to explore the realms of your submission, and guide you towards the vistas of personal growth that await. So, with every fiber of my being, every ounce of my heart, I ask you now. Will you permit me to intertwine our fates in an unbreakable bond? Will you consent to wearing my collar?"

"May I say something first, Sir?"

"Yes."

"I'm so undeserving of your collar," she murmurs, her voice tinged with a self-deprecating undertone. I hate hearing her negativity, but in this moment, I choose to let her continue, to allow her voice to weave its thread into the tapestry of vulnerability we're creating. "I know I'm not perfect. I'm acutely aware of my flaws. For most of my life, I've been content with ignoring anything that caused me pain," she reveals, peeling back the layers of her past with candid honesty. "The ache of losing our child and being apart from you were among the most devastating experiences I've endured. Instead of seeking your comfort, I ran and, in doing so, caused us both unspeakable pain. But I've learned an important lesson—a lesson etched in the depths of my being. Regardless of how far I might try to run, I cannot escape the inescapable grip of truth." She looks up at me, and her beautiful blue eyes sparkle.

"As your submissive, I promise to trust you not only with the simple things but, more importantly, with the complexities that reside within the deepest corners of my heart. I recognize that true strength lies in the willingness to share the unfiltered truth, to expose the most fragile facets of my being to you. I do this knowing that everything I tell you will be held with the utmost reverence. With all my heart, I trust that you're strong enough—that we're strong enough to withstand anything life throws at us."

"I vow never to stop learning and growing in my submission. I can't promise to be perfect, but I can promise to work hard to be a better person, a better submissive, than the day before. I'll stand before you as a willing canvas, trusting and open to your guidance and direction. Knowing you'll safeguard my limits while molding me into the submissive I aspire to be." She swipes at the tears streaming down her cheeks in rivulets. "Thank you for allowing me the privilege of being your submissive. I love you, Sir."

Her words humble me, and I kneel before her. "You're everything I could ever imagine in a submissive. Especially on the days you challenge me. It's as if the universe took every hidden desire I've ever had and fashioned you for me." I smile through my tears. "But, *papillon*, you still didn't answer my question. Will you consent to wearing my collar?"

"I can't think of anything I'd love more. Yes, I consent to wear your collar."

Opening the box, I allow Lana to see it for the first time. Four silver chains extend from a silver ring designed to rest at the base of her throat. Suspended from the ring is a delicate emerald butterfly. "It's exquisite," she breathes, her voice carrying a sense of awe and reverence.

"Green symbolizes growth and new beginnings. You are the butterfly transformation and beauty," I explain, rising from my knees and stepping behind her. As I gently place the collar around her neck, my fingers brush against her skin with the utmost tenderness. "This signifies not only everything you are but everything you've yet to become, *papillon*," I continue, my voice carrying a mixture of conviction and adoration. Securing the collar in place, I extend my hand to her, a silent invitation for her to rise to her feet.

She looks fucking incredible wearing nothing but my ring and collar. My cock is already hard, and we haven't even gotten started.

"Stage one is set for us," I say, waiting for her reaction.

The same St. Andrew's Cross she was restrained to for our first public scene awaits her. My whip rests on the small table beside it, waiting to mark her body.

"I thought we were—"

"Yes, we were going to do a scene in a private room while the club was open. I'm hoping you'll indulge me." She looks at me curiously. "You asked me to be able to have sex with you at the club. I know you meant when there are people here. While I'm unable to fully give you what you've asked for, I want to begin working toward that goal. I've arranged for it to be just you and me tonight. If you let me, I'd love to see you in those cuffs and allow you to feel the caress of the leather against your skin before I fuck you on that stage."

"I would love nothing more, Sir."

She steps up to the cross, keeping her back to me. "Turn around. I have one more gift for you." I pull another set of thin chains from my pocket. "May I?"

"Yes, please."

I attach the top of the chain to the ring of her collar. Her nipples are already hard, but I can't resist bending and taking one into my mouth, sucking and tugging while my fingers play with the other. Releasing it, I take the first clip and tighten the clamp over her nipple, and then I do the same with the other.

I kiss my way down her toned abdomen as I get to my knees. "I've missed tasting you," I say a second before sucking on her clit. Lana lets out a moan. The sound encourages me to continue, and I add my fingers, sliding them in and out while my tongue continues its assault. Her body tenses, and I know she's getting close. With a final nip, I pull away, and she groans. Then, I take the clamp and put it on her swollen clit.

"Turn around," I growl, fighting the urge to skip the scene and fuck her now.

She turns to face the cross, spreading her legs and raising her arms. One by one, I secure her wrists and ankles. I take a few seconds to appreciate the erotic sight before me. Without warning, my hand makes contact with her ass. Over and over, I strike her until her skin is warm and pink.

Tonight, I'm going to test her limits. Svetlana didn't see the small bottle of lube nestled in the coiled leather. Opening it, I squeeze some on my finger. I massage her tight hole before sliding my finger in. She drops her head back with a groan, and I add another finger, stretching her. "Are you ready for more?"

"Mhm," she murmurs softly.

"That isn't consent, papillon," I remind her firmly.

"Yes, Sir. I'm ready for anything you wish to give me," she responds, her voice steady and determined.

When I'm sure she's relaxed and ready, I withdraw my fingers and pick up the silicone toy. After applying a generous amount of lube, I hold it against her. "I'll go slow. Tell me if it's too much." At one time, Lana's body was used to such an invasion, but it's been several years. I don't want to injure her by going too fast.

I begin putting some pressure and pushing the edge of the toy in—her body tenses. "You have to relax," I say, reaching my free hand around her waist and between her legs. With her attention on my fingers in her pussy, her body relaxes, and the toy slides in without further resistance.

I pick up my whip, appreciating the familiar feel of the handle and the way the leather tails soar through the air. After a few practice swings, I turn to face her and pull my arm back, the implement matching my movements until the first lash lands against her skin.

Lana doesn't cry out. Her body relaxes with each strike. I pause, reach into my pocket, and push the button on the tiny remote that controls the butt plug. When it begins vibrating, Lana lets out another seductive moan. My cock is rock hard and begging to sink into her wet heat.

I'm mindful of how long she's had the clamps and know this part of our scene can't last long. Not wanting to waste a second, I allow the whip to make contact over and over in quick succession. The lashes aren't hard, just enough to redden her skin and allow her to forget everything other than what we're doing here.

When I can't take it anymore, I drop my whip and step up behind her. "What's your color?"

"Green, Sir."

Bending down, I undo the restraints around her ankles. Instead of opening the cuffs from her wrists, I release them from the cross, turn her around, and reclip them to the wood.

Lana watches me pull my t-shirt over my head and discard it on the floor. Then I open my jeans, push them and my boxer briefs down my legs, and kick them off to the side. My hard cock is already dripping precum in anticipation of sliding inside her.

I close the distance between us and put my hands under her thighs. She hooks them around my waist. Her body quivers with need. "This is going to be hard and fast, *papillon*."

The words are barely out of my mouth as I spear my dick inside her and pull the clamp from her clit at the same time. Her body shatters in my arms, squeezing my cock.

"Oh my God, Sir," she says, panting.

I pull out and thrust back inside. It isn't going to take much for me to explode, but I want her to come again. My lips crash against hers as I continue my punishing rhythm. "I missed you so fucking much, Svetlana." I manage to get out between kisses.

"So did I."

"Don't ever leave me again," I warn.

"Never, Sir. I promise."

My hands grasp the remaining clamps. Lana's eyes meet mine just as I tug them off. Her body convulses from the force of her orgasm. I thrust one more time and let go, spilling everything I have into her. After the final waves of pleasure subside, I pull out and carefully set her feet on the floor.

Reaching up, I release her hands. "Are you okay?"

"Yes."

Only when I'm sure she's steady on her feet do I step away to find my jeans to turn the butt plug off.

"Thank you, Brandon. This meant so much to me."

"I know it's not exactly what you asked for, but I promise I'm trying, and one day, we'll do this with a full club."

"I don't care if that ever happens." She cups my cheek. "You don't have to change. I love you exactly the way you are."

Svetlana

I'M COLLARED AND ENGAGED TO THE MOST WONDERFUL MAN in the world. Nothing has ever felt more right. Despite everyone hounding us for an answer, we're not setting a date to get married. Eventually, we'll do the whole wedding thing to satisfy everyone who wants to see us say *I do*. But neither of us needs a piece of paper to prove our commitment to one another. As far as we're concerned, the vows we said at Fire and Ice before he collared me are all we need.

The loss of a child and confronting the profound truth that we'll never experience the joy of conceiving a biological child has undoubtedly transformed us, but it hasn't broken us. We know the various alternatives available to us if we should change our minds in the future. Right now, we find ourselves in a place of serene acceptance. Brandon leaves no space for me to question how much he desires me. He leaves no doubt that I'm not any less of a woman because of my inability to conceive a child.

When I stop and look back at my life, I often wish I made better choices and done things differently to spare myself and everyone I love from enduring pain. Yet, in those moments of introspection, Brandon's words resonate with truth. Every decision, regardless of its outcome, has woven the intricate tapestry of my life and has led me to the exact point where destiny intended me to be.

Every day, Brandon embodies the essence of selflessness and unconditional love. In a way that no one else ever could, he's achieved what seemed impossible. He's taught me I don't have to run unless I'm running to him.

He's the quiet to my chaotic mind. The light to my darkness.

We may not have the power to stop life's storms and trials, but as long as we're together, we can withstand anything that dares to cross our path.

Together, we've picked up the pieces of our shattered dreams, taken the lives I believed were fractured, and mended our hearts.

Vmeste na veki.

Thank you for joining Lana and Brandon on their journey. Now, get ready for a powerful and emotional story in *Love Hurts*. Anthony and Leopold's journey will pull at your heartstrings and leave you breathless. Start reading today and experience their unforgettable love story.

If you're ready for another dark and emotional romance, don't miss *Beneath the Shadows*. This dark mafia standalone, an Edgar Allan Poe retelling of *The Cask of Amontillado*, will take you on a thrilling ride filled with passion, betrayal, and redemption. Start reading today and uncover the secrets waiting in the shadows.

Acknowledgments

George--my Dominant, my husband, my soulmate, my world: this book would not have been possible without Your support and encouragement. Writing about some of the worst times of our lives was not easy, but it was a story that needed to be told, and it was Lana's story that she wanted to share. Thank you for giving me the courage to keep writing, especially on the days I wanted to delete it and pretend it didn't exist. And thank you for being by my side when the doctors told us that each of our babies were no longer with us. Your arms and whispered words of love are the only things that got me through some of those darkest days. I love You.

Dana- I'm humbled you chose to share your story with me. I'd been fighting what I knew Lana's story was supposed to be, but when you told me yours, I knew I had to write it. My heart is bursting watching you start your journey as a mom to a very lucky little girl.

To My Readers- Thank you for taking this journey with Brandon, Lana, and me. It was a rocky road filled with less-than-ideal choices and tragic events, but unfortunately, life isn't always kind. It's about realizing none of us are alone on this crazy adventure. Support is out there —you are NEVER alone.

~Tara

Resources for miscarriage and infertility support: https://resolve.org/get-help/helpline/

https://www.postpartum.net/get-help/loss-grief-in-pregnancy-postpartum/

Also by Tara Conrad

Find Tara's Books Here

About Tara

Tara Conrad is the author behind sizzling and passionate love stories that ignite the senses. Her novels celebrate the fiery intensity of desire. They're known for having a blend of deep emotional connections, relatable characters, and captivating plots that ensnare readers from the very first page to the last.

Tara's married to her soulmate and Dominant, George. They are about to celebrate their 30th anniversary and are more in love today than yesterday. George encouraged Tara to start writing, and with each passing day, she's more thankful for his insistence that she tell her stories and his partnership on this journey. There's no one else in this world she'd ever want by her side. He is her happily ever after.

www.ingramcontent.com/pod-product-compliance
Lightning Source LLC
Chambersburg PA
CBHW061030310726
48969CB00004B/897